Wend

the brave, beloved teenu

eradicated Elizabeth Wither, m

creature with an insatiable ap

WITHER'S LEGACY
The end was just the beginning.

Praise for the previous novels in John Passarella's terrifying trilogy

WITHER'S RAIN

Wither's Legacy is also available as an eBook

WITHER

Bram Stoker Award–winner for
Superior Achievement in a First Novel

An Amazon.com bestseller and a
10-best horror pick

"Passarella hits the groove that makes TV's *Buffy the Vampire Slayer* such a kick."

—*San Francisco Chronicle*

"[A] hair-raising novel. . . . I predict *Wither* will become a classic in the supernatural genre. . . . The tale winds tighter and tighter until it snaps open in a climax that leaves you breathless."

—Clive Cussler

"Stephen King fans will love this one."

—*Critic's Choice*

"J. G. Passarella keep[s] the action cranked high. The female characters display . . . intelligence, heroism, and quirkiness. *Wither* is a lot of fun."

—*San Francisco Examiner & Chronicle*

"[A] suspenseful horror story. . . . Readers who savor supernatural menace will enjoy its edge."

—*Publishers Weekly*

COMHAIRLE CHONTAE ÁTHA CLIATH THEAS
SOUTH DUBLIN COUNTY LIBRARIES

STEWARTS HOSPITAL BRANCH
TO RENEW ANY ITEM TEL:

Items should be returned on or before the last date below. Fines, as displayed in the Library, will be charged on overdue items.

3/9/07		

An *Original* Publication of POCKET BOOKS

 POCKET BOOKS, a division of Simon & Schuster, Inc.
1230 Avenue of the Americas, New York, NY 10020

Copyright © 2004 by John Passarella

ISBN: 0-7434-8479-7

First Pocket Books printing October 2004

10 9 8 7 6 5 4 3 2 1

POCKET and colophon are registered trademarks of Simon & Schuster, Inc.

Cover design by Anna Dorfman
Cover illustration by Mark Gerber

Manufactured in the United States of America

For information regarding special discounts for bulk purchases, please contact Simon & Schuster Special Sales at 1-800-456-6798 or business@simonandschuster.com.

To my father, William Passarella,

and my father-in-law, Glenn Wagner,

fighting a common foe with

courage and determination

ACKNOWLEDGMENTS

Thanks to Marcus Wojtas (Destination Winnipeg, www.tourism.winnipeg.mb.ca) for answering all my Winnipeg questions; the Greater Minneapolis Convention and Visitors Association (www.minneapolis.org) for the Twin Cities information; the Logan Township, New Jersey Police Department for the behind-the-scenes look at police operations; Doug Clegg for sharing his experiences, and for letting me bend his ear; Greg Schauer for fighting the good fight, over twenty years running now; and final thanks to Gordon Kato, and to my editor, Mitchell Ivers, who helped make this book happen.

"Thus Winter falls,
A heavy gloom oppressive o'er the world
Through Nature shedding influence malign,
And rouses up the seeds of dark disease.
The soul of man dies in him, loathing life,
And black with more than melancholy views."

—James Thomson (1700–1748)

"Evil is easy, and has infinite forms."

—Blaise Pascal (1623–1662)

WITHER'S
LEGACY

PROLOGUE

HUDSON FALLS, MANITOBA
CANADA
AUGUST 6, 2000

       Hidden beneath a rotting deadfall, more than half submerged in the soft ground and uncomfortable warmth, it shudders into semiconsciousness, the psychic echoes of a tortured scream ripping through its dreamless oblivion of living death. More than an agonized scream, the sound is also an urgent yet confusing command, given potency by wild magic.

Seventy years have passed since it crawled into its meager shelter beneath a blanket of frost and the frozen tides of snow. And for each of those seventy seasons, it has ignored the call of winter, ignored its season of hunting and feeding, to remain in its contented oblivion, in what has become a slow wasting away. But the call of wild magic has infused it with new, destructive purpose.

In the darkness of its underground lair, its yellow eyes flicker open, its long, narrow nostrils flare, and rows of uneven, pointed teeth gnash in its wide, carnivorous maw. Its fingers twitch, power-

ful claws rasping together. Yet it must remain patient. It is out of season, a dangerous time for its kind, and too far from the one it must kill, this Wendy Ward.

The wild magic whispers, "You are the first."

Still, it must wait.

"The time will come."

Claws curl back into fists . . .

"She will come."

The toothy maw clenches shut . . .

"She will call!"

Yellow eyes close to the darkness . . .

"And she will die!"

Over the next hour, it slips down into hibernation, but its powerful body continues to thrum with the energy of wild magic. Above its lair, a rare August snowfall blankets the landscape of Hudson Falls, the purity of white hiding an unseen evil that now bides its time. Waiting . . .

As its consciousness slips deeper into purposeful hibernation, the voice in its mind fades. The last word the magic whispers, a sigh into the silence of approaching darkness without thought, is its own name. "Wither . . ."

PART ONE

WINTER'S BLIGHT
NEW YEAR'S EVE

CHAPTER ONE

Nightfall.

A dusk red smudge in the western sky fades to a purplish bruise.

She is flying over Windale—yet this is a Windale strange to her . . . smaller, divided by dirt roads with wagon-wheel ruts, as if she has flown into the town's past, more than a century gone. She banks to the left, swooping down across a tall field of corn, her night-adapted eyes attracted to movement.

A man in threadbare coveralls walks an unsteady line, pausing every few moments to take a swig from a jug. The whiskey dribbles down his chin. He wipes it away with the back of a sunburnt arm. Perhaps he had fallen asleep drunk in the fields, and is wandering homeward, careless of his surroundings, unaware of what is above.

She drops from the sky with the deadly grace of a hawk striking a rabbit, arms extended, her fingers flashing wicked claws.

The whiskey jug explodes with the sudden impact, bursting in the man's hand. Before he can react, both sets of claws have gouged *into his flesh, crushing ribs and forcefully expelling the air from his lean torso.*

She arcs upward with her burden, banking again, this time into the branches of an old oak tree. She wedges the stunned man into the Y-fork of a branch, and with one swipe of her powerful claws, savages his throat to prevent him from screaming.

Wide lips pull back from bristling rows of jagged teeth and her dark, leathery skinned head darts forward. Ravenous, she begins to feed . . .

. . . DECEMBER 31, 2001

Gasping, Kayla Zanella awoke, her eyes opening wide to darkness.

She tossed the blankets aside and swung her feet to the floor to counter her disorientation. The last image, so real and visceral, came back to her unbidden and she clamped a hand over her mouth, her gaze darting around in search of her trash can.

The hell with it, she thought, and raced to the bathroom. She flung back the toilet seat lid and dropped to her knees, breathless. "Gotta love the taste of bile in the morning," she whispered, her voice weak. Then, "What the hell *was* that?" But she knew what it was. Or rather, *who* it was. Wither. "Evil bitch."

Kayla splashed cold water on her face, fingers brushing against the sterling silver posts, which pierced the edge of each eyebrow like single quotation marks. At least they distracted from the recent bags she was sporting under each eye, as did the ring through the right side of her nose. *Let's not be picky,* she thought. *My rat's nest of black hair pretty much steals the show.*

In place of a nightgown or pajamas, she wore an oversized Animaniacs T-shirt, and had just arrived at the epiphanic realization that Yakko, Wakko and Dot looked too damn jolly at three o'clock in the morning. She was certain it was three o'clock or so, because that's when the nightmares usually woke her.

She whispered to her reflection in the mirror, "I'm still me, right?"

With no answer forthcoming, she shook her head and bumbled her way across the hall back to her bedroom, navigating by the amber glow of the hallway night-light. Back in her room, the unrelenting night sky pressed against her window like a dark, smothering hand, no hint of the dawn still hours away. The bedside digital clock radio confirmed her nightmarish appointment with blood-red numerals: 3:13. *Major apologies to Ralph Waldo Emerson, but consistency seems to be the little hobgoblin in my mind.*

Before climbing under the tangled coils of sweat-damp bed sheets, she decided to pull the window shades, if only to blot out the oppressive darkness. As she turned on her heel toward the window, she froze with a gasp. An inhuman face leered in at her.

A heartbeat later and her frightened blink removed the staring face, though a hideous afterimage still cavorted on her retina in some kind of hallucinatory echo. She ran to the window and yanked the shade down, but not before glimpsing the skeletal silhouettes of bare trees, spattered with the clinging remnants of the last snowfall. *Nothing human or inhuman out there,* she thought. "Oh-kay," she told herself. "I'll prove it." With a snap of her wrist, she raised the blind to half-mast again and—

—a ghostly woman stared in at her.

"Jesus!" Kayla screamed and yanked the blind down so hard the roller jangled in its brackets. Her hands trembled, her heart pounding and her mouth dry. *In the look-on-the-bright-side column, at least I didn't wet myself.* Then, a whispered refrain. "Just my imagination . . . just my imagination . . ."

But the image of the woman remained vivid in her memory. Dark hair gathered under a head rail and widow's peak, a hard face, brooding eyes and a thin, cruel mouth. Doublet under a riding cloak . . . clothing from the colonial period, over three hundred years past. "It's the bitch—gotta be the bitch," Kayla whispered. "How she looked before she turned into a monster." *Check that,* Kayla amended. *Elizabeth Wither had always been a monster. Even if she only looked the part in the last two centuries of her three-hundred-year life cycle. Because evil, despite all the seductive propaganda, does not age like a fine wine.*

"Maybe I'm *still* dreaming," Kayla muttered. "What would Wendy call it, a false awakening?" She nodded to herself. "Sure. That's why I'm still seeing this crazy stuff." She ran her hands through her unruly hair, a nervous gesture denied her during the daytime when she sported stiff hair-gel spikes.

She pinched her forearm between red fingernails and yelped in pain. "Okay, so I'm awake now. Unless this is lucid dreaming, but . . . Stop! You're babbling and, if you don't mind my saying so, you're really starting to scare me."

Slipping a hand along the edge of the blind, she peeked out into the night—and sighed. *Nothing but trees and some Frosty-was-here melting clumps of snow. Satisfied? So go to sleep already.*

Kayla climbed into bed, sitting with the pillows propped against the headboard, blankets pulled up to her underarms. And stared at the window. After a while, she envisioned shadows passing behind the pulled blind. *And if I stare a little* longer, I'll probably start to imagine fairies dancing around a Maypole—not that I've studied fairy habits extensively, but the Maypole is a phallic symbol, so maybe.

One thing became obvious. Despite the early hour, as long as she stayed in her own room, sleep would elude her. With a weary sigh, Kayla climbed out of bed with a pillow tucked under her arm. She crossed the hall to her mother's bedroom, slipped into bed beside her and placed her right hand on her mother's shoulder.

Her mother, always a light sleeper, murmured, "Nightmares again?"

"Doozies," Kayla said, yawned, and eventually drifted off to sleep.

WINNIPEG, MANITOBA
CANADA

Wendy Ward, twenty-year-old Wiccan and one-year-past college dropout, frowned in her sleep, spoke under her breath and sought control of her dream, a dream that was more memory than anything else . . .

The flames roar upward, engulfing Gina Thorne, most recent host to the ancient evil formerly known as Wither, an evil that has existed in dozens of human hosts over the thousands of years of its existence.

Wendy, in her protective magic sphere, is flung away from the inferno, untouched by the heat of the gas explosion but momentarily blinded by the flash.

Neither Gina nor the entity possessing her dies instantly. For tortured moments, she screams in agony, while inside her mind shrieks a curse on Wendy, a potent magical imprecation, searing the ether with utter loathing and vehemence, even as the flames sear Gina's flesh. The unspoken words are a compressed jumble of hate empowered by enchantment. Wendy attempts to untangle them in hope that, by decoding the curse, she may be able to neutralize it.

"... dark shall ... blight ..."

"... chaos forever ..."

Too soon time reels out and Wendy spins away, out of control.

Gina's image is lost, her screams silenced moments after they began, and her mental imprecation, blasted away by cleansing fire and purifying light, returns vile echoes slow to die ... but at last Gina herself is dead.

"She's dead," Wendy whispered as she opened her eyes. The fingers of her right hand strayed from her left wrist where, she knew, they'd been touching the amethyst on her multi-bead bracelet. She grabbed the pad and pen she'd left beside her on the table. Absenting her conscious self from the act, she let her hand write on the pad, in the dark, trusting in the subconscious direction. When her hand stopped moving, seemingly of its own accord, she dropped the pad and pen on the table and sat up in bed.

Well, sofa, if you want to get all technical about it.

Pushing aside the homemade quilt she'd been using as a blanket, Wendy switched on the lamp beside the sofa, scrunched up her eyes and leaned over the pad on the coffee table to examine her chicken scratch. Combining automatic writing with dream magic was an idea suggested a couple weeks ago by Tara, her host, a Winnipeg Wiccan. The results had been somewhat encouraging. Enough to stop Wendy from giving up hope she'd ever

unravel Wither's curse. She frowned at the two lines she'd
scrawled.

*the dark shall come
and blight her days*

"Okay, so my subconscious isn't real particular about dot-
ting i's and crossing t's," Wendy said. "Looks like, 'the dark
shall come; and blight her days.'" She sighed. "Grim bit of
free verse. But not telling me much I don't already know."

Wendy walked to the window of the garden apartment,
beside the living Yule tree decorated with garlands of pop-
corn, tiny bags of fragrant spices, and crystal icicles. Tara had
moved her altar to the bedroom of her small apartment to
make room for the potted tree, otherwise they'd be tripping
over themselves and each other.

Wendy adjusted the vertical blinds so she could watch
the hypnotizing fall of snowflakes, perhaps to seek solace in
the wintry beauty of nature. But all she felt was a vague
uneasiness. Facing the night, she shuddered, a quick twist of
her spine. Her cotton pajamas, patterned with a blue sky
and puffy clouds more reminiscent of summer days than
the dead of winter, should have kept her reasonably warm,
but her bare feet on the hardwood floor seemed to connect
her to the bitter cold that gripped the city. Might explain the
chill in her bones, but it was far from the only explanation.

Wendy crossed and rubbed her arms.

"Good, you're awake," Tara Pepper said, startling Wendy
more than she cared to admit.

Tara crossed from her bedroom, along the edge of the living room into the compact kitchen, where she switched on
the soft white forty-watt bulb over the stove. She cinched

the belt of her pink terrycloth robe before running the fingers of both hands through the tangles of her shoulder-length, medium brown hair. Snowball, her kitten, darted between and around her legs, a feline honor guard no doubt lamenting the lack of shoelaces on her mistress's bedroom slippers. "We'll have tea," Tara said, smiling as if it were midday instead of four in the morning. She filled a kettle, put it on a front burner, then removed two cups from the cupboard and two tea bags from a decorative tin featuring a Currier & Ives winter scene of a horse-drawn sleigh. "Don't worry, it's herbal decaf."

Tara suffered from chronic back pain, the result of an awkward rooftop escape from an overnight fire in her parents' home while she was still a teenager, and the continued discomfort was enough to prevent her from sleeping for any substantial length of time. She compensated by taking naps throughout the day, even during breaks at the dress shop she managed. Somehow she accumulated six or seven hours of shut-eye in most twenty-four hour-periods. Secretly and, as it turned out, futilely, Wendy had cast a magic spell to alleviate Tara's back pain. Wendy suspected the old injury might be somewhat psychosomatic at this point, a subconscious defense mechanism to guard Tara from another late-night fire. "You're awake already," Tara said. "C'mon."

Wendy nodded, shooed Snowball from the chair and sat opposite Tara at the small breakfast table. She rubbed sleep from her eyes.

"So why are you up at this wee hour?"

"Restless, I guess," Wendy said.

"Now, now. Remember, I'm your surrogate big sis. You must confide in me all your woes." Tara claimed to be twenty-eight, but admitted to Wendy she'd been making that same claim for a couple years running. "The dream again, right?"

Wendy nodded. "I just have this feeling the dream won't stop until I've figured it out."

Tara flipped open the lid of a white pastry box and pursed her lips as she considered her sugary choices. Snowball had jumped into her lap and was peering over the edge of the table. "Most dreams don't make a whole lotta sense. They're just subconscious . . . garage sales. Unloading all the psychic junk and clutter."

"I've pretty much lived this dream."

"Oh, yeah. Forgot that little detail."

Tara removed an oblong confection from the box, coated with powdered sugar, slathered with candied fruit and, no doubt, injected with a generous dollop of cream filling. Wendy figured it must be about ten thousand calories. Despite Tara's frequent mega-caloric indulgences, she had the bone-jutting physique of the chronically undernourished.

Wendy thought enviously, *I eat that thing, it takes the express train to my hips.*

Tara looked at her and indicated the contents of the box. "Want one?"

"No thanks."

"Don't know what you're missing."

Oh, but I do!

Tara bit off a good third of the pastry, then licked powdered sugar from her upper lip. Her eye-rolling gaze of rapturous contentment was comical.

Wendy asked, "How can you—?"

"Hummingbird metabolism."

"Lucky you."

"Can't sleep," Tara said. "Good thing I can eat."

"Who says life isn't fair?"

Snowball took a swing and a miss at the pastry.

"How about some milk for you, Furball?" Tara insisted cats in general and Snowball in particular never responded to their given names so she might as well subvert them. Wendy had heard Tara employ at least half a dozen playful variations on Snowball, including Furball, Snowflake, Fluff and Lump.

After filling the cat's dish with whole milk warmed a bit in the microwave, Tara returned to the table and worked her way, in peace, through the midpoint of her pre-breakfast treat. When the teakettle began to whistle, she turned off the flame and poured boiling water into both cups. With the tea steeping, she sat down and contemplated the remainder of her morsel. She pursed her lips. Wendy knew the look.

"What are you thinking?"

"That you should stick around, hang out with me and the girls at Donovan's, give the noisemakers a good workout tonight, get tipsy on bubbly and sleep in tomorrow?"

"Love to, but," Wendy said, clearing her throat, "places to go, people to see." The truth was, Wendy had been uncomfortable celebrating—for lack of a better word—sentimental holidays with anyone. For the past year, she'd made a point of being in transit during holidays. Not too difficult since she'd been sightseeing for a good part of that year. Still, she often thought of her parents, killed by Gina Thorne a year ago August. They'd spent so many wonderful holidays together as a family. Being an only child, Wendy had never had to share her parents' affections with siblings. Most of her childhood memories were of her being the focus of their love, feeling special whenever she was around them. But that exclusivity had its price in her current loneliness, in not having anyone close with whom to share her grief. The prospect of staying in Windale, of being the center of so much well-meaning sympathy from virtual strangers, had literally sent her packing, first emotionally and then physically. To stay would have been like putting all her grief under a microscope for public inspection. She couldn't bear the brunt of so much dutiful kindness. At the same time, she knew that avoiding her emotions wasn't exactly a healthy way of dealing with them.

Sometimes she thought ridding herself of the recurrent dream would allow her to accept their deaths, to move on with life, to regain her sense of balance. Then maybe holidays spent in the company of others wouldn't bring a fierce ache to her chest, an intense longing to be with those who had been taken away from her. For now, better to be alone and not even think about the holidays. Get away, and let the good times and good cheer happen without her, with no reminders of what she'd lost.

"I've imposed too long, Tara."

"Hon, you are not an imposition," Tara said prior to taking the final bite of her pastry. She licked a blob of cream filling from her index finger, then stood to finish preparing their tea. Wendy took herbal tea black and unsweetened but Tara, naturally, needed three scoops of sugar to make hers palatable. "Besides," Tara said, laughing, her back to Wendy, "if you're not here, who will I talk to at three in the morning?"

Wendy had put a temporary halt to her travels in Manitoba, after the Winnipeg Wiccans' Samhain Festival. In the company of such kindred spirits, she'd befriended Tara Pepper, who offered her a place to stay. Since Tara had repeatedly refused Wendy's offers to share the rent, Wendy picked up most of their restaurant checks and entertainment expenses. Otherwise, she would have felt like a complete freeloader. The arrangement had worked out well, weeks had turned into months and the weather—but certainly not the companionship—had become progressively more inhospitable. Recently, Wendy had been experiencing what she thought of as Wiccan intuition, telling her it was time to pack up and move on. More often than not, she tended to trust her inner voices. "Snowball's always around."

Tara squeezed the last hint of herbal flavor out of the tea bags. "Snowball only sits still if I tickle her belly."

"Never underestimate the power of a good belly-rub."

"Ah—comes the light!" Tara said, smiling as she turned with a steaming cup in each hand. "Minneapolis beckons. Alex . . . Dunkirk, wasn't it?"

"I haven't seen Alex in months."

"My point exactly," Tara said. "You've got it bad, hon."

Wendy felt herself blushing. "I just meant that things aren't the way—"

Tara screamed, eyes wide, both cups of tea slipping from her numb fingers.

Wendy jumped out of her chair, knocking it over. The ceramic cups hit the kitchen tiles first, spraying hot tea across the kitchen. Snowball was a bounding white blur of motion, then gone.

Tara gasped. "A g-ghost!"

"Wendy . . ."

Not a ghost, Wendy realized, and *saw* a split second later. "The Crone," she whispered.

Despite the past-through-tomorrow metaphysics of the Crone's appearances with which Wendy was familiar, she understood how someone might mistake the old woman's manifestations for a ghostly visitation. The Crone's image was white and translucent, hovering inches above the sodden floor. Framed by long white-gray hair, her face was her most well-defined feature, seemingly sculpted from mist, with a magical tint of blue to her eyes and a pale flush to her cheeks and lips. *Maybe a bit of vanity there,* Wendy thought. Well-formed hands disappeared into the voluminous sleeves of a gauzy robe whose folds became more indistinct the farther down one's gaze traveled, finally dissipating into thin air.

"Tara," Wendy said calmly, "it's okay."

"Okay? What do you mean it's okay? There's a ghost in my—!"

"I know her," Wendy said. "She a friend—a friendly spirit."

The Crone flashed a brief, reassuring smile to lend credence to Wendy's words, but to Wendy's eye the Crone seemed agitated, concerned about something. Wendy hadn't seen or spoken to the Crone in months, since before her long Winnipeg stay. Now, in addition to Wendy's own uneasy intuition, the appearance of the Crone did not bode well. *She's dead,* Wendy told herself for the thousandth time. *Wither's dead.*

"*Wendy, something is happening here. You are the center of it.*"

With a quick glance at Tara, Wendy phrased her question carefully. "What can you tell me?"

"*A turning point,*" the Crone said. "*Divergent futures.*"

Oh, joy, Wendy thought. *A fork in the temporal road. One way probably leads to disaster, the other to calamity.* "You're here to tell me which path I should take?"

"*I only know that you must be prepared.*" The Crone shimmered, her astral image losing some definition. "*There is . . . other magic at work. Strong magic.*"

That hesitation in the Crone's statement made Wendy shudder. *She's talking about evil. Doesn't want Tara to catch on. This has something to do with Wither's curse. And the dreams have been some sort of early warning system. But all I have to show for them are notebook pages filled with a lot of automatic writing gibberish.* "I understand."

Tara spared Wendy an awed glance. "You do? How?"

"It's . . . complicated. I'll explain later."

"Be . . . ready, Wendy," the Crone said, her voice fading.

It always comes back to my magical training. "I'll try."

"Wendy, you must . . ." the Crone said, the edges of her image dissipating like smoke rings in a fitful breeze. "*You must go. As soon as you are able, you must go . . .*"

And with that warning, the Crone vanished.

Tara was shaking her head in disbelief. "I just—did you see . . . ?" she asked, pointing to where the Crone had hovered moments ago.

"Yes," Wendy said with a slight smile. "You weren't hallucinating."

"You've s-seen that—her before?"

"Now and then."

"I heard—you called her—the Crone?" Tara asked, still trembling. "As in Maiden, Mother, Crone? *That* Crone?"

"Not really," Wendy said, mentally backpedaling. "Just something I call her."

The entity Wendy would always think of as the third and final aspect of the Wiccan Goddess was actually two-year-old Hannah Glazer's future-self, channeled—or, maybe, astrally projected, Wendy wasn't really clear on the actual mechanism of the manifestations—by the girl into the present, so far appearing only to Wendy and, by extension, anyone who happened to be in Wendy's immediate vicinity.

Tara plopped down in her chair, her bedroom slippers sending ripples of herbal tea across the kitchen floor. Wendy grabbed a roll of paper towels from the counter and began blotting up the mess. Although she'd spent some time around dedicated Wiccans, she had, with the exception of a few close friends, kept the details of her extreme magical experiences to herself. Because they were too hard to explain, would evoke disbelief or elicit a thousand questions. Instead, Wendy had traveled quietly and respectfully in the midst of her fellow Wiccans.

Tara was still trying to come to grips with what she had seen. "She's like . . . a guardian angel or something?"

"Close enough," Wendy said. Then she looked up from the wet clump of paper towels to where the Crone had appeared. "But it's been a while since she last . . ."

"Don't you think that's kind of amazing?"

"Yes," Wendy said, unable to suppress a grin at Tara's excitement. But the smile soon faltered. Amazement succumbed to fright because, in addition to her Wiccan intuition, the Crone's living spirit, relayed from the future, had now warned Wendy it was time for her to leave.

MENLO PARK, CALIFORNIA

"—go! Wendy, go!" Hannah screamed as she thrashed in her bed, dislodging her blankets.

A moment later, Karen flicked on the light switch and sat down on the edge of Hannah's bed. "Hannah, wake up."

"Wendy—go!"

"Hannah!" Karen yelled, shaking her daughter's shoulders.

A stranger would have guessed the little girl was six years old, but Karen had given birth to Hannah Nicole Glazer twenty-six months ago, a little over two years. Rebecca Cole—one of the three murderous Windale witches, all of whom had survived hanging in 1699 and had endured long periods of hibernation, eventually transforming into vicious, demonic creatures—had tried to possess Karen's baby before she was born. Rebecca Cole's malevolent taint had somehow changed Hannah. Despite having been born healthy and never having suffered from so much as a common cold or ear infection, Hannah had aged at an accelerated pace from the date of her birth, Halloween 1999. None of the pediatricians Karen consulted could explain her condition. Most of them wanted to keep Hannah in a lab and study her, but Karen refused to allow that. She had turned to Wendy Ward, a practicing witch—a white witch—for answers, mostly because Wendy had been targeted by Wither, the leader of the evil coven, and she seemed to have a good idea what had happened to all of them two long years ago. Unfortunately, in this respect, Wendy was as puzzled as the doctors were.

Karen lived in daily fear that something bad would happen to her little girl. More so, she imagined, than parents with normal children, children untouched by evil. The idea of staying in Windale, so close to the horror they had experienced, including the loss of Hannah's father, Paul, had been abhorrent. When Stanford offered her a position in their English department, she had taken it without hesitation or regrets. She, Hannah and Paul's brother, Art Leeson had begun to build a new life in California. Yet even on the opposite coast, three thousand miles from Windale, Karen still worried. No matter how far they ran, they could never escape what was inside Hannah.

Hannah's blue eyes flew open. "Momma!"

Karen hugged her, felt the young girl's body trembling in her arms. "Just a bad dream, honey." *Oh, God, I pray that's all it is.*

"No, Momma, it wasn't a dream. Not really."

"Right, a nightmare."

"No, Momma. It was something that's gonna happen."

"Wanna talk about it?" Karen couldn't discount the possibility of Hannah having another premonition. Her uncanny awareness of the Gina Thorne situation last year, of the mortal danger Wendy faced from the resurrected spirit of Wither, would have convinced anyone of the girl's psychic abilities. The last two years with Hannah had succeeded in purging Karen of supernatural skepticism.

Hannah frowned. "It's hard to remember . . ."

Karen held Hannah at arm's length, fussed with the little rosebud buttons on the girl's white flannel nightgown and then, with a resigned sigh, looked into her daughter's eyes. "You were screaming, baby. About Wendy. Telling her to run, to go somewhere."

"Don't remember Wendy in my dream—I mean, in my . . ."

"Your vision?"

"Vision."

"What do you remember?"

"Snow . . . it was snowing . . . and there was something big and scary. A monster. All big and it had . . ." Hannah curled the fingers of both hands and stared at her fingernails. "It had claws and there was—Momma, I think there was blood."

"Oh, baby," Karen said, hugging her daughter again, wishing she could pluck the horrible images right out of Hannah's mind. "I'm so sorry."

Hannah whispered against her mother's chest. "And I heard her voice."

"Whose voice? Wendy's?"

"No. That girl . . . Gina."

Karen shuddered. Hannah had never met Gina Thorne. The eighteen-year-old girl had died before their plane landed at Logan International. No way Hannah could know the sound of Gina's voice. No *natural* way . . .

"But it wasn't just Gina's voice, Momma," Hannah said. "It was *her* voice too. Wither's."

"I'm not sure what it means, Hannah," Karen said. "Maybe we should call Wendy in the morning. Would that be a good idea?" She waited for Hannah's response, maybe even just a simple nod. "Hannah?"

Hannah's body began to shake. At first Karen thought her daughter was sobbing, unable to maintain a brave face against overwhelming fear. Sometimes, it was more than Karen herself could handle. How could she expect Hannah to—?

Hannah's shaking became violent.

"Baby?"

Karen held Hannah away from her and saw her daughter's eyes had rolled back in her head, only the whites showing. A thin line of drool ran down Hannah's chin as her body was wracked by the violent seizure. To prevent Hannah from swallowing her tongue and choking, Karen shoved two fingers into her daughter's mouth, then winced as Hannah bit down hard. *Never the flu or a cold, but now this! What's happening to my baby?* "Art! Oh, Jesus! Art! Call nine-one-one!" But with Hannah clutched in her arms, Karen was already running for the phone.

WINDALE, MASSACHUSETTS

Christina Nottingham, wife of Windale's sheriff, was alone in the kitchen, making pancakes for breakfast, and lamenting the fact that the sheriff of a small town was not exempt from working holidays. Some adult company would have been pleasant for a change, but at least the house was quiet. All four children, accompanied by Rowdy, their chocolate Lab, were playing in the backyard while Christina labored over a hot griddle. Max and Ben had requested dinosaur-shaped pancakes, Erica wanted a princess or a kitty cat, while Abby, their adopted daughter, had specifically asked for a wolf. Not a nice, cute little doggie. A wolf. Christina managed as well as she could, her artistic acumen challenged by and limited to careful dollops of batter here and there to form legs, claws, tiaras, whatever. Brushing an errant strand of blond hair away from her eyes, she smiled and said to herself, "It's not the meal; it's the presentation."

Rowdy began barking.

A few moments later, Erica ran into the kitchen, eyes wide with alarm.

"Are your brothers upsetting the dog?" Christina asked. Erica wasn't exactly a tattletale, but she made sure her mother was apprised of all the little household dramas with the unabashed eagerness of a cub reporter.

"Not Max and Ben," Erica said, shaking her head. "It's Abby."

Christina's hand involuntarily jerked, slopping batter over the ladle, and the princess's tiara became a turban. Christina loved Abby, but always worried about the little girl, more than she fretted over her natural children.

Abby had already been through so much, and it seemed as if her trials never ended: first living with an abusive father, who'd later been murdered, then the car accident that had left Abby temporarily quadriplegic. She had inexplicably recovered the use of her limbs in the wake of a strange mutation of her bones, a mutation since healed as well. In the past year, she'd fallen victim to nocturnal wanderings—or maybe it *was* just sleepwalking, a phase she would outgrow . . . But with Abby, who knew? Because Sarah Hutchins, one of the infamous Windale monster-witches in Elizabeth Wither's coven, had tried to take possession of Abby's body. Christina wanted to forget all that, to put it behind them, which was impossible. That unknown would always be there, an X factor in Abby's life, for as long as she lived.

"What about Abby?" Christina asked Erica, her throat tight. *What's happened now?*

"She's on the roof!"

Christina switched off the burner, scooped Erica up in her arms and ran out back.

Max and Ben were enjoying the show. Rowdy, a responsible minority of one, seemed to think Abby was putting herself at risk and, as family protector, was vocally displeased and making sure everyone within barking distance knew about it.

"Oh, my God," Christina whispered.

Even though their house was a rancher, seeing Abby standing on the roof, arms held out parallel to her shoulders as she turned in slow circles, eyes closed as her boots crunched in the covering of snow, put Christina's heart in her throat. "Abby! Get down here right now!"

Eyes still closed, Abby smiled and continued her slow rotation. A gusting breeze stirred the fine strands of her ash blond hair beneath her powder blue knit cap. "I just want to fly, Mrs. Nottingham. Just for a little while."

"I want you down from that roof this minute, young lady!"

Abby opened her eyes and frowned. "Oh, all right," she said, heaving a dramatic sigh.

Christina Nottingham walked toward the edge of the roof, intending to help her down, but Abby darted across the slanted roof tiles and leapt to the narrow deck railing without a moment's pause, never losing her balance as she spun on her heel and dropped to the deck with a kind of animal grace. *The fearlessness of youth,* Christina thought. But she couldn't shake a strange, nameless feeling that overcame her while watching Abby's descent. Something distracted her. "What's that in your hair?"

Abby reached behind her right ear and withdrew the long feather she had tucked there. "An eagle feather," Abby said, giving it an appreciative look. "I—found it on the roof. Do you think eagles fly over our house?"

"They may," Christina said. "But you're not a bird, Abby. I forbid you to go on the roof. Understand?"

Abby looked down at her feet, the eagle feather clutched in her hand, and mumbled, "Yes, ma'am."

"Good," Christina said, then looked around to take in the other children and softened her tone. "Now, everyone inside for pancakes."

The boys cheered and ran into the house, Rowdy close on their heels. Erica started in, then returned to Abby's side, clutched her hand and tugged her into the house. For a moment, Christina stared after them and realized with shock that her nameless feeling had been something akin to fear.

Was it possible? When she wasn't afraid *for* Abby, was she afraid *of* Abby? Afraid of what the girl might become if the taint of Sarah Hutchins took control of her? Ridiculous, Christina knew. Sarah Hutchins was gone forever. Nevertheless, as she returned to the comfort of her home, hands clasped before her, Christina couldn't help but shudder at the persistent thought.

WINNIPEG, MANITOBA
CANADA

Wendy jogged along Portage Avenue toward its intersection with Main Street, often referred to as the windiest corner in North America. While snowplows had made the street passable, the resulting mounds of snow piled everywhere else made foot travel treacherous. With utmost care, bundled lunchtime crowds made their plodding way along the busy street.

She'd dressed in layers, cotton below, a green-striped black jogging suit over that, and a waist-length, hooded Gore-Tex jacket. She tugged the hood strings tight, leaving only the oval of her face exposed to the numbing blast of wintry air. Unfortunately, at ground level the harsh weather was winning the battle of attrition, having already soaked through her Skechers, rendering her double layer of tube socks a cold, soggy mess.

Getting in her daily quota of jogged miles was always a matter of mind over matter. Whenever Wendy jogged, she tried to distance herself from the immediacy of the physical act, entering what she called her *zone of disconnect*, sort of a Zen state of disregard for minor discomforts. Usually she blocked out the early, false signs of exhaustion, her body's way of complaining that she was about to embark on this exercise business again. Later in the run, she tried not to think about the muscle fatigue, the ragged breath or the stitch in her side. Comfort meant lack of progress. She raised her heart rate by making the journey more difficult, either by jogging the same distance faster or by jogging farther than she had before. Of course, she wasn't about to run till she dropped, but she was aware of her real and imagined limits. As with most endeavors in life, progress followed effort. Despite her desire to enter the zone of disconnect while jogging, she always stayed alert to her surroundings. She'd been attacked once while jogging, and probably would have been raped and killed if Abby, in wolf form, hadn't come to her aid. Not an incident she was likely to forget. Consequently, she never jogged alone at night and confined her routes to public places. And though she struggled to become detached from her own discomfort, she remained aware of her surroundings . . .

. . . and noticed the change as soon as it happened.

The glass and steel monoliths of downtown Winnipeg shimmered and shifted across the skyline before her eyes. She blinked, eyes tearing in the cold, thinking she'd experienced some sort of optical illusion. But the change was permanent. She was no longer running down Portage Avenue. Now she was jogging along the tree-lined river walkway . . . alone. Everyone gone. And something else was wrong.

On either side of her, the skeletal deciduous trees and resilient evergreens clumped with snow were bathed in golden twilight. She'd changed location—and slipped forward in time! *Or backward*, she thought. *Anything's possible.* But she had remained in The Forks, the junction of the Red and Assiniboine Rivers. A place with a six-thousand-year-old history of hunting, trading and ceremonial rites. She recognized the area from her months spent in Winnipeg. So she hadn't moved all that far. Nevertheless . . .

It occurred to Wendy that she was dreaming. At the same time, she couldn't discount the altered state of consciousness. Important information had come to her before in the guise of dreams.

A man awaited her in the distance, wearing the red and black uniform of a Downtown Watch ambassador, one of Winnipeg's official tourist guides. *Why here?* she wondered. *A dream guide?*

Wendy sensed that she would find answers from the Downtown Watch ambassador. She tried to jog faster, to reach the man before he left or simply vanished, but her legs felt leaden, each step forward an ordeal of exertion. She looked down at her feet and saw them sinking into the snow, then deeper, into the concrete! Each time she raised a leg, the ground pulled up with her shoe, like warm taffy. Impeding progress further was the bitter wind, stinging her face, blurring her vision. To either side, the bare trees bent toward her, whipping branches at her face, stinging her flesh. Hands shielding her face, she lurched down the walkway, finally stumbling and falling to one knee.

Extricating herself from the sucking concrete was almost impossible, and sapped all her strength. She looked up, helpless, and gasped in exhaustion as the Downtown Watch ambassador looked down impassively at her. "Help me," she said. "Please!"

"You've come the wrong way," the old man said, his eyes a blind white under his black and red cap.

"Show me—the right way."

"Too late."

"Why?"

"The curse."

"Wither's curse? This is about Wither's curse?"

"It encircles your life."

"You're right," Wendy said. "I should know how to piece it together—remember all of it."

The blind man turned, started to walk away, unimpeded.

Wendy tried to follow, but stumbled, one leg sinking up to her knee in the soft, clingy concrete. "Wait!"

"Can't wait," the man called over his shoulder. "No time left."

Wendy stretched forward, overbalanced and fell face-first onto and *into* the ground. With her face submerged in cold cement, she couldn't move, couldn't scream—couldn't breathe!

Wendy gasped, rolling away from the blanket that had snagged around her legs and arms. She dropped to the floor, between the sofa and the coffee table, and tried to reorient herself. Although she'd packed her bags early in the morning, she'd decided to take a nap before the first leg of a long drive to Minneapolis, before New Year's Eve celebrations began in earnest.

Early-afternoon light streamed through the window near the Yule tree in Tara's apartment, enough illumination for Wendy to read the pages of her dream notebook without needing to turn on a lamp or light the two tea candles in ceramic cat holders at either end of the coffee table. She skimmed the automatic writing sessions, glancing at each page long enough for the words to register without comprehension, snapshots of fragments of thoughts, the ingredients of the curse, out of context.

Gradually, an image formed in her mind ...

... *and Wendy relives the memory of Wither's destruction.*

Gina Thorne, Wither's final host, enveloped in the flash and roar of white hot flames, flames she must know will, at last, destroy her. A soul-shattering scream, a desperate, demented wail until her human lungs are ruined. Yet inside Wendy's mind, Wither's thought-voice surges again and again, "I CURSE YOU . . . CURSE YOU . . . CURSE!"

Summoning the last of her dark-hearted will, Gina Thorne blasts Wendy's mind with the curse, a spell cobbled together in these dying moments of agony, a spell electrified with all her wild, chaotic magic. The sheer power of the spell buffets Wendy, even inside her protective sphere, covering her skin with gooseflesh.

Now, as the words flowed back and slipped through Wendy's lips, as if compelled by a distant ripple of that wild magic, she shivered again, and the hair at the nape of her neck rose.

"Creatures of chaos, rise! Rise and hear my call.
Come for this one—this Wiccan Wendy Ward—that
*   she may fall!*
One by one—and by one more—seek her out,
*   forevermore.*
Know her course and know her ways,
For the dark shall come and blight her days."
Both tea candle wicks burst into flame.
Wendy gasped.

The walls of the apartment trembled and the floor beneath her feet seemed to rise and fall, as if the ground beneath the building had flinched.

"Magic," she whispered. The air seemed charged with electricity. Wendy had a premonition she was about to be struck by lightning . . . or something worse. "Okay," she said, attempting to calm herself. "What the *hell* just happened?"

Her gaze settled on the tea candles, the flames she'd some-how lit with magic, but not her own magic. *Wither's magic,*

Wendy thought. *I've been carrying it inside my head since that night in August. A spell—with a time-release formula. Not a big guess, but something tells me I won't like her prescription.*

HUDSON FALLS, MANITOBA
CANADA

It rouses itself from the long, dreamless sleep.

Pushes its way up through shifting debris, shoves off the crumbling deadwood log that has concealed it for so long. Takes a deep breath of the frost-scented air.

Winter!

Snow coats the forest floor and the branches of the trees in this quiet place. Above, the low gray sky hints at more snow to come. Over a year has passed since it first heard the demanding call of wild magic. And now a powerful echo has sounded, but this time in its season, in the time of cold and snow, its time to roam the land and sate its unending hunger for human flesh. Yet now it must do more than simply feed. It must find and destroy a particular victim. For the magical call is like a fever, driving it toward this particular prey. While its season lasts, it will know no rest until it has answered that call.

It shambles through the woods, its hunger awakening in stages. Before all else, it must find sustenance. Its large, toothy head sweeps back and forth on a powerful neck as long, narrow nostrils flare, scenting the air for prey. As expected, the immediate area is deserted but it knows much of patience and stalks through the pine forest, lumbering toward the remembered direction of water.

Around seven feet tall, broad across the chest but cadaverously thin from its long hibernation, it walks hunched over, deep-set yellow eyes glittering as it seeks any sign of movement. Covered with a ragged pelt, black across its muscular arms and legs, but white across its torso, it appears as much simian as human, but strides with a solemnity of dark intent more appropriate to the latter. Across the color-bleached landscape, under an overcast sky, its passage is like a rippling, repeating pattern of light and shadow.

It pauses at a break in the woods, staring far ahead at a solitary dwelling made of logs, amber light spilling from an upstairs window. In anticipation, its fingers twitch, powerful claws clicking together. Once human itself—though the memories are more than a century or two distant—it recognizes a human place . . . just as it knows it will soon feed.

Loping toward the dwelling, it hears a dog begin to bark and slowly gathers the cold around itself . . .

Earl Cady sat in his reading chair near the floor lamp, working his way through Tom Clancy's *Clear and Present Danger*. He had no intention of staying up to ring in the New Year. After decades spent as a night watchman, he'd enjoyed spending the last five years trooping up to bed at a decent hour. Amanda and he would have their champagne toast after dinner, maybe watch one of the old classics on television, then head up to bed long before most of the New Year's Eve parties had reached full volume. *Tomorrow's just another day*, he thought.

Amanda had a roast in the oven, and the mouthwatering aroma had just set Earl's stomach to anticipatory grumbling, when Cody began to bark. Cody had never been a casual barker, and this current canine tirade seemed damned purposeful, part warning, part threat. With a resigned sigh, Earl set his book down on the small table beside his chair and walked to the bay window, which looked out on their wide yard. The German shepherd was running back and forth, frantic, pulling at the end of his chain. Earl rapped on the window and shouted, "Cody! What is it, boy?"

The dog stopped in his tracks, stared at his master's face through the window for a moment, then barked even louder, transitioning into a full-fledged howl.

"Earl?" Amanda called from the kitchen. "What's wrong with the dog?"

"I don't—" Earl's voice caught in his throat. Thick snowflakes were drifting down out of the overcast sky. "I'll be damned," he whispered. Snow hadn't been in the forecast. Earl looked back toward the kitchen. "It's snowing."

"Maybe he wants to be let in."

"Doesn't sound like—"

Cody squealed, a tortured sound of abrupt pain, followed by a brief whimper, then silence.

Again Earl peered though the bay window, now rimed with frost, looking for the dog. His gaze followed the length of chain, stretched straight across the yard, all the way to the end, expecting . . . not knowing what to expect, but certainly not an empty collar. No sign of Cody. "Stay here!" he shouted to Amanda. "I'll be right back."

What happened to the damn fool dog? Earl thought as he shrugged on his mackinaw. "Probably hurt himself good pulling free of that collar," Earl muttered to himself without believing it. "Maybe a bear . . ." Earl chose not to finish that particular thought. More likely the dog had chased after a skunk or a raccoon that made the mistake of nosing around his yard.

"Probably all it is," Earl concluded. Nevertheless, he removed his double-barreled shotgun from the closet, along with a box of shells. He pushed a shell into each chamber and slipped a handful into the pockets of his mackinaw. Grabbing his keys from the peg by the front door, he hit the switch to turn on the exterior lights, then stepped outside and locked the door behind him. Not that he expected a hungry bear to open the front door while he was around back, and Hudson Falls wasn't exactly downtown Winnipeg, but Earl was cautious by nature. Snow swirled around him, melting when it made contact with the too-warm ground.

First he walked around the side of the house to examine the dog's chain and collar. Earl had decided that choke collars were inhumane, so Cody wore a tough leather collar. *Had worn one*, he corrected, *up until a few minutes ago*. Earl placed one knee on the damp ground—his crouching days were a thing of the distant past—and picked up the empty collar. Still intact, but . . . stained. Wet. He ran a finger along the dark patch and held his hand up to the exterior lights for close inspection. "Blood," he whispered. *Cody's blood? Or the blood of the critter Cody chased after?*

Earl stood and walked beyond the reach of the lights, in the direction Cody had pulled his chain, toward the line of trees and the gathering darkness. He hoisted the shotgun a little higher, bracing the barrel with his left hand, and stepped into the deep shadows cast by the coniferous trees. He stopped when he saw Cody lying on the ground, peeking out from under a spruce, staring back at him. "Hey, Cody! Why you hiding back here, boy?" Earl dropped to one knee again and extended his hand toward the dog, expecting the rough tongue to lap his fingers in canine contrition. But Cody remained still, eyes staring . . . but not at Earl. Cody was staring off into the distance, almost as if . . .

Earl's eyes had begun to adjust to the shadows, enough

for him to notice something was wrong. Left hand trembling, he reached behind Cody's head and found nothing, nothing at all. "Dear Lord," he whispered. Almost absently, Earl placed the shotgun at his side and cradled Cody's head with both hands. Odd the way it came up, so easily, nothing attached to it but a few strands of gore and the pale gleam of spinal cord, violently severed. Earl began to shiver, gooseflesh covering his arms and legs. Mist plumed from his mouth and nostrils as snowflakes whirled around his face in dizzy abundance.

A twig snapped.

Earl dropped the dog's severed head, hoping Cody would forgive the disrespectful treatment, and snatched the shotgun from the ground as he climbed to his feet. The branch of a spruce tree swept aside with a blur of darkness and white, flowing toward him from his left.

A moment too late, Earl swung the barrel of the shotgun around. Something struck him low in the gut with tremendous force, knocking his left arm aside. His knees buckled and the shotgun dipped in his numb hands, but whatever held him wouldn't let him fall to the ground. Pressure moving upward—*tearing him open!*—like a handful of knives—or claws!

His universe was reduced to agonizing, unendurable pain, but one last image rushed down at him, down into the vortex of darkness that swirled up to claim him: a large head, matted with white and gray fur, pointed, fur-tufted ears, deep-set, burning yellow eyes, long nostril slits and a maw bristling with long, pointed teeth. A maw stretching wide.

Amanda Cady had been puttering around the kitchen, checking her cabinets and making out a grocery list as she waited for the roast to finish. By the time she slipped on her oven mitts and removed the roast from the oven, she realized she hadn't heard from Earl in a while. Not since he'd left to check on Cody. She'd assumed he'd gone back to his book. But now she was worried and her concern rose by degrees when she found his chair empty.

The house seemed unnaturally quiet, expectant.

She had the odd sense that somebody was watching her. Ridiculous really. They were isolated in Hudson Falls, a good distance from their nearest neighbor. She pushed aside the bay window's gauzy white curtains and peered outside. Earl had turned on the exterior lights, and, even with the heavy snowfall, she had no trouble scanning their property. No shadows to conceal a potential intruder, and the bright lights would discourage anyone from prowling around outside. Nevertheless, the length of chain ending in an empty dog collar, combined with Earl's absence, was a little unnerving.

Already she felt alone, abandoned, and frightened in the quiet house. She fought the urge to turn on all the interior lights. With a fire roaring in the hearth, the relative darkness of a log cabin home was usually warm and inviting. Now it just seemed dark and foreboding. And cold. She walked nervously through the house, rubbing her shoulders over her sweater to ward off a sudden chill.

She had insisted on drywall in the kitchen so that the off-white paint and flower-trimmed wallpaper would provide a brighter kind of warmth in their home. Now she thought of returning to the kitchen, perhaps to call the police and report her husband missing. They'd probably think she was a silly old fool, but she was long past the point in her life where she cared much what others thought of her. Still, he hadn't been gone too long. And she imagined the police had more important matters to handle on New Year's Eve than finding an old man looking for his runaway dog.

She decided she could wait a while before making the call. She would sit in the bright kitchen, and try to shed her chill in the warm afterglow of the oven. Time enough for—

A strange pattern of movement outside the bay window caught her eye. A trick of the light or . . .

She returned to the window, slipped the curtain aside and her breath plumed in front of her face. She glimpsed sudden movement, racing toward the window. Then a terrible shriek unhinged her spine as—

—the bay window exploded into the house, cutting her body with shards of glass and splinters of wood. Instinctively, she covered her face, but not before she saw a blur of shadow, a streak of white in a swirling torrent of snow, and a wrenching splash of red . . .

Sated on its feast of raw human flesh, it feels again the insistent pressure of the wild magic, the call to do its bidding, to seek the special one it must destroy.

It recalls her name, whispered to it so long ago. Yet the name alone is meaningless. Useless, if the strange magic had not also marked her, and provided a supernatural means to track her. Though she is far away, the wild magic reveals a blue-white psychic cord—a thread of glowing light—that leads to her. This glowing cord—suspended in the air like a pulsing psychic vein—is the path it must now follow. It senses she is young, so her raw flesh will be choice, worthy of a long hunt.

Yet, to find her, it will need to walk among men again, as it has before, which is but a small concern. When it stalks among men, its own magic provides a human guise, a predator's camouflage born of enchantment. Its true appearance will lie hidden until it strikes. It cannot be known. It cannot be stopped.

Soon it will find her. And to rid itself of the feverish witchery, to be free again, it will joyously feast upon the young flesh of the one called Wendy Ward.

CHAPTER TWO

Looking back, Kayla would realize that on Monday, New Year's Eve, her nightmares started to consume her waking life. Of course, the day began innocently enough. Too soon to question her sanity or her humanity. But if she had possessed an ounce of foresight, she would have stayed in bed.

With the Crystal Path closed on New Year's Eve and Tuesday, New Year's Day, Kayla had anticipated what she referred to as a deferred weekend pass from work. Selena Zanella, Kayla's mother and a waitress at the Witches' Stewpot, was less fortunate. She dutifully answered her alarm clock's shrill predawn reveille without a single snooze-button delaying tactic. Lena was showered, dressed and out the door before the sun's first rays knifed through the vertical blinds to disturb Kayla's fitful slumber. Refusing to capitulate after the sun's first volley, Kayla yanked the blankets over her head with a mumbled complaint and turned her back to the window.

Three hours later, she was ready to face the day. An hour after that, she was ready to face the world. Besides, the thought of staying in their Cape Cod while plagued with recent memories of leering bedroom-window faces helped drive Kayla outdoors and away from the quiet house. Never a morning or, by extension, a breakfast person, Kayla decided she wouldn't mind a little brunch at the Witches' Stewpot. A *three-for*, Kayla thought, *warm meal, deep family discount, and a chance to visit Mom.*

Open twenty-four hours a day, the Witches' Stewpot was an old-fashioned American diner on Main Street. Good, reasonably priced food made the Stewpot a favorite stop for truckers, tourists, Danfield undergrads and local Windalers—or *Windaliens*, as Kayla sometimes referred to them. Fortunately for her, the summer and fall tourist seasons were long past, and the undergrads were between semesters, lounging back home, recuperating from too many exams or too many keg parties, probably both. All of which meant the Stewpot's asphalt parking lot was only half full: two semis, both independents, a handful of delivery or business vans, a dozen cars and one white panel truck, Danfield Furniture Emporium painted on its side in peeling gold letters.

Long, narrow and painted a dull black, the diner's exterior was highlighted by cascading, stylized lightning bolts and speckled with something meant to resemble pixie dust, all in glittery silver paint. At night, truck and car headlights reflected off these silver decorations, which appeared to shower down from the cartoonish sign atop the roof of the diner. The sign itself depicted three stereotypical witches—

pointed black hats and wart-riddled noses—hunched over a cauldron expelling wiggly green neon fumes. Beneath the cauldron, red neon *flames* spelled out the diner's name. The silhouettes of the witches were outlined in white neon tubing, the better to display their black attire. Naturally, they represented Elizabeth Wither's coven. While Kayla might shudder at the loony tunes treatment bestowed upon the murderous trio, she was reconciled to the fact that most Windaliens considered them harmless. The town logically assumed that three cold centuries separated present-day Windale from the witches' evil. *They'd ditch these caricatures in a heartbeat if they knew Wither's life force—in the body of Gina Thorne—was responsible for almost a dozen murders sixteen months ago.*

Because of her work association with Wendy Ward, Kayla had caught the attention of Gina Thorne, the reborn Wither. Gina had tried to draft Kayla into her new coven by forcing Kayla to drink the black Wither blood that coursed through Gina's veins. Kayla had escaped the coven induction by making herself vomit up the infectious blood. Later, Wendy assured Kayla she was cured, completely free of Wither's influence. *So why have the nightmares returned?* she wondered. Gina Thorne was dead, but Kayla was far from convinced she'd witnessed the last of Wither's reign.

Kayla walked faster, in part to counter the winter chill, but mostly to shake off her grim thoughts. Despite the blustery day, Kayla had walked to the Stewpot, as had her mother. They lived less than a half mile from the diner, just a few blocks off Main. Walking represented a fraction of the time it would take to exhume their car from the snow barriers raised and reinforced with each passing of the plows down their narrow street.

The Stewpot's parking lot had also been plowed. Twin hillocks of snow punctuated each end of the lot like frozen parentheses. Small puddles and dirty slush mounds littered the exposed asphalt. Rock salt crunched under Kayla's black boots as she veered toward the diner's entrance. She paused at the *Windale Record* newspaper box to scan the above-the-fold stories but saw nothing worth fifty cents, so she moved on to the diner's entrance.

The metal handles on the glass double doors were shaped like broomsticks, painted solid black to give the impression of silhouettes, and were cold as a dot-com stock portfolio against her bare hands. No wonder the sterling silver posts bracketing her eyebrows felt like tiny icicles skewering her flesh. *At least my tongue stud stays warm,* she thought.

Inside the diner, a long counter with a phalanx of orange stools on black posts bolted to the floor faced a row of booths with black Formica tables and orange vinyl seats. The permanent Halloween color scheme was by design, regardless of the season or any interim decorations proclaiming otherwise. Per the ubiquitous Chamber of Commerce brochures, "It's always Halloween in Windale!"

The variety of aromas, from powdered sugar and frying bacon to hamburgers and pastries, made Kayla's stomach grumble in anticipation. And, of course, the air was filled with a jumble of familiar sounds. Along with the hypnotic sound of spoons swirling in bottomless coffee cups and the staccato clinking of knives and forks against plates, she heard the rustle of newspapers and intermingled conversations expounding on everything from the Patriots' playoff chances to foreign policy initiatives in an age of global terrorism. Not really something she bragged about, but the Stewpot was as familiar to Kayla as her own home, and she found herself comfortably ensconced in the familiar surroundings.

Shrugging off her black leather jacket, with its faux fur collar and cuff trim, Kayla tossed it on one of the black, wrought iron coatracks, each in the shape of a broom-riding witch, that were mounted on the posts between booths. Underneath the jacket, Kayla had dressed in a silver sweater and black jeans. Her Betty Boop earrings—Betty in a red minidress—provided the only spot of true color in her ensemble. Her outfit was much too warm for the Stewpot's tireless heating system, but under the sweater was a black bra and bare skin. Not even a baby-T. Too bad. Next time she'd remember to dress in layers and bring gloves.

After smiling and nodding to a couple of the regulars who called out to her by name, Kayla sat on the stool nearest the cash register. From her unofficial sociological survey of the Stewpot, she knew it would be the last stool chosen by any regular customer. Since she practically ate for free, the least she could do was take one of the cheap seats. She grabbed the edge of the counter and spun herself around once, in a complete circle, for luck—something she'd done since she was a kid, every time she came into the Stewpot, even before her mother started working there.

"Hey, Kayla," Bethany said. "Need a menu? Or just visiting your mom?"

As hostess and cashier of the Stewpot, Bethany was occasionally called upon to wait tables. At twenty, Bethany was a year younger than Kayla—although Kayla was only five in Leap Day Baby years, a technicality she figured would come in handy much later in life. Back in their high school days, Bethany had always seemed malnourished, a condition echoed by her flat, dishwater blond hair. Since working at the Stewpot, her fondness—some might say weakness—for German chocolate cake had helped her move up a few black and orange uniform sizes. Although she seemed healthier for the change, her hair remained as lifeless as ever.

"I'm here to brunch and bond," Kayla said. "Don't need a menu. Just my mom."

"Right," Bethany said. "I'll tell her you're here."

At that moment, the double doors to the kitchen swung open with Lena Zanella backing through them, several plates of sandwiches and French fry baskets balanced on one forearm, a tray of brimming soda glasses held in her other hand. "Who's here?" Lena said, then noticed her daughter next to the cash register.

A couple inches taller than Kayla, Lena also had a figure with more pronounced curves. Both had pale blue eyes and black hair, though Lena's was longer and bound in a French braid. While Lena's lips were wide, often slipping into an easy, generous smile, Kayla's lips were full, prone to unconscious pouting whenever she was thoughtful or angry. Otherwise, the family resemblance was unmistakable.

Lena wore the Stewpot's standard-issue waitress uniform, black with an orange apron. "Oh, Kayla! Hi, Babe. Get you something?"

"When you have a minute."

Kayla started off with a stack of pancakes and syrup and a large glass of orange juice followed by a fruit cup and coffee, black but with artificial sweetener. While she ate, her mother would stop by to chat, at least until the next order or coffee refill request. Mostly their conversation circled around Kayla's trouble sleeping. "But that's an asset tonight, being New Year's Eve and all."

"Never mind New Year's Eve. We need to figure out why you're having these dreams."

Kayla had described the dreams in a roundabout way, leaving out the little, unimportant details, such as the consumption of kicking-and-screaming human flesh. Kayla's mother actually had more dream analysis books than the Crystal Path, and Kayla could only imagine her mother's reaction upon hearing the full litany of horrors visited upon Kayla's mind around three o'clock every morning. That reaction would, no doubt, be followed by the suggestion that Kayla seek voluntary commitment at the nearest mental health facility. "Well, I don't know why," Kayla said with a shrug. "Post-traumatic stress, maybe. Although it's not like I'm having flashbacks." *At least not flashbacks to events in my life.*

"The Gina Thorne thing?"

Kayla nodded.

As far as Kayla's mother knew, Gina Thorne had been a demented teenager with delusions of being the infamous Elizabeth Wither. In a small town, a murderous teenager was scary enough. Kayla had decided not to burden her mother with the supernatural specifics of Gina's possession and killing spree. As a single, working mother, Lena had raised Kayla from the carefree end of the parenting scale. Kayla had continued to reap the benefits of her mother's laissez-faire approach to child rearing by not piling up too many adolescent abuses of privilege. Though Kayla doubted her mother could ever be shocked, she had ceased making overt attempts at piercing her sangfroid about three years ago. Hoping and praying that the whole Wither affair was now, officially, history, Kayla had decided the less her mother knew, the better, for her own peace of mind. Beyond worrying about her own sanity, Kayla had to consider her mother's safety. *What if Wendy's wrong? What if I'm not cured?*

Kayla clung to the hope that her dreams were a result of her morbid imagination running wild, that she wasn't really reliving experiences in Wither's life. Because the alternative . . .

"Maybe you should see somebody."

What? An exorcist? "We can't afford a shrink."

Her mother shrugged. "We'll figure something out."

Yep. She already thinks I'm nuts. "You know what they charge per hour?" Kayla said, finishing her coffee. "And you don't even get a full hour. Just fifty minutes. Anyway, it's no big deal. Bad dreams, that's all." *Stop thinking about faces staring through the bedroom window!* "I'll swear off spicy nachos before bed."

"Kayla . . ."

"Hey! Why'd nobody tell me Miss Kayla was here? Huh?" Bill Borkowski burst through the kitchen's double doors, wearing his cook's whites and wiping his meaty hands on a dish towel. Known as Wild Bill since his college football days playing defensive end, Borkowski was six-four and barrel-chested, with a receding crew cut as white as his uniform. Back in the early sixties, he'd done a stint in the Navy, mostly as a cook, and now worked part-time in a similar capacity at the Stewpot, usually when construction work was hard to come by. As recently as the fall of 1999, after the centennial return of Wither's Coven and the resulting freak storms and fires, the Windale economy had experienced a boom in the demolition and construction sectors that lasted well over a year. Wild Bill had earned enough income in one season to buy the motorboat of his dreams, promptly christened *Millennium Madness*. "Or the

M *and* M," as Wild Bill would sometimes say, adding, "But not after that rapper fella."

Wild Bill lifted the counter flap next to the cash register, squeezed through the gap, and gave Kayla a bear hug, lifting her off the stool. "Hello, Wild Bill," Kayla squeaked.

"How's my little girl?"

"Breath—less!"

Ever since Wild Bill found out Kayla had grown up with a single mom—and despite the fact that he was old enough to be Lena's father, or that Kayla was presently over twenty-one years old—Bill had unilaterally decided to be a surrogate father for her, at least until Lena settled down with some "stand-up fella." In Bill's book, *stand-up* was the sine qua non measure of quality, although he'd never express it in quite those terms. Adjectives such as brave, loyal, dependable, hardworking and honorable were all rolled up into one's being a stand-up individual. It was an all or nothing proposition.

Wild Bill set Kayla down and noticed her empty plate. "I bet you're not eating enough, huh? Lena, look at her, she's wasting away." Kayla's mother just grinned. "Whatever you want, you tell me. I'll whip it up, no time flat."

"That—that's okay. Really. I'm stuffed." *And squashed, and far from wasting away, thank you.*

A delivery man wearing a brown bomber jacket over a brown uniform flashed a grin as he edged by Wild Bill and took a seat at a stool one down from Kayla's. She gave him only passing notice, but then, out of the corner of her eye, she saw him placing something on the counter and, for a long moment, the size and shape were all wrong. Her head swiveled as the object seemed to descend in slow motion and made a prolonged, hollow impact. Voices faded around her. Lights dimmed. The air seemed weighty and pressurized, with insufficient oxygen. Judging by their actions, nobody else realized time had slowed to a crawl. Ignoring them, Kayla focused on the object. Eventually, she was unable to look anywhere else. It was a dark, leather-bound tome—book was too modern a term for what she saw—with brittle yellow pages, their edges uneven and crinkled, flaking. Further, her protracted, hypnotized gaze was drawn to the center of the leather cover and the large, monogrammed W branded there.

Driven by a need to possess the tome, to know its contents, Kayla's hands reached toward it, ignoring the delivery man who had brought it into the Witches' Stewpot. She pulled it toward her and tried to open the cover. It wouldn't budge.

"Mm . . . m . . . i . . . ss . . . ss?"

Time snapped back to normal. After the protracted moment of breathlessness, Kayla sucked in fresh air, felt her heart racing. In her hands, she clutched the edges of an aluminum clipboard, the boxy kind, with a storage compartment under the writing surface.

"Miss? You okay?"

Kayla nodded several times, shoved the clipboard back toward him and climbed off her stool with rubbery legs. "S-sorry. I don't—don't know what I was thinking." She fumbled with her coin purse, dropped a crumpled up ten-dollar bill on the counter without waiting for change, and stumbled back toward the coatrack. Her mother called her name.

"What's wrong?" Wild Bill asked.

Kayla shook her head. "Nothing," she said. "Just need some air."

She pulled on her coat and stepped back into the brisk morning air, hoping it would clear the fog that had swirled around her mind. Tucking her chin down against her chest, she shoved her hands deep in her jacket pockets and, her concerns elsewhere, all but ignored the echoing footfalls behind her.

A strong hand caught her arm and pulled her hand free of the jacket pocket. She felt cold steel slap against her bare wrist, followed by the ratcheting click of—handcuffs!

"I'm placing you under arrest."

STANFORD UNIVERSITY HOSPITAL
PALO ALTO, CALIFORNIA

Karen Glazer sat in an uncomfortable hospital chair, staring at her amazing little daughter, too big and yet too small all at the same time. Sound asleep. Slow breathing against a backdrop of muted lighting and beeping monitors. To look at Hannah now, and that's all Karen had been doing for the past several hours, one would never know what she'd been through in the two-plus years since her birth, or in the last twelve hours.

Hannah's seizure had been short-lived, but no less frightening for its brevity. With Art behind the wheel of Karen's white 1995 Camry, they had rushed her to the hospital's emergency room, while in the backseat, Hannah had fallen asleep. At first Karen worried she wouldn't be able to wake Hannah, but she responded to shaking by wondering what all the fuss was about and telling them she just wanted to go back to sleep now. Okay? The emergency room physician scheduled her for a CT scan and an EEG, and decided to admit her for observation. Karen hadn't slept a wink.

The heavy hospital door swung inward, catching Karen's attention. A shadow cast from the bright hall lights played across the far wall of Hannah's room, revealing the silhouette of Art's head with its familiar ponytail. He'd opened the door with his hip because he was balancing a tray with two large coffees in a cardboard container. Scattered on the tray were creamers, sweeteners and stirrers, along with a bag of pretzels and a pack of peanut butter crackers. He set the tray down on the table behind her and said, "I miss anything?"

"The pediatric neurologist stopped in," Karen said, already shaking her head in futility.

"Dr. Montoya?" Art asked. Karen nodded. They'd met Dr. Elena Montoya about an hour after Hannah had been admitted, and talked while the doctor performed a cursory physical exam. "The test results?"

"The CT scan, the EEG, both were normal," Karen said. "Everything's normal." Karen choked back a sob and Art took her in his arms. "They never find anything, Art. What's the point?"

"Well, whatever these things are, we know we're not imagining them, right?" Art said. "Science and medicine haven't caught up . . ."

"I think she knows about Hannah's condition," Karen said softly into Art's shoulder. Of course, she was talking about Hannah's rapid aging and physical development. "She talked about keeping Hannah for long-term study."

"What did you say?"

Karen leaned back and gave him the look.

"Uh, right. So, when do we check out?"

Groggy in her hospital bed, Hannah murmured something.

Exchanging a brief glance of curiosity and concern, Karen and Art approached the bed. Karen leaned over the bed rail. "What, baby?"

"Wanna go home now," Hannah mumbled. Her voice had a faraway quality, almost as if she were speaking from a dream.

Karen brushed Hannah's hair back from her forehead, careful not to disturb the circular adhesive pads or the wires trailing from them. "We're in the hospital, Hannah. The doctors want to make sure you're okay before we take you home."

"Better now, Momma."

"You feel better?"

Hannah nodded, her eyes still closed as she poised on the brink of sleep. "Everything was . . . mixed up . . . inside my head."

"You don't feel that way anymore?"

Hannah shook her head twice.

"Do you know why?" *The doctors are baffled*, Karen thought, *might as well ask Hannah herself.*

"Two ways . . . for things to happen," Hannah said. "Too confusing. One way or the other way. Keeping both inside . . . hurt my head. Trying to know . . . best way was hurting."

"But now you know?"

Hannah nodded.

"There's just one . . . way now, Hannah?"

Again, the little girl nodded.

"Hannah, is this one way . . . a good thing?"

Head shake, then a frown. "No. None good. Both bad."

"Why?" Karen said, her voice unsteady, trying to control her fear. "Why is this *way* bad, baby?"

"Because . . ." Hannah said softly, weighted with exhaustion. "Because it's coming now."

"What's coming, Hannah?"

But Hannah had drifted back into a deep sleep.

She awoke three hours later with no memory of the conversation.

WINDALE, MASSACHUSETTS

"I'm placing you under arrest."

The authoritative voice resonated in the cold morning air.

Kayla felt herself pulled backward, off balance, by her handcuffed wrist. As she turned, she stumbled into strong hands that caught her by her upper arms and supported her. The young police officer was a half foot taller than Kayla's five-seven, wearing a black leather coat—complete with a bulky utility belt and holstered .357 Magnum—with a silver badge affixed to the breast pocket, gold-striped charcoal gray pants and shiny black leather boots. Though his close-cropped brown hair was a medium brown, his trimmed mustache had hints of rust-red. Ruggedly handsome, he had hard, jade green eyes, a square jaw and a nose that looked as if it had been broken twice, set once. He projected the air of someone not to be trifled with, an important quality in a police officer. "Deputy McKay, are you taking me into custody?"

"That's standard operating procedure, ma'am."

Still facing her, he stepped forward and held her handcuffed wrist behind her back with his right hand. With his left, he caught her free wrist and brought it back next to the manacled one. With a ratcheting click he closed the other cuff around that hand. Now both wrists were cuffed behind her back.

She smiled. "Well, you are an . . . arresting officer."

"Snug?"

She worked her wrists against the cuffs. "Oh, very."

"Good." He was close enough to kiss her. And he did.

Taking her face in his callused hands, he bent down and pressed his lips against hers. She leaned into him, let her mouth open, felt his tongue slip inside and jostle her tongue stud. She mumbled, "Is this also standard operating procedure?"

"I have a very unconventional technique," he mumbled back at her. "Frowned upon at the Police Academy."

"Um," Kayla murmured, grinding into his hips a bit. "No complaints here."

"So, we won't have any problems with you resisting arrest."

"How could I? You once told me I was irresistible."

He laughed. "How could I forget?"

"My mother's probably watching us right now," Kayla said, tilting her head back and away from him. "Maybe it's time you took me to a *holding* cell."

"Worried she'll find out you're in trouble with the law?"

"Too late for that," Kayla said. "But let's keep it out of the *Record*'s gossip column, hmm?"

"Papers, maybe. Grapevine? Too late," he said. "Town this small, hard to step out your front door without putting your nose in somebody else's business." He circled behind her and removed the cuffs. "Miss Zanella, I'm letting you off with a warning this time."

She flashed a saucy grin. "But next time you'll be getting me off, right?"

"Listen, I'm going off duty now," he said. "Ride with me to the Public Safety Building and we'll see about that holding cell."

"Ooh! Can we turn on the siren and run a few traffic lights?"

They walked to the black and white Crown Victoria police cruiser, its white door panels decorated with the silhouette of a broom-riding witch next to 911 painted in thick white numerals against a round black circle, which represented a full moon. Beneath witch and moon were the words WINDALE POLICE and the police department's non-emergency telephone number. He held the passenger side door open for her. "Promise to behave or I'll put you in back, behind the bulletproof glass."

"What about my rebel reputation?" Kayla said.

"You get the reputation. I get the reprimands," Bobby said, and hurried around the front of the cruiser.

Kayla slid into the front seat and eyed the enticing dashboard, with all its tempting switches and blinking lights. She was always amazed at how much equipment the police department had managed to cram into the front of a patrol car. Above the windshield was a self-contained video camera system with a small color monitor that began recording automatically whenever the roof lights were switched on. Mounted over the dashboard was a radar gun, while in front of it was the twelve-inch touch screen of the Mobile Data Terminal. The MDT keyboard rested on the blocky console between the front seats, overshadowing the radio display and microphone. Mounted and locked above the bulletproof glass partition behind them was a black Remington 870 shotgun. But Kayla's attention was drawn to the row of red rocker switches on the console in front of the radio controls, switches that controlled all the whistles and sirens and lights—oh my.

Making practiced allowances for the bulkiness of his utility belt, Bobby situated himself behind the wheel of the patrol car, then frowned when he noticed where her fingers were roaming. He lifted her hand away from the rocker switches and placed it in her lap.

"How about this?" she said. "If Sheriff Nottingham slaps your wrist, you can slap my bottom."

"No siren. No flashing lights."

"Spoilsport."

Despite her threats of mischief, Kayla sank back in her seat, arms crossed, and stared off into space, hardly aware of Bobby's occasional, inquisitive glances or the police radio's muted chatter, which assumed the quality of white noise.

Kayla always wondered how she and Bobby had hooked up, become an item. Wondered too why she felt so comfortable in his presence. Only in the last few days had the answer crystallized for her. Knowing the reason and handling its repercussions were two different things.

On the surface, they were an unusual pairing. He was by the book; she was outside the box. He was law and order; she was rebel without a new millennial cause. How they met wasn't unusual. In the aftermath of the Gina Thorne's brief but devastating reign of terror, Sheriff Nottingham had assigned Bobby to check on the Crystal Path and its employees on a regular basis, specifically Kayla. Bobby hadn't been working in Windale during Gina's murder spree, but he'd been hired as a direct result of it. Jen Hoyt, who'd become part of Gina's coven, had killed one of Sheriff Nottingham's deputies, the second deputy killed in the line of duty in less than a year. (The remaining deputy, Jeff Schaeffer—deciding law enforcement life would be sweeter and much safer out west—had packed his bags for Wyoming.) Following the murders and destruction in the autumn of 1999 and the summer of 2000, the police department's budget had been reviewed and increased. Because the department was woefully understaffed, Sheriff Nottingham received three new police cruisers and authorization to hire a total of four deputies through 2001, and another four patrol officers in 2002. With Jeff long gone, that meant four new hires. Robert Louis McKay, a transplant from Baltimore, was the first, and he saw firsthand a lot of the devastation Gina Thorne had left behind, which led him right to Kayla.

The Crystal Path's entire inventory had been vandalized or destroyed, while all three employees had been the victims of direct or indirect violence. Tristan Rogers had been killed in the store and no amount of civic attention could remedy that. Kayla had witnessed Tristan's murder; then she'd been abducted, physically abused and forced to submit to Gina's infectious blood. (Of the surviving victims, Wendy had suffered the most, losing both parents.) As a result of being the focal point of so much of the death and destruction, the Crystal Path had merited increased police sweeps and drop-in visits. This assignment had become a regular part of Bobby McKay's daily rounds.

Although Kayla had declined the town's offers to pay for psychological counseling—against her mother's advice—she found she enjoyed Deputy McKay's daily visits to the Crystal Path during the extended period of repair and restocking. With the source of the threat gone, they both realized the extra attention was more a courtesy than protection. But they both played their part.

Over the course of several months—the time she needed for the memories of Tristan's murder to become blurred and distant, but never forgotten—the alchemy of polite conversa-

tion and growing attraction transmuted their regular interactions through the realm of innocent flirtation until, one
bright and inspiring day, Bobby had asked her out, as con-
ventionally as possible, to dinner and a movie. Almost surprising herself, she'd accepted. Dinner was an enjoyable mix
of tentative but interested conversation, the food playing a
less than secondary role. The movie, however, was lame con-
ventionally or otherwise and they agreed to bail after the
first half hour. Bobby suggested dancing and Kayla suggested a rave in the Boston area.

Sporadic dating followed, Bobby limited by all the over-
time and shift changes while the sheriff recruited more
deputies. Weeks bled into months and the hours improved.
Bobby and Kayla found themselves spending more and
more of that free time in each other's company.

In all that time, Kayla never asked herself why they had
become Windale's most unusual couple.

She suspected Bobby had an inner rebel, and that was the
part of him most drawn to her, someone who defied and
flaunted conventions. Maybe Kayla had even fooled herself
into thinking her goal in the relationship was to free that
inner rebel, to chip away at his wall of propriety and confor-
mity. Now she suspected her subconscious had had other
motives all along. Her recent nightmares had just brought
that reason to the surface. Even though Bobby appreciated
her individuality, that wasn't the main reason she felt comfortable around him. It was because he made her feel safe.
Public guardian becomes personal protector, she thought. She
recalled their early interactions, her jokes about liking a
man in uniform. Had the joking masked a deeper need for a
sense of security? *If I had accepted those offers for counseling,
maybe I could answer that question.* The cold truth was, Kayla

had witnessed two of Gina's henchmen—her *cat's-paws*—murder Tristan then threaten Kayla with a knife. And even though Gina and her goons were dead and gone, part of Kayla still felt vulnerable and raw, exposed. Maybe it was just Windale. Lately, the town had a way of getting under her skin. *Do I feel safe?* Kayla wondered. *Or do I just feel safe when I'm around Bobby? Is that all he means to me? Or do we really have something? Okay, that's too many questions and not enough answers.*

"What are you thinking about?" Bobby asked as he steered into the municipal parking lot.

"What—? Oh . . ." Kayla sighed, noticed she'd been slouching and sat up. Her left hand rose to her gel-spiked hair. "Changing my hair, maybe. The spikes are kinda carbon-dated."

"Oh, really?" He parked the police cruiser next to the Public Safety Building, two slots from his cherry red Mustang GT, and switched off the ignition. "What did you have in mind?"

"Blue," Kayla said, nodding. "Would you be ashamed to be seen in public with me if I had iridescent blue hair? You're Windale Blue and I'd be Kayla Blue."

"You'd be easy to spot in a crowd," he said casually, rubbing his arm after she punched it in reply. "It's your hair. Who am I not to admire it?"

"You're my boyfriend, that's who," Kayla said. "God, that sounds corny."

"Is it really?"

"What? Corny?"

"No. Your hair. What you were thinking about before?"

"We'll talk. Later," Kayla said. Off his doubtful look, she sighed. "Promise. Now go change into your streets, and let's jet before I get the urge to confess to crimes I didn't commit."

Ten minutes later, when Bobby came out of the Public Safety Building, Kayla was sitting on the hood of his Mustang, legs crossed, back resting against the slope of the windshield, eyes closed. She wasn't asleep, just replaying the image in her mind of the ancient tome, the brief illusion she'd experienced when the brown-uniformed delivery guy dropped his clipboard on the Stewpot's counter. Everything was still so clear: the branded monogram, a scar in the shape of a W, the dark, coarse grain of the leather cover, the cracked and yellowed edges of the pages within. She was now convinced it had been more than a hallucination. *It was some kind of vision.* The aluminum clipboard had been a trigger, a means to inform her of the ancient book's existence. *Maybe it still exists.*

"Bad news," Bobby said.

Kayla's eyelids fluttered open, as if she were rousing herself from a self-induced trance—not to mention the numbing cold. *Maybe it was a trance,* she thought. *Autohypnosis!* The Crystal Path had a dozen books on the topic. "Tell me."

Bobby had changed into a watch cap, pea coat, faded jeans and Timberland boots, the image of a sailor on leave. *Well, maybe not the boots,* she thought.

She swung her legs over the side of the car and extended her hand for assistance. He gripped her hand and lower back, helping her down. Then, as she landed beside him, he playfully swatted her rear. "That's a car hood, not a park bench."

Kayla rubbed her behind and frowned. "The last time you caught me sitting on your car, we had sex on the hood. As I recall, you had no complaints then."

"As I recall, that was a spring night, and far from municipal parking lots."

"Okay then, what about the picnic at Harrison Park? Or that morning in Round-the-Clock Laundromat. And what about—?"

"Well, we were a little discreet then."

"Discretion and passion, by definition, are incompatible."

"And yet somehow they coexist in a civilized society," Bobby said, grinning even as he shook his head. "Now get in."

She rolled her eyes, but complied. Once he was inside the car, had started the ignition and switched on the heater, she asked, "So, was that a personal assessment or were you trying to tell me something."

"What?"

"The 'bad news'?"

"Oh, no. Not you. You're sugar and spice, Kay," Bobby said, smiling. "Mostly spice."

"And everything nice, right?"

He shrugged. "When you're not being naughty."

"Get back to the subject, McKay."

He sighed. "I have to work tonight. Back by eleven."

"Oh, no."

"Oh, yes."

"But it's New Year's Eve. You were supposed to be off duty tonight."

He nodded. "True. Right up until Captain Kirk came down with some heinous intestinal bug." Known somewhat affectionately as "Captain Kirk" by his fellow officers, James Kirkbride himself was good-naturedly unappreciative of the sobriquet. "Nottingham is up, and wants Curtis and me with him, at least till dawn. Just in case there's trouble."

"What about Auto Club?"

Angelo Ambrose Antonelli was low man on the seniority list. Just one problem. "Disney World, remember," Bobby said. "Drove down with the family week before Christmas. Two weeks of long lines and animatronics. Out till January third."

"He could fly back in time," Kayla said petulantly.

"Kayla . . ."

"I know," she said, reaching over to squeeze his thigh. "But it's such short notice for me."

"For you?"

"Sure. Gives me less than twelve hours to find somebody else to kiss at midnight."

"Ha, ha," he said, driving from the municipal lot and into the flow of midday traffic. "You could give your mother a peck on the cheek."

"You could play hooky tonight."

"No can do."

"What if I report a prowler at a quarter till midnight?"

He pursed his lips. "That might work."

Kayla smiled, then looked out her window as they drove past the new Witch Museum. At first she thought it strange she hadn't visited the place. Then she remembered it had reopened for business after the whole Gina Thorne affair, a time when Kayla had wanted lots of distance from all things related to Wither and her murderous coven. She shuddered.

"Cold?"

"No," Kayla said. "Let's go somewhere, get naked and hold each other."

"I like the way you think," he said. "My place?"

"Chicken."

"With the windchill, I think it's about fifty below outside," Bobby said. "Those hair-gel spikes of yours will snap off like icicles. And you honestly want to get naked outside?" Her bluff called, she shook her head and stared at the open road. "Hey, you haven't told me what you were really thinking about before."

"Imagine that."

"Should I be worried?"

She squeezed his thigh again. "You worry too much."

"Job hazard."

"Just drive. Okay?"

With a nod, he gave her one last curious glance, then turned his attention to the road. Kayla stared absently out her window at downtown Windale. They passed the squat, red-brick post office, a taxidermist, Windale Dry Cleaners, Beckett Books with the cartoon bespectacled bookworm sign and, on the next corner, the grand Palace Cinema with its overhanging wedge-shaped marquee. Closed for months now—after being condemned for structural damage to and a partial collapse of the roof—the old-fashioned, elegant theater had already been in a state of steady economic decline owing to the competitive depredations of multiplexes in Harrison and Peabody. Fiscal anemia probably explained the owner's lack of insurance. With no movie posters in the display cases and a marquee that proclaimed FOR SALE, the Palace was an uncharacteristic bit of urban decay in Windale. Kayla looked away from the abandoned building.

A companionable silence wrapped around them as they left the downtown area. Soon the houses were farther apart, suburban sprawl becoming rural woodlands, and the two-lane asphalt road narrowed, with muddy mounds of plowed snow all but eliminating the shoulder. Due to much lighter traffic, the outlying roads were quick to ice up and become treacherous. Lonely, potentially deadly places. And crowding both sides of the winding road, like an assemblage of quiet sentinels, skeletal deciduous trees intermingled with pines and spruces impervious to winter's blight.

The silence became eerie. Even the hum of the car's snow tires seemed to fade away. Kayla could feel herself drifting into that semi-hypnotic state she'd experienced earlier. Then the Mustang fishtailed —

—and an electric charge contorted Kayla's spine. "You feel that?"

"Patch of black ice," Bobby said, taking his foot off the accelerator as he steered into the skid and regained control of the Mustang. "Keep telling myself, 'Trade it in on a four-wheel drive.' This car was hardly practical for Baltimore winters. Up here, it's a death wish on wheels."

"That's not what I meant—I felt something . . . else."

"What?"

Kayla looked toward the trees to her right and gasped. "Stop the car!"

Before the Mustang came to a complete stop, Kayla pushed her door open and stepped out onto the slick asphalt road. Beyond the row of trees, something called out to her, but not with a voice, certainly not with spoken words or any audible sound. The communication occurred on a deeper level, primal, maybe instinctual, part urge, part exhortation. A summoning? Whatever she was experiencing, she sensed it was too important to ignore, no matter how hard to explain. The sensation seemed too fragile and fleeting to examine, like trying to hold a snowflake in the palm of her hand. Her only recourse was to respond to the call.

"Kayla! Kayla, wait!"

Kayla glanced back over her shoulder. Bobby had wedged the Mustang against the piled snow and switched on his hazard blinkers. Circling around the back of the car, he leapt over the uneven mounds of snow and followed her down the gradual slope to the tree line.

"Hurry," she shouted.

Perhaps as a result of the distraction, the call began to fade.

Kayla turned back to the woods. Impatient, she worried her bottom lip, tolerating only the briefest hesitation before resuming her course into the trees. Her passage was slowed by four inches of virgin snow and deeper drifts. She plodded along, wrenching her ankle once, another time tripping over an aboveground tree root. Bobby closed the distance behind her, but she reached the clearing first. In the center was a tumbled mound of charred, brittle wood, the remains of an old, unchecked fire.

"I know this place," Bobby said as he closed the distance between them. "Sheriff brought me here soon after I signed on. Said it was a barn belonged to a man named Stone, Matthias Stone. That he aided and abetted a group of women who thought they were reincarnated versions of the original Windale witches."

For weeks, Sheriff Nottingham had kept the area sealed, an official crime scene, no doubt the most infamous crime scene in Windale's storied history. Dismembered human remains in various stages of decay, from several days to hundreds of years old, had been buried all over Stone's property. Inside the barn, assorted bones had been found, stripped clean of flesh, the marrow sucked out.

Two years had passed since those remains had been removed for proper burials. *But this place is still evil,* she thought. *It should feel evil, somehow. Maybe at night the ghosts return.* Kayla whispered, "Not reincarnations. They were the same witches."

"That's impossible," Bobby said. "That would have made them three hundred years old."

"Yes," Kayla said. "But Wither herself was much older than that."

"C'mon, that's just a campfire tale for tourists."

"You have no idea," Kayla said, shaking her head. "Anyway, it's not here."

"What isn't?"

"Not here . . . but close," Kayla said softly. "I can feel it."

"This is crazy," Bobby said. "I have no idea what you're talking about."

"Makes two of us," Kayla said, walking away from the charred wreckage of Matthias Stone's barn. She followed a path leading from the barn through the trees.

Confused, Bobby held his hands out at his sides, shaking his head in surrender before dropping them. Without further protest, he followed her. Ahead, they saw an abandoned, ramshackle farmhouse, white paint all but weathered away, porch floorboards warped, windows long gone. "Stone's house," Bobby said.

The house held no interest for Kayla. She turned right, down a narrow path, which seemed invisible until you were on it, somehow playing tricks on the eye. From both sides, tree trunks leaned inward, closing around them, and though it was early afternoon, the sky became dark as dusk. Bobby looked back and forth, as if lost. He had a hard time catching his breath. Simple breathing felt labored here. "Kayla, this doesn't feel right. We should turn back."

"It's meant to discourage intruders."

"What is?"

"The location."

"How?"

"Don't know. Some kind of enchantment, maybe. A spell."

"If you say so," Bobby said. "It's all hocus-pocus to me."

"But you feel it. Don't you?"

Frowning, Bobby rubbed the back of his neck. Kayla thought she saw him shudder. "You feel that too?" he asked.

Kayla nodded.

"So why are we still walking toward it, whatever *it* is?"

"Because something else is stronger."

Eventually, the claustrophobic path in the woods opened into a small clearing, less than ten feet in diameter. At the far side was a smooth, oblong gray stone, wide as a park bench, but tilted at a ten-degree angle. Kayla looked up at the section of sky exposed by the ring of trees. Still too dark. "What time is it?"

Bobby glanced at his watch and shook his head. "Can't be right. Should be noon, twelve-thirty at the latest."

"What's it say?"

Frowning, he said, "Five-thirty."

"Figures."

"How? We haven't been walking that long."

"Once we stepped into the clearing it hit me. I'm starving. Like I haven't eaten for a long time." She looked back the way they'd come. "First the feeling of dread, now this. Somehow time slows down when you come this way. She could corrupt nature. Why not the flow of time?"

"It's more likely my watch needs a new battery."

"More comforting maybe. But the dark sky and my stomach both agree with your watch." Kayla looked around the clearing again. Here the snow had melted . . . or had never fallen. The ground was hard and barren. Featureless, aside from the smooth stone. This was a special place. *She hid something here!*

Kayla approached the long stone and kneeled down before it. She ran her palm along the surface, from left to right. The stone was gray, splotchy dark in places, and seemed to vibrate under her touch. "Maybe this was an altar."

"Maybe you should get away from it," Bobby countered, taking a few hesitant steps toward her. "Whatever it is, it may not be safe."

Kayla whipped her head around and glared at him. "I don't need you to protect me, McKay. I'm a big girl."

"I just meant—"

She began to shake, as if from severe cold, her teeth chattering. "I know what you meant. That I'm—helpless, that I need my own personal—bodyguard to keep me out—out of trouble."

"Kayla—?"

"Well, I have news for—for you, mister," Kayla said, beginning to sway, her balance uncertain. "I can take—care of myself."

"Kayla, your nose," Bobby said, pointing. "It's bleeding."

She pressed the fingers of her right hand to her nostrils, felt the moisture, pulled them away and examined the blood. "Oh, God! Oh, God, no . . ." *Maybe it's just the light—it's so dark and maybe it's not . . .* She teetered on the edge of hysteria, leaning over an abyss that could steal her sanity.

Bobby sensed something was wrong, something more than a simple nosebleed. He closed the distance between them, knelt down in front of her and took her shoulders in his hands. "What's wrong? Tell me."

Silent tears rolled down her cheeks. Kayla bit the fingers of her other hand. "Bobby, look!" She raised her trembling, bloodied hand so he could see. "Oh, God, Bobby, it's black—my blood is black!"

"I don't understand—"

"We have to leave," she said, panic gnawing at her insides. "Have to get out of here. Now!"

She reached back to the smooth stone to push herself up, to help herself stand on weak legs, to run away from the clearing, from the woods, from all the evil that had seeped into the ground like radiation contamination from the spent fuel rods of a nuclear reactor. As she pushed against the stone, the air flared around her—a burst of light and a muffled roar of sound.

Kayla plunged forward into darkness, unconscious before her body hit the hard, unforgiving ground.

FARGO, NORTH DAKOTA

The front desk clerk at the Fargo Motor Lodge asked, "How long will you be staying with us?"

Wendy nibbled the corner of her thumbnail. "Just tonight."

"All by yourself?"

The intimate tone of the question and his too-familiar, lopsided grin startled Wendy out of her complacency. In the span of an eye blink, her estimation of the man switched from innocuous clerk to potential threat, and brought him into focus. Late thirties, going soft around the middle, dirty blond hair thinning on top, pale eyes, pudgy face and an ill-advised, droopy mustache bracketing a weak chin. He wore a rumpled white dress shirt with several crescent layers of yellow pit stains, like the strata of an archeological dig, along with a navy blue clip-on tie and pale jeans over scuffed brown leather boots. No wedding ring.

"Got a problem with that"—Wendy checked his white-on-green name tag—"Lloyd?"

"Who? Me? No, no, no," he said, hands raised in a placating gesture. "No problems here." He cleared his throat. "Just a might unusual, is all, since it's, you know, New Year's Eve." He shrugged. "Just assumed a pretty young girl would—"

"It's been a long drive," Wendy said. "Could I just have the room key, please?"

"Right," he said. "Key." He placed a brass key with a white plastic fob on top of her credit card and slid both across the counter. "Room two-thirteen. This side, upper level."

"Thanks."

"You need any help getting your bags upstairs, Miss Ward, you just let me know. Be my pleasure. Surely would."

"I'll manage."

"Don't be too sure. Elevator's broken."

"I'm stronger than I look."

Lloyd took that as an excuse to give her an appraising gaze, which verged on a lingering leer. Not that she was revealing much in a bulky, goose down jacket over black jeans and waterproof boots. "Well then, enjoy your stay."

Wendy stepped back outside, and a blast of cold air took her breath away. *What a creep,* she thought. Countering her urge for an immediate, cleansing shower was the vivid screen memory of Janet Leigh's exit scene in *Psycho.* She was beginning to rethink the wisdom of splitting her trip into two parts. Winnipeg to Minneapolis would have been a nine-hour drive, maybe less, depending on road conditions and rest breaks. Not impossible . . . if she had wanted to be in Minneapolis with Alex for New Year's Eve. Of course, the alternative would have been to check into a hotel in Minneapolis and not call to tell him she'd arrived, but she doubted her willpower. That close, she might have caved. Had to remind herself she'd left Winnipeg to be alone for the holiday. Besides, the strange spell she had cast following her automatic writing had unnerved her. Add in the Crone's message warning her to hit the road and all signs, not just her fragile emotions, pointed south.

Wendy had left the forest green Nissan Pathfinder parked under the motel's portico. She sighed, hopped into the SUV and slammed the door shut with a little more force than necessary. Dangling from the rearview mirror, swaying side to side with a honey pot clutched under one arm, was the wooden Winnie-the-Pooh Christmas tree ornament she'd picked up in Winnipeg after learning the fictional Winnie had been named after a real bear named Winnipeg. She could imagine this dangling Pooh saying in sympathy, "Oh, bother."

Wendy drove the Pathfinder to the back of the parking lot and found a parking spot close to the exterior stairs, snugging the front tires up against the mounds of plowed snow. The Fargo Motor Lodge was a long, two-leveled rectangle surrounded by a U-shaped parking lot. The out-of-service elevator, flanked by vending and ice machines, was located near the front of the motel, the highway end. The stairs were in back, near a pair of Dumpsters wafting a sour odor more potent than the natural fragrance provided by the jagged line of spruces just beyond the lot.

Wendy removed only her overnight bag from the storage compartment. The Pathfinder had been her mother's car and was a better choice for cross-country travel than her Civic, even discounting the constant threat of snow-covered roads. But driving the Pathfinder was a constant reminder to Wendy that her mother was gone, as was her father, both killed by Gina Thorne in the lightning storm that had also destroyed the college president's mansion along with most of her parents' belongings. Wendy had placed in storage the few items that had survived. She hadn't disposed of anything, deciding to wait a year before making any decisions. That year had stretched into sixteen months. Easier to stay away from home, away from the memories that lived there among her parents' possessions. Someday she would be strong enough to deal with them. Just not today. And probably not tomorrow.

She wheeled her bag along the green outdoor carpeting of the covered, exterior walkway, holding onto the extendable handle with a loose grip as she scanned for her room. Tarnished brass numerals on a white door with chipped, weather-beaten paint. *Probably a high lead content in every chip and flake,* Wendy thought.

Since motel management hadn't converted the room locks to electronic card readers, she could practice her magical lock picking. She ran her right index finger along the grooves and ridges of the brass key, a delicate caress, before stuffing it and the plastic fob into her jeans pocket. A slight cheat for what was to come, but it would save a lot of time. She slipped off her multi-bead bracelet, spinning it around until her left thumb and index finger pinched the agate geode and the quartz crystal beside it. Quartz crystal helped with many magical tasks, so she had paired many of the beads with a crystal in order to touch both simultaneously. The power beads helped her focus, pulling the magical energy in through her receptive hand and shaping it to her will. She'd been practicing magic without using the beads, but visualization always came much faster with them. Whenever the Crone was in mentor mode, she deemed the bracelet a magical crutch, reminding Wendy that in her Wiccan infancy she had also needed another crutch, the ritual of the protective circle, to perform magic. *Easy for her to call it a crutch,* Wendy thought. *I can still travel five miles a helluva lot faster with the crutch of a car than I can on foot.* Sometimes expediency won out.

Next Wendy extended her right, projective hand to the door lock, centering her awareness there, sensing the inner mechanism of the lock. Her first locks had been of the pushbutton variety. Keyed locks were much harder, but her right index finger still held the tactile memory of the room key. She visualized the energy as golden light, solidifying into the shape of the key and, as she released the energy, she turned her right wrist, twisting the phantom key into the lock. She grinned as she heard the bolt retract into its housing. *The Crone would be proud,* Wendy thought. *Well, except for the cheating key caress part.* Of course, the irony of working this type of magic was that she could have opened the door with the real key in a fraction of the time. Naturally, she was preparing for the day she lost or forgot a key or for when, should the occasion arise, she needed to break into a room.

A moment later she was inside room two-thirteen, assessing her overnight accommodations. She flicked on a light, raised her eyebrows and sighed. "At least it's clean," she consoled herself, but crinkled her nose at the faint, sour odor. The blankets were thin and ratty, the threadbare carpeting sported a half dozen cigarette burns and the wallpaper featured a plethora of Rorschachian stains. After locking and chaining her door, she tossed her bag on the lone chair and sat down at the foot of the bed. Loud voices and classic rock bled through the cheap walls on both sides of her room. Sounded like a party in one room, an argument in the other.

Wendy placed her elbows on her knees, chin on her palms. "And why, exactly, did I want to spend tonight isolated and alone?"

SOMEWHERE ALONG I-29
140 MILES MORTH OF FARGO, NORTH DAKOTA

It sees the path to her—its special prey—and the path stretches along the paved road made by man. So it runs parallel to the road—almost tireless and ever hungry—but still envious of the machines roaring by unthinkably fast. Even its best loping speed is no match for the gleaming vehicles. She too must travel in one of them, for it senses she is much farther away now than she was in the morning. If it ever hopes to remove the compulsion from its mind by destroying her, it will have to adapt to human ways and human tools. It must look for an opportunity to travel as humans now travel. Then, and only then, will it close the distance and end the chase.

Slipping into its human glamour, it veers toward the road and slows to an intolerable pace—a human pace—and waits for an opportunity . . .

CHAPTER THREE

"Pull over."

"Aw, Christ, Clay! Don't tell me you gotta piss now. You'll freeze your dick off."

"No, I don't gotta piss, Hank," Thomas Clay said indignantly from the passenger side of the rust-spotted navy blue Dodge Ram pickup truck. "Just pull over, would ya?"

Henry Turner swung the pickup onto the side of the road, tires crunching over the remnants of the last snowfall. "Jesus, we're still a couple hours from Fargo. This better be good." He talked with an unlit Marlboro dangling from the corner of his lips. Couple weeks since he'd decided to quit. Again. Sometimes just holding one between his lips was enough. Now and again he gave in to the urge to light up. *Fuck cold turkey*, he thought, and was often heard to say moments before he fished a Zippo out of his jacket.

"That old-timer back there," Clay indicated with a backward jerk of his thumb. "Let's give him a ride to Grand Forks or something 'fore he keels over."

"What old-timer?" Hank said, frowning as he looked at the rearview mirror. Finally, he turned around and stared out the back window, casting about until he saw the lumbering, hunched over figure, about a hundred yards behind them, and ten yards from the edge of the lonely interstate highway. Wild mane of white-gray hair, long black cloak. "Tall son of a bitch, ain't he?"

Clay nodded.

"What the hell's he doing out here in the middle of goddamn nowhere?"

"Car broke down, maybe."

"I never saw it."

"Me neither, but he's a long ways from anywhere . . ."

"Fast for a geezer, I'll give him that."

"Wanna back up some?"

"What the hell for? He sees us stopped. Look at that. Gotta little spring in his step now, don't he?" Hank rubbed his hands in front of the heating vents. "Long goddamn way to Fargo. Janet's friend better be as hot and horny as you say she is." Clay nodded, cleared his throat and reached for the bill of his Minnesota Twins baseball cap, bending the sides down. Nervous gesture. Hank caught it, figured something was up. "Ah, fuck, man! You fed me some bullshit. Didn't you?"

"Hell, Hank, you ain't gotta worry. Trust me. Janet told me Lisette's real cute."

Hank Turner had a sun-weathered face, narrow gray eyes the color of dirty ice, a bushy mustache and two days' worth of stubble on his chin. While the stubble gave him a rugged look, he'd been thinking about growing a beard to hide his weak chin. Ever since Maria ran off, he'd been concerned about his appearance. "Never actually saw this Lisette yourself, is what you're telling me."

"No, not personally," Clay admitted. "But she's divorced, like you. And she's got an impressive rack, from what I hear."

"And a double-wide ass to go with it?"

"No way, Hank," Clay said, shaking his head. "Janet's got a good figure, right? Well, those two swap outfits. Wear the same size. Don't worry about it."

Hank nodded. "Bet she's got a horse face, then."

"You're just a miserable bastard, Hank. No wonder you don't get laid."

"Get laid plenty."

"Not counting sheep?"

"Fuck you, Clay," Hank said, reaching for his Zippo. "Look, your geezer's here."

"Fine. Now stop worrying about Lisette, Hank. It's New Year's Eve. You will get drunk. And you will get laid. Guaranteed."

The old-timer walked up beside the passenger window and stood there, hunched over, staring in at them. His hair was an untamed mess around his head. His face—or what they could see of it through the bushy eyebrows, wild mustache and beard—was pale and unnaturally still.

As a kid, Hank had visited a wax museum in Las Vegas once. He remembered the lifeless faces, lacking all animation, the unseeing glass eyes. Remembered they scared the shit out of him too. Gave him nightmares for weeks. The old man had the same glassy eyes as those celebrity replicas in the wax museum. They seemed to stare without seeing. His clothes were unremarkable, the coat long and black, open to reveal a white shirt or sweater. For some reason it was hard to make out any details, like an out-of-focus photograph.

Clay rolled down the window. "Where you headed?" Without speaking, the old man pointed south, along the interstate. "Consider this your lucky day. Hop in. We'll make room."

As Clay opened the door, a breeze swirled into the cab of the pickup truck, bringing with it a foul odor. Hank wrinkled his nose in disgust. "Fuck that, Clay. He ain't riding up here. Smelly bastard can sit in back."

"Outside? Exposed?"

"Better than walking."

Clay shrugged at the old man and hooked his arm around, indicating the bed of the pickup truck. "Man says you gotta ride in back, old-timer."

The old man nodded, stepped back and climbed over the side panel of the truck, which creaked and groaned under the sudden increase in weight. For a moment, Hank pictured the front wheels of the pickup rising off the ground and gave a nervous laugh. The old guy was about seven feet tall, seemed scrawny but his build must have been deceptive. Something definitely odd about him, aside from the glassy eyes and funky odor. *Maybe he ain't right in the head,* Hank thought. The old man just sat there, still as a statue, broad back to the cab, knees drawn up to his chest, arms wrapped around them.

After Clay rolled up the window, Hank put the Dodge Ram in gear and pulled out onto I-29 again. "Some fucking smell, ain't it?" Hank said. Clay nodded. "Like the son of a bitch forgot how to wipe."

"Maybe he's got no control down there," Clay suggested. "Happens to some, they get real old."

"Feel sorry for the bastard if you want," Hank said. "But

New Year's Eve or not, neither of us is gonna be dipping our wicks tonight if we smell like a backed-up sewer."

"Well, he's in back now," Clay said. "So there's no problem. Trust me."

Some primal instinct warned Hank not to have faith in Clay's assurances. As premonitions go, it was a good one. Fortunately, Hank would have only one brief, painful moment to regret not heeding it.

WINDALE, MASSACHUSETTS

Kayla's neck was stiff. She mumbled, then frowned because the words hadn't come out right. The right side of her forehead was pressed against a cold window.

"Kayla?"

Her eyes fluttered open. Awareness returned, her surroundings coming into slow focus. She'd been unconscious, slouched sideways in the passenger seat of Bobby's Mustang. She pushed herself upright, clapped a hand over a jaw-cracking yawn and noticed the sky was dark. On either side of the moving car, the trees were gloomy silhouettes towering over the oddly incandescent white carpet of snow. "Had the weirdest dream . . ." Kayla shook her head. "We were in the woods and—"

"That wasn't a dream."

Silent, Kayla stared at him for a moment; then her hand touched beneath her nostrils. The bleeding had stopped.

"I'm taking you to Windale General."

"No," she said. "No hospitals."

"Kayla, you passed out back there."

"I'm fine now," she said, but he remained unconvinced.

"Look, I haven't been sleeping well, okay? Everything just . . . caught up with me. That's all." She took a deep, nervous breath. "My nose, was it . . . ?"

"You had a nosebleed."

"The blood—was it . . . ?"

"You thought it was black."

"It wasn't black?"

"It was dark back there," Bobby said. "You probably just imagined your blood was black." Kayla looked at her fingers, to examine the blood stains, but found none. "I cleaned you up. To avoid staining your clothes." He shrugged. "Rubbed snow on a handkerchief. And before you ask, I don't have the handkerchief. Lost it back there somewhere. Must have fallen out of my pocket."

"You carried me back to the car?"

"Couldn't wake you. And I wasn't about to leave you lying there unconscious while I ran for help."

"That's a long way to carry someone."

"Hardly noticed."

She grinned. "Stronger than you look, huh?"

"Pure adrenaline, Kay. I was worried about you."

"Did you . . . lose time on your way out?"

He shook his head. "Not that I checked my watch, but I came out fast, no change in the sky. Whatever that effect is, I guess it only works one way. Personally, I think we imagined it and spooked ourselves."

Knowing the truth of it, Kayla shivered, but chose not to argue the point. "Anyway, I'm fine now. Let's stick to the original plan. Take me to your place."

"I'd feel better if a doctor examined you."

She rubbed his upper arm. "I'd feel better if you examined me."

"Well," he said, studying her with his jade green eyes, his resolve weakening. "I can't exactly drag you to the hospital."

"No, you can't," Kayla said. "So take me to your place while the night's still young." *Besides,* she thought, *the hospital would be a waste of time.* Doctors weren't equipped to diagnose what she thought was wrong with her. *Maybe Wendy . . .* But Wendy hadn't been in Windale in months and even then only briefly. *I'm on my own.* She grabbed Bobby's right hand where it rested on the gear shift and squeezed.

They were silent the rest of the drive.

Bobby rented both sides of a twin house from a little old lady who spent nine months of the year in Florida. During the fall and spring semesters at Danfield, Bobby would sublet the left side to undergrads who had their own transportation and didn't mind living several miles from campus. Some even preferred the distance for the privacy and perspective it granted. Once these students discovered their landlord was a policeman, they scaled back any ideas they might have had regarding wild, all-night keg parties, which in turn kept the neighbors pacified.

A morning person by nature, Bobby had chosen the right side of the twin for himself, enjoying the early-morning light that spilled through the windows of that unit. Also, the right-side driveway had a carport, which protected the Mustang's shiny red coat from the ravages of sun, sleet and bird bombardment. Bobby would have preferred a garage, but the carport was sufficient for a rental home.

Kayla always teased Bobby that the house was too big for him. He'd brought precious few belongings with him from Baltimore and hadn't put much effort into furnishing the place since he'd moved to Windale. Lack of time was his refrain. Some rooms were furnished and seemed complete, others completely forgotten. The dining room featured a floor lamp, a wicker umbrella stand and a Navajo throw rug in the middle of the hardwood floor. Nothing else. In the second bedroom, he kept an underused personal computer on an old metal desk, along with an uncomfortable looking cot for a potential guest. Potted cacti, in various shapes and sizes, were scattered throughout the house. On the walls were some family photographs, scenes of the southwestern United States, and several framed reproductions of Wanted posters from the days of the Wild West.

Bobby hung their coats in the hall closet. When he offered to make them steaks and baked potatoes, Kayla suggested they order pizza instead. Even though Kayla hadn't given up meat entirely, Bobby's tastes in beef ran to medium rare and Kayla hadn't been in the mood to watch blood ooze across a dinner plate since her nightmares began. With an accommodating shrug, Bobby picked up the phone and placed the order. "Looks like we have an hour to kill before the pizza gets here."

Kayla stepped close to him and placed her hands on his shoulders. "Wrong."

"What?"

"It's not an hour to kill," Kayla said. "It's an hour to thrill."

"Interesting perspective," Bobby said, touching his index finger to the thin metal ring that pierced the middle of her lower lip. "Have any specific ideas?"

"Let's start with a steaming hot shower." Kayla brought his face down to hers, kissed his lips in two soft passes, left to right and back again. "After that, let's just improvise."

"I'm in."

"Soon," Kayla said with a mischievous grin. "But first, undress me, sir."

She unzipped and kicked off her boots, then raised her arms high. Bobby pulled her sweater over her head, waiting for her to tug her head and arms free. Underneath she wore a black bra with a front clasp, which Bobby promptly unfastened. The released weight of her breasts pressed sensually against the back of his hands. "Hmm . . . you always wear a bra."

"Fashion tip," Kayla said, her breath catching as he slipped his hands inside the satin cups of the bra. "Never mix sweaters with nipple rings." Only her left nipple was pierced—with a tiny surgical steel ring—but the first sweater snag had been so painful she'd sworn it would be the last.

She turned within the circle of his arms, feeling a delicious chill of excitement as he held her breasts in the palms of his hands and stroked her nipples with his thumbs, paying extra attention to the ring looping through the left one.

What Kayla called her public piercings consisted of the steel posts beside her eyebrows, the right nostril ring, the bottom lip ring—and of course her earlobes and cartilage were fair game for numerous piercings along with some decorative ear cuffs. Her navel ring was seasonally public, exposed during the warmer months, concealed the rest of the year. The tongue stud was a year-round wildcard, sometimes noticed, sometimes overlooked. She'd worked hard to lose the telltale lisp and, to compensate for the obstruction in her mouth, she often spoke with precise, clipped diction.

Bobby's hands slid down her abdomen to unbutton and unzip her jeans. He slipped his thumbs and index fingers inside the black denim and pulled down her pants. For a moment, his right hand lingered over her black panties, pressing against the mound of her sex. Soon he gave into temptation and slipped off her underpants as well.

While Bobby hardly noticed, or at least rarely commented on Kayla's public piercings, both of her private piercings were an endless source of fascination for him. In addition to having her left nipple pierced, and only after a couple shots of vodka to bolster her courage, she'd had her prepuce—the hood of her clitoris—pierced. So, a second little ring down there, but this one held a tiny metal ball that dangled against that particularly pleasurable spot of the female anatomy. While Kayla had no regrets about this most intimate of her piercings, it had tripped some sort of social circuit breaker in her brain, basically a simple note-to-self: *that's enough.* She'd heard the stories about people who became addicted to plastic surgery or tattoos, to the point where self-expression failed to pay heed to self-censorship. She didn't mind others thinking she was a freak. Actually, she encouraged that and found it amusing, her little rebel yell. But she couldn't tolerate thinking of herself as a freak. *We all draw the line somewhere,* she thought. *Or should.* For now and forever, she hoped she would remain satisfied with the quantity and variety of her piercings.

Kayla shuddered with a wave of pleasure when Bobby's hands slid down to her sex again, pressed against the tiny ring and ball, rolling it against her flesh. She smiled to herself when she felt his hands stop moving. "Yes?"

"You're, um, completely bare down there."

"Ah, you noticed."

"Hard to miss."

"I've been in an anti-hair mood lately," Kayla said. "I figured, why stop with shaving my legs and underarms. Thought about shaving my head too, but maybe the blue dye job will be enough of a change, for now." She laughed, then gasped as she felt his hands roaming lower. "You like?"

"Hmm . ."

"I think that's a yes," she said, leaning back against his chest while she enjoyed the exploration of his hands at the juncture of her thighs. "Ooh—definitely a yes."

She turned around again, letting his hands slide across her hips and down to cup her bare bottom. Kayla swiped her tongue across the ring in her bottom lip. Her suddenly clumsy fingers unfastened the buttons of his flannel shirt, then the button of his jeans. Within a minute they were both naked. "Boop boop be doop," Kayla said in her best Betty Boop impression. She took Bobby by the hand and led him back to the bathroom and the promised steaming hot shower.

They both knew the shower was merely prelude. Teasing each other with the caress of hands and lips and tongues, they stoked the heat of each other's desire to unbearable levels. A soapy tangle of sliding, bumping, jostling limbs, eyes closed but mouths agape and gasping against the hot spray of water and swelling waves of pleasure. Half unwrapped in plush towels, they stumbled together into the bedroom, falling across the bed, still slippery skin wetting blankets as they rolled about, not quite thrashing yet impatient, seeking a comfortable position of mutual satisfaction.

In terms of energetic expression of passion, Bobby had the initial edge, perhaps inflamed by the visual novelty of her clean-shaven sex above the gleaming prepuce accessory. His brow furrowed in pleasurable concentration, he held her upraised knees apart to accommodate his deep thrusts inside her. He punctuated each downward thrust by grinding his pelvis against hers, exciting her with the movement and pressure of the metal ring and ball. She countered each of his thrusts with a sharp intake of breath, her eyes fluttering back as she tried to cling to each moment, each sensation, each rolling surge of pleasure. When Bobby finally shuddered with an exhausting release of his own, sagging against her, she pulled him even closer and pressed her mouth to his. She worked her tongue between his lips and into his mouth, to the sound of the tongue stud clicking against her teeth and his. But soon she turned her attentions elsewhere.

A short while later, after coaxing him into new life with her mouth and tongue, she straddled him, taking him deep inside her in one long, shuddering stroke. This time she took it slow, her legs still trembling and weak with the sweet aftershocks of ecstasy as she watched the deep rise and fall of his broad chest. His hands stroked the outside of her thighs, cupped her bottom and, when she leaned forward to kiss his hairy chest, found and teased her breasts. Her flesh tingled everywhere and each moment was a distillation of fresh pleasure. Almost unconsciously, she increased the tempo of their lovemaking to a feverish pace. Her breath grew short. When Bobby closed his eyes, she closed hers. That way she could concentrate on the feeling of him inside her, filling her, pulsing and swelling, approaching the brink . . . and passing it with a rush of breath and a shuddering release of taut muscles, a sweet surrender.

With a weary sigh, she collapsed against him, luxuriating in the warmth of their mingled sweat and shared breathing, letting each moment pulse by without protest, feeling him slip at last from inside her. She curled up beside him, right arm across his chest and said, "Hmm . . ."

"That's all? Hmm?"

"Too tired to talk."

"Hmm," he agreed. After a few minutes, he said, "What's it feel like . . . down there?" To clarify matters, he turned toward her and let his left hand scout the area in question.

"Ah, well, everything is very sensitive to touch," she said and placed her hand over his, holding it still. Then she reached up to his face and stroked his mustache with her index finger. "Like I can feel every whisker." He smiled, but a moment later she looked down at his chest and frowned. "Oh! I scratched you." Her fingers traced two parallel scratches from his collarbone to the bottom of his chest, stippled red in the middle, where her nails had cut deepest. She pressed her fingertips against his flesh for a moment, then held them up to her face, lips pursed.

"You got a little carried away there at the end," he said, a nervous smile on his face. She could tell he wasn't too thrilled with the way she was examining his blood. "Don't worry about it."

The doorbell chimed before she could respond.

Kayla hopped out of bed without bothering to cover her nudity. She looked at her fingers again. "Wait here," she said. "I have an idea."

As she strode from the bedroom, he jumped up, grabbed a bathrobe from his closet and followed her. "Answer the door like that, you better not tip the pizza guy."

At the bottom of the stairs, she turned toward the kitchen. "Pizza guy?" The doorbell chimed again. "Oh—that pizza guy. She glanced down at her own nakedness, accessorized with gleaming surgical steel. "Then keep him out of the kitchen."

As Bobby belted his robe and picked through some bills

he'd left on the small table near the front door, Kayla walked down the hallway into the kitchen and flipped on the overhead lights. She wasn't too concerned with staying out of the line of sight of the front door—the frozen delivery boy was hustling to make a buck on New Year's Eve, so the exhibitionist in her hated to deny him a cheap thrill—but she was preoccupied with rifling through the kitchen drawers searching for what she needed.

Her back was to Bobby as he joined her in the kitchen. Dropping the pizza box on the table, he turned to the cabinet over the sink, opened it and removed two paper plates. "Pizza cutter's in the back of—" He looked at her face, then his gaze followed hers, down to the paring knife clutched in her white-knuckled right hand. "Kayla . . . ?"

She blinked, looking up at him as if she'd just come out of a trance. "Huh?"

"What's with the knife?"

She swallowed, nervous. "I—I need to make myself bleed."

Wendy Ward's Mirror Book
December 31, 2001
Moon: waning gibbous, day 16
Fargo, North Dakota

Wendy Ward, reporting live from the claustrophobic confines of Fargo Motor Lodge's room 213, where, after several hours of mind-numbing boredom, I've successfully deconstructed the strange and sour mélange of odors into its constituent components of old beer, old vomit and fresh Lysol. But, hey, points to management for the Lysol. Lost cause, but at least they're trying.

Went down to the vending machines for a Diet Coke a

little while ago and saw Creepy-Desk-Clerk-Lloyd lurking
by the ice machine like a junkie near an ATM. Told me to
consider myself invited to a *private* party in Room 240.
Emphasis on the private. Probably him and a couple of
his buddies watching the Spice channel. I thanked him
and, as they say, beat a hasty retreat. Maybe if he thinks
I'll show up at his skanky party he'll leave me alone for
now. (sigh)

Meanwhile, I'm worried about Hannah . . . the Crone
never returned to Tara's place, and I've had this feeling,
okay premonition, that I should call Karen to check on
Hannah. Called twice, but nobody home. Left a message
on the machine. Who knows? Maybe Karen and Art went
to a New Year's Eve party and left Hannah with a sitter.
Hope so. If I don't stop worrying about everything out of
my control, I'll go bat guano.

Bigger question: How did I end up here? Even before
I *activated* the time-release spell lodged in my back-brain
for over a year, the Crone had warned me to leave Winnipeg. Too afraid to stay . . . and too chicken to drive the
rest of the way to Minneapolis. Couldn't take the chance
Alex would pull me into his orbit. Alone with Alex on
New Year's Eve . . . Okay, that is *so* not happening. I'd
burn up in the atmosphere. Tomorrow is soon enough.
So maybe I picked this dump to punish myself, my cowardice. Maybe I deserve the funky smell, the cigarette-
scarred carpet and the corrugated cardboard walls.

Seems I've been punishing myself a lot lately. Well, if
I'm being honest with myself—and what else is a mirror
book for?—there's no "lately" about it. I've been punishing myself since . . . Wither murdered my parents to punish me. (Ironic how I keep finding ways to continue her

work.) More honesty? I haven't been traveling or sight-seeing, I've been running away. Hiding from everyone and everything that meant anything to me. Out of sight, out of mind. Pretending that when I return, all will be magically restored.

Magic . . .

I miss you, Mom and Dad. So much. More with each passing day. Hard to believe a whole calendar year has passed. Every day of an entire year spent without seeing you or hearing you or . . . They say time heals all wounds, but it also destroys. The past is cold and immutable and unforgiving. That's what I've learned.

It's a lie, though, that part about out of sight, out of mind. When I close my eyes, I still see your faces. I re-member you and our times together and I smile. But I also remember what she did to you, because of me, and then it hurts so much inside I can't breathe. Magic can't fix that. Nothing can fix that. I should have warned you. I should have . . . All I ever wanted was for you both to be proud of me as your daughter. Instead, I failed you, in the worst possible way. I sacrificed you because of my own arrogance. I thought I knew . . .

I realize now that I'm alone in this awful place not be-cause the dead can't grant forgiveness, but because I don't deserve their forgiveness. Mom and Dad, I know you don't feel that way—you are both kind, gentle souls with a remarkable capacity for compassion—and maybe you don't even blame me, but you know how stubborn I am. Leopards and spots.

I can't imagine a day when I am not completely sorry for the mess I made of everything, nor can I foresee a day where that makes one bit of difference. Yet that is how I

live now, day to day. Most days are hard. The rest are unbearable.

If I had any delusions about sleeping through the
changeover to the New Year, oblivious to the festivities,
those delusions have been raucously obliterated. The
neighbors (i.e., rooms 212 and 214) are already getting
into the holiday spirit—make that spirits. And why wait
until midnight to make good use of noisemakers?

Can't sleep. Might as well practice my spheres and
such.

Tomorrow's another year.

Wendy clicked the toolbar button to save her mirror
book entry to her notebook's hard drive, then switched off
the computer and slipped it back into the carrying case. She
hadn't bothered to connect to the hotel's phone line to check
e-mail. Although she'd switched to a national Internet
provider at the start of her travels and could probably find a
local dial-up number—*well, maybe not, this being North
Dakota*—tonight she preferred to stay out of touch with
everyone.

She'd changed into her blue-sky-and-clouds pajamas and
pulled back the blankets on the bed so she could sit on the
relatively clean sheets to type on her computer. Now she
assumed a modified lotus position, back straight, legs
crossed, but with hands resting palm up on her knees, as if
she were cupping water. With the room's fan turned to high,
hot air from the heater rattled through the vents and flowed
around her. Hotter than was comfortable, but she needed
that fuel to aid her magic. Though it had been a tough concept for a native New Englander to grasp, she'd learned in a
long-ago science class that there was no such thing as cold,

only the relative absence of heat. A refrigerator worked not by making things cold, but by removing heat from its interior. Wendy's task was not to remove the heat from her room, but to manipulate the ambient heat into a concentrated form. Fire.

She'd had nominal success with this magical art. The idea of conjuring flame, inviting burns, was a little unnerving. Her first time had been under extreme duress, while pinned to the ground, threatened with rape and mutilation. Compared to the threat posed by her attacker, the risk of minor burns seemed trivial. Since then, she'd managed to conjure flame without a literal knife at her throat, but her progress was slow, her flames unimpressive.

After a deep, cleansing breath, she began a regular breathing pattern of inhaling through her nostrils, exhaling through her mouth. The steady, disciplined respiration helped her focus, was an almost instant trigger to the concentration needed for magic, and allowed her to block out the wailing heavy metal bass of AC/DC shaking the walls of her room. After more than a year of magical studies, she could center herself with little effort. Long moments passed and she was aware of her slow, steady heartbeat as she willed the heat in the room toward her through the power of advanced visualization. She imagined shimmering heat waves rolling toward her, swirling into dense spheres an inch above her palms. And she began to compress the spheres, willing them from basketball size to bowling ball, to softball, tennis ball, Ping-Pong ball and then marble, glowing with amber light. She squeezed again hard, imagining them shrunk to pinpoints of unblinking light—then singularities. At that moment, twin flames erupted above her cupped palms.

She tempered her excitement with a measured exhalation, maintaining the flames, continuing to feed them with the heat she siphoned from the surrounding air. *Now for the hard part*, she thought. She always converted the gathered heat into flame by visualizing a critical level of compression, smaller being hotter. As the Crone often reminded her, conjured, supernatural flame differed from the natural variety. Having no fuel to consume, supernatural flame's existence depended solely on the concentration of the magic user, unless and until it was applied to a fuel source, at which point it could take on a—for want of a better word—life of its own. Supernatural flame conjured in midair was fleeting, difficult to maintain, harder to vary. Wendy concentrated on gathering more heat to feed her two-inch flames. Gooseflesh raced along her arms and legs. Later she would notice the room thermostat's reading had dipped several degrees during her exercise. For now, she fed her supernatural flames and could not suppress a smile as they swelled above her palms, pure blue base with flickering orange tongues. Yet, as the flames grew—almost wider than her hands now—their center of . . . origin dipped, closing the narrow gap between fire and flesh. Instead of hovering above her cupped palms, the flames were sinking, about to make contact with her bare flesh. Maintaining her concentration, she skirted the image of charred and smoking flesh, seeking comfort from the Crone's assurances that the flame was in her control, literally in her hands. *Unless I'm careless, it won't burn me. I control its expression.*

The moment the flame touched her palm—a feathery, fluttering sensation, but warm and comfortable, not hot, *not hot!*—something banged against the wall, hard enough to dislodge an old painting from its hook and send it crashing to the floor. The print of a deer drinking from a stream slipped from the broken frame. And Wendy lost her concentration. As she looked away from the flames bobbing above and around her hands, she yelped in pain.

She whipped her hands side to side, but the supernatural flames had disappeared a moment after her concentration stopped feeding them. Only that brief moment of lost control burned because the next moment her loss of concentration extinguished the fire. *Just lucky the flame hadn't dipped low enough to touch my pajamas when I lost control,* she thought. *Otherwise, the supernatural flame would have had a natural fuel source for a Wendy roast.* She muttered to herself, "If I'm gonna play with fire in bed, I'd better stock up on flame-retardant undies."

A fist pounded on her wall. "Hey! Dude! Sorry about that New Year's Eve clumsiness! Won't happen again!"

Wendy examined her palms. Tender and a little pink, maybe, but otherwise none the worse for juggling cantaloupe-sized fireballs. *I'll find carnival work yet,* she thought. "Don't worry about it," she yelled back, then realized her mistake.

"Cool!" It took him a moment longer. In a lower but still loud voice, "Hey, man, it's a *dudette.*" Calling through the wall again, "Hey! C'mon over! We got a keg and weed and some serious party tunes!"

"*We're* fine!" Wendy called. "Thanks, anyway."

A considering pause, then, "Whatever, man. Rock on!"

Whatever, Wendy thought. She resumed her breathing pattern, but this time worked on conjuring her protective magic sphere. The fastest she'd ever conjured a protective sphere was the day her parents died, during her failed attempt to rescue them. Again, extreme stress had been the key, either breaking through her mental blocks or aiding her visualization. Maybe both. Using her athame, the black-handled ritual knife, as her *crutch*, she could conjure a sphere in several seconds. Without it, maybe twenty seconds. In either case, her sphere was about nine feet in diameter, large enough to protect several stationary people huddled close to the center. The size was fine, but her conjuration speed needed work. The Crone had told Wendy her goal should be to raise a sphere as fast as she could flip a light switch. Her life and the lives of others would depend on it.

Now, however, instead of improving, Wendy's concentration began to deteriorate. As much as she blocked out the heavy metal music and loud voices, one imagined sound dominated all of them and set her skin to itching. The ticking of the clock in her head. *The midnight hour's close at hand*, she thought. *And I'm at party central*. But what were her options? Wherever she went, somebody would be celebrating, ringing in the New Year with loved ones and friends or casual but enthusiastic acquaintances.

"I'd have to hide in my car to avoid . . ." Wendy's voice trailed off. "Of course, the car, stupid! Wasn't looking forward to sleeping in this dump anyway."

Despite the late hour, anxiety replaced exhaustion. *Check out now, drive to Minneapolis. By the time I arrive, midnight will be past, all parties avoided. Find a hotel in the wee hours. Call Alex in the morning. Sure there's a chance Alex will stay up all night, but I wouldn't be inconsiderate enough to call and find out.*

She hopped off the bed and flipped open her suitcase.

Fifteen minutes later she was dressed and checking out of the Fargo Motor Lodge. To her relief, creepy Lloyd had been relieved by Sylvester, a sallow, paunchy night clerk in his late fifties with an air of total boredom. No questions about her stay or why she was leaving, just handed her a receipt with the phlegmatic parting words, "Come again."

She wheeled her suitcase along the narrow parking lot to the rear of the Pathfinder, then fished her car keys out of her coat pocket. A weak light mounted on a pole beside the twin, pungent Dumpsters cast a wan glow over the parking lot. The only other illumination came from lights mounted along the exterior walkway on the second floor of the lodge. At that moment, all she wanted was a quick exit from the cold, smelly parking lot.

As she fitted the key to the lock, she heard the steady tap-tap of approaching footfalls. *Not again*, she thought, sighing, even before she looked up.

"Can't leave yet," Lloyd said, a cigar in one hand, an open bottle of champagne in the other. He sported a sloppy grin, but there was nothing amused about his eyes. "It's time to party."

I-29, FARGO, NORTH DAKOTA

Hank figured it was nerves. After the long drive in the rickety old Dodge Ram pickup, they were finally in Fargo, which meant they were just a few miles from their rendezvous with Janet and Lisette, the cute friend with the big rack. Hank always let bluster do the work of self-confidence and now he was wondering if, as Clay had all but guaranteed, he would be getting laid tonight. Prospects seemed good, as long as Hank didn't fuck up the meet and greet. He mumbled something to himself and reached into his jacket pocket.

"What?"

"Fuck cold turkey." Hank chuckled, but his mouth had gone dry. He lit the cigarette that had been dangling from the corner of his mouth. He inhaled, savoring the taste of the first cigarette he'd allowed himself in the last two days. *Hell,* he thought, *I can quit tomorrow just as easy as today.* He blew out a forceful stream of smoke, already feeling a boost in his confidence. *Bitch better not think she's too good for Hank Turner.* "Hand me the flask in the glove box, will ya?"

Clay passed him the whiskey without comment. Hank unscrewed the cap and took two quick swigs, no more than a shot and a half, he figured. Just to take the edge off. *Haven't even met the bitch yet and she's making me nervous as hell.* The last thing on his mind was the big smelly bastard hunkered down in the truck bed. Until it was too late.

Ahead, a traffic light blinked to yellow.

Both hands on the wheel, cigarette pinched between the fingers of his left and the flask clutched in his right, Hank figured he could make the light easy. He gunned the accelerator.

STOP!

"What the fuck?"

Clay winced, hands clapped over his ears.

Hank glanced in the rearview mirror and saw the reflected image of the long gaunt face staring through the back window, big mitts pressed to the glass. "Bastard yelling at me . . ." But the loud voice, almost a roar, seemed to come from inside Hank's head. "Sit tight, old-timer!" Hank yelled.

"Hank!"

One glance back at the road showed a van coming across the intersection. "Ah, shit!" Hank floored the gas pedal to jump through the intersection before the van plowed into his door panel.

At the same moment, the scream blasted in his mind again. STOP!

Hank's hands jerked on the wheel. He dropped the flask, but managed to swerve around the van, even as the horn wailed an indignant protest. For a frozen moment, the sudden crash of breaking glass refused to register. He'd missed the van, so how—?

He saw what appeared to be a furred arm smash through the back window, a large clawed hand grabbing Clay under the chin and pulling him back—just as Hank's own head was wrenched back into the shattered glass. His foot shot out straight, flooring the accelerator as thick claws gouged his flesh. A warm flood gushed down his chest. Darkness seeped in from the edges of his vision. The next to last thing Hank saw was Clay's head ripped from his body with a sickening crunch of yielding bone and a fountain of blood. Then the claws of the other hand burrowed deeper into Hank's throat.

The pickup swerved, bounced over a median in excess of sixty miles an hour, showering sparks from the screeching undercarriage as it lurched up the driveway of the Fargo Motor Lodge.

The last thing Hank Turner saw was the front office of the Fargo Motor Lodge, its wide plate-glass window with a red neon sign centered high, a one word enticement: VACANCY.

Unfortunately, Hank was checking out.

It is unpracticed in human communication. Although its glamour has allowed it to pass as human, decades of mindless sleep have atrophied its ability to interact with men. Vocal chords not yet nimble enough to mimic human speech. Yet when the pulsing blue path grows bright, almost too bright to bear, it commands the humans to stop their rushing vehicle, commands in the only way possible, with a directive from its mind. A simple, forceful command to—STOP!

The human hears but does not obey. Instead, the vehicle seems to travel even faster than before. The human to his left, the one holding the wheel, yells back, defiant, refusing to stop. It shrieks its command again to no avail.

Impatient, it reacts with the simple logic of violence. If the humans are dead, they are powerless and their vehicle will stop.

Shoving its arms through the glass barrier, it grabs their heads, claws gouging deep into the soft flesh of their necks. Human spinal chords are no match for its inhuman strength. Bone and cartilage protest for a futile moment or two before yielding. Geysers of blood. The heads come spinning through the shattered barrier, bouncing around in the back of the vehicle, which continues to hurtle over the paved roads despite the death of its masters.

Bewildered, it decides it must leap from the speeding vehicle. But too late—it glances up from the slumped humans in time to see the vehicle about to strike a large human structure.

The impact is devastating, crushing the front end of the vehicle, which finally stops—violently.

Unsecured and unprepared, it flips over the roof, finding its own brutal impact . . .

WINDALE, MASSACHUSETTS

"Kayla, put the knife down." Bobby's voice was measured calm.

Determined, Kayla shook her head. "No," she said. "Why didn't I think of this before? Cutting myself. So obvious!"

Bobby saw something primal in her, standing there stark naked in his kitchen, the knife clutched in her right hand.

Primal, and unnerving. "Kayla, please put the knife down," he said, inching toward her. "It's very sharp."

"Sure hope so," Kayla said, a flare of anger or sarcasm lighting her eyes. "Bobby, you don't have to protect me. I don't need my own private bodyguard."

Calmly, "I know."

"Then stop acting like one," she said. She took a deep breath. "I can take care of myself."

"I realize that."

"We're more than that, aren't we?"

"Sure we are," he said. "But I'm afraid you're gonna hurt yourself."

Kayla pressed the gleaming blade of the black-handled paring knife against her bare left forearm. "I am. But only a little."

Bobby grabbed for the knife, but Kayla stepped out of reach, as if anticipating his move. "Kayla—knew I should've taken you to—why are you doing this?"

"Get some paper towels ready," she said. "I won't cut deep."

"I don't want you to cut at all! This is crazy."

"But I need to see it," she said. "It's the only way to be sure."

"Be sure about what?"

"My blood," Kayla said softly. "I need to be sure it's still my blood."

Bobby shook his head. "Kayla, you're not making sense. Of course it's your blood! How could it be anybody else's blood?"

Kayla shook her head. "Too complicated to explain right now," Kayla said. "Just let me do this."

"No—!"

He lunged—

—but was too late to stop her.

A moment of nightmarish inevitability as, with one quick slice, she opened up her arm. True to her word, she didn't cut deep, but ripe blood welled up from the wound in an instant. She tossed the knife in the sink, then looked up at him, smiling. He wondered if he was staring at the face of incipient madness. Had his rebel girl—while standing in his kitchen waiting for a slice of pizza—had she really gone insane, as simple as that?

Confused by the expression, or lack of expression, on his face, she shook her head, telling him he had it all wrong. She laughed, ran her right index finger along the bleeding cut, scooping up fresh blood as if it were cake frosting, and held it up for him to examine. "Don't you see?" she said. "It's red. Red! I'm still me."

And he wondered, *Why was that ever a question?*

FARGO, NORTH DAKOTA

"Don't tell me you forgot about my party invite," Lloyd said, his champagne-abetted smile not quite reaching his cold, pale eyes.

"Sorry," Wendy said. Going for nonchalance, she opened the back of the forest green Pathfinder and tossed the small overnight suitcase on top of her long-term luggage. "Too pooped to party."

He stroked his droopy mustache with the thumb of the hand holding the cigar, a gesture that drew unfortunate attention to his weak chin. "C'mon, it's New Year's Eve!"

"Even so," she said, slamming the overhead door shut, then checking to make sure the latch had engaged. "Gotta run."

He took a step closer, took another slug of champagne

from the bottle. "Gotta be something I can do, persuade you to hang around for a little while."

Wendy's left hand rose to her throat, almost casually touching the teardrop crystal pendant dangling from the silver chain around her neck. At the moment of contact, she felt a warm tingle, like a mild static shock, and her concentration compressed to a pinpoint of focus. Centered, she willed the pinpoint to bloom around her, an expanding bubble—a sphere to protect her. When she spoke, her voice was flat, emotionless. "Forget it, Lloyd."

"Aw, c'mon," he said, spreading his hands—see I'm harmless old Lloyd here. "Give a guy a chance."

"Back off! We're done here."

"How 'bout a taste of champagne?" He held the bottle toward her, taking another step closer. "It'll change your whole attitude."

Initially, Wendy had visualized her first protective spheres as rigid, kind of like a transparent, impervious alloy, but the Crone had told her that in the future Wendy would become creative with her use of protective spheres. Since then, Wendy always visualized her spheres as rigid from the outside in, malleable to her from the inside out.

As Lloyd moved another step closer, Wendy *pushed*, imagining a section of the sphere stretching out, a quick jab of protective shielding striking the creepy desk clerk in the solar plexus.

Lloyd gasped, taking two overbalanced steps backward before falling on his ass, the champagne bottle shattering on the ground, his cigar falling in his lap. He sputtered, confused, unable to speak.

Wendy heard a metallic screech from the front of the motel. She looked up just as a dark pickup truck careened across the front of the motel's parking lot at highway speed, trailing sparks, and plowed into the plate-glass window of the front office. The truck almost flipped over as the front end disappeared into the building, then the rear axle came crashing down. For a split second, Wendy thought somebody had been standing in the bed of the pickup truck, which would have been suicide. Then she remembered the tired old night clerk, Sylvester.

Maintaining her protective sphere, Wendy ran to the office. She could have blasted through the glass side door with the front of her sphere, but that would have meant another potentially lethal shower of glass shards inside the ruined office. She focused on the malleable interior of her sphere, clutched the door handle, which felt padded beneath the protection of the sphere, pulled it toward her and slipped inside.

A moment to survey the damage. The front end of the pickup had, of course, taken out the plate-glass window, crushed the television set and coffeemaker that had rested on a table in front of the window, then lurched across the office with enough force to demolish the clerk's desk before coming to a halt.

She heard a prolonged moan from beneath the shattered desk. Sylvester?

Inside the cab of the pickup, obscured by blood splattered on the cracked side windows, she saw the flickering amber glow of a raging fire. Oily black coils of smoke issued from the cab's shattered rear window. Tongues of flame were already ravaging the upholstery, along with the clothes of the men inside the cab. Wendy could heal burns, especially if she caught them early. Her protected hand folded around the door handle and pulled, but the door was crushed into

the frame of the truck. Something odd about the men. Two
of them. Partially blocked from view by the blood-smeared
windows, but if she looked in the gaps, maybe she could—
Oh, God! Goddess, no!

Nausea clutched her stomach like a greasy fist. She
gagged as a burning line of bile surged up her throat.

The bodies—the bodies—headless! Both decapitated in
the accident. *Too late, too late,* Wendy thought. *I can't—can't
help them . . .* If she saw the severed heads, she'd lose it. She
was afraid to look—anywhere!

Another moan from behind the collapsed desk.

Sylvester!

Wendy backed away from the pickup truck, casting her
gaze from the headless corpses, and slipped on the floor. She
glanced down. Gasoline! Pooling out from underneath the
truck, probably from a ruptured gas line. She had to move fast.

She gripped the edge of the desk in her protected hands
and tried to squeeze behind it, but she wasn't strong enough
to move it. With a deep, calming breath, she centered herself
again and, as she exhaled, imagined her sphere inflating, its
impervious exterior shoving outward—

—and the ruined desk screeched and cracked as it pushed
back, jostling the crumpled front end of the pickup truck a
foot or two. Sylvester was curled in a frightened ball on the
floor, arms over his face. Wendy reached down from her
malleable interior, caught his sweater at the shoulder and
tugged him out from behind the desk.

"Never slowed—just came crashing—crashing through
the—"

"I know," Wendy said. "We gotta get out of here."

At any moment the gasoline could ignite, the gas tank
could blow. She needed to get Sylvester inside her sphere of

protection, but she couldn't pull him through the magical membrane. No choice! If she had no confidence in her own abilities, what good were they? Putting herself at risk, Wendy released her sphere, absorbing the energy of its creation inside her, and pulled Sylvester close with one hand, clutching her crystal pendant with the other. *Raise it again*, she urged herself, distracted by the strong odor of gasoline and the hungry crackle of flames inside the truck. She heard a *whoosh!* as the gasoline ignited, felt a flare of intense heat on her face and hands. A burning ember must have fluttered down to the—*Now or never!*

Belatedly, the overhead sprinklers engaged, spraying the office with cold, pressurized water, matting Wendy's hair to her face but providing some relief from the scorching heat.

Attempting to block out the many distractions around her, Wendy concentrated on the crystal in her hand, on the warm tingle that washed over her hand, and felt the calm take hold, her renewed focus rendering the moment in frozen clarity. A pinpoint of energy swelled from her chest outward, enclosing her . . . and Sylvester just as the truck's gas tank exploded, lifting the pickup off the ground with the force of the blast. The noise was deafening, the light blinding. The shockwave slammed into Wendy's sphere, still in the making, and blasted it through the side door with another explosion of glass.

Inside the sphere, they both tumbled head over heels.

Wendy's mind flashed back to the gas explosion that had killed Gina Thorne, reliving that memory in vivid detail one moment—rolling across the sidewalk, unprotected, the next. The distraction had destroyed her focus, enough that the incomplete sphere had popped, fragile as a soap bubble without her will to enforce the supernatural physics—oxymoron or not. She rolled onto her hands and knees, then climbed to her feet, gasping, and staggered sideways a step or two.

Sylvester, whimpering even though he'd only suffered a few minor abrasions, was crawling away from the office and the fire roaring within. Lloyd, having recovered from the magical blow to his solar plexus, helped the old man to his feet and said something about having called the fire department on his cell phone.

Wendy looked back at the office, remembering the fleeting image of the body hurtling over the roof of the pickup as it slammed into the office. Had she imagined it? Or was somebody still in there, possibly alive but in need of immediate medical help? Logic warned her away from the blaze, self-preservation making itself loud and clear. But she had the ability to protect herself even if, on some primal level, she couldn't accept that. Somehow, she felt a deeper warning, a premonition of . . . ? The feeling was too visceral, a rational explanation eluded her. *No time!* She clutched the crystal pendant again, and took several steps forward, toward the office and the shattered doorway, and the raging flames beyond.

Someone caught her arm, causing her to whip her head around, glaring. Lloyd. "Are you nuts? You can't go back in there!"

She shrugged off his arm. "I think somebody's inside."

From a few feet farther back, Sylvester shook his head. "I was alone."

Fire engine sirens wailed in the night, approaching fast.

Wendy shook her head. "I thought I saw somebody in the bed of the pickup," she said, moving forward again. Even though the crystal was clutched in her hand, she felt no warm tingle, no trigger of renewed focus. Nothing. *No problem*, she thought. *That's just a signal. I can conjure a sphere without it.*

Three steps closer to the door, no sphere. She edged around to the front of the office, casting glances around the debris, looking on both sides of the truck. Even without a sphere, maybe she could make a mad dash into the chaos, grab hold of the person and try to pull—nothing!

Had she imagined the person in the truck bed? Doubting herself. Maybe that's why she couldn't conjure another sphere. Again the instinct, the premonition tugged at her from somewhere in her subconscious. But now the message was about her magic. Her magic was gone. Something about the way her incomplete sphere had dispersed had damaged her—her what? Her psyche?

She shook her head again in frustration. What was the point of rushing into the flames if there was nobody to rescue? With a sigh, she stepped back, finally releasing the urge to dash into the inferno, only to jump out of her skin as the approaching fire truck blasted its horn several times. She ran to the sidewalk as the fire truck swung into the driveway, several firemen already jumping down and scrambling into action.

Wendy decided to leave the fire to the professionals and backed toward her Pathfinder, sparing a glance for Sylvester and Lloyd. Both men ignored her, and Lloyd was already approaching the fire truck to explain how he had been the one to place the emergency call moments after the accident.

As she drove the Pathfinder around to the back of the motel, Wendy figured Lloyd, once he realized she'd fled, would waste no time taking credit for saving Sylvester. The poor night clerk was so befuddled, he'd believe the story himself. And Lloyd would probably end up with his picture in the local newspaper, and receive a big hero's reward. *Couldn't happen to a bigger jerk,* Wendy thought. She had no interest in publicity herself, and no desire to spend the holiday night fielding questions from the fire chief or the chief of police.

As she began the long drive to Minneapolis, she tried to put the incident out of her mind but failed. Her thoughts kept returning to the damage she'd sustained. Not the minor physical injuries. Bumps and bruises would heal in time. No, it was the *magical* injury that concerned her. What if that never healed? What if she could never perform magic again?

The impact was sudden and violent.

It lies stunned on the far side of the damaged, burning vehicle. After a few moments it regains enough strength to climb to its hands and knees. Then the broken, wooden structure and the vehicle are pushed toward it by an invisible hand, and it stumbles away, confused. Moments later, the hated fire roars across the floor of the manmade dwelling, igniting its fur. More than the physical pain of its burning flesh, the circle of heat almost drives it mad. It tries to bring the cold, the freezing air, the soothing snow . . . but the damaging impact, the burning flames, the agony of its flesh all prove too much to overcome. Moments slip by as it struggles silently, swatting at the flames attempting to devour its arms and legs, even as it rolls away from the sweeping wall of fire on the floor.

It tries to rise just as an explosion lifts the vehicle off the ground with a deafening roar and a painful flash of light, and even more dreaded, unbearable heat. It is blown away from the vehicle, crashing through a doorway—engulfed in flames now. It staggers away from the human lodge, almost mad with pain . . .

. . . but it sees the woods, the bare trees and the evergreens, standing in a field of crusty snow, and it lumbers there, unable to breathe, almost unable to think, the scent of its burning flesh coiling up into its raw nostrils.

The pads of its feet rush across the cool snow and it drops, rolling against the cold and the moisture, the devouring flames hissing in protest and surrender, rolling deeper and deeper into the darkness of the woods and the comfort of the snow until the last of the flames are extinguished. It crawls, scuttles almost, toward the darkest spot it can find, the lowest depression. Severely injured, it will need time to heal, time spent hidden away from man during a long, vulnerable period.

To take its mind off the throbbing, searing pain along its limbs, it thinks about the special prey, marveling that the path to her had been so bright right there at the end, that its task would have been finished if not for one moment of lost control. Humans are weak, inconsequential things to be preyed upon, but it now has respect for their vehicles, which are monstrous things, capable of inflicting serious injury, even on such a creature as itself. Times have changed since last it walked and fed among mankind. It has much to learn.

In time, it will heal. And it will feed to restore itself, both its body and its ability to call the cold. Its prey was lucky to escape this time. But all luck is fleeting, and hers will not last. It will find her. And it will feast on her flesh. Soon now . . .

PART TWO

WITHER'S
LEGACY

CHAPTER FOUR

Wendy Ward's Mirror Book
January 1, 2002
Moon: waning gibbous, day 17
Minneapolis, Minnesota

       Rough night. Long drive. Checked into a hotel in Minneapolis in the wee hours, just in time to catch a few hours shut-eye before dawn. Of course, nightmares robbed those scant few hours of any restful quality. Let's see . . . Burning, headless men in exploding pickup trucks; a large, shadowy image floating over the destruction; glowing yellow eyes and razor claws, something monstrous yet indistinct. That was one batch. Later, I'm holding magic fireballs in both hands, but I lose control and my clothes catch fire. I run screaming into the night, burning head to toe.

After waking from this nightmare-induced stress test, the dream analyst side of me took over and summarized:

something bad is coming and I am in no way prepared to handle it. Real comforting.

Too early to call Alex. Wonder how he's been . . .

"Do I even have the right to know?" Wendy asked herself as she looked away from the glowing laptop screen. Sitting cross-legged on the bed in her sky-and-cloud pajamas, Wendy had the lightweight computer balanced on her thighs, running on battery power. The screen was the only source of artificial illumination in the hotel room. Darkness surrounded her and isolated her from the room, from the world. Not that she minded being alone. She deserved to be alone, quarantined.

She had abandoned Alex in Windale over a year ago, believing it was for the best. Bad things happened to people who were close to her. She couldn't protect everyone around her. Too much responsibility. Too easy to fail them. And with so much time having passed, Alex might have moved on. How could she expect him to put his life on hold, as she had? She recognized the real possibility that she had burned her bridge to him.

Despite her self-enforced isolation, Wendy resented her nomadic lifestyle, not simply because it represented a victory for Wither. Truth be told, she missed living. Simple living without fear or guilt or grief. Though she had defeated Wither twice, in two different forms, Wendy had surrendered everything that meant anything to her. Maybe that was the sum of Wither's curse. *If only it were that easy,* Wendy thought bitterly, *something a few years of therapy could cure.* She knew better. Something nasty was on the way and she had a supernatural bull's-eye between her shoulder blades.

The laptop's glowing screen winked out, plunging her into total darkness. Wendy gasped, then chuckled at her own timidity when she realized the cause was nothing more sinister than her laptop switching into power-conserving sleep mode. A tap of the space bar restored the light.

With a nervous sigh, she directed her attention to the glowing screen and resumed her entry . . .

Wendy Ward's Mirror Book (continued)

Find myself in need of advice from the Crone. Her vantage point is in the future. She has the answers. Knows things I have yet to muddle through. Or rather, she has the ability to know some of these things, but they may or may not happen. The Crone is Hannah's channeled future self, astrally projected to me via present-Hannah's subconscious. I visualize Hannah shining a supernatural mirror on her future self and the Crone is the image that bounces back to our time. Hannah's future self is not the messenger. Rather, Hannah's "foreknowledge" (not quite the right word, but the right word probably hasn't been coined yet) of her future self, interpreted through Hannah's childish mind, is what appears to me and informs me. Unfortunately, Hannah has no conscious control over the Crone's manifestations; she can't dial up her future self on a whim.

Another complication, one that tends to confuse the temporally fainthearted—yes, my hand is raised here too—is that the Crone's past is fixed, but my future is not, even though it's the same time frame. Meaning, I can alter what the Crone perceives as her past. From my perspective, her past is merely a potential time line. And if I alter her time line, the Crone only *remembers* the new version of her past. Must be scary to realize your past, as well as your future, is uncertain. Doesn't bother the Crone though. She calls the gap between my present and her present the "temporal flux."

We talk about fate and destiny and all that preordained stuff, but the future is just the sum of one's past and present choices. We do have choices. Generally, we try to make the right ones. And we become the sum of our choices because they reflect our values, our willpower, our integrity and our commitment. All of it defines us, determines how we will react and respond to circumstances. The result is that the time line, that temporal flux, doesn't fluctuate all that much. Maybe the Crone has reason not to be worried.

Finally, the Crone is far from the perfect crystal ball for future gazing. The information she provides relates to my current . . . predicament. That is, when something magical happens in the present, it triggers the angle or direction of focus of Hannah's future "mirror." Maybe I should call it precognitive intuition. But the Crone is much more to me than a peek into the possible future. She's also my friend. Unfortunately, she's a friend I can never call or visit. I have to wait on her to make an appearance.

The next best option is to contact Hannah herself, through Karen, and it's too early for that. Something is definitely up, and I need to know what that *something* is.

A subject I've been avoiding in this journal is magic . . . my magic. I have yet to try any magic since my sphere implosion in Fargo. Too bone-tired. And—fess up—a little worried. Part of me is scared the magic will never return. Another part wonders if that would be such a bad thing. Maybe I'd be better off without it, without the responsibility. Ah, normalcy . . .

WINDALE, MASSACHUSETTS

A blanket rolled up under his arm, Sheriff Nottingham walked with care along the narrow path, an animal trail, through the forest behind his home. Low-hanging branches and exposed tree roots ranked, for the many four-legged woodland denizens who followed the trail, as minor nuisances, but for a full grown man they were legitimate hiking hazards. Especially when that man had worked through New Year's Eve into the wee hours of New Year's Day, protecting the local citizenry from their holiday excesses. *At least I won't have to deal with a hangover this morning,* he thought. *A throbbing headache from prolonged lack of sleep, maybe, but no hangover.*

He'd returned to his dark, quiet home a little after four in the morning to find almost everyone in bed. Even Rowdy had been too tired to more than lift his head up from the foot of Ben's bed to grumble a canine greeting. One bed was unoccupied. And the sheriff was not surprised. After all, the moon was nearly full. She would have been itching to get out, impatient for everyone to fall asleep so she could make her escape. Christina would have been the last in bed, the last to fall asleep, despite having allowed the kids to stay awake past midnight. How could he begrudge his wife's wanting some company to ring in the New Year? The sheriff had placed a call to her around the stroke of midnight, to send a kiss over his cell phone since he couldn't deliver one in person. The kids had paused long enough in their whooping and hollering, and banging on pots and pans, to wish him a happy New Year. Christina had made them snacks throughout the evening, and he had no doubt she'd had quite a chore settling them down for bed. Except for Abby.

She would have waited them out, one by one, as they drifted off to sleep. Once the house was still, she would have wasted no time taking to the woods . . . after shape-shifting into her other form.

Although the sheriff and Abby had reached an accommodation regarding Abby's ability and apparent need to shape-shift, Christina remained unaware of her secret. First there had been his promise to Abby. She had pleaded with him not to tell anyone else in the family lest they view her as a freak. Later . . . well, there is never a good time to tell your wife that your adopted ten-year-old daughter shape-shifts into a wolf about a dozen nights each month.

Maybe his belief that Christina would worry more about Abby if she knew the truth was a mere rationalization, because he couldn't ignore the little nagging kernel of doubt in Christina, in her willingness to accept Abby if she knew the little girl's true nature. Would Christina reject Abby if she knew? The sheriff had witnessed things he could never expect the rational world to believe, let alone accept as gospel. The expression "you had to be there" came to mind. *And if you haven't been there, well the world probably still seems sane to you, or as sane as it ever was.* If Christina turned her back on Abby, she would be devastated . . . and Abby MacNeil—correction Abby MacNeil Nottingham—

had already been through too much for a girl her age. How could the sheriff consciously expose her to more grief and heartache?

He hated having doubts about his wife, but compared to the possibility of Abby's emotional devastation, keeping a secret from Christina seemed the lesser of two evils.

Dawn arrived while he was finding his way along the cramped animal trail. No burst of sunshine, simply a lightening of an overcast sky, the silhouettes of skeletal trees resolving from the lessening gloom.

Ahead, beyond the tree line, he heard the sound of the trickling stream. Trudging through the carpet of snow, he marveled that the stream hadn't frozen solid. He emerged from the trees and looked first right then left before spotting her—a white wolf gazing up into the sky, almost invisible against the backdrop of pure snow. Blue eyes above the black snout as the wolf's head turned toward him. "Figured you were out here."

Abby had become adept at retaining her own identity and intelligence while in wolf form. Thus she would recognize him and not feel threatened by his presence. In the early days, she would sometimes lose herself to the instinctual part of the wolf, the raw desire to hunt and run wild. She had described the feeling as "being along for the ride." Though the loss of control had worried her, the wolf had always been guided by her human conscience, her sense of loyalty to her family and, certainly, to Wendy. In her wolf form, Abby had saved Wendy's life. The sheriff's life as well. After those two incidents, the sheriff felt he'd lost any right he might have had to order her to remain in human form. Instead he'd demanded only that she stay close to home, to eliminate the chance that a frightened homeowner, a hunter or another policeman might take a shot at her.

"Getting late, Abby," he said. "Come home before everyone wakes up, finds you missing and worries."

Taking several steps forward, the wolf stared intently at the sheriff before nudging the blanket roll with her nose. The sheriff nodded and unrolled the blanket, revealing a change of clothes in a plastic bag at its core, and draped the blanket around her shoulders. Again the wolf stared at him, then gave a flick of her head, emitting a little yowl for emphasis. "Oh, right, no problem," the sheriff said, turning his back to her. While not overly modest about nudity, Abby was embarrassed by the idea of anyone watching her transform from wolf to girl or vice versa. No doubt she remembered his disturbed reaction when he'd witnessed a partial change—hand to paw.

With his back turned, he heard the unsettling array of sounds involved in her transformation without any visual context, which was enough to open a dark door into his imagination. After a few moments of squishing, cracking and muffled crunching, combined with Abby's short moans and grunts of effort, the sheriff squeezed his eyes shut, as if that could somehow lessen the enormity of what was happening a few yards behind him.

"All done," she said. "You can toss me my clothes now."

The sheriff turned a bit, enough to see her squatting with the blanket wrapped around her naked, shivering body, clutched to her throat. He tossed the plastic bag of clothes at her feet and averted his gaze while she dressed herself.

Without the insulating wolf fur, she was vulnerable to the cold, just like a normal girl. That thought made the sheriff question his own objectivity in lying to his wife. He did treat Abby differently, but how could he not? While he wouldn't classify Abby as normal, that hardly meant she was abnormal or, in her own words, a freak. Instead, he forced himself to think of her as a very unusual little girl. Semantics? Maybe. Still, he wondered if his own buried prejudice might be coloring his lack of faith in his wife. *Have I been unfair to you, Christina? Painting you with the brush of my own intolerance? And since I'm unable to see the world objectively anymore, how will I ever know? I'm certainly beyond questioning my own sanity. But if I am insane, I'm in good company.*

"You can look now."

Aside from her tousled hair, one would never know this towheaded little girl had spent a good part of the night as a wolf. He shook his head again, momentarily at a loss for words. Instead he dropped to one knee and held out his arms. With a smile, she dropped the blanket, ran forward into the hug and squeezed him hard. He patted her back, then stroked her hair. "Ugh," he said, feigning a grimace. "Sure you're not part bear?"

She laughed and stepped back to look at him. "You know I can't do a bear."

"Good thing for me, huh? I'd never survive a real bear hug."

Wistful, Abby looked up into the sky. A frown creased her pale forehead.

"What's wrong?"

"I don't want to be a bear," Abby said with a sigh. "I want to fly."

"A flying wolf?" he teased.

"No! You know, an eagle."

Combing her hair with his fingers, he said with a straight face, "Why would you ever want to be a bald eagle?"

She laughed at him. "Silly, they're not really bald. They just have white feathers on their head. Kinda like the color of my hair."

"And you want to . . . shape-shift into an eagle."

Gazing skyward again, Abby flashed the broadest smile he could imagine. "To soar up in the sky, high above the trees. How cool would that be?"

"Very high on the cool meter, I'm sure," the sheriff said. "But, Abby, sometimes we must accept our own limitations. You already have this wonderful . . . ability, to change into a wolf. That's more than the rest of us."

"I know," Abby said, a little apologetically. "But my bones . . . Sometimes, when I'm almost asleep but not quite . . . it's like my bones talk to me, and they want me to become other . . . things."

"Talk how, Abby?"

She shrugged in the way only children can shrug. "Not really words, I guess. It's just that they . . . move, under my skin. I can feel them shifting, testing what they can do. Like they think I'm not paying attention."

"Abby, does it hurt when this happens, when your bones move?"

"Doesn't hurt, but it kinda tickles," she said. "Sometimes it just feels . . . strange. Makes it hard to go to sleep."

"Does it scare you?"

"No. I'm not scared. I mean, I was scared about all the wolf stuff at first, but now it just seems natural." Again, the shrug. "You know how, sometimes, your eyelid jumps and you can't make it stop."

"Ah, the twitch," he said, nodding. With lack of sleep, and especially after a day heavy with paperwork, his eyelid would twitch. Whether the result of fatigue, middle age or declining vision, the tiny, involuntary spasms were a minor distraction. But the sheriff tried to imagine what it would feel like to have his entire skeletal structure twitching while he was trying to fall asleep and, for a moment, had an inkling of what Abby must go through on an almost daily basis. *No wonder she can't resist the urge to shape-shift. Probably the only way for her to scratch that itch.* "I think I understand. Well, as much as a non-shape-shifter can ever understand. But what makes you think your bones twitching isn't just your inner wolf trying to get out?"

"Because I know how they move when I become a wolf," Abby explained. "It's always the same, like they remember what to do. But this . . . twitching is different. It's like my bones are experimenting."

At that moment, the sheriff was supremely grateful Abby's changeable bones did not frighten her, because they terrified him. In an attempt to hide this sudden unease from her, he cleared his throat, placed one hand on her shoulder and pointed back through the woods with the other. "We should start back."

"Okay," Abby said. "I'll go first. I know the way by heart."

By her wolf's heart, he thought but did not say. He scooped up the blanket and the plastic bag. "Look, Abby," he said. "I know you want to fly, that you want to shape-shift into an eagle form, but try to be patient. If it's meant to be, it will happen. Give it time. Meanwhile, promise me you won't force something you may be unable to control."

"I'll be careful, Sheriff—I mean, Dad," Abby said. "Promise."

Calling the sheriff "Dad" was still an adjustment-in-progress for Abby, but she was getting there. "Good girl," he said, giving her an approving smile. "Now lead the way home."

Wendy Ward's Mirror Book
January 1, 2002 (continued)
Moon: waning gibbous, day 17
Minneapolis, Minnesota

Just got off the phone with Karen. She and Art spent the night in the hospital with Hannah after she had a seizure. Oh, that poor baby! Wish there was something I could do to help Hannah, or somehow help her mother and Art cope with this. I may be their long-distance magical expert, but I'm clueless.

Karen checked her messages when they got home from the hospital, and left a message on my cell phone voice mail. I heard her tired, dejected message when I turned on my cell this morning to give Alex a call. I bumped Alex back in the queue, and called Karen at home while she was—in her words—"piddling around in the kitchen." Art and Hannah had both fallen asleep an hour earlier.

Though Karen whispered throughout our conversation, her frustration with the hospital was loud and clear. Unsurprisingly, all Hannah's tests had come back negative. Whatever causes Hannah's rapid aging is undetectable to modern medicine. Her seizure has no apparent physiological cause. One more manifestation of the supernatural ripple effect surrounding those chosen as hosts by Wither's coven, namely Hannah, Abby and me.

Karen related the events leading up to Hannah's seizure, describing Hannah's nightmare, which was probably a vision or prophecy, and how Hannah had shouted in her sleep for me to run away, echoing the Crone's warning.

What concerns me most is the timing. Hannah's vision and her seizure happened about the same time I was *remembering* and, dare I even entertain this chilling thought, invoking Wither's curse. I'd be a fool to think the two events were unrelated, but—the Crone's here!!

Wendy saved her mirror book file, powered off the notebook computer and slipped it back into the vinyl carrying case. She'd had room service deliver an "All American" breakfast, and so was still in her pajamas, enjoying the luxury of lounging after a mostly sleepless night. "Glad you're back. We need to talk."

The Crone, who had appeared at the foot of her hotel bed while Wendy was typing her mirror book entry, nodded. "*Yes, we do.*"

"Something happened last night. I just . . . lost my magic. Tried to raise a sphere and I couldn't."

"*Tell me what happened.*"

Wendy summarized the events leading up to the pickup's fuel tank explosion and her failure to raise another sphere after the second one was struck by the blast while it was assuming its regular dimensions. "Did I burn out my magic?"

"*You haven't attempted magic since the failed sphere?*"

"No. For some reason, I haven't felt like trying."

"*Don't worry, Wendy,*" the Crone said. "*I'm sure it's only a temporary loss. Since you were channeling your own magical energies when the explosion occurred, you probably tripped a psychic circuit breaker in your mind.*"

"Wasn't aware I had one of those installed."

"*It's the part of your mind designed to protect you from absorbing too much energy too fast.*"

"I could absorb an explosion? And channel that energy into my magic?"

"*Wendy, don't even think about trying such a thing! Not for a long time!*" the Crone said. "*You could incinerate yourself from the inside out. Promise me you won't try something so dangerous.*"

"Okay," Wendy said. "Just asking. Body surfing gasoline explosions is not exactly on my preferred extreme sports list. Next topic. What can you tell me about the whole Winnipeg incident?"

"*I'm not sure how helpful my information will be.*"

"You told me to get out of Dodge—well, Winnipeg—but I got the gist."

The Crone was opaque, yet she assumed a degree of solidity whenever Wendy focused exclusively on her astral-and-temporal projected image. Sometimes, Wendy had to remind herself she could see through the body that wasn't physically present, that it was merely a visual and vocal supernatural projection.

The Crone frowned. "*Cause and effect were a little mixed up.*"

"The obvious question is, 'Huh?'"

"*The reason you needed to leave Winnipeg had not yet happened.*"

"But in the running-for-your-life context, that's even better, right?"

"*I gave you a warning, but it was the wrong warning. You were the reason you needed to leave Winnipeg.*"

"I'm my own worst enemy? Okay, now you've lost me . . . Oh, crap! It was the spell, wasn't it? Wither's curse?"

The Crone nodded. "*In my past, somewhere in the temporal flux period between us, you had already reactivated the curse. The problem was that it happened twice in my past.*"

"I made the same dumb mistake twice?"

"Not exactly," the Crone said. "Hence my confusion. When I gave you the warning, you were at a temporal crossroads, a place where the time line is capable of broad shifts. As I've explained before, the time line is not as changeable as one might suspect. Broad shifts, even the potential for broad shifts, are rare. I responded to this temporal . . . fulcrum instead of responding to the real issue."

"The spell?"

"Yes. Because of your position at the fulcrum, what you call a 'hot spot,' I—"

"I call them hot spots?"

"Not yet, but you will."

"Ah," Wendy said, knowing enough not to go off on that tangent.

"Because of your position at that crossroads, I experienced something I'd never experienced before, something unusual and . . . unexpected."

"And that caused Hannah's seizure?"

"Yes. The seizure occurred when I recalled both time lines simultaneously."

"So, at that moment, instead of one past, you had two? Two completely different sets of memories?"

"I'm afraid my younger self was unable to resolve or tolerate so many contradictions, although for her, neither set of memories has actually happened."

"Two possible pasts of her future self," Wendy murmured. "Two sets of memories experienced through the prism of her future. Even I'm having a problem resolving it!" At least now Wendy could try to explain to Karen what had happened, assuring her that there had been a reason for the seizure and that it was unlikely to happen again. She hoped. "Does Hannah know what you're telling me?"

"Not consciously. Although she may intuit some of it."

"But you're a projection from her mind . . ."

"I am something of an altered state of consciousness created by her mind. Just as she has no conscious control over my appearances here, she has no conscious knowledge of my thoughts and memories."

"Like a split personality?"

"In a crude manner of speaking," the Crone said. "But there is some . . . leakage between us, leakage that is probably the cause of her occasional premonitions. That's probably the reason I am able to exist here at all."

"I'll take that on faith," Wendy said, smiling. "But what was the cause and effect problem with your warning?"

The Crone spread her hands. "I thought, erroneously, that you had already reactivated the dormant curse, that you were already in danger in Winnipeg."

"But I wasn't?"

"Not at the time . . ." the Crone said, but stopped short of completing her thought.

"And now?"

"I sense that you were in danger, but the threat is no longer immediate."

"Hannah talked about a monster with bloody claws, something big and scary."

"Wither's curse was designed to resonate with creatures of chaos."

"From the description, her monster qualifies."

"In the overlapped time lines I remembered you reactivating the curse on that day, but also much later in your life."

"So it happened in both time lines?"

"Yes, but in one time line, you had more time to prepare."

"And that would have been a good thing."

"Yes, but the . . . monster killed you in that time line. You were *more knowledgeable, but less cautious. Years of peace had insulated you, left you unprepared for supernatural threats."*

"But in the other time line—the one I accidentally . . . selected by reciting Wither's spell—I live to tell the tale in that one?"

"Yes, but we must always consider the temporal flux."

"Meaning, if you tell me I will survive the encounter with Old Bloody Claws, I might go into the battle overconfident or unprepared and . . ."

"Exactly," the Crone said. *"And, if that does happen, if you were to die, I would remember yet another time line."*

"One in which I died in the battle."

"Yes. And I would never remember it had been otherwise."

"Gotcha. No guarantees in temporal gamesmanship."

"I'm glad you understand, Wendy. My presence here is a kind of temporal cheating, a bending of the rules," the Crone said. *"But you must never take anything I tell you for granted. Nothing is a given. I . . . interact with you at risk of altering my past and your future. Of course, my intentions are good. I want to help. Otherwise I would not make contact. Nevertheless, the decision to appear is always a difficult one."*

"So now we're back to one time line from your end?"

The Crone nodded.

"Which means Hannah shouldn't have any more seizures, right?"

Another nod.

"What's the story with Old Bloody Claws?"

"Soon after you recast Wither's curse spell, the creature began to pursue you. Unfortunately, this happened while I was . . . incapacitated," the Crone said. *"I no longer sense its presence . . . I've lost it. I believe it is dormant again."*

"I don't understand. Should I be worried?"

"Without sensing the exact nature of this threat, I am unable to guide the direction of your training. Continue practicing your current exercises. As always, you should work to improve your timing, the time needed to achieve focus and to conjure your protective sphere. Practice your ability to maintain focus under duress and with distractions, improve the quality of your visualization and, above all else, remain cautious. Unfortunately, when I am able to be more specific, it will mean the threat is imminent, that the creature is again in pursuit of you and your training time will be limited." The Crone's image rippled. She glanced down at her translucent hands. "Hannah grows weary. I must leave soon."

"Okay, but explain how it—I mean, why did it wait for me to recite Wither's curse to awaken? Is this some sort of, I don't know, practical joke Gina Thorne is playing on me from beyond the grave?"

"Her spell was effective, but thwarted by bad timing," the Crone said. "The first creature of chaos her incantation attempted to summon is one which lies dormant during warm seasons."

"Gina died in August."

"The creature attempted to come after you then, but succumbed to the stronger urge to resume its hibernation."

"How can you know that?"

Another ripple of the projected image before the Crone replied, "Your own investigation of . . . the Winnipeg area led you to that conclusion."

"The first creature called to exact Wither's revenge just happened to be hibernating in the Winnipeg area which, sixteen months later, I just happened to visit for an extended stay. That seems a little too freakish in the coincidence department."

"Don't assume coincidence, Wendy. Either the residual effects of the curse led you . . . Winnipeg or a possible ancillary effect of the *curse is . . . place you, whenever possible, in closest proximity to the danger you . . . face."*

"Maybe. But knowing that doesn't help me," Wendy said. The Crone's image was approaching transparency now. She's losing her connection to me. "I can't make assumptions about foreknowledge. If I stay put, that could be what the curse needs for me to become vulnerable. And if I run, I could be rushing right toward the big nastiness."

"True, unfortunately. You can't know the path not taken. By definition, it doesn't exist. Again . . . advice to you is to re . . . cautious."

"Anything else?"

"No. Unfortunately, while the creature . . . dormant, Hannah's knowledge of events in the time line . . . my own past . . . murky. You suggested . . . me once—will suggest to . . . one day—that flares of supernatural energies in . . . present . . . responsible for burning prescient holes in the temporal fog . . . obscures the future."

"Hold on while I grab a pen," Wendy said, with a wry grin. "That's a great theory I'll have. I'd like to remember it."

"—is one other thing . . ." The Crone's image wavered again, becoming wispy around the edges like a dissipating smoke ring. When she spoke again her voice was much fainter. *"Made clear, in a man—of speaking, by supernatural energy—other type."*

"Tell me."

"Talk . . . Kayla. She is close to discover—something you need to know, something we all need . . ."

"What?"

"Wither's plans for us . . ."

"Wait!"

Too late. With those final words, the Crone had faded from Wendy's hotel room.

Wendy Ward's Mirror Book
January 1, 2002 (continued)
Moon: waning gibbous, day 17
Minneapolis, Minnesota

Unfortunately, even after Wither's death, her evil influence continues to spread. I had hoped and assumed only the three of us—Hannah, Abby and I—would have to spend the rest of our lives worrying about the aftereffects of Wither's coven having chosen us. It's as if we've been infected with a fatal illness but are in a collective state of remission. Living with the fear and uncertainty has become our norm. Now the Crone tells me Kayla is in the mix, which can only mean one thing: Kayla is not free of the taint of Gina Thorne's black blood.

Though Kayla had been forced to imbibe the demonic blood, she subsequently purged it from her system with a well-placed finger down her throat. Because she and I worried that might be an insufficient remedy, I attempted to heal Kayla, magically. Fortunately, I found nothing to heal, nothing of Wither lurking inside her mind. I prayed Kayla was free of this. Time gave us some comfort, most of it unspoken, since Kayla has showed no signs of what would amount to an infection of evil . . . And that is how we begin to deceive ourselves, believe our own lies.

I'm still so new to all this magic stuff. Back then, I was pure neophyte. What did I know? Maybe there's another explanation besides the most logical one, but that's the explanation that gives me the grandmother of all willies . . . What if the taint has been inside Kayla all this time? Maybe I was too inexperienced back then to detect it. Maybe it's been festering inside her, and only now is it ready to erupt with—educated guess here, folks—hideous consequences.

Okay, calm down Wendy. If it was that bad, the Crone would have been more concerned. Unless, of course, she was trying not to alarm me. No, no, stop that! The information was almost an afterthought. She said Kayla is close to uncovering some information about Wither. Nothing more.

Time to contact the outside world . . .

Back again. Hoped to talk this over with Kayla. Got her mother's machine instead. (Yes, voice mail tango is really beginning to red-line my patience meters. Calming breath, calming breath . . .) Left a message for her to call my cell.

Alex, on the other hand, was awake at home to take my call. Seemed in good spirits, but the conversation became awkward. It's been too long since we saw each other, too long since we even talked over the phone or even e-mailed. We definitely need a face-to-face. So, we're meeting at the Mall of America, Bloomington, MN. Yes, a couple miles from my hotel du jour is the largest mall in North America. (On your marks, get set, *shop!*) Alex said he'd bring a compass, tent and sleeping bags. Hope he's kidding. Anyway, if I can't find something to buy there, I'll be shamed into cutting up my assortment of credit cards, which probably isn't such a bad idea. Still, I could use a solid round of shopping-as-therapy.

And now, my shower beckons . . .

BLOOMINGTON, MINNESOTA

"So, what do you think?"

"My bags are already packed," Wendy said. "Can I move into Camp Snoopy now?" Camp Snoopy, a seven-acre amusement park located in the center of the multilevel Mall of America, featured rides, games, stages and restaurants but, unfortunately, no public housing. "Bad things don't happen in Camp Snoopy, do they?"

"Don't know about that," Alex Dunkirk said. "Charlie Brown lost his hair at a very early age, never has much luck kicking a football and, from what I hear, Lucy's curbside psychiatric stand is doing a bang-up business. I'm thinking those little guys with the big heads have a lot of personal issues."

"So no different from the rest of us?"

Alex shook his head. "But the beagle's cool."

Alex stood almost six feet tall with a slender build. He had brown hair, tucked under a Minnesota Wild baseball cap at the moment, green eyes with a scar over the right eyelid, and a pair of Wayfarers riding low on the bridge of his nose. When Wendy had first met Alex, he'd told her his eyes were extra sensitive to light and that, whenever he forgot to wear the sunglasses, he'd invariably develop a nasty headache. She imagined the condition was better now, that the sunglasses had become more casual affectation than necessity, but never gave him a hard time about it. Actually, she was thinking a better match for the brown leather bomber jacket, tan corduroys and dark boots he was wearing would be a pair of aviator sunglasses. Thinking, maybe she'd buy him a pair before they left the mall.

Under a belted, full-length, dark green wool coat she'd bought in Winnipeg, she was wearing an emerald green sweater paired with a long black skirt with a Celtic design embroidered in silver thread around the hem. Dressier than her standard winter ensemble of sweater, jeans and goose down jacket, but she hadn't seen Alex in ages, and had—she was ashamed to admit—dressed to impress. In addition to her everyday crystal pendant and multi-bead power bracelet, she'd accessorized with a pair of dangly, sterling silver five-pointed star earrings. Right before leaving her hotel, Wendy had decided to apply burgundy lipstick and a touch of eye shadow. One night back in Winnipeg, when Tara and Wendy were goofing around, experimenting with different *looks*, they had chanced upon that color combination for Wendy and Tara had declared, "It makes your eyes more dramatic, brings out the green." Wendy couldn't be sure if her dramatic eyes had worked any cosmetic magic on Alex, but the first words out of his mouth upon seeing her had been, "You look great!" Of course, that could have been a knee-jerk response. Alex was as unaccustomed to seeing Wendy in makeup as she was to wearing it.

She looked at the rows of shops, most of them familiar names from national advertising campaigns and their sheer ubiquity in the United States and, probably, around the world. In the Mall of America—and if ever there was an appropriate name for the mother of all malls, that was it—chain store homogeneity on a grand scale was a testament to the power of capitalism. "Don't see many mom-and-pop shops in malls."

Alex, in true business-major form, scratched his chin thoughtfully and said, "Capitalism is the survival of the entrepreneurial fittest. Chains mean greater volume of customers than the mom-and-pop stores, which translates into volume purchase discounts, resulting in more competitive pricing, generating even more sales, swelling the bottom line and producing even more franchises. An ever-expanding circle."

"And it helps that we Americans prefer known quantities," Wendy said. "Probably goes back to tribal acceptance. And the national advertising campaigns co-opt some of that mindshare, telling us how we can *belong*."

Grinning, Alex said, "I want to be like Mike."

"You're too short," Wendy said and laughed. She turned in a slow circle, looking up from the first level of the mall. "Would it be an understatement to say this place is huge?"

"A vast understatement, milady," Alex said. "Did you know you could fit seven Yankee Stadiums in this place?"

"One would be sufficient," Wendy said. "But I came for boots. Two pairs, actually. I need an outdoor, snow-trudgy kind, and a dressy pair, mid-calf height maybe. Oh, and some earrings."

"Shouldn't be a problem here."

"It's good to see you again, Alex."

"Same here. Been a long time."

"Too long." After a moment of indecision, she planted a chaste kiss on his cheek. "Taking care of yourself?"

"Got a new cane," Alex said, showing off a gargoyle-headed cane. "From the same shop that made the first one." When his mobility had been limited, Alex needed a cane and figured he might as well have one that doubled as a weapon. The press of a button flipped up the head of the cane, releasing the short sword from the camouflaged housing. "I hardly ever need it for support, though."

"That's great, Alex."

"Well, after very long walks, my legs still get fatigued. Although I manage to jog a couple times a week without any pain."

"I'm so glad," Wendy said. She continued to feel guilt over his injuries, inflicted by Wither in her failed attempt to kill Alex and thus remove him from Wendy's life. Even with rehab, Alex would have suffered long-term, possibly permanent damage and chronic pain if Wendy hadn't intervened with healing magic. The remarkable effects of that healing spell had convinced Wendy she really could wield magic, something she'd come to doubt after Wither entered her life. Wendy had assumed all evidence of her own magical power was the result of an elaborate set of illusions created by Wither in some twisted, psychological game. The healing spell for Alex convinced her otherwise. When Alex returned to Windale, Wendy channeled power and continued Alex's healing with direct, physical contact.

"Not a hundred percent yet," he admitted. "But somewhere in the nineties."

"Excellent!"

"Well, I have you to thank," he said and gave her a chaste kiss of his own.

"You put in the months of rehab."

"But your"— he glanced around the mall to see if anyone might be eavesdropping —"your *medicine* worked wonders."

"That's me," Wendy said. "Ms. Wonderful."

"You are," Alex said with a lopsided grin. "Wonderful, that is."

"Check your mailbox in four to six weeks for my fan club packet," Wendy said. "You're now an official member."

Alex clapped a hand against his chest. "Hey! I thought I was the president."

"Okay, seriously, more flattery and my head will explode," Wendy said. "Let's go over the plan. How do we conquer this mall?"

"Find your boots, pet a shark, picture with Snoopy, lunch at Café Odyssey—they have some cool backdrops—maybe a movie, some dancing—"

"Whoa, slow down, tiger," Wendy said. "Aren't you forgetting something? Like, dinner with your family?"

"Oh, right," Alex said. "Forgot I'm supposed to share you. Have to keep reminding myself it's only January first. We have a whole week together."

That had been the original plan, assuming Wendy made it to Minneapolis around the first of the year. A week together, then Alex would fly back to Danfield College, while Wendy drove the Pathfinder back to Windale to meet him. However, things had changed since her last day in Winnipeg. Wendy couldn't risk staying in Minneapolis more than a day or so. But how could she tell Alex she'd be leaving so soon? Their relationship—whatever remained of it—had been stalled for over a year now. Because of those long months of anticipation, regrets and expectations, every word and gesture would be magnified out of proportion. But everything had changed. Wheels had been set in motion, magical levers and gears, and with each passing hour, Wendy's anxiety increased. If she wasn't careful, she'd fall into the supernatural contraption and be crushed.

All she could do now was enjoy the moment. With a deep calming breath, she temporarily set aside her weighty concerns and slipped her arm through his. "I'm ready," she said. "Let's go."

CHAPTER FIVE

Several hours later, as Wendy and Alex were returning to Nordstrom's, from which their mall tour had begun, Wendy consolidated several small shopping bags into the large one that held her new boots. Bagless himself, but sporting a brand-new pair of aviator sunglasses, Alex walked with both hands stuffed into the pockets of his cords, cane tucked under his right arm. Wendy looped her free hand inside his left arm and gave a gentle upward tug. He glanced at her, smiled, and grasped her hand in his.

"That was fun," she said. "Never petted a shark before."

"No?"

Wendy shook her head. "Thought the skin would be rougher, tough."

"That is hardly the roughest, toughest bunch of sharks in the world. Shark gang initiation requires that they eat at least one license plate or an old rubber boot, whole. Those little guys couldn't make the cut, so they're stuck working at UnderWater Adventures earning minimum wage."

Wendy chuckled. "Minimum wage, huh?"

"Sure. They aren't allowed to accept tips. Not even a little chum."

"Then I'd better toss all those fish heads I've been saving."

"Fish heads?" Alex asked, quirking an eyebrow. "I thought that was your new perfume."

Wendy banged her hip into him, knocking him off stride. "You've just lost nighttime nuzzling privileges, Mr. Dunkirk."

"Ouch! That's cold."

"Like Winter in Minnesota, baby," Wendy said, laughing. "Hey, did I tell you how much I like your new sunglasses?"

Alex grinned. "When you picked them out, and again when you paid for them. Did I thank you?"

"Yes. And it was my pleasure. Your birthday's in four days," Wendy said. "Hey, you'll be twenty-one! So, I can cajole you into buying liquor for me. Least till I turn the big two-one in August."

"Drink much, do you?"

"No, not really. Okay, a few times up in Canada, but I think I was legal there."

"Ever wonder why, at eighteen, a guy can be drafted into the armed forces and be asked to die for his country, but it's illegal for him to buy a beer till he's twenty-one?"

"Too irresponsible to drink at eighteen, but responsible enough to carry lethal weapons? Kinda warped logic, but no draft worries these days." Wendy stopped. "Oh—where are you parked? I'm on level three, I think."

"Suzanne dropped me off," Alex said. "Figured you could drive me home."

"So your sister will be at dinner tonight?"

"We might catch her," Alex said. "But not for long. She has a hot date."

Later, as they were leaving the parking facility, Wendy behind the wheel of the Pathfinder, she said, "You said your parents bought a home in Roseville?"

"Just north of St. Paul. Take 494 eastbound here. I'll tell you when to turn."

"Okay," Wendy said. "Hey, I saw signs for a wildlife refuge nearby."

"Yep. Minnesota Valley National Wildlife Refuge. Open year round."

"Figures I'd visit during the coldest month of the year."

"January's fine," Alex said. He held up his hand and began ticking off his fingers. "The newly incorporated Dunkirk Travel Agency has us penciled in for cross-country skiing tomorrow, snowmobile rentals on Thursday and the Milwaukee Depot ice rink on Friday. We'll save ice fishing for Saturday. Unless you'd rather ice fish on Friday and skate on Saturday."

"Brrrr," Wendy said with mock shivering. "And again, brrrr. Anything on your agenda not involving ice or snow?"

"Well, the Minnesota Zoo," Alex said. "But there's bound to be snow there. Can't force it to melt. Oh, how about the Institute of Arts, or the Weisman Museum? And, um, I was thinking Saturday night, maybe a romantic dinner at the St. Paul Grill or Kincaid's."

"Alex . . ."

"What? Candlelight ban in effect too?"

"About this week," Wendy began, "I know you have all these plans, but—"

At that moment, her cell phone chirped. She fished it out of her purse and pressed the TALK button.

WINDALE, MASSACHUSETTS

Kayla felt lost, sitting in the middle of her made bed, tossing the portable phone from hand to hand. Now and then she looked up at the Harley Davidson poster taped to the back of her bedroom door, staring through the picture of the Softail Night Train, her dream bike, but not really seeing it at all. More appropriate to her current state of mind were the framed Escher prints decorating her walls, images that were optical illusions, leading the eye astray, playing tricks on visual perception. *When you're not sure who you are anymore,* she wondered, *can you really be sure which end is up?*

Though Bobby had freaked the previous night when she sliced her forearm open, she had maintained that it was a shallow cut, just deep enough to draw blood—*red blood!*—and not some half-assed suicide attempt. Not that her assurances counted for much. Long after he bandaged her arm with his home first-aid kit, he continued to look at her as if she were an escaped mental patient. Took her the rest of the evening to convince him she wasn't psychotic. Nevertheless, when he left for his graveyard shift and dropped her off at her house, she saw the unasked question in his eyes. *Is it safe for me to leave you alone all night?*

In the harsh light of day, she could imagine how nutso her impulsive arm-slicing routine must have looked to Mr. Rational Cop. Bleeding red was certainly no guarantee of sanity. Making oneself bleed would seem to favor the opposing argument. How then could she convince Bobby she was normal, at least as normal as she'd ever been, without telling him the whole truth about Wither and Gina Thorne? *That* truth could prove more damning than a convenient lie.

Yet, as the day wore on, she began to think time would fix everything. She *was* normal. She remained Kayla Zanella. Nothing more, nothing less. Bobby would see that in time. *Time heals all wounds, right? Including this stupid cut on my arm.*

She had even begun to anticipate a gradual return to normalcy. Until she listened to Wendy's answering machine message. "Kayla. Hi, it's Wendy. Long time, no speak. I'm sorry about that, and sorry I've been so scarce. Lots of traveling, and too much time bouncing around inside my own head." A sigh. "Listen, I need to talk to you about something. Ugh—I wish this was you, not a machine . . . Anyway, the Cr—that is, my old mentor dropped by. She said I should touch base with you, that you might have some news for me about—about a mutual acquaintance of ours. I'll explain when we do this live. Call my cell, please. Soon. Bye."

Until she listened to Wendy's message, Kayla had hoped her nightmares and visions were the result of her overactive imagination, and she had rationalized her fainting spell in the woods as the result of exhaustion, a by-product of sleepless nights and pointless worries. First she'd make herself believe that, then Bobby, in that order. But Wendy's nervous message changed everything. Something was happening. The reference to the old mentor obviously meant the Crone, and the Crone was plugged into the temporal switchboard. And if the Crone thought Kayla was screwed up, chances were Kayla was screwed. *If I stop being me, will Wendy become my enemy? Will she be forced to destroy whoever or whatever I become? And will I try to destroy her?* Kayla shuddered. *If I call her, will I confirm her suspicions? What if she can perform a magical litmus test over the phone, and she finds out I'm some sort of evil seedling about to sprout in Windale's tainted ground?*

Earlier in the day, while procrastinating about making the return call, Kayla had clipped her hair short and, as promised, dyed it electric blue. For a while she stared at her reflection in the bathroom mirror, absently tapping her tongue stud against her front teeth, as she finger-combed her hair and debated dying her eyebrows blue. Since her eyes were a pale blue, almost gray, she decided against blue eyebrows, thinking the combination would make her already pale complexion look completely washed out. "But blue hair or not," she told herself, "I'm still me."

The simple decision spurred the more difficult one and, in the end, Kayla had no choice but to trust in Wendy's friendship. *If she's calling, she must be able to help. Knowing Wendy, she's being proactive. Trying to nip me in the bud, my evil bud.* With that last thought, Kayla chuckled. *Yes, that's all it is,* she decided. *I still know the difference between a chuckle and a mad cackle.*

After a few deep breaths to steady her nerves, Kayla dialed Wendy's cell phone number, and noticed a slight tremor in her fingers as she pushed each button. After four rings, Wendy answered, her voice clear, but faint and distant, as if she were on the far side of a dimensional portal. "Hello?"

"Uh—hi, Wendy. It's Kayla. Just, um, returning your call."

"Oh, hi, Kayla! Sorry for the cryptic message. Right in the middle of it I realized your mother might hear it first. You still haven't told her all . . . ?"

"No, I've been quiet on that subject. I think it's for the best. No reason to worry her, right? It's old news."

With a slight hesitation in her voice, Wendy said, "That's why I'm calling."

"You mentioned an old mentor," Kayla said. "The Crone dropped in?"

"That she did," Wendy said. "And before she disappeared, she said I should contact you. She said you'd have some sort of news about Wither. Any idea what that means?"

Kayla took a deep breath. "No, I'm sorry, Wendy. I don't have a clue."

"Anything strange happen there? Anything unusual?"

Kayla heard Alex say, "Make the left here."

She bit down on her lip ring. "You realize I can't speak for the whole town. But, well, it just seems silly to talk about this . . ." *So why am I tensing up?*

"Please, Kayla, go on. It might be important."

"I—I don't see how, but . . . well, I've had bad dreams, that's all. Probably just revenge of the late-night tacos. A few nightmares. No biggie, right?"

"Nightmares about Wither, I presume?"

"I don't—maybe. Maybe they're about Wither."

"Veridical dreams of colonial Windale? Past life, walking-in-the-shoes stuff?"

"Not exactly." Kayla let out a resigned sigh. "Not the Puritan Junction type you experienced. I think it's later . . . Like maybe two hundred years later."

"1899? But Wither would have already started to—"

"Change," Kayla finished for her. "Not quite the hulking, nine-foot-tall beastie you got to party with a few years ago . . . but big enough to play a mean center in the NBA."

"Not just big," Wendy said. "She'd be part . . ."

Monster was the word Wendy left unsaid. "Ugly. Butt-ugly," Kayla said, opting for a euphemism. "And no chance at winning Miss Congeniality."

Wendy guessed the truth. "You witnessed her . . . feeding?"

Kayla closed her eyes. "It's like those dreams where you're falling from a great height, but you wake up before you hit bottom."

"Gotcha," Wendy said. "Think it's trying to tell you something?"

"'Abandon those late-night taco fests.' Or, maybe, 'Get therapy.'"

"I know what it's like," Wendy said. Then a thoughtful silence. "What else?"

"Who said there *was* anything else?"

"The Crone indicated you might tell me something about Wither's plans for us."

"Wither's dead and gone," Kayla said, getting angry. "Who cares about the bitch's plans anymore?"

"Hannah for one," Wendy said. "Abby for another. And, something happened to me, in Winnipeg, something Wither had a hand in."

Goosebumps covered Kayla's bare arms. "Wendy, what happened?"

"We can talk about that when I get back to Windale."

"You're coming back?" Kayla couldn't keep a note of resignation out of her voice, resignation and a hint of relief.

"Soon," Wendy said. "And, Kayla, I think you should have some interest in finding out Wither's plans for the three of us. Gina Thorne tried to recruit you into her coven. That's not so different from what almost happened to Abby, Hannah and me."

"I know, Wendy, I know," Kayla said, and felt a sob rising in the back of her throat. "I try not to obsess about this twisted shit. I just want my life back the way it was. It may not have been normal, but it was mine."

"Kayla, is there anything else I should know?"

A heavy sigh. "I think I may have . . ."—*been drawn to*—"stumbled upon a secret place of hers. In the woods, near that barn, the one that burned down."

"Matthias Stone's barn?" Wendy said. "The lair of Wither's coven?"

"That's the one," Kayla said. She explained how she'd jumped out of Bobby's car and wandered through the woods, how time seemed to slow down on the way to the clearing with the long flat rock. She admitted fainting, but left out the part about her nosebleed and seeing her own blood as black. She also made no mention of the New Year's Eve paring knife incident. If she ever revealed those details, she wanted to be watching Wendy's face, to gauge her reaction in person, not over the phone. "What do you think it means?"

"I'm not certain," Wendy said. "That flat rock could be an altar. Maybe Wither performed ceremonies in that clearing back in the seventeenth century. It must be important if the protective spell hanging over the place still has power."

Though fearful of the answers, Kayla asked the fateful questions. "What led me there? And why?"

"You had contact with Wither's blood," Wendy said, putting voice to Kayla's fear. "I . . . triggered something back in Winnipeg. About the same time, Hannah had a seizure in California, and you passed out in Windale. I might have stirred up a magical hornet's nest."

Wendy thinks it's her fault. But I've been having the nightmares for weeks. "Hannah? Is she okay?"

"She's fine," Wendy said. "Medically fine, anyway. Her affliction was supernatural in origin, but it's over now. At least, the Crone seems to think so."

"Good."

"One thing's obvious, though."

Kayla held her breath. Then, "What?"

"You need to take me to that clearing."

"I was afraid you were going to say that." Actually, Kayla had expected something much worse. "Guess we're not out of the woods yet."

"Literally, and figuratively," Wendy said, with an uneasy laugh.

"Wendy, about this . . . thing you triggered in Winnipeg," Kayla said. "Should I be worried?"

"If it's as bad as I fear," Wendy said. "We should all be worried."

ROSEVILLE, MINNESOTA

"Take care, Kayla. See ya soon." Wendy took the cell phone away from her ear and, with a slight shake of her head, pressed the END button to terminate the call.

"Take this left," Alex said.

At the entrance to the upscale housing development, rising from mounds of snow, was a wide green wooden sign with engraved golden letters announcing HORIZON ESTATES. Wendy turned the Pathfinder down the entrance lane, on the far side of an elaborately landscaped median. Packed snow crunched under their tires. If not for the bracketing mounds of plowed snow, the entrance and exit lanes would have been wide enough to accommodate two SUVs abreast with room enough for the driver of a subcompact to dart between them. Wendy had grown accustomed to clogged arterial highways ever since November began in Canada. Something about the prospect of a paralyzing snowfall always made her long for the comforts of home, as meager as they were these days. A simple human response, she supposed, to the potential for inconvenience and discomfort. Rather than give in to the anxiety and mild depression, she attempted to shrug it off as irrational and unproductive. So far, she'd been successful.

Horizon Estates boasted big sprawling homes, most five to ten years old, in combinations of stone and siding, with two-door garages, elaborate, often tiered redwood decks overlooking several acres of land. She caught glimpses of sunrooms and other additions, late-afternoon sunlight reflecting off skylights above two-story foyers.

"How's Kayla?"

Wendy cleared her throat. "Not good. She's worried. And she was a little evasive. I think it's worse than she's letting on."

"I know the feeling."

Wendy frowned, not tracking. "What?"

"Wendy, you could give lessons in the art of being a closed book."

"I'm not like that."

"You know it's true," Alex said. "I just don't understand why. You don't trust me. Or maybe you don't want to share your secret world."

Wendy laughed, shook her head. "You make it sound like a secret society."

"Well, sometimes . . ."

"Look, I've shared . . . things with you. Lots of things."

"You've also shut me out, kept me in the dark."

"Listen, I'm kinda lost here."

"I'm talking about the way you—"

"No, no—I mean these streets," Wendy said, indicating the road in front of her. "Where's your house?"

"Sorry. Next left. First right. Third house on the right. 1480 Orchard Drive."

Wendy nodded. "Look, Alex, I'm sorry you think I'm shutting you out," she said. "It's not intentional. It's just . . . well, we haven't seen each other in a long time." Wendy turned left, paused longer than necessary at the next stop sign, then took the right.

"You're the one taking an extended road trip."

"I know, Alex, but it's not about that." Wendy sighed. "Don't you see? I just want things between us to be normal. For a little while. I thought they could be. I really did, but then . . ."

"What's that supposed to mean?"

"I haven't seen you in months, almost a year," Wendy said, shaking her head. "So I don't want the first words out of my mouth to be all magical doom and gloom. You'll think—I don't want you to think I'm crazy, all right?"

"How could I? I was there, remember? I saw demon Wither up close and way too personal when she tried to kill me. I know you're not crazy."

"Maybe not personally," Wendy said. "But my life sure is." She pulled up to the curb, shifted the SUV into park and dropped her head to her hands on the steering wheel. "That's the problem. My life is insane. That's what I have to offer."

Alex tugged her right arm, lifted her hand from the steering wheel and clasped it in his. "That's not all you have to offer."

"Sometimes it's all that seems to matter."

"That's because you keep it to yourself," Alex said. "Eventually, you *will* go crazy, after you've pushed everyone else away."

Wendy looked over at him, tears brimming in her eyes. "You know what I'm afraid of?" He shook his head. "That maybe it would be for the best. Maybe I *should* push everyone away."

"Why?"

"Haven't you heard?" Wendy asked, bitterness and guilt tingeing her voice. "It's dangerous to get too close to me."

"Now that you mention it, there was that story in the newspaper."

She sat up straight. "What—what story?"

"The one about the surgeon general wanting to tattoo a warning on your forehead," Alex said. " 'Caution: Wendy Ward may be hazardous to your health.' "

Wendy laughed, "Oh, that old story. Wasn't aware the wire services had picked it up."

"Don't worry. It ran under the fold," Alex said. "I'm sure nobody noticed."

"Small favors," Wendy said. She grabbed a tissue from a travel pack on the dashboard, blotted the tears from her eyes, and laughed again. "Because, you know, that kind of thing can turn you into a social pariah." She sighed. "You think I'm feeling sorry for myself, don't you?"

He squeezed her hand. "No, not really. Maybe you don't have enough faith in the people who care about you."

"It's *because* I have faith in them," Wendy said. "I don't want to be responsible when things go wrong—and things always go horribly wrong! I can't bear the thought of—"

"Wendy, you can't protect everyone. There are dangerous people out there. Always have been. We're only now starting to realize how dangerous and inhuman they really are." Alex sighed. "These days everyone's afraid. They may not admit it, but they don't really feel safe anymore."

"What's your point?"

"Simply that safety has always been an illusion. Most car accidents happen within a few miles of home. Believe it or not, it's still safer to fly than to drive, but you never hear about people afraid to drive to the grocery store."

"Guess it's about being in control."

"Of course it is," Alex said. "But the real illusion is that any of us ever have control over what happens in our lives. We can save for a rainy day, prepare for a lucrative career and obey all traffic laws, but none of that protects us from the drunk driver who swerves into our lane, or an incurable illness, or an industrial accident or a terrorist act, or—"

"Okay, okay," Wendy said. "But the planning and the preparing improve your odds."

"Sometimes, maybe—probably not as much as we'd like to think. Maybe just enough to let us sleep at night."

"Well, staying close to me is one surefire way to significantly decrease your odds of survival."

Alex shrugged. "Like Paul Newman said in Hud, 'Nobody gets out of life alive.'"

Wendy squeezed his hand between both of hers. "You really want to know?"

"Guess that's the gist of what I've been saying. Can't back out now."

"But you can," Wendy said, a wry smile on her face. "Say the magic word and you're out of it. Completely."

"Tell me."

"Okay," she said. "After everything you've been through because of me—"

"Not because of you," Alex insisted. "Because of Wither. Don't blame yourself."

Wendy disagreed, but was disinclined to renew the circular argument. She simply nodded and continued. "Anyway, after what you've been through, you deserve the truth about what's happening." She sighed. "Problem is, I'm not too sure myself."

"Start by telling me what happened in Winnipeg."

"I made a mistake," Wendy said. "Maybe a costly mistake." Alex waited, not interrupting. "In the gas explosion, Gina Thorne did not die instantly. For a moment or two, she sensed—*Wither* sensed—that she was finally doomed. And before her evil life force was snuffed out, she . . . cursed me."

"I'm guessing you don't mean she swore like a sailor?"

"No," Wendy said and grinned despite herself. "A magical curse. At the time, it seemed as if she spoke the words, screamed them at me, but there really wasn't time for that. Instead, she screamed them inside my head, telepathically."

"But that was sixteen months ago," Alex said. "That was sour grapes, bitterness or futility on her part. You won. She lost and she knew it. She's dead. Case closed."

Wendy shook her head. "That's what I thought too. But now, not so much. Her mental curse spread across . . . let's call it the telepathic ether. It called out to other creatures of chaos, maybe only one. And it almost worked."

"Almost? How? And how do you know?"

"Because of the season, the creature summoned first by the curse was hibernating. Apparently this creature tried to come after me but failed. It slipped back into hibernation."

"So the curse was a dud. She had her last chance. Game over."

"She had a backup plan."

"Who? Gina? Wither?"

"Wither was calling the shots by then," Wendy said. "Gina was just the latest in a long line of hosts."

"What was this backup plan?"

Wendy tapped her temple. "The curse was planted inside my own mind, like a weird posthypnotic suggestion. But that's not quite right. It was more like an itch under my skin. Something I would keep scratching mentally to relieve the itch. I thought I needed to decipher the curse. Because it was hidden from my conscious mind, I tried various experiments, including automatic writing, dream magic, anything I could think of to unlock this . . . information locked in my head."

"Oh, Wendy, don't tell me . . ."

She nodded. "Yep. I finally unlocked it. With my own magic power. By speaking it, invoking it, reenergizing it."

"So you applied jumper cables to a dead battery."

"Afraid so," Wendy said, combing fingers through her auburn hair. "I don't know, Alex. Maybe this bogeyman, whatever it is, would have stayed in blissful hibernation forever, or at least long enough to forget about avenging Wither."

"So where is this bogeyman?"

"We—I don't know," Wendy said. "Dormant for the moment."

"But you think this reactivated spell somehow affected Hannah and Kayla?"

"That's what worries me," Wendy said. She switched off the ignition, killing the warm blast from the vents. Almost immediately the Pathfinder's interior began to chill. "Let's talk about that later."

"Fair enough," Alex said. "Let's go inside."

Darkness had begun to fall like a shroud from the overcast sky. Along the street, strings of Christmas lights had begun to come on, outlining windows and rooftops as all color faded from the homes, transforming them into silhouettes. After they climbed out of the Pathfinder and closed the doors with muffled *thunks* in the still evening, Wendy pressed the button on the remote to engage the locks.

She circled around front of the SUV and stepped over a mound of snow onto the shoveled and salted sidewalk to join Alex, who then pointed toward the empty driveway leading up to the two-car garage attached to his house. "Looks like we missed Suzanne."

"Hot date couldn't wait?"

Alex nodded. "Just as well. She would have done her best to embarrass me as only an older sibling can."

"Explain please," Wendy said innocently. "I'm an only child."

"You know," Alex said. "Goofy stuff I did as a kid. Jumping off the garage roof with a towel tied around my neck, pretending I was Superman, and spraining my non-super ankle. Tales of drool and other unsightly bodily excretions. My toddler days of chewing on electrical wires."

"Chewing through wires?"

"That's a shocking story."

Wendy laughed. "I've heard more embarrassing stories."

"And of course, she would have brought up Allison."

Wendy stopped halfway up the walkway. "Allison? Who's Allison?"

"Allison Kramer," Alex said dismissively. "Girl I dated back in high school."

"And that would be embarrassing because . . . ?"

"No reason," Alex said, but he could tell she wasn't buying it. He sighed. "Okay, so maybe I . . . bumped into her a couple times during break."

"Bumped into her? Help me with that visual."

"It's nothing. Really."

"Alex, I'm the one who made a mess of things. I don't blame you for—"

"Allison and I are friends. That's it. End of story. The rest is past tense."

"Okay," Wendy said. "Say no more." Despite her attempt at nonchalance, Wendy's stomach had performed a nauseating little flip that made her wonder if she had lost something precious. As they started forward again, Wendy frowned and wondered, *If this Allison is old news, why's Alex so defensive?* Neither spoke as their boots crunched and crushed Jiffy Melt crystals strewn liberally along the pavement.

At the front steps, Wendy panicked for a different reason and caught Alex's arm. "Wait! What should I know? Tell me about your family. I'm totally unprepared!"

"You want the Cliff Notes on the Dunkirk family?" Wendy nodded briskly. "Okay, let's see, Suzanne works for Readi-Set-Tech, a computer consulting firm. She's a systems analyst or hardware specialist, something like that, but she's talking to headhunters. She's had a job offer in Boston and keeps threatening surprise visits to my dorm room if she relocates. Talk about sibling harassment!"

"And your parents?"

"Dad's the CIO—chief information officer—at Waterman Pharmaceuticals in St. Paul. Been there a year. Mom works in the human resources department at TCFPC, a financial services company in Minneapolis. Between them, they have the Twin Cities covered. They're serious but harmless. Don't worry." Alex snapped his fingers. "Forgot to mention, Suzanne's boyfriend Jeremy works part-time at a ticket agency. He can hook us up with tickets to the Wild tomorrow or the Timberwolves on Friday. That's basketball and hockey. Both indoors for the faint of Minnesotan heart. Your choice."

"Tomorrow or Friday, huh?" As much as Wendy tried to enjoy the moment, her nagging anxiety cautioned her against making long-term plans in Minneapolis.

Ever amenable, Alex said, "If you'd rather skip sports, we could catch The Nutcracker. I figured we'd hang out for a few days. I'm not due at Danfield until next week and you don't . . ." Wendy stared at the sidewalk, avoiding eye contact. "It's about the Winnipeg spell, isn't it?"

She finally met his crestfallen gaze. "I need to piece this all together before it sneaks up on me. Kayla may have a piece of the puzzle. The Crone may have news any day now, maybe any hour."

"But, you are staying for dinner?"

Wendy smiled and nodded. "That I can do."

"And then we'll talk?"

"Then we'll talk."

Wendy discovered that Scott Dunkirk, Alex's father, found cooking to be a relaxing pastime, one in which he rarely had time to indulge, other than on weekends. While he prepared the chicken parmesan, Kate Dunkirk, Alex's mother, made them each a fresh, tossed salad.

Around a poinsettia centerpiece, Alex and Wendy set the long dining room table for four. Everywhere in the house were reminders of the Christmas so recently past. An abundance of greeting cards featuring Santa, reindeer and nativity scenes were taped to the back of the closet door and around an archway into the kitchen, from which dangled an inviting sprig of mistletoe. A natural Scottish fir, in full Christmas regalia, dominated the huge family room, with a splay of opened boxes and plastic containers around the tree stand and its green felt skirt.

As they sat down to eat, Kate Dunkirk expressed Suzanne's regrets that she couldn't share the meal with them. Alex suggested that sparing him an evening of embarrassing stories was probably Suzanne's final Christmas present to him. His mother said, "Oh, but I have a few stories I could tell." Alex almost knocked over his water glass, blurting out, "Don't you dare!" Everyone laughed and Wendy patted his hand in a show of support. Alex actually seemed more nervous than she was which, strangely, helped calm her own nerves.

After they had dispensed with the casual conversational gambits—Wendy expressing appreciation for the Dunkirk's lovely home, Kate asking how Wendy enjoyed Canada, Scott inquiring about road conditions up north—their discussion turned to Danfield, Alex's return and, inevitably, Wendy's decision to drop out in her sophomore year. Alex jumped into the conversational fray at that point to comment on the aviator sunglasses Wendy had given him as an early birthday present.

Unperturbed, Scott Dunkirk, a tall man sporting rust-colored hair streaked with gray, took a direct course back to inquiring about Wendy's career path. "Have you given any thought to your future? How you'll earn a living?"

"Scott, please," Kate said, with a warning look. "She just needed some time off, away from all the pressures."

"Now, Kate, all I'm saying is, this younger generation could do with a little guidance, a little focus. Never too soon to start thinking about the rest of your life. I'm sure Wendy agrees."

"Yes, I think about it all the time."

"For instance," Scott said, "Alex has been a business

administration major since his freshman year. Made a decision and gives maximum effort to reach his goal. Too many kids today bumble through college as undeclared majors. What the hell is that?"

"Wendy had a major," Alex said. "She just dropped out after . . ."

"Scott, the poor girl lost both her parents in a horrible accident," Kate said, looking to Wendy for a moment with a sympathetic frown. "Nothing wrong with her taking some time to decide what to do with her—"

"You know what," Wendy said, "I need some fresh air. Please, excuse me, everyone." Dropping her napkin on her chair, she hurried out of the dining room.

By the time she grabbed her coat from the closet, Alex was beside her, speaking softly. "Wendy, I'm sorry—"

"It's not your fault," Wendy said. "It's nobody's fault. Okay? I just need to get out for a few minutes."

Alex grabbed his coat and followed her out the door. As they descended the steps side by side, Alex said, "They can be a little intense."

"They don't approve of me," Wendy said. "Fine. At this point in my life, I'm not seeking anyone's approval."

"It's not you," Alex said. "It's my father. His philosophy in life is, if you're not going somewhere you aren't going anywhere."

Where the Dunkirk walkway intersected the public sidewalk, Wendy stopped and looked at him. "What have you told them about me?"

"I told them how we met in Professor Glazer's class, that we dated for a while . . ."

"That my parents were killed in a 'horrible accident' and I dropped out of college to find myself?"

"Well, I had to leave out the magic stuff," Alex said. "They'd assume I was on drugs or was a candidate for psychotherapy. And, if I leave out the magic, that doesn't leave much to tell them about you." Alex shrugged. "I think they're just curious."

"Curious?"

"My mother, mostly. When my father sees what he perceives is a problem, he wants to roll up his sleeves and fix it."

"So he wants to *fix* me?"

Alex chuckled. "In his own concerned-adult role model way, yes. Then it's on to the next problem."

"What about you?" Wendy asked, arching her eyebrow. "Think I need to be fixed?"

"Are you trying to pick a fight?"

"No."

"Fishing for a compliment?"

"Maybe," Wendy said, grinning. "Got any?"

"You're lovely," Alex said. "And talented. And amazing."

"But close-mouthed?"

"Mysteriously secretive."

Wendy laughed. "And directionless?"

"Not as far as I'm concerned," Alex said. "You've got some sort of cosmic GPS signal navigating your life."

"Wish it were that simple."

"I know," Alex said. "Let's walk. You can tell me about Winnipeg."

"What about your parents?"

"Let 'em see the error of their overbearing ways."

They strolled through the development, bracing themselves against the occasional stiff, cold wind. Wendy walked with her arms crossed under her chest, Alex with his hands stuffed in his pockets. Too cold to hold hands, and their discussion, far from engendering romantic gestures, resembled a military debriefing. Wendy brought Alex up to speed on the magical happenings in her life. She began by talking about the progression of her training, then segued into related recent events, including the Crone's warning—although she referred to the Crone as an 'old Wiccan friend and mentor' with psychic ability rather than try to explain the Crone's complicated history—Hannah's seizure and Kayla locating Wither's magically guarded clearing. Finally, she told him about the pickup truck crashing into the office of her motel the previous night and how attempting to conjure a sphere right before the explosion may have short-circuited her magical abilities.

"But this old Wiccan friend of yours thinks it's a temporary loss?"

Wendy nodded. "I might already be cured or fixed or whatever the proper term is. I just haven't had the need or the urge to attempt anything magical."

"Shouldn't you get back on that horse?"

"It's not that I'm afraid," Wendy said. "Maybe I'm magically exhausted."

Alex gave a tentative nod. "In need of a mental recharge."

They had completed a loop around the development and were approaching the Dunkirk house again. Wendy stopped and looked at him. "You think I'm afraid to try, don't you?"

Carefully, "I believe you trust yourself and your instincts . . ."

"Okay, watch."

"Wendy, if you're not ready, don't force it!"

"I am ready," she said, reaching inside the flap of her jacket to grasp the crystal pendant dangling from her neck. She held her other hand out, palm up, took several calming breaths, focusing breaths, concentrating on the spot above her cupped palm. The evening was so cold she struggled to pull heat toward her, to focus it into the igniting pinpoint she needed. After a few minutes of concentrating to no avail, perspiration beaded her forehead.

"Wendy, you don't have to prove—"

"Shhh," she whispered, then renewed her focus. Another half minute ticked by, long seconds. Wendy shivered with a new chill, gooseflesh rippling across her arms and legs even though they were bundled in wool. She felt almost feverish, realized she was siphoning heat right out of her own body to feed the flame she was conjuring. Still, she focused on achieving the pinpoint of heat, visualizing the coalescing energy contracting tighter and tighter until it came to golden light and sparked a tiny blue flame with a darting orange tip.

Alex whispered, awestruck, "That's incredible."

Wendy gave a little more of herself to the flame, making it swell and poof before vanishing. "That was harder than I . . ."

Her knees became unhinged and she stumbled, but Alex caught her in his arms. "You okay?"

Wendy nodded. "I draw heat from my surroundings." She looked up and down the deserted street, the bordering mounds of snow. "Not much to work with." Alex steadied her, waiting as she recovered her strength and balance. "Of course, the Cr—I mean, my old Wiccan friend—would probably say it's several hundred degrees above absolute zero so I should have no problem conjuring a few dozen fireballs."

"Your reach should exceed your grasp."

"Hey! Has she been talking to you too?"

Alex chuckled. "Just something my father always says."

"Hmm."

"Guess he has something in common with your friend."

"Maybe he does at that."

"Gotta say, though, that flame thing is pretty damn amazing."

"I was hoping for something a little more ostentatious," Wendy said. "But at least I know the magic's still there in me." *Maybe that little demonstration wasn't for Alex's benefit alone,* she thought. *Was I trying to prove something to myself?*

"Mind if we go back inside?" Alex said. "My feet are numb. And, besides, you're looking a little blue around the gills."

Wendy reached up, placed both hands to her neck. "Gills? She promised me there wouldn't be any side effects."

"Hey, watch the gill jokes!" Alex said. "Remember, you're talking to a guy with webbed toes."

As soon as they returned to the Dunkirk residence, Wendy endured a barrage of sincere and profuse apologies. She heard "I'm sorry" so many times, she began to apologize for being too sensitive. Once order and goodwill was restored, Kate announced a surprise, left for the kitchen and returned a minute later with a sheet cake—alight at each corner with a crackling, sizzling sparkler—which proclaimed in looping pink cursive icing, WENDY, WELCOME TO OUR HOME! A second trip to the kitchen by Mrs. Dunkirk yielded a half gallon container of chocolate-chocolate chip ice cream. Mr. Dunkirk brought out a stack of frosted glass plates.

The decompression of conversational seriousness was evidenced by the animated debate over the relative merits of regular chocolate chip ice cream versus mint chocolate chip and chocolate-chocolate chip. Mr. Dunkirk preferred the original, a "classic" in his opinion, while Mrs. Dunkirk favored mint chocolate chip, "but only the kind with green ice cream, not the white." Alex and Wendy thought chocolate-chocolate chip ruled supreme as the inevitable evolutionary endpoint of chocolate chip ice cream or, in Wendy's words, "chock-full of chocolaty goodness."

Later, Alex's parents retired to the family room to watch *It's a Wonderful Life*, which Alex's mother had videotaped a few weeks prior and, according to Alex, had already watched at least three times this holiday season.

"More cake?" Alex asked.

"No, thanks. Stuffed to my blue gills."

"Actually, they're a cute shade of pink right now." Wendy smiled, but didn't respond. She'd been moving her fork around her plate as if it required all her attention. After a companionable silence, Alex asked, "How soon?"

"What?"

"I can take a few dozen hints," Alex said. "Every time I've mentioned plans for the week, you frown. So, how soon are you leaving?"

Wendy thought it might be dangerous to wait around while Kayla might have a clue as to what was happening, and she was determined not to face the impending nightmare from Winnipeg unprepared. Unable to delay the inevitable any longer, she heaved a sigh and said, "Tomorrow."

CHAPTER SIX

On the trip back to her hotel in Minneapolis, Wendy couldn't help but think back to the disappointed expression on Alex's face. He'd been unusually quiet for the remainder of her stay, and she couldn't help think she'd let him down again, maybe for the last time. Wendy shook her head, tears stinging her eyes. She cared about Alex. He'd been someone special in her life. Was that the problem? That he was past tense? She had hoped it wasn't too late to set things right, but feared otherwise. How many times could she run off and expect him to hang around with his life in neutral and no idea what their relationship meant?

"Maybe it's for the best," she said, dabbing at a tear that threatened to spill down her cheek. "Clean break." She nodded to convince herself. "Get over it and move on."

The Pathfinder's windows had begun to fog up, cocooning her inside the SUV. Beyond the clotted windshield, houses were outlined with strands of Christmas tree lights, the glowing bulbs like smears of brightly colored paint now, an impressionist rendering of a holiday season in which she had little to celebrate. She pressed the defrost button, turned the fan on high and waited for the images to resolve into cold clarity.

A light snow had begun to fall, a swirling chaos exposed by the parallel beams of her headlights, snowflakes hypnotic in their random, tireless descent.

FARGO, NORTH DAKOTA

Too weak to hunt . . .

It awakens to unbearable pain.

. . . unable to feed and thus unable to heal . . .

Writhing on scorched flesh and raw nerve endings. Pain too intense to endure for more than a few moments without screaming or release. A survival instinct honed over hundreds of years won't allow it to scream, which would reveal its presence, so it blacks out, slipping into the fleeting relief of tortured unconsciousness.

This sleep, far from dreamless, is rife with nightmare, and the nightmare is a bitter memory, nearly two hundred and forty years old, long suppressed and all but forgotten . . . until now. This is the memory of its birth or, rather, its rebirth. And the memory feeds this nightmare of a different kind of pain, different but no less unbearable.

As it will survive now, it survived then, though forever changed. Born a man, reborn a monster . . .

RUPERT'S LAND, RED RIVER VALLEY
CANADA
OCTOBER, 1768

They have been rowing the birchbark canoe without rest since

several hours before dawn. Gerard Lambert, the shorter and older of
the two, sits in front, Jacques Robitaille in back. Their bundled fur
trapping gear and trade goods fill most of the space between them.
Endless miles pass on waterways too feeble to be named, too
insignificant to earn distinction on any maps. When one stream
becomes too shallow to navigate, they portage their canoe and gear
to the next nameless stream. And so it goes.

They are French voyageurs also known as coureurs de bois,
wood rangers, living in the years after the French and Indian Wars,
in the wake of overwhelming British victories which have left the
French out in the cold in more ways than those accounted for by the
fierce Canadian winter. As other voyageurs must, Jacques and
Gerard continue to trap and trade on lands licensed to the Hudson
Bay Company. While French-controlled forts are a thing of the
past, the trading posts won't turn away any furs. The market
remains strong in Europe, even if the hunting grounds in the Red
River Valley have thinned over the years. The Indians hunt farther
and farther west, the Cree taking to horses to chase after the abundance of beaver, otter, fox, lynx, marten and mink, but here that
abundance is becoming no more than a fond memory. The traders
follow westward, though the most fertile hunting grounds have
become ever more distant from their company offices.

Jacques believes he is part of a dying breed. He has a Cree wife,
Little Doe, and a Métis child with her, four-year-old François,
named for his paternal grandfather. Half-breeds are not uncommon in Rupert's Land, the necessities of this society having accom-
modated a new way of life, and for all that, this land has become a
new home for Jacques. Years from now, he may be forced to trade
farther west, away from Little Doe and François, but he will stay
the course while he can.

Gerard, though, is a loner and while he has his share of hired
women, he has no family and no attachments. Since the end of last

year, he has talked of heading west. Jacques has wished him well, making clear his own intent to stay close to his new home.

An hour after dawn, they decide to stop for breakfast, but a turn in the stream reveals an isolated stretch of prairie grass coated with snow. There the edges of the stream have begun to freeze, but what draws their attention is less the stream than the splash of crimson marking the snow field.

They paddle faster, hurrying toward the waterline. Along the way, they see a trap pole—rays from the low sun glinting off the metal—protruding from the stream in a parallel waterway, where a beaver has begun building a dam. Indian trappers at work with European gear purchased in trade for furs, a repeating cycle.

Near the pole is the telltale willow branch rising from the water. Its tip will have been baited, daubed with beaver scent. The beaver is a territorial animal by nature and will investigate any intrusion on its territory. The fresh-cut branch, shoved into the bottom of the streambed with its tip exposed and baited with the foreign scent, lures the beaver to the trap.

Jacques and Gerard ship the oars and hop out of the canoe in knee-deep water. Almost instantly, they feel the frigid bite of the stream through their buckskin trousers, leggings and homemade moccasins. With a practiced economy of motion, they haul the canoe up onto the bank, then reach inside the boat for their flint-lock rifles, which are never far from hand. Jacques removes the fringed buckskin case Little Doe made for him and tosses it into the canoe. Not one for excessive ornamentation, Gerard has but a simple calf's knee gun protector on his rifle, which keeps the powder charge dry. He tosses this into the canoe and nods to Jacques.

Together they stalk forward, hunched over even though the wide expanse of prairie offers little cover. The fringes on their buckskin shirts flutter in the cold, steady wind. Jacques is grateful for the thick beard that insulates his face from the icy blasts. In contrast,

Gerard sports only a droopy handlebar mustache, a feature that gives him a perpetual ruminative quality.

Although Gerard takes a marginal vanguard, Jacques makes the first assessment of the victims of the carnage. "Cree," he whispers to Gerard, indicating the three ravaged bodies sprawled in the middle of the snowfield. The two nearest bodies are no more than steaming internal organs exposed to the cold light of day, tatters of skin barely covering cracked and gleaming bones. Scattered around the bodies are camp supplies and a dozen beaver pelts, some already scraped and laced to willow sapling frames to dry out. Jacques notes a broken rifle nearby, and two knives lying in the blood-spattered grass.

The third Cree is in better shape, but only because most of his exposed organs remain inside his body. Across his torso, blood has soaked through his shredded buckskin shirt, and two cracked ribs are visible, the bones stark white against the field of red. Lower, a chunk of flesh is missing from his ruined right thigh. The edges of the grievous wound are ragged, the result not of weapons but of teeth.

Beyond this mostly intact victim is a considerable mound of snow. Jacques wonders if another body lies beneath it. More likely supplies, covered with a cured buffalo hide concealed under a blanket of snow. Yet the kills are fresh, spilled blood still warm, and the third Cree might still be alive, though not for long by the look of him.

Possibly they were set upon when they arrived to check their beaver traps. But what animal could be so thorough, so ravenous . . .

"Grizzly?" Gerard wonders.

Jacques scans the prairie grass for a lumbering brown shape, shrugs when he sees nothing. "Maybe," he says. As good a guess as any.

"This one's still alive," Gerard says, approaching the third Indian.

Jacques notices a bloodstained hand rise slightly, fingers trembling, then drop. In a pained, quavering voice, the Cree says, "Wîcihin . . ." Help me.

Gerard kneels beside the third Indian, placing his rifle beside his leg before taking the man's head in his hands. "What did this?" Gerard asks. There is nothing either man can do to help the Indian. He's lost too much blood, suffered more than one mortal wound. All they can do is try to understand what happened here.

"Win—winti—" the Indian coughs, tries to speak again, his mouth working open and shut with effort, but only a gurgling sound comes out, followed by a gush of blood.

Jacques glances around once more, but they are alone on the prairie. When he looks back to Gerard and the dying Cree, snow begins to fall around them. Fat snowflakes swirling in the stiff breeze. A deeper chill grabs Jacques' bones, raising the short hairs on the back of his neck. The heart of winter is many weeks away but, at that moment, it seems as if it has already come.

Something shrieks nearby. Too close!

Jacques stops in his tracks.

Gerard falls back from the now-dead Indian, watching horrified as the mound of snow just a few feet away seems to erupt from the prairie grass, revealing black furred arms and legs, and a white face with a dripping-red maw filled with razor teeth.

Having faced more than one grizzly in his fur-trading days, Gerard has enough presence of mind to grab his flintlock rifle and aim it at the monstrosity rising from the prairie grass. Whatever it is, it's hellishly fast, faster than Gerard, and swats the barrel of his rifle aside. The powder charge roars, but the lead ball soars wide of the mark. Though covered in white and black fur, the creature resembles an oversized man more than a bear. Its legs are longer than a bear's, made to walk upright, and the arms are powerful and fast, ending in clawed fingers, not paws.

As Gerard's lead ball arcs harmlessly across the stream, Jacques raises his own rifle to his shoulder, prepared to fire, but hesitates. Although the creature stands eight feet tall, it huddles over Gerard, blocking a clear shot. Jacques' hesitation, however prudent under normal circumstances, proves fatal for Gerard.

The next moment, the creature swats at Gerard with deadly force. One set of claws disembowels Gerard, the other slices through his neck, almost decapitating him in one stroke.

Jacques knows his friend is dead. As the creature sinks its fearsome teeth into the exposed flesh of Gerard's throat, Jacques fires, aiming for its right eye. Jacques is an excellent shot, but the creature's head is bobbing grotesquely, its maw coated with fresh gore. The lead ball tears through the side of the creature's throat instead. Blood the color of pus erupts from the furred neck and now Jacques finally has the creature's undivided attention.

It drops Gerard's corpse to the grass beside the third Indian and, with a bloodcurdling roar, charges Jacques.

But Jacques has not been idle. As soon as he fired the first ball, he began reloading his rifle. The acrid tang of gunpowder lingering in his nostrils, he reaches for his ball block, attached by a leather thong to his shooting bag. Even before he pops a lead ball free of the wooden block and into his palm, he rushes backward through the grass, trying to maintain some distance from the creature, la bête.

Yet it gains ground, surprisingly fast considering the arc of blood spurting from its neck wound. The snow around it is awash in crimson, the blood of men, and the pus-yellow blood of la bête itself.

Honed frontier instincts have contributed to Jacques' survival. He relies on them now, refusing himself the luxury of blind panic. Live in this moment, he tells himself, worry not for the next. Without conscious thought, he has dumped a premeasured powder charge from a drilled antler tip into the rifle muzzle, tamped it down with the ramrod and placed the ball. In those few seconds, the creature is upon him, within its considerable arm's length—

No time to raise the rifle to his shoulder, no time to aim—

From the hip, Jacques pulls the trigger.

Flint strikes a spark, igniting the powder, blasting the lead ball toward the creature, but nowhere near the fatal head-shot he would have attempted. Instead the lead ball rips into the creature's gut, under the ribs, driving up—Jacques hopes—into vital organs.

A yellow bloom erupts in the creature's white-furred belly.

It's not enough . . .

The creature barrels into Jacques, staggering him backward. A clawed hand whacks the rifle just below the trigger guard, cracking the wooden stock, ripping the rifle painfully from Jacques' grasp. It spirals in the air and disappears in the tall prairie grass beyond the field of snow. Jacques knows he will never reload again. His right hand drops to his knife sheath, but his fingers are numb and he fumbles an instant too long with the hilt.

The creature's backhanded blow snaps Jacques' head to the side, stunning him, buckling his knees. The claws have slashed open his forehead and his own blood splatters his cheeks and nose. Jacques stumbles, trying to catch his balance, but the creature rams into him again, hurling him to the ground.

La bête . . .

Its monstrous bulk blots out the low sun, casting a shadow over Jacques' face. In that darkness is the chill of death. Snowflakes trace a dizzy course in the air above Jacques. They cling to his blood-stained eyelashes and refuse to melt. His body feels immersed in ice. He shivers, teeth chattering, but his hand continues to fumble at the knife hilt.

The creature crouches astride him, its gore-strewn maw gaping.

Jacques' gaze is drawn to its yellow eyes, aglow in the pall of darkness cast by its own hellish shadow, aglow with a malevolent intelligence that has little in common with simple animal hunger or pain-driven rage. In that moment, sure of his own death, Jacques knows that this creature is evil incarnate. He whispers, "Démon . . ."

With what seems an acknowledging smile, broadened to display even more fearsome teeth—a mouthful of blood-drenched fangs!—it lowers its head and, with a blast of fetid breath, rips into the meat of Jacques' shoulder.

But Jacques has freed his knife . . .

When the creature tears into his flesh, Jacques cannot help but scream in agony. Yet he swears to himself that it will not be his last act. With what strength he retains, he drives the point of his knife into the creature's belly wound, then pulls the blade up, and up some more until the edge of the blade digs into its sternum.

While each single wound was insufficient to kill the creature, Jacques hopes the accumulation of blood loss and damaged organs have taken their toll. The creature rears back, scrambling away from Jacques, who pants in pain and exhaustion. It clutches its torn gut, staring at Jacques with all the hate in Hell. Jacques swallows hard, determined to hide his fear. Die already, he thinks, die damn you!

Jacques has no fight left in him. His strength has fled, though his will has not. He can bluff. He is determined to hide his fear, to ignore his fear and stare down la bête to the bitter end. For long, agonizing moments, they watch each other, measuring each other. Jacques' knife, where it is not covered with the creature's strange yellow blood, gleams in the morning light. His hand wavers not. He will not allow it.

The creature nods once, backs up one step, then another, finally turning to lumber away into the high prairie grass far beyond the collection of streams that have led Gerard and Jacques to their doom.

Jacques does not flatter himself. He has not won a battle, merely forced a draw. The creature would have had the better of him. Maybe its stomach was simply too full for it to bother with one last, thorny morsel. Yet Jacques' neck continues to bleed. He is too weak to travel, too weak to run. His only choice is to wait for the creature's hunger to return, to wait for la bête itself to return. If he has not bled out by then . . .

If the creature has not bled out by then . . .

He chuckles, and the pain is intense. "If it is not enough to win the day, I will be content with the prize of morning . . ."

But as Jacques soon learns, he has won nothing. The creature has doomed him in its own way. Already, the fever has set in.

FARGO, NORTH DAKOTA
JANUARY 1, 2002

It stirs from its troubled sleep.

The remembered pain is so intense, the nightmare so visceral, that it rouses itself from the darkness of long-buried, disturbing memories to agonized consciousness. Upon waking, it senses a change. Either it has grown numb to the torment of its own seared flesh, or the pain has eased. It rolls to a fresh patch of snow and savors the cool embrace of the crystallized water.

The bleeding has stopped.

Its blackened skin has begun to peel off, charred flakes, exposing fresh, tender skin underneath. From its long years, it knows that it heals preternaturally fast and has the inhuman ability to regenerate lost limbs. A mere human, suffering the same degree and extent of burns would have died many hours ago. But it is no longer human.

Remembered faces hover behind the dissipating mist that has cloaked distant memories. A name attaches to a face with a droopy mustache . . . Gerard. Gerard Lambert! Dead over two hundred years.

Disturbed by these unearthed memories, it rolls to its hands and knees, tries to stand, leaning against a pine tree for support. The pain flares anew, a second unrelenting fire across its limbs. It stumbles, falls to its knees, then collapses in the snow. For long moments it trembles in fresh agony. Motionless, it waits . . .

. . . And another face appears—ghostly reflection on the surface of still waters—before cupped hands disturb the surface, dispelling the visage, forever lost. That face was its own, before it was reborn, back when it was human, a man named Jacques Robitaille.

Useless knowledge. Nothing remains of Robitaille but jumbled memories. The fever was the start of it, but Jacques took care of the rest. Jacques knew the way home and what la bête could not touch, Jacques himself destroyed.

With a deep roar, it raises clawed hands to its head, presses sharp claws into the raw flesh of its burnt scalp until they draw new blood. In the burst of stark white pain, it pants, fighting an urge to shriek.

Through some trick of twisted logic, an invented survival mechanism invested with the power of its own pain-driven conviction, it convinces itself that killing the special prey will end its own suffering, the nightmares, the agony of its burns, and all the tortured memories . . . kill the one called Wendy Ward and it will find its way back to dreamless sleep and oblivion.

Moments pass, its breathing slows and consciousness fades, but the nightmares linger, waiting just below the surface—while she yet lives.

MINNEAPOLIS, MINNESOTA

Too distracted to sleep or practice magic, Wendy paced her hotel room and although it was well-appointed and spacious, she nonetheless felt caged. For a while, she thought about checking out in the middle of the night, climbing into the Pathfinder and heading east. Fortunately, logic prevailed. The road to Windale was a lot farther than the Fargo to Minneapolis run. *Couple days at least,* she thought. Therefore, she should rest, but first she needed to unwind.

"Relaxation bath," she said to herself. "Good place to start."

After adjusting the water flow—hot enough to last without scalding—she placed several lit candles on the sink and one at each corner of the bathtub. This allowed her to switch off the harsh artificial lighting. Next she withdrew lavender flower petals from a pouch she kept in her overnight bag and tossed them into the water. As she waited for the water to reach optimum immersion level, her thoughts drifted back to the Alex and Allison equation again. She needed something to turn that page in a hurry. But what?

She removed her emerald green sweater, along with her long black skirt with the Celtic hem design and placed both on a hanger in the narrow hotel closet. "Not *what*," she said aloud. "*Who.*" She stripped off her matching black bra and panties, tossed them onto the bed, then retrieved her cell phone from her pocketbook and returned with it to the bathroom.

As she placed her silver wristwatch on the counter, she glanced at the time and nodded. Depending on the state of her back, Tara Pepper was a night owl, an insomniac or a light sleeper. Still time to make a polite phone call.

Wendy slipped into the bath and sighed as the hot, soothing water embraced her. This far north, the cold seeped into one's bones and lingered there like a waiting case of hypothermia. A hot bath was just the thing . . .

After a few minutes of relaxing, thoughtless calm, she speed-dialed Tara and, in a few rings, had the ebullient Winnipeg Wiccan on the phone. "Hope I didn't wake you."

"Not at all," Tara said, her voice sounding unimaginably distant. "Nursing a New Year's Eve hangover, but no sleeping in the mix yet."

"Glad I caught you, then."

"What's up, hon? Wait—don't tell me! You're coming back to Winnipeg."

Wendy chuckled, felt the muscles in her forehead relax. "No."

"Well, if you change your mind, you have a place to stay, surrogate little sis."

"Thanks, surrogate big sis," Wendy said. "Anyway, I was wondering if you could do me a favor."

"Right after I hear the Alex update."

Wendy frowned. "We're heading in opposite directions."

"I'm sorry, hon," Tara said, sounding genuinely apologetic. "Keep looking forward. You'll forget about him in no time. Now what's this favor? Spirit's willing, long as it's not illegal, immoral or impractical."

"Nothing illegal," Wendy said. "But it may involve a little digging."

"Please, not grave digging?" Tara asked. "After seeing that ghost lady of yours, grave digging wouldn't seem that far-fetched."

"No cemetery visits," Wendy said, smiling. "Promise. At least, I hope not. Just a library and maybe a morgue—the newspaper kind. Here's what you should look for . . ."

After Wendy finished, Tara asked, "You're sure about the date?"

"No. But definitely not before that date."

"Okay, then," Tara said. "I'll call if I find something."

"Thanks, Tara," Wendy said. "Call either way. I'd like us to stay in touch." Before ending the call, she gave Tara her number at the cottage in Windale. Wendy had continued to pay her portion of the rent on the cottage she'd planned to share with Frankie Lenard, simply because it was the only place left in Windale she could reasonably call home. Most of her things remained there in the empty bedroom.

Leaning across the bathroom, Wendy placed her cell phone on the counter before settling back into the hot water, sinking down until her chin was even with the waterline. With a hot washcloth draped over her forehead, she cleared her mind of distracting thoughts, visualizing instead a restful place, summer in a peaceful meadow under azure skies with cottony tufts of cloud drifting past the noonday sun, birdsong lilting down from nearby trees . . .

. . . Wendy is drifting across the wild grass, bodiless, and notices a patch of glistening white. Willing herself closer, she is surprised to find snow here, even more surprised when the sun sinks in the sky, its golden light tinged with red, painting the snow crimson . . . but now the snow is splattered with the blood of a bearded man wearing torn, blood-soaked buckskin. Her attention shifts to his grizzled face, the slash marks across his forehead and the fresh blood welling from these wounds. She wonders if he's dead, but the frozen moment of uncertainty ends when his eyelids flutter open and he glares at her—with glowing amber eyes! He opens his mouth to speak and all his teeth are sharp, dripping with gore. Blood spraying from his mouth, he hisses, "WENDY!"

Wendy awoke with the startling and unpleasant sensation of a spasm wracking her body in the now-tepid bathwater. She flung the washcloth from her face and sat up, hugging her knees to her chest. Water diamonds beaded her eyelashes, lavender petals clung to her arms and legs, now covered with goosebumps.

A *face from the past*, she thought.

A past connected to her future.

Her lips trembled and the cold returned to her bones.

"Wither, you sick bitch," Wendy said, shaking her head. "What have you done to me?"

RUPERT'S LAND, RED RIVER VALLEY
CANADA
OCTOBER, 1768

A day and a night pass and la bête does not return.

Jacques begins to hope the creature has died after all.

Soon Jacques wishes he himself were dead.

Fever wracks his body, while deep within him, an unnatural hunger grows. Jacques raids his supplies, and Gerard's as well, but pemmican and cornmeal only make him vomit. He uses his flint to strike a spark into some kindling, nurses a fire to life, and roasts a couple beaver tails he found in the remains of the Cree camp. Unfortunately, the tails make him gag. Nothing, save water, will stay down.

He huddles in the grass, trembling, scratching at his arms and legs at an itch that remains agonizingly beneath the skin. Again and again he returns to the corpses, stroking the exposed flesh, a morbid fascination spreading inside him.

His shoulder and neck wounds stop bleeding on their own, without any compression or treatment, so too the claw wounds on his forehead. He no longer worries about infection or gangrene. A new instinct informs him of his relative invulnerability. Fever is a sign of the change, not sickness, although one might consider the change itself an illness. Actually, it is much worse. It is the loss of his humanity.

A second night falls and his eyes seem unnaturally adapted to perceive its depths. He spends the coldest hours of the night staring at the corpse of the third Indian, but mostly at Gerard, hardly touched by la bête. He wonders if the creature has left Gerard's body for his sustenance, but he doubts there is any consideration in the creature's actions. It is selfish. All else is happenstance. Soon Jacques must eat that which will sustain him or die. Despite the cold, a cold that no longer troubles Jacques as before, he worries that Gerard's flesh has already begun to rot. Morbid fascination gradually transforms into distaste, but not at the idea he's been avoiding. The idea is no longer anathema to him, simply the sense that the meat is now too old. Whatever it is that Jacques is becoming, that part of him understands he needs fresh meat to survive.

Unfortunately, the prairie is a wide and lonely place . . . he must travel far to locate fresh meat that will suffice. Yet there is one place he knows, a place that calls to him like a beacon to satisfy his hellish hunger . . . a place he once knew as home.

Wendy Ward's Mirror Book
January 2, 2002
Moon: waning gibbous, day 18
Minneapolis, Minnesota

Sleepless nights becoming entirely too routine. Looks like I'll have three overnight bags from now on, counting the two under my eyes. Checkout's not until eleven, but I want to be on the road long before then. Open road, fresh start.

—

Okay, so it won't be that simple. With the Alex chapter of my life just about over, it's probably better this way for both of us. Safer for Alex, less emotionally draining for me. Clean break. Rinse. Repeat. Yeah, that'll do it. (sigh)

Now I have a more pressing concern. What I believe was a veridical dream—well, an image more than a real dream—of a buckskin-clad man from the 17th or 18th century, but a man with glowing yellow eyes! Not sure what the mini-dream means. No real context. I woke too soon—thankfully! But he called my name from the past. It's some kind of warning, a result of Wither's curse. Maybe the Crone will know.

Many miles ahead of me today.

Meanwhile, bet your ass I steer clear of guys in fringed buckskin.

Since she was cutting her stay short, Wendy checked out the old-fashioned way, at the hotel's front desk. Her mind was already on the long day ahead. According to her mapping software, Minneapolis to Windale was fourteen hundred–plus miles, which she figured to tackle in three days of steady driving. Anticipating a lot of time behind the wheel of the Pathfinder, she'd dressed comfortably in a black cable-knit sweater and old comfy jeans. Deciding against her new casual boots, she'd laced up her green Skechers. Less chance of lead-footing her way to a speeding ticket, though she hoped to cruise-control most of the trip.

Wendy crossed the lobby, wheeling her overnight suitcase, shopping bag dangling from her free hand. She paused at the automatic revolving door to button her coat and loop her green scarf once around her neck. Bracing herself for a

Minnesota winter morning, she fished the valet parking stub out of her jeans and walked outside.

She started to turn left, toward the valet parking window, when something—rather, someone—out of place caught her eye. She stopped, turned to the right and looked across the covered driveway at the hotel entrance and saw him leaning against the half wall there, in a navy blue ski parka and gloves, tan cords, scuffed Timberland boots and, of course, his new steel-rimmed, aviator sunglasses. He stood next to a brown metal bench, a Minnesota Timberwolves duffel bag at his feet, black leather computer bag hanging from his right shoulder.

She walked toward him, a frown creasing her forehead. "Alex . . . ?" she said. "What are you doing here?"

Tentative smile. "Thought I might catch a lift to Windale."

"What?"

Grinning. "You are headed that way, right?"

She nodded. Though he was bundled up neck to toe, his head was uncovered, brown hair blowing in the stiff breeze, and his face was red. "How long have you been waiting out here?"

"About an hour," he said. "In the lobby, an hour before that. Afraid I'd miss your early departure."

Wendy's lips were already numb. "Alex, it's freezing out here. You're crazy, you know that?"

"So I've been told."

"And you want a ride to Windale?"

"I'll chip in for gas."

"Classes don't start for what, five days?"

Alex shrugged. "Why arrive at the last minute?"

A valet parking attendant walked over to Wendy, took the ticket stub from her and promised to have her car out in five minutes. She thanked him, then turned back to Alex. "One condition. Besides the gas money."

"Name it."

"What's the real deal with Allison?"

"I told you," Alex said. "We dated in high school. It was over in high school. Past tense. Recently, I happened to run into her at the mall. We started hanging out. Not dating. Strictly platonic."

"Reminiscing about the good old days?"

"A little, maybe," Alex said. "But nothing serious. Harmless, kidding around stuff. Look, the only reason I even . . ." Alex took a deep breath. "I've been wondering about us. Hoping what we had—what we have—might still be salvageable. But sometimes I couldn't help thinking it was a lost cause."

If Alex had been dating this Allison person again, Wendy could hardly justify being mad at him. When she abandoned Windale, she'd left Alex on shaky relationship ground. She still wasn't sure if she'd gone to his house last night to patch up their differences or to say a final good-bye. She'd been ready to face the end, but not without a dull ache when faced with the real possibility that Alex had already begun to move on. Just imagining the two of them—the high school sweethearts—rediscovering each other years later, brought a painful lump to her throat.

"I thought I was deluding myself," Alex said.

"Me too." A cold blast of air made Wendy shiver. She cupped her hands over her face, and breathed into them to warm herself. "It's freezing out here."

"Wanna go inside?"

"Nah," Wendy said. "Better than a coffee kick. Besides, the car will be here in a minute."

Alex nodded. "When you first left Windale, I just thought you needed some time away—"

"The wounds were too raw, especially there. Every day something would remind me of my parents. And every time I saw you, I felt guilty about keeping you in the dark. I almost got you killed—twice!"

Alex chuckled. "Okay, the first time you had no way of knowing, and the second time, well, your intentions were good. Misguided, but good." Alex shrugged. "Far as I'm concerned, that's in the past. Aren't we supposed to learn from our mistakes?"

Wendy sighed. "Alex, I'm not sure what you want from me."

"Makes two of us," Alex said. "But I'd like to spend some time with you while we figure it out."

Fresh from its sabbatical in the secret valet parking zone, her green Pathfinder swung around the driveway and came to a stop a few feet in front of them. The attendant hopped out and asked if she needed help stowing her bags. Wendy declined, thanked him for the offer and tipped him for his trouble.

She looked back to Alex, who tilted his head toward the Pathfinder, eyebrow arched. She smiled. "Road trip, huh?"

"We'll take turns driving," Alex said enthusiastically. "Cut the trip in half."

"Alex, maybe this isn't such a—"

"Look, you said it was important to return to Windale pronto, find out what Kayla knows and look into Wither's secret forest place. So, sharing the ride makes sense, right? Besides, what's the worst that could happen?"

I *could fall for you all over again.* "Your luck runs out next time and you get killed all the way."

"Said it before. I'm willing to take that risk."

"Maybe I'm not willing to let you."

"I can't force you to take me," Alex said. "But one way or another, sooner or later, I will be returning to Windale. Since I can't make myself stop caring about you, I will worry. So I will be watching over you, which will probably put me in the supernatural line of fire anyway. Wouldn't it be better if we had a chance to pursue a somewhat normal life together in the meantime, just to find out if what's between us is viable?"

Wendy grinned. "Viable?"

"Sorry. My impending business degree requires jargon loading," Alex said. "Sometimes when I'm eating breakfast I blurt out PE ratios. Can't help myself. Life hasn't been the same since my father gave me a subscription to the *Wall Street Journal*."

Wendy laughed. "Poor boy. Maybe there's a support group in Windale." She looked around the looping hotel entrance driveway. "How'd you get here? Walk? Hitch? Carpool?"

"D, none of the above," Alex said. "Mom's Taxi Service."

"Then I can't very well strand you out here. Well, I could, but it would be a little heartless, right?"

"And completely out of character."

"Lucky for you," Wendy said with a wry grin. "Let's pack and hit the road."

A minute's work to stow their luggage in back, then Wendy hopped into the driver's seat, switched the heat to high and bathed her face in the welcome rush of warmth. Alex climbed into the passenger side and slammed the door against the bitter cold. He pulled off his gloves and rubbed his hands together in front of the blower.

Wendy disengaged the emergency brake, shifted into drive and left the hotel's driveway, looking for signs directing her to I-94. "You're traveling light."

"Folks are flying in for a visit in about a week," Alex said. "They offered to bring the rest. I have the essentials. Toiletries, change of clothes and my notebook computer."

"New computer?"

"Birthday present from Mom and Dad," Alex said. "Some software from Suzanne. Of course, my Christmas allotment kinda rolled into the whole thing too. No complaints though."

The on-ramp to eastbound I-94 was only a mile or so from the hotel. They'd stay on the Interstate for over a hundred and seventy miles. In about thirty miles they'd be in Wisconsin. *Smooth sailing, so to speak,* she thought. *If the weather and the snow plows cooperate.* "As far as . . . arrangements for this trip," Wendy said. "We'll take turns driving. One of us will be behind the wheel at all times?"

"Except for rest stops, meals, whatever."

"What 'whatever'?"

Alex shrugged. "I don't know. Something might come up. Certainly can't discount the possibility of something coming up."

"Uh-huh," Wendy said, smiling at his mischievousness. "And you'll chip in for gas."

Alex patted his hip pocket. "Funds in hand. We'll alternate fill-ups."

"Sounds reasonable," Wendy said. "Anything else I should know? Any . . . expectations?"

"You should expect entertainment. For instance, I'm full of fun yet useless factoids."

"Such as?"

"Let's see," Alex said, tugging thoughtfully on his lower lip. "Did you know way back in the 1840s, St. Paul was called Pig's Eye Landing?"

"Good move changing the name."

"Classic no-brainer."

Wendy laughed. It was good to be around Alex again. Maybe she could allow herself to expect something more than entertainment, something salvageable.

FARGO, NORTH DAKOTA

The long fitful night was plagued by nightmares of its prior life, but morning brings consciousness and a growing hunger. Somehow it must find prey. Fresh meat will give it strength and speed the healing process. That is the only way it will find her. Already the path to her fades. It senses she is on the move again, stretching the distance between them.

At first it crawls on its raw belly through the underbrush, but soon it climbs to hands and knees, progressing on all fours like a sick animal. Humans will not stumble upon it here, deep in the woods, so it must move to where they will be, near their dwellings and contraptions, the places where they believe themselves safe.

It pants with effort, clambers over a deadfall and collapses in the brush, its face washed in snow. After a moment's rest, it will move again . . . after a moment . . .

RUPERT'S LAND, RED RIVER VALLEY
CANADA
OCTOBER, 1768

Jacques abandons the birchbark canoe after a futile hour of awkward, inefficient strokes. His muscles are strong, perhaps stronger than ever, but they have lost the discipline and patience for repetitive, mechanical motion. As he becomes more inhuman, the tools of man lose their appeal. Yet he tires easily. From hunger? And thus his progress toward home is hindered.

The hunger and rage grow hand in hand. He becomes desperate to feed and angry that food is scarce. Cold days and frigid nights pass as he roams the prairie, head sweeping side to side, absently rubbing his newly clawed hands along rough-skinned arms. His jaw hangs wide, unaccustomed to the mouthful of jagged teeth that have sprouted there. Teeth with which he's sliced his own lips numerous times.

He has undergone many changes, some gradual, others abrupt, most after a long night of fitful dreams. While his inhuman hunger and night vision manifested early, his increase in height and the toughening of his hide occurred over the span of a fortnight. In contrast, one fateful morning all his human teeth fell out. The next morning, his prodding fingers detected the tips of fangs.

Over the course of two nights he sprouts fur, white on his face and torso, black on his arms and legs. Since then it has grown thicker, become matted, and the cold is a comfort to him . . . unlike the buckskin hides covering his body, which chafe and confine his every movement. One day he rips the human clothing from his furred body.

He has become as the creature which attacked him, as la bête, but he does not know the ways of it. The small and receding part of him that is still Jacques Robitaille craves death and oblivion, release from the living nightmare. But each day that internal voice grows fainter, less insistent, and more unfamiliar to that which he has become. The hunger is all that he knows, but not how to satisfy it.

A beaver caught fresh in a trap does little to sustain him. A small feast, devoured whole and raw, his drool mixing freely with the puny creature's warm blood, merely stokes the fire of his inhuman hunger. Disgusted with the meager fare, he tosses aside the remaining clotted bones, prepared to stride toward the places of man, but pauses, his yellow-eyed gaze settling on the gleaming pole in the water.

Man is never far from the tools of man . . .

Ah this, now, is the way of la bête.

The promise of food quells his impatience. He will set his own trap for the trappers. Backing away, his head swings side to side, his gaze scanning the prairie grass for any movement. See, yet be unseen.

A trap must be disguised, but how?

A light snow has begun to fall. Jacques, or that which was Jacques, casts his amber gaze up to the overcast sky, arms spread to receive the snow. The cool drops of snow melt on his furred hide, calming him, quenching a fever of hunger. He sinks to the ground and tucks arms and legs beneath his torso, thinking only of the cold and the snow. Minutes dissolve away into an immeasurable span of time, yet he remains still, ears attuned for any sign of man. Once, he opens his eyes and marvels at the field of snow, the wind-driven mounds around his own humped body. See, yet be unseen . . .

Lost in his predatory trance, a stillness that sinks into his bones, he is unaware of the passage of time before he catches the scent of man. His ears, now pointed and covered with tufts of white fur, twitch at the rustle in the grass, the muffled beat of wet footfalls, and the faint creak of buckskin. In a moment, the man curses at finding the sprung trap empty and the words are almost foreign to Jacques' mutated ears.

More rustling, the clink of metal tossed carelessly to the ground then . . . stillness. Jacques knows the man has discovered the bloody remains of the beaver and believes an animal has eaten his prize. The chain, attached to the pole placed in the middle of the stream, allows the beaver to swim to deeper water, where it drowns before it can chew off its own foot to escape. But here, here something has pulled the chain and the beaver up onto land, and devoured the animal whole.

While the man attempts to solve his little riddle, his back upwind to Jacques' position, Jacques rises from the new fallen snow and lumbers forward with a preternatural grace, the merest whisper of sound, closing the distance with long strides.

Perhaps a change in the wind or the snap of a twig alerts the trapper, but his reactions seem slow to Jacques. Pivoting on his heel, the man takes up his rifle, bringing it to bear before he sees the danger.

Still in a crouch, the man's eyes open wide when he sees what is charging him. Jacques experiences a strange, fleeting moment of sympathy and inevitability. For a split second, the face staring at him in horror is his own. He is the man but also la bête. They are one. Yet the moment passes and Jacques does not stop to wield his vicious claws, for he knows the real threat of the rifle. He never slows his charge, never gives the trapper a chance to wound him as Jacques once wounded the creature of his own worst nightmares. Before the barrel of the rifle can stare him down, spit its lethal lead ball in his face, Jacques shrieks, but not in fear. The terrible, ear-splitting sound is a war cry, a spontaneous instinct from within.

Unnerved by the shrill cry, the man freezes for an instant, long enough to forfeit his life.

Jacques smashes into the man with hellish force. The man

grunts as the impact cracks several of his ribs. His rifle flips end over end, far from his numb hands. Jacques spins around, his clawed toes gouging the dirt, seeking purchase. Wheezing in pain, the man has curled over on his side, reaching for a knife in a sheath at his waist. Jacques swings his arm overhead, like a club or an ax, a wood-chopping motion, striking and shattering the man's wrist. The trapper roars in agony, but Jacques pounces on him, rows of razor teeth clamping down on the man's bearded throat, biting deep, tearing into warm flesh.

As the man lies still, Jacques savors the hot gush of blood.

Truly, he has become la bête. There is no turning back, no salvation.

Lowering an already bloodied maw, it feeds . . .

CHAPTER SEVEN

Abby leaps from the roof of a three-story Victorian house, spreads her considerable wings and feels the updraft first support her weight, then lift her high, as an exhilarating rush of winter air streams over her face. Her gliding flight traces a circular path around the outlying rural sections of Windale until she veers inward, tilting one wing down to bank into a narrow turn. Gradually, she closes the circle, watching as the scattered chimneys far below start to clump together in bunches, as if huddling together for support until finally becoming rows and phalanxes, order pulled from chaos.

Above the heart of the commercial district, she recognizes the ACME by its long parking lot and Gibson's Package Store by the green-striped awnings. She glimpses the rotating red and white 1-STOP sign of the One-Stop Mini-Mart, and notices that the old-fashioned, overhanging movie marquee on the corner, protruding from the Palace Cinema, still announces the building is FOR SALE. Atop the roof is the reason why. A black tarp, like a square hole, held down by loose cinder blocks marks the spot where part of the roof caved in after years of water damage, abetted by Wither's fateful hailstorm. Farther along, Abby flies over the humorous bookworm sign for Beckett Books, then the drab brick Windale Post Office, and the Public Safety Building and . . .

. . . an unusual shape catches her eye, a new building, glossy black marble walls, but from above, its geometry represents more than architectural convenience. Unlike the procession of squares and rectangles surrounding it, this building is a circle with the back of a crescent touching opposing sides. It is the waxing-full-waning moon symbol of the Wiccan Goddess. Abby knows it is Windale's new witch museum, vital economic center of Windale tourism. Yet, to Abby's keen eyes, it is something more, something sinister. While it does not profess to commemorate the lives and deaths of innocent women persecuted by a hysterical populace and convicted by a flawed legal system, its symbolism encourages that assumption. Abby sees it as a memorial to evil, a diseased heart pumping blood into an ailing economy. Windale thrives on the darkness, the chaos it embraces and celebrates. Just as she . . .

Abby's wings falter at the incomplete thought. She wobbles in her flight, terrified. Her bones contort, bend and melt like hot wax. A modern-day Icarus, she's flown too close to the sun. But her sun is a dark orb and lies below, flaring black and tugging at her with its own merciless gravity.

Feathers flutter away from her sickened wings, twirling down into the circle of darkness, giving shape to the vortex that has firm hold of her. She spirals out of control, unable to fly, unable to glide, able only to fall into that darkness.

The ground rises to meet her.

Abby would have screamed, but she was breathless.

In darkness, she awoke in extreme discomfort, covered

with a sheen of sweat. Her right arm twisted impossibly far behind her back, as if someone were trying to wrench it from the socket like a Thanksgiving Day drumstick. Her fingers were too long, thin and feeble as straws, almost lifeless. "Oh, God," she moaned, rolling onto her left side, away from the deformity.

She clawed at the mattress with her left hand, tried to crawl away from that side of her body, the impossible side. With a heave, she rolled over the edge of the bed and toppled awkwardly to the floor. Fingers scrabbling at the carpeting, feet shoving against the floor, she pushed and pulled her way into the corner, almost mindless, huddling in a ball. Whimpering with the unrelieved, uncomfortable sensation, she banged the side of her head against the wall—not to cause herself further injury, merely to clear her thoughts.

Across the room, Erica was sound asleep. *Having pleasant dreams probably*, Abby thought enviously.

Abby had one thought. Nobody, not even Sheriff Nottingham, must see her this way, trapped in the middle of a skeletal deformity. The sheriff had never been comfortable with her ability to shape-shift, but even if he never understood it, at least he accepted it. *If he sees me like this*, Abby thought, *he won't allow me to become a wolf ever again. But I can't stop—and when he finds out, he'll send me to a foster home.*

Dreams of flight, of becoming an eagle, had become commonplace for her lately. But never before had the dream flight seemed so real, her human form so distant. Somehow she had begun to shape-shift in her sleep, but the vision of the witch museum had unsettled her mind, aborting the process.

No, no, no!

Distractions. All her panicked thoughts were distracting

her from the task at hand. She had to correct the problem with her bones. If she could fix that, nothing else would matter. Closing her eyes, she began to breathe deeply. Her muscles had been tight, her bones stiff and achy. The more she panicked, the worse the stiffness became. Now, as she relaxed and stopped fighting the change in her bones, her joints began to ease. Gradually, over the course of several minutes, her bones untangled themselves. Her right arm flopped forward, her elbow reformed its human hinge, and her fingers, long, thin and splayed, contracted and thickened. She flexed them, then made a fist.

Down the hall, from the bedroom shared by Max and Ben, came a familiar thump, followed by the rush of four padded feet. Abby looked toward the door just as a black nose nudged it open, permitting Rowdy entrance to the girls' bedroom. The chocolate Lab took a quick survey of the bedroom, then crossed to the corner where Abby was just beginning to feel like a normal ten-year-old girl again.

"Hey, boy," Abby said, stroking the dog's sleek neck.

Rowdy sniffed at her, paying particular attention to her re-formed right arm. A moment later, the tongue lapped at her face. The canine seal of approval, she supposed.

"Abby? You okay?"

Abby looked across the room at Erica, sitting up in bed in her Powerpuff Girls nightgown, clutching a stuffed Blossom to her chest with one hand, rubbing her eyes with the other. "Fine, Erica. Go back to sleep now."

"Okay. Why are you sitting on the floor?"

"Bad dream," Abby said. Not much of an explanation, but enough to satisfy eight-year-old girl logic, because Erica nodded solemnly, curled up on her side and pulled the blankets up to her chin.

Rowdy stepped back from Abby, sat and appraised her for a long moment, then spun around and leapt onto Erica's bed, finding a suitable spot at the foot, where he lay down, lowered his head on his front paws and closed his eyes.

"Weirdest dream . . ." Abby whispered to herself as she climbed into bed again. She stroked her right arm with her left. The flesh still tingled. "Like I fell and broke my wing." *Wrong,* she thought. She hadn't shape-shifted into a bird. The dream represented one more failure.

She drifted back to sleep before the sun rose, before the darkness of night was chased across the floor, revealing three eagle feathers beside her bed.

Deputy Bobby McKay might be content with a large black coffee, but Kayla was determined to have a full breakfast before driving her ailing Dodge Neon to the Crystal Path to start her workday.

Bobby sat on the stool beside hers in the Witches' Stewpot, tapping his boot on the counter's stainless steel foot rail. "If my not eating bothers you," Bobby said with a grin, "I could reinforce the cop stereotype and have a donut."

"Live dangerously," Kayla said. "Have a cinnamon bun."

"No time. Five-minute break."

Lena, Kayla's mother, was busy at one of the corner booths, while Bethany, the dishwater blond cashier-slash-hostess, leaned against the wall near the kitchen door with a smile on her face, pretending not to notice their discussion. *Or maybe she finds my electric-blue hair amusing,* Kayla thought with a frown.

She clutched Bobby's bouncing thigh just above the

knee, to stop his incessant rail tapping. "Where do you get your energy?"

"Noontime double-cheeseburger and fries."

"Ah, so you spackle your arteries with grease when I'm not around."

"Righteous indignation coming from a lady with bacon strips and breakfast sausage on her plate."

"They came with the breakfast special."

"So you won't mind if I eat one," Bobby said as he reached for a bacon strip.

"Stop!" She slapped his hand. "You'll ruin the symmetry of the plate."

"What?"

"Just ask Wild Bill," Kayla said, pausing for a sip of orange juice. "With cooks, presentation is everything."

Laughing, "Okay, then how about if I just steal a kiss?" Before she could respond, he leaned sideways and gave her a peck on the cheek.

Kayla dropped her right hand under the counter to his knee again, but this time she ran it up the length of his thigh. With her left hand she plucked a brittle strip of bacon from her plate and steered it toward his mouth. He opened his mouth and she popped it in. Under the counter, she gave him a healthy squeeze with her right hand. "Ah—that hit the spot."

The chimes mounted on the Stewpot's front door announced a new customer chased by a swirl of cold air. Both Kayla and Bobby looked at the newcomer. "Hi, Sheriff," Kayla said, smiling. "I'm innocent."

"What they all say," Sheriff Nottingham replied with a grin. "Almost didn't recognize you, Kayla, without the spikes."

"This is my blue debut."

"She's a little blue belle," Bobby said, just managing to dodge Kayla's elbow jab.

"Apparently with a few thorns," the Sheriff said, then turned his attention to Bobby. "You wanted to talk?"

Bobby cleared his throat. "Uh, yes, Sheriff." He hopped off the stool, but not fast enough to avoid Kayla's questioning look. He shrugged in a "nothing serious" way. "Some paperwork I'm having a problem with . . ."

"Paperwork," the sheriff repeated, looking back and forth between them, and caught the pleading look in Bobby's eyes. "That's right. Bane of the job."

Kayla gave a slow, measured nod. "All-righty. See ya later, McKay."

"With bells on," he said.

Just loud enough for Bobby alone to hear, Kayla said, "Leave the body ornamentation to me." She almost thought she saw him blush before he hurried outside with Sheriff Nottingham.

Kayla waited until they were both gone, then pushed up the sleeve of her sweater, exposing the long, narrow white gauze of a homemade bandage. She massaged her arm through the bandage and tried not to moan with relief. Itch had been driving her crazy the whole time Bobby was sitting beside her. Though she was sure nothing was wrong with the wound—already scabbing, edged with pink, puckered flesh—she dreaded the thought of drawing Bobby's attention to what he no doubt believed was an act of incipient madness. Just that morning, before applying a fresh dressing, she'd examined the wound. No inflammation, so probably no infection. The paring knife had been clean and she'd treated the wound right away. To convince herself nothing was amiss inside her own body, she'd picked at the bottom of the long scab, enough to draw some blood—red blood. Satisfied, she'd applied more Neosporin and covered the whole mess with fresh sterile bandages and white medical tape.

Bethany stood over her, holding a pot of coffee, but staring at Kayla's bandaged arm. "Yes?" Kayla said.

"I, uh, wondered if you wanted a refill."

"That's decaf," Kayla said, indicating the pot's orange handle. "Never drink the stuff."

"Oh, right. Sorry," Bethany said. "Couldn't help noticing . . ."

"Cut myself."

"Ah."

"Moving boxes around in the basement," Kayla said. "Staple scraped my arm."

"If it itches, could be infected."

"Thanks," Kayla said. "And since you mentioned refills, how about some more of the high octane stuff."

"Sure," Bethany said, sparing a quick glance through the long front window of the restaurant. "Right away."

As Bethany wandered away, Kayla spun around on her orange vinyl stool to look out the window. Bobby and Sheriff Nottingham were talking near the sheriff's car. The sheriff seemed to be carrying the conversation, but Bobby's back blocked her view. Unaware she was watching him through the garlands of tinsel looped along the windows, he nodded every few moments, the attentive listener.

Kayla doubted Bobby had told Sheriff Nottingham about her cutting herself with a paring knife, but he was nervous about something, hiding something from her. *Probably asking the sheriff if he thinks I'm missing a full complement of marbles.* Kayla sighed. *And it's only gonna get worse.* Wendy was on her way to Windale to find out what Kayla knew about Wither's secret place in Matthias Stone's woods. *She probably thinks I'm Wither reborn. God knows, I sometimes wonder that myself—especially at three in the morning.*

She looked at her half-eaten breakfast without much of an appetite and forced herself to nibble on a cold strip of bacon, wondering why it had ever appealed to her.

As soon as they stepped outside the Witches' Stewpot, the New England winter wind reintroduced itself, tugging at their hats and bringing tears to their eyes. Bobby pulled the zipper of his jacket up to his throat, then shoved his bare hands into the pockets, following Sheriff Nottingham to his black-and-white Crown Vic parked at the far end of the lot. Above the witch-riding-a-broom silhouette on both front-door panels of Nottingham's squad car was the word SHERIFF in large block letters.

The sheriff stopped, turned around and leaned against the right front panel of his car, arms crossed over his chest. Bobby stood before him, unsure how to proceed with his concerns. Fortunately, the sheriff sensed his unease and jump-started the conversation with a question. "So, you and Kayla are ... ?"

"Dating, yes."

"Exclusive?"

"Not by royal decree," Bobby said, smiling. "But it's worked out that way."

"She's a good kid."

"You don't think she's a little ... ?"

"Unusual?" the sheriff said. "Absolutely." Bobby had been about to say *odd*, but preferred the sheriff's term. "Won't hold it against her. She's made of stern stuff. You could do worse. A lot worse."

"That's what I wanted to talk to you about."

"You want a character reference for Ms. Kayla Zanella?" The sheriff grinned, amused. "Little bit late, isn't it?"

"No—I mean, that's not what I'm asking."

"Then what? No need to be bashful, Bobby."

Bobby shook his head. "When I came onboard, you gave me a rundown of the town's recent history. The mutilation murders of 1999, how you lost a deputy in '99 and another one in 2000, the freak hailstorm that damaged the town in '99 and the lightning storm that destroyed the college president's mansion."

"We've had our share of foul weather." The words were lighthearted, but the sheriff's face and tone were grim.

"Then there's Matthias Stone's murder spree, Gina Thorne and her goons . . ."

"What are you getting at, Bobby?"

"Well, Kayla was mixed up in the Gina Thorne mess and . . ."

"And you two have been talking?"

Bobby nodded. "Kayla's said some things, hinted at others, and I've experienced some stuff myself that's hard to explain."

The sheriff pushed off the car, stood straight, more alert. "Anything I should know about?"

"Something odd happened near the Stone property," Bobby said. "Back in the woods."

"Care to tell me why you were traipsing around on private property?"

"Kayla made me stop the car. Said something drew her there," Bobby explained. "Anyway, what happened was, time seemed to . . . get away from us."

"Lost time?"

"I suppose that's the phrase," Bobby said. "But I shrugged it off. Figured it wasn't lost time, just time we lost track of, if you know what I mean."

"My advice is stay out of those woods," the sheriff said.

"Don't have to tell me twice, but . . ." Bobby sighed. "Sir, I don't mean any disrespect, but this whole town has a 'you had to be there' feel to it. Some weird stuff happened here—is still happening here and I'm having a hard time understanding it."

"Bobby," the sheriff began, rubbing his chin thoughtfully as he leaned against the car again. "When you signed on, I told you what I thought you needed to know to be successful here."

"Sure."

"Thing is, I didn't tell you everything that went on here. Some of it, I still don't believe, and I saw it with my own eyes. Damned if I can explain it."

"Sir?"

"Are you serious about that young lady in there?"

"I might be," Bobby said. "But—"

"You see, Bobby," the sheriff interrupted before Bobby could commit himself to the thought. "Kayla was there for the weirdness of 2000. And she knows about the weirdness of 1999. You only had to experience a little to believe the rest. Witness the unexplainable and it changes you. Hell, it changes you forever. Bobby, there's an old expression. Ignorance is bliss. Sometimes I have an old-fashioned craving for ignorance."

"I don't understand."

"Are you willing to have your worldview forever changed? Once you open your mind, it won't be so easy to close it again. Of course, you and I, as police officers, it's not in our nature to remain ignorant."

"What exactly are you saying, Sheriff?"

"The truth, if you're willing to hear it. But be careful what you wish for."

Bobby shifted his stance, frowned. "I want to know. Hell, sir, I think I need to know. Don't keep me in the dark on this."

"Bobby, you said the whole town has a 'you had to be there' feel to it. But that's not entirely true. I have my own theory."

"Which is?"

"That this town still vibrates from prior bouts of weirdness, if you will. Like a tuning fork continues to hum after being struck. But the whole town did not bear witness to these unexplainable phenomena. Only a few of us were there. That young lady in there, she's a believer. That makes her different. In that regard, electric-blue hair is the tip of the iceberg. But if you are serious about her, you'd better understand that and accept it."

"I am, and I do ... but it's not easy."

"Never imagined it would be," the sheriff said with a wry grin. "But you said you yourself experienced something bizarre. Get close to that fire and it burns you, scars you, and that means your mind opens to other possibilities, extreme possibilities."

"What about you, Sheriff?"

"What about me?"

"Are you a believer?"

The sheriff laughed, a dry, resigned sound having little to do with humor on a cold January morning. "Bobby, I have scars you would not believe."

FARGO, NORTH DAKOTA

It awakens with the approach of dusk, rises from a light covering of fresh snow. Muscles stiff, but the agony has receded to a full body ache, uncomfortable but tolerable. A quick examination of its arms and legs reveals that the raw, blood-oozing flesh has healed. The skin is sensitive, but no longer burns. And its thick pelt has begun to grow back. In another night, perhaps two, it will be whole. With the release from excruciating pain, its thoughts turn once more to its hunger.

It is RAVENOUS!

Supernatural healing has taken a toll on its body. A complete recovery will come with a full stomach. Yet it remains under the compulsion to find and kill the special prey. Lifting its large head, it casts about with its other sense, the one that detects the magical path to her. For long moments it agonizes over the missing path. It must kill her! But how, if she remains invisible, hidden from it. Must it wander the world endlessly in search of—?

—its breath catches.

There! Like an unbroken gossamer tendril of smoke before it surrenders to the breeze and is absorbed. It glows—but so pale—a whitish blue that slips in and out of transparency. More imagined than real, the path to her is a magical construct, a witch's compass spelled into its brain to facilitate its murderous task. And it has almost lost the way . . . With that thought comes the realization of another compulsion, hidden underneath its grim task. Should it fail, should it lose the path to the special prey—this Wendy—it must destroy itself. The threat has always been there, unseen, unnecessary until now, when the way seems nearly lost. It is twice-damned by this magical curse! Roused from its contented oblivion to be goaded into a long, arduous trek for a specific kill, and punished by death should it fail. But only if it fails. Kill the special prey and its life, its freedom is granted. Her raw flesh will taste all the sweeter for the price of it.

Yet this Wendy has traveled far while it has lain feeble and impotent in the woods. It must feed soon, regain its strength and follow the fading thread that leads to her death and its own freedom.

Creeping through the woods, finding by instinct the silent path through the underbrush, it approaches a manmade clearing, a paved place where humans leave their vehicles gathered around a two-story dwelling. A stench of rotting food wafts back through the trees, unpalatable. Its head swivels, locates the source of the stench, two brown metal containers, lids flipped open, piled with refuse.

With a predator's instinct, it becomes preternaturally still.

Standing beside the rightmost container, smoking a cigarette, is a man.

It stalks forward, draws the cold around its body like a cloak, bringing the snow, but the effort is weak, the flakes puny things that melt when they touch the paved area where the man stands. Weakness is the price for healing, but a full stomach will restore its powers. Though weakened, it is more than capable of bringing down a mere human.

Lloyd wasn't supposed to smoke in the Fargo Motor Lodge office. Not that the prohibition had ever stopped him before. A smokeless ashtray under the counter avoided any unpleasantness with Carl, the motel's manager. That was before New Year's Eve. Before the pickup truck had plowed through the front lobby and burst into flames, before that strange chick traveling solo had checked in, then checked out a few hours later, just minutes before the collision. *Maybe she had a premonition or something,* Lloyd thought as he took a long drag of his Marlboro. *Certainly wanted no part of my party, the stuck-up little bitch.* But now Lloyd was willing to be magnanimous. He'd moved on to the world of bigger and better. Human interest story in the local paper featuring Lloyd Fetty, with a personal account of how he'd pulled old Sylvester's goose out of the frying pan *and* the fire just seconds before the pickup exploded. Never mind that it had been the stuck-up bitch who had saved Sly, because old Sly was too confused about the whole chain of events to remember who plucked his scrawny ass out of the fire. So Lloyd came out of that freaky New Year's Eve with a little notoriety courtesy of the morning edition, and Carl's promise of a raise. *Better make me employee of the fucking month,* Lloyd figured. *With my own parking space. And I probably won't need to buy my own drinks until the spring thaw.*

No, the real reason Lloyd was smoking outside and freezing his newfound celebrity ass off was the damn fumes. The smashed windows had been boarded up, and that only intensified the heavy odors of wet paint and lacquer. Gave him one hellacious headache, but that wasn't the worst of it. All that smelly shit was damn flammable and Lloyd had no desire to make like a marshmallow on a campfire stick.

Besides, all but a few guests had checked out already and nobody was looking to check into the 'pardon our appearance' dump anytime soon, which meant Lloyd was just marking time, racking up some easy hours at his new and improved hourly rate. Somebody had to be on duty, though. *Might as well be me.*

Truth be told, the foul reek wafting from the Dumpsters actually cleared his head of the fumes. Aside from the bone-chilling cold, he had no complaints.

Then it began to snow.

Sudden movement behind him.

Lloyd spun around, almost dropping the cigarette from his lips. "Shit! Scared me half to death, old-timer. What the fuck you doin' out here, Dumpster diving?" Old Graybeard, wearing a black jacket over a white shirt just stared at him, motionless. *Eerie old fuck,* he thought. *Some of these homeless are crazy.* "Takin' a piss in the woods, that it? Out here, buddy, you're liable to freeze your balls off. Little icicles and shit hanging down there." Lloyd laughed at his own joke. "Jeez, you're a somber son of a bitch."

Without a sound, the old man stepped forward.

Reflexively, Lloyd stepped back. Old Graybeard reached out with his black-cloaked arm. "Oh—you wanna bum a smoke. That it?" Lloyd shrugged. "Sure, buddy. Guess I can afford a little generosity." Lloyd reached into his jacket pocket for the crumpled box of cigarettes. "Don't suppose you read the story about me in—"

Lloyd choked on his words.

The old man's hand had darted forward with the suddenness of a striking cobra, but instead of fangs, strong claws dug into Lloyd's throat.

What the fuck!?

The old man squeezed his fingers together, making a fist and, in the process, ripping out a substantial portion of Lloyd's throat.

Already Lloyd's vision grew dim, playing tricks on his panicked mind. The old man seemed to have swelled in size, to have become something covered in fur, something inhuman. *A fucking monst—!*

The thought froze stillborn in Lloyd's mind. A gurgling sound came up through his ruined throat. Darkness continued to close around him. His last sight was a toothy maw descending, glowing yellow eyes staring at him a moment before rows of razor teeth tore into the exposed flesh of his neck.

It makes short work of the plump meal, leaving little more than a skeleton with cracked bones where it sucked out the marrow. It stuffs these meager remains into the nearest of the two refuse containers and slips back into the woods. Satisfied, but hardly sated, it lopes through the cover provided by the trees. With each nourishing mouthful of its human meal, it felt its physical strength return, its supernatural power expanding. Now it is determined to make up for lost time.

First it draws the cold, bolsters the meager snowfall into a full-fledged storm, a steady swirl of fat flakes to blanket vehicles and roads, but more importantly to decrease visibility, first to a hundred yards, then no more than fifty. With the heavy snowfall, it may forego its glamour, its illusion of humanity, and travel freely.

Camouflaged in this storm of its own making, it breaks from the cover of trees and races for the wide paved roads that seem to connect all the burgeoning human cities, civilization's arteries it must use for its own purposes. Again it will need to ride on one of the demonically swift human vehicles. It casts about for the magical path to its special prey, finally locating the pulsing blue-white thread that spirals south and east. Freedom waits at its end, the one named Wendy, she who must die to release it from its magical compulsion. Then—if it chooses—a return to oblivion. But another tantalizing choice beckons, revealed by present circumstances. In the long years it has spent in oblivious hibernation, the hunting grounds have grown bountiful with weak, almost helpless prey. Instead of turning away, why not spend the years ahead feasting on easy prey? It begins to salivate at the prospect . . .

But first, the girl must die.

TRAVELING: ILLINOIS TO OHIO, I-90 EAST AND I-80 EAST

The plan had been for Alex to begin driving after they reached the first rest stop beyond the Illinois state line. Wendy would have been at the wheel nonstop for almost six hours by then, having already passed through several snow squalls and sections of I-90 where the Interstate surrendered a lane or two to plowed snow. But as they neared the rest stop, Wendy vetoed the plan, insisting she could hold out for the ninety or so miles to Chicago, where they planned to stop for a late lunch slash early dinner. Alex agreed to the revised agenda, but only after convincing himself she remained alert enough to respond to any traffic emergencies. They'd kept small talk to a minimum so Wendy could stay focused on the road and, as a result, monotony loomed over the trip. All they had to eat were prepackaged snacks they'd plucked form the aisles of a mini-mart attached to a gas station during their sole refueling stop.

His heart set on a thick, juicy steak, Alex wanted to stop at the first Chicago steak house they saw, and promised to pick up the tab. Wendy frowned at the thought of passing so much time literally sitting still. "Sorry, Alex," Wendy said, "but I have this . . ."

"Premonition about tainted meat?"

"No, not about meat," Wendy said. "But I have this sense that time is precious. Anxiety that something has happened or is about to happen. We need to keep moving."

In the end, they settled for drive-thru, and ate in the parked SUV. Alex had a cheeseburger and fries; Wendy veered toward the reasonably healthy choices of a salad, grilled chicken sandwich and a baked potato. Though they lost only thirty minutes, by the time they were back on the road with Alex behind the wheel, night had fallen.

In the passenger seat, Wendy closed her bleary eyes. If she'd been alone, she would no doubt have pushed herself another couple hundred miles, fatigue setting in as road conditions deteriorated. Letting Alex accompany her on the long drive back to Windale had been a good decision. She smiled, her early reservations all but forgotten.

At some point, she fell asleep. When next she glanced at the LED clock display, almost two hours had passed. They were fifty miles from Ohio, making good time. "How far from Windale," Wendy asked, rubbing her stiff neck.

Alex's eyes stayed focused on the unspooling Interstate. "Too damn far," he said. "And too depressing to think about. Go back to sleep. If you feel up for it, you can take over near Toledo. If not, we'll crash there for the night. Okay, considering the workout I'm giving the antilock brakes, *crash* was probably a poor word choice."

"If you feel yourself getting sleepy, promise you'll wake me."

Alex nodded.

"Good. Maybe we can make New York before we call it a day."

"Doable," Alex said. "If the weather and road conditions cooperate. Buffalo's been hit with eighty-plus inches of snow since Christmas."

"Jeez, we might have to tunnel our way through New York," Wendy said. Thinking about the weather brought to mind both Wither's and Gina's prodigious command of the weather, including hailstorms and lethal summer thunderstorms. The extent of Wendy's weather power, and the first tangible proof of the effectiveness of her magic, had been one gentle rain shower. *Someday, maybe I'll be able to hold off these snowstorms,* Wendy thought. Unfortunately, she lacked the knowledge and, probably, the power to stop a snowstorm in its tracks. Considering the devastating consequences of Wither's storm manipulation, Wendy doubted she'd *ever* want that much magical power. The sheer scale was frightening to contemplate.

Alex gave her a concerned look. "Stock option for your thoughts."

Wendy smiled, shrugged. "Nothing. Weather, that's all."

"Wendy . . ."

Wendy sighed. "Okay, okay, I was thinking about *controlling* the weather."

"You'd really want to try something like that?" Alex said. "I know you . . . conjured rain, but juggling arctic cold fronts and winter snowstorms seems . . ."

"Risky?"

"Scary!"

Wendy patted his arm. "Don't worry. I won't try to shove the snowstorms out of our way. I was thinking about Wither's control of weather. Far as I know, she only demonstrated destructive control. Weather was one more weapon in her magic arsenal. Nothing to gain from calming a storm."

"Maybe calming storms is more difficult."

"Sweet of you, trying to bring her powers down to my scale," Wendy said. "But it's unnecessary. I'm not in competition with her. Don't want to be anything like her." Wendy yawned. "Okay, Alex, I'll take you at your word. You're alert. You're in charge. I'll try to catch a few more z's so I can relieve you later." Wendy reclined her seat, crossed her hands in her lap, tilted her head back and tried to empty her mind of distracting thoughts.

Alex whispered, "Pleasant dreams."

Drifting off to sleep, Wendy smiled—

—and the Pathfinder swerved violently, slamming her head against the passenger window.

MENLO PARK, CALIFORNIA

Karen Glazer had trouble focusing on the childhood brain development article featured in *Psychology Today*. Far more interesting was the picture her remarkable daughter was drawing on a blank sheet of paper with an assortment of Crayolas. Though Hannah's attention seemed riveted to her composition, Karen knew her little girl was uncannily aware of overt observation. If Karen stared over Hannah's shoulder, she would become self-conscious and abandon the picture. So Karen satisfied herself with the occasional quick peek at the outlined white house and picket fence, under a shade tree, round yellow sun and impressive rainbow, rendered in wax on twenty-pound bond.

Karen had rinsed all the dinner dishes, loading the dishwasher while Art made a run to the mini-mart for his one real food indulgence, one that Karen and Hannah were happy to share with him, a couple of pints of Cherry Garcia ice cream. She glanced at the wall clock and estimated he'd be back in another five minutes. "I'll get out some bowls and spoons," she said, but doubted Hannah heard.

By the calendar, Hannah was just over two years old, but physically and mentally she seemed ready for first or even second grade. The point was moot, though, as Karen had come to a decision with Art to homeschool the girl. Other children just wouldn't understand or accept Hannah, for whom the phase "growth spurt" was an understatement. Sometimes it seemed to Karen that she could measure Hannah's height before breakfast and by bedtime detect a noticeable change. Her child's mental development was as impressive. Whatever class she was placed in would soon fall behind her. A teacher in a busy classroom would never give Hannah all the attention she required to stay interested. Yet new clothes and new lessons were minor problems. Karen worried about Hannah's emotional development. Was there any real substitute for experience? Emotional maturity came through life's adventures and misadventures, successes and failures. Life would be so much simpler if they could just slow Hannah down to normal. Though medical science was unable to stop Hannah's accelerated growth, Karen hoped that someday Wendy would find the secret spell or arcane incantation necessary to unravel the hex Rebecca Hutchins had placed on Hannah.

As Karen placed three bowls and spoons around the table, she noticed Hannah's coloring had become a little frenetic. For some reason she'd taken a black crayon and blotted out the summer sun and filled the sky with tiny little circles.

"What are you drawing, Hannah?"

Without looking up from the paper, "Snow, Momma."

"Snow on such a sunny day?"

"Lotsa snow, Momma," Hannah said. "That's what happens."

Karen sat beside her, in growing alarm, as Hannah drew a large figure, taller than the house, arms raised menacingly, with claws for fingers. She held the crayon tight, pressing hard on the paper, grinding the soft wax tip. Her motions became jerky, her face a frozen grimace, as if she was determined to complete an unpleasant chore. "Tell her, Momma. Tell her."

"What Hannah?"

Hannah grabbed a new crayon and smeared red streaks on the clawed hands. "Wendy, Wendy, Wendy . . ."

"What should I tell Wendy?"

Now heavy red lines from the mouth, a mouth filled with pointed teeth. Karen could no longer pretend her daughter wasn't drawing blood on the large, blocky figure's hands and mouth. "Tell her, Wendy go! Tell Wendy! Wendy go, Momma! Tell her!"

"Where should Wendy go, baby?"

Slashing red lines across the house. "No! No! Tell her!"

Karen grabbed Hannah's hand and held it still. "Hannah! Look at me!"

Hannah looked up from her violent drawing and stared at her mother. Tears were spilling down her cheeks. "I'm tired, Momma. Can I go to sleep now?"

"Okay, okay, baby," Karen said. "Let's get you to bed."

Karen picked her up, cradling her neck as she climbed the stairs.

Hannah murmured against her throat. "Can I have my ice cream tomorrow, Momma?"

"We'll save you a big bowl, Hannah," Karen said, fighting back her own tears. "You rest now. Everything will be better in the morning."

After Hannah brushed her teeth, Karen tucked her into her bed and stroked her hair for a while. A few minutes earlier, she'd heard Art come home and toss his keys on the counter, but she said nothing to Hannah, afraid she'd want to go downstairs for some ice cream after all. "Feel better, baby?"

Hannah nodded. "Better, but sleepy . . ." She punctuated the sentence with a yawn.

"My little sleepy girl." Karen kissed her forehead and whispered, "Go to sleep now, baby."

"Mm-hmm. Tell her, Momma. Okay?"

"I'll call Wendy tonight, Hannah. Promise."

"Good . . . and tell her I'll see her soon, Momma."

"I will, dear." Karen stood by the doorway. "Okay to turn the light off?" Hannah nodded, eyes already closed. "Night-light's on. If you need anything, call me."

"Mm-hmm."

Karen hurried down to the kitchen and saw Art sitting at the kitchen table, two stacked pints of Cherry Garcia resting under his chin. He was staring at Hannah's *blood*-drenched drawing. "Not a happy sketch," he mumbled.

Karen sat beside him and placed a hand on his shoulder. "It started out happy, rainbow and everything."

Art tugged at his ponytail, rubbed the stubble on his jaw, then pushed his eyeglasses up the bridge of his nose. "Then what happened?"

"She became . . . agitated. Drew that thing with the claws, started yelling about Wendy again."

"No seizures, I hope."

Karen shook her head. "But whatever it was, it wiped her out. She wanted to sleep. Think she's out already."

"What now?"

Karen stood up, spent a few seconds trying to work a kink out of her neck, heaved a sigh and reached for the phone. "Time to call somebody."

"Her doctor?"

"No," Karen said. She walked over to the fridge and placed her index finger on the magnetic notepad where she'd written the cell phone number. "Wendy."

TRAVELING: OHIO, I-80 EAST

Head throbbing, Wendy leaned forward and clutched the dashboard. "What happened?" The airbags hadn't deployed, so they hadn't hit anything, at least not head-on. "Deer in the road?"

Alex clutched the steering wheel in a white-knuckled grip, his gaze ricocheting from the endless dance of snowflakes revealed in the headlight beams to something glimpsed in the rearview mirror. He swallowed hard. "Not a deer. A hallucination . . . a little night-driving hallucination, that's all."

"Want me to take over?"

"One little problem," Alex said, glancing in the rearview mirror again.

"What?"

"It—I mean, *she* is still there." Small backward jerk of his head. "Actually, she's right behind you."

"What are you—?" Wendy swiveled in her seat to look behind the car, worrying that Alex had hit something or someone in the road. But Alex had meant literally behind her. Sitting behind Wendy with an uncomfortable frown on her face. "Oh," Wendy said. "It's you." Mini-wave with her right hand. "Welcome back."

"Wait!" Alex said. "You *know* my hallucination? How do you—ah, shit! This is like that story, isn't it, 'An Occurrence at Owl Creek Bridge.' They hang the guy, the rope snaps, he gets away, then we realize he fantasized the whole getaway in the time it takes for the rope to break his neck. That's it! I'm asleep at the wheel and we're about to drive off a cliff or something."

"No, Alex," Wendy said. "Stay calm. You're fine. Trust me."

"*Hello, Wendy—and Alex,*" the Crone said. "*Impossible to find you alone, Wendy. Hadn't realized you were asleep and I . . .*"

startled Alex." She could have spoken inside Wendy's mind, but the one-sided silence might have disturbed Alex even more.

"Okay, everything's copacetic," Alex said. "You're just talking to a ghost in the back of a Nissan Pathfinder on I-80 in Ohio. Perfectly natural."

Wendy reached over and kissed his cheek. "If you were with any other girl right now, you'd be wise to question your sanity."

"So, in addition to being a witch, you're also haunted?"

"She's not a ghost."

"But she just—popped in! And I can see through her. She's transparent, I mean, translucent. Not really here."

"True, on all counts," Wendy said. "She's, well, I call her the Crone."

"As in Maiden, Mother, Crone? Aspects of the Goddess?"

"Hey! Have you been reading up on Wicca?"

"Skimming," Alex said with a grin. "Not that I'm thinking of converting or anything. Uh, no offense."

"None taken," Wendy and the Crone replied simultaneously.

"Just, uh, give me a heads-up, maybe, if you're expecting the Maiden or the Mother to drop in anytime soon."

Wendy laughed. "No need to worry about that. Besides, this Crone isn't really the Crone. That's just how I first imagined her. The name stuck. Mostly to avoid confusion with Hannah."

"Little Hannah? Out in California? What confusion?"

The Crone answered before Wendy launched into the full explanation, "*Because my name is also Hannah.*"

"Ah," Alex said, nodding. "Common enough name I suppose. Suzanne, my sister, has a friend with the same name, but we call her Susie. So, uh, Crone Lady, no offense, but what *are* you?"

Wendy said, "She's . . . from the future. Kind of a living premonition." *That answers what if not who.*

"The future? Really? Hey, do the Timberwolves make the finals this year?"

"*Sorry*," the Crone said. "*I don't follow sports.*"

"How 'bout winning lottery numbers? Super Bowl? Kentucky Derby?"

The Crone smiled and shook her head. "*Who remembers years-old trivia?*"

"Right," Alex said. Then, to Wendy, "Wait a minute. She's your old Wiccan mentor, isn't she?"

"Yes," Wendy said. "I would have explained yesterday, but obviously it's a bit complicated."

"Jeez, if she's your mentor, no wonder you call her the Crone."

"*More like the student instructing the teacher,*" the Crone said. "*Well, after the teacher teaches—never mind. Wendy's right, it is complicated.*"

"Her temporal perspective gives me the equivalent of a crash course in magic," Wendy said. "She shows me where to focus my studies."

"*As I am here now, to tell Wendy what she needs to know before I must leave.*"

"Alex, I promise to bring you up to speed on this after . . .'" Wendy looked back at the Crone, remembering her interruption when Wendy had begun to explain how Hannah the Crone was a future representation of Hannah Glazer manifesting in the present. "Assuming you're okay with that, Hannah."

Hannah closed her eyes. Accessing her memories of events awaiting young Hannah, Wendy imagined, before deciding how much Alex should know. At last, the Crone said, "I trust your judgment, Wendy. I sense no issue either way. Tell Alex, if you wish, but I would request, as should you, that he tell no other." Alex nodded his agreement. "Good. Then we should discuss the matter at hand. This new threat."

"It's on the move again," Wendy guessed.

"Yes, unfortunately," the Crone says. "I sense that it has almost completely healed itself, and has taken more than one victim since its awakening. It is still far away, but less than a thousand miles."

"But it's on foot, right?" Alex said. "Or can this thing fly, like Wither?"

"It has no inherent capacity for flight," the Crone said. "But it is relentless."

Alex continued, "And what exactly do you mean by taken victims?"

The Crone's face was grim. "It eats the raw flesh of human beings."

"The Wither diet, but without the fly-thru window."

"Can we attach a name to this thing already?" Wendy said, anxiety creeping into her voice. Not knowing exactly what it was that was hell-bent on turning her into Wendy sashimi was a little unnerving. Naming the thing might settle her frazzled nerves a bit. Emphasis on the might. "What exactly is this big nasty thing Wither's curse has whipped into a frenzy?"

"The creature is a demon with origins described in the Cree and Algonquian folklore of the Manitoba province of Canada, although the first sightings—by Jesuit missionaries in the seventeenth century—predate the legal formation of the province. There are many references to the creature in the eighteenth century journals of the Hudson Bay Company. It is known by the Ojibwa name wintiko or wendigo, which translates roughly as evil spirit and cannibal."

"Wonderful," Alex said, shaking his head.

"Name's familiar," Wendy said. "What does this *wendigo* look like?"

"The Cree and Ojibwa believed the wendigo was a human possessed by an evil spirit, and turned to cannibalism. However, a human who became a wendigo would be much smaller than a true wendigo, which would be as tall as a tree. Of course, we must allow for some exaggeration."

"Ah, regular and lite versions," Alex said. "How does a human become one?"

"The wendigo's bite is thought to be infectious."

"How does that matter if it eats you?"

"If it eats you," the Crone said evenly. *"I don't suppose it does matter."*

"Which type is after me?" Wendy asked. "Giant-sized or human-hybrid?"

"I have no memory of a tree-sized giant," the Crone said. *"Actually, I have no firsthand memory of the creature at all. I was never there. What I know comes from your own description, Wendy. An unusually large creature with a white-furred torso, black-furred arms and legs."*

"What are its powers? Any kind of supernatural whammy?"

Alex looked wide-eyed at Wendy. "You mean a cannibaistic, evil-spirited, plague-carrying, witch-cursed bounty hunter isn't scary enough for you?"

"Girl likes to be prepared," Wendy said, shrugging with a touch of false bravado. *My choices here are false bravado or blind, screaming panic.*

"It thrives in cold weather," the Crone said. *"It attacks with the snow and blizzards. And its scream supposedly has the power to petrify its victims."*

Wendy held up her hands, palms out. "That's quite enough of the *wendigo's* résumé. Let's get to the part where you tell me how to fight it—how I fought it."

"She already knows how this battle plays out?"

"Somewhat," Wendy hedged. "There's the problem of changing time lines. I—we can't take anything for granted." She looked to the Crone, who seemed noticeably more transparent. Hannah was tiring. Wendy had to speed the briefing along. "I did beat it, though, right?" The Crone nodded, but her expression was pained. "What . . . ? Tell me! What went wrong?"

The Crone shook her head, *"In my time line, as the past exists for me now, you defeated the* wendigo, *but at great personal cost."*

"Oh, God," Wendy's hands covered her mouth. She closed her eyes for a moment and shook her head. "No. Not again," she whispered. "Please not again."

"What?" Alex looked back and forth between them. The Crone's image was dissolving around the edges. "Somebody clue me in."

Wendy looked at him, her green eyes wide. "Somebody dies, Alex. Somebody close to me."

"Oh," Alex said. He cleared his throat. "I—I see."

"Before this is over," the Crone said softly, *"many will die."*

CHAPTER EIGHT

Wendy was trembling. Terrified to pose the question. But she had to ask the Crone, had to know if bringing Alex along had been a horrible mistake. "Is Alex—?" Wendy's voice caught in her throat before she could complete the question. "No, I don't want to know!" Maybe when he was asleep, when she and the Crone had some privacy, maybe then she could ask, but not now. "Alex, when we reach Windale, I want you to stay away from me, far away."

Alex turned to the Crone, and showed the courage Wendy couldn't muster. "Am I one of those who died—uh, will die?"

"Grief blinds me here," the Crone said. "Faces swirl in my memory, yours and Wendy's, among others, but I don't know which survived. All I know, all I remember is a devastating battle. Wendy, I've told you before about the malleable nature of the time lines."

"Wendy, what is she saying? It doesn't necessarily turn out the way she remembers it?"

"Maybe better. Maybe worse."

"What about your preemptive training?" Alex asked. "Forewarned is forearmed."

"Good point," Wendy said, seizing the positive as she turned to the Crone. "Where should I focus my training?"

"*When the* wendigo *awoke, I sensed three vital magical areas.*" As the Crone spoke, the edges of her voice faded out and her image lost some definition.

"Since this thing thrives on cold, I'm assuming *fire* is one of them."

"*Fire may play a part, but won't be instrumental in the battle,*" the Crone said. "*Or perhaps . . . seems that way because . . . already know fire . . .*"

"Then tell me the three."

"*Astral projection, border vision . . . sphere . . .*"

"Sphere? I already—"

"*More versatile . . . not vulnerable to . . .*"

"Okay, more tricks with protective spheres. Astral projection, understood. And third was . . . border vision?"

The Crone nodded and the motion caused her head to melt away. "*See the betweens . . . rest . . . be back . . . have time, you . . .*" And then she was gone.

"Damn it!" Wendy said bitterly. "We wasted too much of her time."

"Sorry. My fault for interrupting."

"No, it was both of us," Wendy said and sighed. "She said she'll be back. That I have time. Only so much training I can do at fifty miles per hour, right? So, I'll start with astral projection. Simple stuff—I hope. When she returns, she can explain the not-so-simple stuff."

"You're the expert."

"I wish." Seemed to her, the more magic she learned, the more she needed to know. "Anyway, time to get started. Clear

my mind of all distractions and begin Astral Projection 101."
Wendy stretched her neck, arms and legs as much as possible
within the confines of the SUV, trying to loosen cramped
muscles and make herself comfortable in the bucket seat.
More than comfortable, serene. Hands folded in her lap, head
against the headrest, she closed her eyes and tried to recall
everything she'd read or heard about astral projection.

BBRREEEEEPP!

"Ah—cell phone!" Might as well have been an electric
cattle prod for the effect it had on her. Several clumsy
moments, fumbling through her pocketbook and snagging
the phone's strap on Alex's gargoyle-headed cane before she
could answer.

BBRREEEEEPP!

"I really need to select one of those soothing musical
ringers." She pressed the TALK button and said, "Hello."

WINNIPEG, MANITOBA
CANADA

"Snowball, down!" Tara commanded. Naturally, her kitten
jumped from the chair to the kitchen table, where the little
white fur ball happily curled up on the legal pad with Tara's
scribbled notes. Frowning, Tara scooped the kitten off the
paper and dropped her in the opposite chair. While she
waited for Wendy to pick up, Tara sipped her herbal tea,
smiling when she heard Wendy's familiar voice on the other
end of the line. "Hi, Wendy, it's your Winnipeg connection."

"Hey, Tara! How are things?"

"Back's been good. I'd forgotten what it feels like to sleep
several hours in a row. And you? Getting over the ex?"

"Not as much over as I thought. More later. Promise."

"Gotcha," Tara said. "I'm calling about your research request."

"Any luck?"

"Maybe," Tara said, running a hand through her short hair. "After digging through some old microfilm issues of the *Winnipeg Sun* and the *Free Press*, starting with the sixth of August, 2000, I thought I had come up empty. The only item that caught my eye was a freak snowstorm up in Hudson Falls."

"On August sixth?"

"Qualifies as unusual in my book," Tara said. "Like some kind of Fortean event. But I might have dismissed it if not for the recent news reports. Probably on the news last night, but I wasn't watching. Generally, I avoid broadcast news. Depresses the hell out of me. But I read the newspaper today and . . ."

"Something bad happened in Hudson Falls?"

"Something *grisly* happened in Hudson Falls on New Year's Eve, and that's putting it mildly."

"Tell me." Wendy's voice was fainter, tense now.

"Well, Hudson Falls is a tiny rural town, northeast of here. Couldn't even find it on a map. Two victims. Three, if you count the dog. Neighbor stopped by to wish them a Happy New Year and found the bodies. Prevailing theory is an animal attack. Rogue, man-eating animal. Officially, they're blaming a grizzly bear. If you ask me, it had to be a rabid grizzly. Do grizzlies get rabies?"

"Don't know."

Tara glanced down at her notes. "Well, it was large and nasty, with powerful claws, lots of sharp teeth, and an incredible appetite. Ate most of the man—Earl Cady, retired night watchman—his wife, Amanda, and their German shepherd. Earl and the dog were found—what was left of them—in the woods nearby the Cady home. Mrs. Cady's body was inside the house. Apparently, the animal crashed through a bay window to attack her."

"Tara," Wendy said. "Have you ever heard of a *wendigo*?"

"Funny you should mention that. The papers interviewed some neighbors to get their reactions—as if we couldn't imagine their reactions! Anyway, one old gent said it reminded him of *wendigo* legends."

"What do you know about them?"

"*Wendigos*? Not much. They're a kind of demon in Native American folklore. Love the cold and snow, definitely cannibals and . . . I think I heard or read that they could infect humans, or humans could become *wendigos* somehow. Never understood why a human would want to become one, though. Anyway, I always imagined a cross between a werewolf and the abominable snowman."

"About sums it up."

"Hey—wait a minute," Tara said. "You really think a *wendigo* . . . ?"

"It's one theory."

"But, Wendy, they're—I always assumed *wendigos* were just folklore bogeymen, the stuff of cautionary fairy tales, or an old-world version of Bigfoot or the Loch Ness Monster. Right?"

"Maybe," Wendy conceded for Tara's benefit. "Maybe it's a psycho impersonating a *wendigo*."

"Either way," Tara said. "Not good."

"No."

"This is gonna give me nightmares, isn't it?"

Traveling: Ohio, I-80 East

Wendy pressed END to terminate the call, and stared down at the phone with a bit of delayed shock. *God, I woke that thing up! Wither pushed my buttons from beyond the grave, and made me wake that damn thing up.* She shook her head, caught Alex's inquiring gaze and fought to regain her composure. "I had Tara check the papers for any type of grisly incidents shortly after August 6, 2000, the day Gina Thorne died, the day of Wither's curse." Wendy related the details of the call.

"Fits the bill," Alex said. "What did she say about *wendigos?*"

"It's a creature from Native American folklore and legend to her. Not real." Wendy thought, *If only it were that simple.* "She pictures a cross between a werewolf and the abominable snowman."

"Not liking that mental image one bit."

BBRREEEEEPP!

Wendy almost dropped the phone, but managed to answer it on the second ring. "Tara? Did you forget—Oh, Karen. Hi!" Wendy still felt as if she should call her former college teacher Professor Glazer, but *Karen* insisted otherwise. "Hannah okay?"

Menlo Park, California

"She's fine," Karen said. "Sleeping now."

Karen sat at the kitchen table. Art stood behind her, massaging her neck and shoulders, which had been tight since Hannah's frenzied drawing. The Cherry Garcia was in the freezer, all but forgotten.

"Good. I'm glad she's—"

Karen interrupted. "But she had another episode. Not a seizure, but she became very agitated. She was drawing with crayons . . ." Karen described the transformation of Hannah's picture from rainbow skies to blood-smeared monster. "It's horrible. I can't imagine—a child having that kind of image in her head! It's . . . I'm sorry . . ."

"No need to apologize, Karen. It's awful, I know," Wendy said. "She's such a precious little angel. Is she okay now?"

"Yes. Very tired. Fell asleep fast, but made me promise to call you. To tell you about the drawing, and to pass along her warning," Karen said. "Same thing she yelled before her seizure. Warning you to run away, or go away. I don't know. Doesn't make sense really. Tell Wendy to go away. She thought it was important, and I promised to tell you."

"What were her exact words? Do you remember?"

"There wasn't much to it," Karen said. "Maybe, 'Tell her to go.' No, wait. It was 'Tell her, Wendy go.' And, 'Tell Wendy, Wendy go.' " Karen chuckled, a dry humorless sound. "Obviously, her grammar needs work."

"No," Wendy said softly over the long distance call. "I think she got it just right."

Karen looked up at Art, a puzzled expression on her face, then leaned forward over the table. "I'm—I'm not sure what you mean."

"She's not telling me to go," Wendy said. "All along she's been telling me what's coming after me. Not two words, 'Wendy go.' One word. W-E-N-D-I-G-O." Wendy described the Native American demon as casually as she could, but it sounded horrendous nonetheless.

"Oh, my God, Wendy," Karen said. "You're sure? This monster is real?"

"We think so. Just another helping of Wither's revenge."

"The curse you told me about? But it's been so long, I just assumed..."

"Revenge is a dish best served cold," Wendy said grimly. "It's complicated."

"And Hannah knows about this?"

"The Crone visited me before you called."

"When Hannah was coloring, she seemed to be in some kind of trance."

"An altered state of consciousness. Makes sense."

"I don't know what to say, Wendy."

"How about 'Good luck'? And promise me you guys will stay on the left coast this time."

"But if Hannah can help..."

"She can," Wendy said. "As the Crone. Promise you'll keep Hannah safe."

"Of course, I will," Karen said, without making the promise. When Wendy fought Gina Thorne, Hannah had to be nearby for her Crone aspect to stay in contact with Wendy. Hannah was never directly in danger, yet her presence had helped. "But Hannah also said to tell you she would see you soon."

"I hope she was talking about a Crone visit," Wendy said. "I don't want to see any cute toddlers on the arctic demon battlefield."

Karen smiled, but it was a pale effort. Already worried about Hannah, she now had to add Wendy to the list. "Take care, Wendy."

"I will," Wendy said. "Take care of that cutie pie for me."

Karen smiled again, broader this time, and hung up the phone. She sighed, but it became a shudder. She stood and turned around to face Art, and when she looked at him there were tears in her eyes.

His expression was grim. Hearing only one side of the conversation had been enough to alarm him. "How bad?"

Karen shook her head, unable to give voice to her concerns. After what she had witnessed, all she had experienced, rational explanations and denial no longer fit into her worldview. In their absence, Karen could only accept that the worst was not simply possible but entirely probable. She stepped forward and wrapped her arms around Art's waist, tucked her head under his chin. He held her in his arms, stroked her hair and waited. Finally, she said, "Oh, Art . . . it's awful." *Dear God, help Wendy through this, and please, please keep my baby safe.*

TRAVELING: OHIO, I-80 EAST AND I-90 EAST
JANUARY 2, 2002 INTO JANUARY 3, 2002

"Now that Hannah knows I received her warning, I hope she can let it go," Wendy said to Alex. "Hate to think of her having nightmares about this. Bad enough I'll be having nightmares."

A light snow was falling. Dry flakes accumulated on the windshield. Alex switched the wipers on to the intermittent setting. Every few seconds, with a rubbery *f-whump*, the blades cleared the windshield. Red taillights glowed along the highway in front of them, flickering in and out of focus as visibility changed. Sometimes they appeared alone on the long dark road, drifting in a sea of night. "But if the Crone knows, won't Hannah . . . ?"

"Think of Hannah and the Crone as two different individuals, two different consciousnesses, with a special bond. Sometimes they overlap. When . . . feedback from the future triggers something in our Hannah's subconscious, the Crone manifests to me. Hannah may sense when the Crone is here, but she doesn't have access to the details of our conversations."

"They never meet and compare notes?"

"Hannah can't manifest the Crone in her own presence. Paradoxical maybe, unable to influence events in her own life, too close to temporal ground zero. But those limitations allow Hannah to have a quasi-normal life, considering how much more traumatic it could be."

Alex nodded. "What happens now?"

"Are you still okay driving?" Wendy asked, and Alex nodded. "We probably won't see the Crone again for a while. Since I need her to explain 'border vision' and to tell me what new tricks I should learn for my protective sphere, my only option is to practice astral projection. I understand the basic concept, but haven't tried it in years."

"What's that about? Stars? Horoscopes?"

Wendy grinned, "As in *astralogy*."

Alex smiled and shook his head. *Probably biting his tongue.* "Where do I sign up for my remedial New Age course?"

Wendy's smile faded. "Oh, Alex, I'm sorry for being a smart-ass. I'm frazzled and tired and scared at the same time."

"I understand. I don't have the supernatural bull's-eye on my back, and I'm scared. All things considered, you're amazingly calm."

"That's me," Wendy said, forcing a smile. "Grace under pressure." While she recognized that she was the primary target, she remained concerned that Alex would be one of the *many* who died in the Crone's remembered past, that he would fall victim to the crossfire surrounding Wither's curse. Worse than facing her own literal demon was the knowledge that those close to her were in grave danger. Her presence put everyone around her at risk. "Alex, I might need to deal with this alone."

"No," he said without hesitation. "I won't let you face it alone."

Wendy took his right hand from the steering wheel and clasped it between hers. He wanted to be brave for her but not out of some overinflated sense of chivalry. He cared for her. Simple as that. How much worse would Wither's curse be if she truly were alone? Yet the possibility remained that, in the final hour, her most selfless act might be to stay away from those she loved. "Thanks, Alex. I hope it doesn't come to that. Wither's spell turned this thing loose. Maybe there's a spell to send it back into hibernation."

"Like defusing a bomb?"

"Exactly." But it wouldn't be that simple. It *never is*, she thought bitterly.

"What's the scoop on astral projection?"

"Oh, right, almost forgot," Wendy said. "Have you heard of 'out of body experiences'?"

"Like near-death experiences?"

"Um, somewhat," Wendy said. "With near-death, the person is clinically dead or nearly so, hence the name. Classic example is when the heart stops beating but CPR or a defibrillator restarts it. The person reports seeing a light at the end of a tunnel, maybe deceased friends and loved ones waiting for them. They may even have looked down on their own physical body as their soul or spirit departed."

Alex nodded for her to continue.

"With astral projection, one experiences the same sense of slipping out of and hovering over one's physical body, but rather than near-death trauma, the trigger event is self-hypnosis."

"How's that work?"

"It's a self-induced trance, an altered state of consciousness. That's how I think of it, and it's the method I've used—or tried to, anyway—to perform astral projection."

"What's the point? Looking down on your physical body sounds kinda morbid."

"Sure, if that's all you do," Wendy said with a wry grin. "I suppose the benefit is that your astral body lacks the limitations of your physical body. In theory, your consciousness can fly through walls, into the clouds and to distant lands. Meanwhile, your physical body stays right where you left it, unmoving."

"Still hypnotized? Then how do you snap out of it? If you can't move, how do you clap your hands or snap your fingers to come out of the trance?"

"You stay in control of your consciousness," Wendy said. "Just bring it back when you're done zooming around. Once your consciousness is back in your body, you just *wake* yourself out of the trance."

"Any chance you could get stuck in a trance? Go into a coma?"

"I've never heard of that happening." Wendy chuckled. "Are you trying to spook me, Mr. Dunkirk?"

"No, not at all," Alex said, a grin tugging the corner of his mouth. "Wondered if I might be called upon to provide mouth-to-mouth resuscitation."

"Hey, mister," Wendy said, shaking a finger at him. "If you try to cop a feel while I'm under, I *will* know about it."

"Don't confuse checking vital signs for copping a feel and we shouldn't have any misunderstandings." Alex was displaying his most innocent, wide-eyed expression. Pure mischief, she knew, waiting for the façade to crumble, but he was too good a poker player for that. "Now start projecting your astral, young lady," he said. "I need to pay attention to the road."

"Aye, aye," Wendy said with mock seriousness. She removed her crystal necklace, cupped it in the palm of her hand, and began her relaxation ritual, progressing through each muscle group. As with much of magic, visualization was key. Relaxation was important for self-hypnosis, and the crystal helped her focus her mind. Now, however, exhaustion proved too big an obstacle. The same relaxation techniques that enabled self-hypnosis also facilitated sleep. Wendy knew the exercise was a bust when her attempts at self-hypnosis resulted in a series of prolonged yawns.

"Maybe you should sleep a bit first."

"Umm . . . think you're right. You mind?"

"Of course not," Alex said. "We should be near Toledo before eleven. Cleveland's another hundred or so miles east of that. I'll try to hold out at least that long. Besides, if you yawn like that one more time I'll fall asleep."

Wendy woke up to discover the Pathfinder wasn't moving. For a moment, she was alarmed, not sure what had happened or where they were. Bright lights shone down into the car, making her squint as she checked her surroundings. Alex was gone.

She leaned across the driver's seat and saw him outside, bundled in his parka, breath creating white plumes in front of his face, as he paid for gas. *That's what I need to shake off this lethargy.* Opening her door, she thought she would be braced for the cold, but was ill-prepared for the blast of frigid air that swirled around her, driving a chill into her bones. In moments her teeth were chattering and her ears ached. She hopped around, patting her arms, letting the cold temperature take the place of caffeine or actual rest. By the time she hopped back into the car, she was awake and alert enough to attempt self-hypnosis again.

Alex climbed back into the driver's seat, looked at her red face for a moment, and smiled. "Cold enough for you?"

"No points for originality. Where are we, wise guy?"

"Toledo."

"You still up for driving?"

"Sure. Especially, if you want to try that out of body thing again."

Once they were back on the Interstate highway, Wendy had a flash of inspiration. She leaned forward to remove her dangly Winnie-the-Pooh from the rearview mirror and stashed it in the glove compartment. "I need a focus," she said, by way of explanation. She removed her crystal pendant again, but this time looped it over the rearview mirror. The clear crystal swayed gently, catching light in one facet, refracting it out another. Not as dazzling as a sun-catcher at noon, but it sparkled and glittered just enough in the ambient lighting to hold her attention, her focus. She performed her relaxation ritual, this time without succumbing to yawns. Next she cleared distracting thoughts from her mind by focusing her undivided attention on the crystal as it gently swung back and forth, back and forth, back . . . and . . . forth . . . back . . . and . . .

When she had achieved a dispassionate state of being, moment-by-moment-by-moment indifference, total passivity, she proceeded to the visualization.

The first step, the simplest step, was to close her eyes, and yet *still* see the crystal pendant, notwithstanding the physical obstruction of her eyelids. She visualized the crystal dangling from the rearview mirror post on its slender silver chain, the flow of its swaying movement uninterrupted by the closing of her eyes. She saw all its gleaming details, each facet, cut and groove, every trick of light it performed as it swung and twirled beneath the mirror. Visualization was the mother of belief. If she opened her eyes at that instant, she knew which side of the crystal would be facing her, where it would be in its gentle arc above the dashboard, how the light would play through and across its surface. She *knew* . . .

And with a giddy sense of weightlessness she elevated that awareness over her body, one slow inch at a time and, now that the crystal had helped her achieve a state of self-hypnosis, an altered state of consciousness, she no longer needed to stay focused on it. She was free, with total detachment from the confines of her body, lifting herself—her awareness—up and away, as if on a mild current of warm air, until she was able to look down and dispassionately examine her own body.

Astral Wendy examined physical Wendy with an odd sense of calm, almost as if she had left all emotions behind, as if they were too weighty for astral flight. *Gives new meaning to the phrase "emotional baggage."* Physical Wendy almost seemed asleep, with her eyes closed, head tilted just to the left. Fingers interlocked, but the slightest outward pressure, the merest bump on the Interstate would probably disentangle them. Astral Wendy couldn't believe how relaxed physical Wendy appeared.

And the details! Everything stood out in stark relief, as if viewed for the first time with perfect eyesight: the grain of the vinyl ceiling, the cross-hatched pattern on the cloth seats, a tangle in physical Wendy's hair, the metallic gleam of the dome light housing, the dewy condensation on Alex's soda can, the creased corner of an old AAA strip map tossed on top of the dashboard, next to a crumpled gasoline receipt, the stubble on Alex's chin and neck, a tiny smudge of gas station grease at the bend of the second joint of his right index finger. One thing, however, remained invisible: astral Wendy herself. She was a drifting awareness but, unlike the Crone, not a visible entity. Looking down, she saw the seats and floor of the Pathfinder, much of it shrouded in darkness, but not her astral body.

Astral Wendy drifted closer to Alex, mischief on her detached mind. She could move with the power of thought, wherever her will directed her, unfettered by gravity, physical constraints, momentum or inertia. Different from and more liberating than the weightlessness of outer space, she imagined, because she needn't push off anything to propel herself in any direction. Her mind alone gave her all the flight control she required. At the moment, she was willing herself to Alex's side, her awareness close to his face, almost touching him in the sense of overlapping her consciousness with the physical boundary of his skin. With an inward smile, she inched forward, intending to give him the equivalent of an astral kiss and was surprised when he shivered, as if tickled with an unseen feather. She wondered if she could pass right through his body but decided not to test it.

Instead she swiveled her awareness around to the front of his face, at first just to the side, but then slipping sideways to cross into his line of sight. She was prepared to withdraw in an instant if she seemed to be obstructing his vision, but she remained an unseen presence in the car. For a few moments, she simply *stared* at his face, noticed the line of scar tissue, like a jagged checkmark, over his right eyelid, then was drawn to his hazel eyes, tiny daubs of green, brown and gold. Something slightly odd about his pupils . . . ? Of course! They seemed strange because she wasn't reflected in them! Had her face been that close to him, she would see a miniature reflection of it in his pupils. Instead, only the receding lines of the highway were there, like a demonstration of perspective.

As he rubbed at his eyes, astral Wendy noticed they were slightly droopy, the whites bloodshot. Night driving was more debilitating over the long haul than daytime driving because the eyes lacked stimulation in the form of visual information. Moreover, the body was accustomed to sleeping while it was dark out. Unless one worked the night shift and had, over time, inverted one's circadian rhythm. Alex covered a yawn with a loose fist, unaware of her astral presence so close to his face.

Astral Wendy tried to whisper his name, an experiment on the limitations of astral projection, not a mischievous prank to scare the hell out of him. Nothing happened, so she tried again and, this time, heard a mumbled sound to her left, from the passenger seat. Physical Wendy had mumbled in her self-hypnotized state, an attempt at speech, but nothing coherent. If astral Wendy tried harder to speak, she might be able to make physical Wendy utter the words, but aside from the vicarious ventriloquistic thrill, she saw no point to the experiment. If astral Wendy could speak, however, that could be very useful and not just for dinner party tricks.

The next logical experiment for astral Wendy would be to pass through the body of the Pathfinder and drift up into the night, but she hesitated. Alex was traveling close to fifty miles per hour. If she lost sight of the SUV, she might be unable to return to her physical body. What happened if an astral body never found its way back? Would physical Wendy remain unconscious, trapped in a self-induced trance, a veritable coma, as Alex had suggested? Could somebody snap her out of the trance if nothing of her conscious mind remained? Not a good time or place for that experiment. Had she been lying on a sofa in her Windale cottage, she would have taken the risk of leaving the building, maybe even the town itself, knowing where she needed to return, where she needed to will herself to end the session. At night, inside a moving car on the Interstate highway system, she was reluctant to gamble on the safety of her ignorance.

Instead she spent a few minutes drifting to the back of the SUV, swirling her awareness around the luggage and souvenir bags she'd accumulated in Winnipeg, through the loop of a camera bag, under the seats, into the smallest crevice, around the tightest corner, as if her awareness were a pinpoint of consciousness, a singularity of Wendy's mind, a boneless, bodiless, mass-less traveler, unconstrained by any physical limitations. *This will come in handy if I ever lose my keys*, she thought with a mental laugh that was a burst of unexpected exhilaration rather than a physical sound. But it was time to end the experiment, at least until they were stationary and she could attempt distant astral travel.

She willed herself to the front of the car and noticed that physical Wendy's hands had come unclasped at some point, and it seemed strange to her that she hadn't felt them shift . . . but then, that had been the whole point of focusing her consciousness on the crystal and nothing else, to achieve the weightless detachment necessary for astral projection.

Almost as if she were snuggling under a blanket, she settled herself within the confines of her body. One moment her consciousness was a separate entity, the next she felt the pressure of her legs against the seat, her fingertips against the cotton of her jeans, and the slight muscle strain of her listing neck. Her eyelids fluttered open as she raised her head. She lifted her hand to rub the back of her neck and frowned at the relative difficulty of a simple movement. Her limbs felt heavy, not with the pins and needles of returning circulation, but with a jarring sense of . . . weightiness, as if they were encased in armor, but . . . "Gravity," she whispered, awed. During her brief experiment of displaced consciousness, she'd been liberated from the shackles of gravity. Not for the first time, she wondered how Wither and her coven had been able to fly, the magical mechanics of it, and tried to imagine the exhilaration they must have felt the first time—the hundredth time! *To know such weightlessness, yet still retain your physical body, flying without wings or any kind of physical effort, complete control . . .* She shook her head, disrupting the pointless reverie. *Is it pointless if it's possible?*

"No luck, huh?"

"What?" Wendy asked, disoriented by the question.

"You fell asleep again."

"No, it worked," Wendy said. "I astrally projected—or projected astrally. Out of body. Adrift in the cosmic ether. The key was focus. Of course, the nap helped."

"Really?" Alex said, covering another yawn. "Not that I don't believe you, but from where I'm sitting, well, I couldn't tell—so much. So . . . really?"

"Yes, really," Wendy said, nodding. She chuckled, a bit giddy from her success, from being able to share it with someone. "I was floating all over the place in here."

"And you're sure it wasn't . . . well, a dream?"

"No, it wasn't a dream," Wendy said. "It was different—liberating. A little strange, but in a fascinating way." She lowered her brows at him. "You're not buying this, are you? You think I'm covering up for another nap?"

"Well, I . . ."

Wendy held up her left hand, thumb and index finger half an inch apart. "I was this close to your face. I stared into your eyes. I even tried to . . ." Heat rose in her cheeks.

"Tried to what?"

"I tried, as an experiment, to see what it would feel like," Wendy began, frowning at her own awkwardness, "to give you an astral kiss." Alex's eyebrows rose noticeably. His right hand reached up, touched his cheek. "That's the spot. Made you shiver."

He looked over at her, stunned. "*You* did that." Wendy nodded, grinning. "I felt something. Like a chill, but . . . It really worked!"

"That's what I've been trying to tell you, silly."

"Wow," Alex said. "I mean . . . wow! What's it like?"

"Couldn't really feel anything. No skin. No tactile sensation. I was weightless, but I could direct my consciousness wherever I wanted to go, into the smallest places, but for some reason I was reluctant to pass through solid objects. I thought about passing right through the car, but I worried I wouldn't find my way back."

"No eyes, but you could see."

"Unlike regular vision, though. It's hard to explain, but what I *saw* just seemed to be an extension of awareness.

Nothing came in or out of focus, everything was just *there*, crystal clear, wherever I directed my awareness."

"Bet the Crone will be"—Alex stopped mid-sentence to unleash a fearsome yawn—"impressed with your self-study program."

"Remember; her motto is 'Your reach should exceed your grasp.'"

"Right. The classic."

"How long was I . . . ?" She'd been about to say *asleep*. "Entranced?"

"Out of body a good hour, I'd estimate. We're approaching Cleveland."

"I was out that long? Guess I lost track of time." If I *ever had a sense of time passing*. Wendy rolled her shoulders. "It was an amazing experience. But coming back down to the physical plane is a literal drag. Like my bones are lined with cement."

"I'll keep driving if you . . ."

"No, no, I'm decompressing or recompressing, I guess," Wendy said. "Besides, you're the one with the chain-link yawns now. I'm fresh. I'll drive. Pull over next rest stop and we'll switch."

FARGO, NORTH DAKOTA
JANUARY 2, 2002

It can run for many miles and many hours without tiring, without resting until its hunger becomes too insistent. Yet compared with the relative speed of human vehicles—and little wonder they have abandoned their horses—the race afoot will be lost the moment it begins. Delayed from reaching its special prey for weeks!

The thought is unbearable. It has no choice but to take advantage of the power and speed of human vehicles to close the gap, to complete the hunt.

As soon as it comes to a paved resting place, set aside from the main road, a place where humans stop their vehicles for several minutes at a time before proceeding on their way, it crouches low, working its silent way through the brush. Many of the paved lanes travel away from the special prey, but just as many lead to her, not as the bird flies, but as men ride. All the vehicles stopping here will soon resume their journey.

The pulsing blue-white thread wavers in the air above the road, following the same general direction. She has traveled this same road and it must follow.

It sees its chance when one of the longest type of vehicles stops at the edge of the rest area, squealing and hissing, like an irritated beast reined in against its will. The driver hops down from the shorter front section of the vehicle, and ambles toward the human dwellings with their bright signs and lights while attempting to tug his pants up against a wide paunch.

It turns its attention to the vehicle, with its driver section attached to a long boxy end riding on many big black wheels. The boxy back end is large as a railroad car. Under cover of pine trees, it stalks forward, wondering if the metal beast can sense its presence so close, if it will react or alert its master somehow. But nothing happens. It steps up to the back, sees a small ledge by the back door and jumps onto it, reaching out with its claws to dig into the steel for support. Hand over hand, claws gouging into the metal, it pulls itself up the back of the vehicle, climbing onto the roof. There it waits, and waits, until . . .

The man returns, whistling . . . a creak as he climbs up into the front section. Moments later, the metallic beast roars to life and rumbles with unleashed power. The vehicle moves, gathers speed.

Wind buffets its exposed position on the vehicle's roof. As the vehicle's speed increases, the force of the wind becomes an uncomfortable distraction. It reaches forward, claws extended, and rips into the metal, half closing its hands into fists with its grip until it is secure.

Maybe it only imagines the pulsing blue-white thread glowing a little brighter, a little more defined, but it is reassured now that it travels as fast as its prey. It is relentless; it will not quit until she is dead and it roams free again.

Minutes fold into hours and the miles seem endless. Despite the buffeting wind and the spray of snow, it holds tight. Soon it sleeps, giving rise to memories lost in Jacques Robitaille's mind for hundreds of years, memories freighted with emotions it abandoned when it gave up its last claim to humanity. Memories of a place it once called home . . .

RUPERT'S LAND, RED RIVER VALLEY
CANADA
NOVEMBER, 1768

Afoot, its northbound wanderings have returned it to the place it remembers as home, a human abode it finds strange now. It lived here, took shelter here, in a former life, a life that is meaningless now. It no longer needs shelter from winter storms. It is a bringer of winter storms! The change is complete, if not thoroughly understood. All that was human inside or out is gone, and what changes remain only put its former humanity farther out of reach. It knows that now. It is incapable of rowing a boat or setting a beaver trap, unable to load or fire a rifle. Instead, it has the power to wrap the snow around itself like a cloak, to blind men and beat them down with a winter storm. While they huddle against the ravages of the cold, it hunts them with impunity.

As it hunts now. Creeping forward, edging nearer the log cabin as black smoke billows from a stack on the roof. It creeps along the blanket of snow. When it pauses, it is inhumanly still, almost a frozen piece of the landscape, camouflaged in the white-blanketed world, while the air is clotted with fat snowflakes. It hears her inside, her voice frail on the wind and a name pops into its mind . . . Little Doe. The name seems important . . . but nothing is important, nothing except hunting and feeding. A human child is crying . . . cold or hungry, maybe both. Another name resolves . . . François. This name also means something to that which was Jacques, but the memories have shattered and only scraps of images remain, shattered beyond repair or recognition. Only hunting and feeding matter . . . everything else is meaningless.

Satisfied that the two are alone, isolated from immediate help, it rises, taking long strides toward the door, loping first, then charging until it smashes into the wood. The first blow is powerful enough to break its way into the feeble human shelter. Wood shatters under its fury, revealing the human female, long black hair, braided behind her, brown flesh, wearing animal skins. The human child stands behind her, mouth hanging.

To the left is a pitiful fire of burning logs. Beyond the fire is a human bed with one side attached to a wall, a smaller child's bed pushed underneath.

It looks at the female for a heartbeat, maybe two—a fractured moment of indecision. She stares in horror at what it has become. In her face is nothing but horror. That she should recognize who it was before the change seems important for that fateful, frozen moment. When she does not, it heeds only the call of its insatiable hunger. She is weaponless, as is the scrawny child. Nothing matters but the hunger . . . and feeding.

It senses she is about to scream and it shrieks at her, its hunting wail piercing the cold like an icicle through the heart. She stares, eyes wide, helpless and paralyzed with fear. Somehow she regains control of her muscles, turns her back and tries to shield the child, a boy whose skin is lighter than hers but darker than . . .

The thought is lost as its teeth rip into the back of her neck, its claws wrap around her hips and slice into the meat of her thighs, gouging deep.

She pulls away, collapsing on the boy, who is screaming now. It falls over them, its weight and its rage crushing them, ravaging flesh and bone until the woman and child are forever silenced by its relentless, ravenous hunger.

And that is all that matters . . .

TRAVELING: I-94 EAST
APPROACHING MINNEAPOLIS
JANUARY 3, 2002

It awakens, remembers scraps of a dream, a dream of feeding, sating its incredible hunger. The memory only reminds it that it grows hungry yet again. It recalls the driver of the vehicle upon which it rides, the plump driver. When the driver stops next to rest, it will eat the man. There are many drivers on the wide road that leads to its special prey. It will have no trouble finding another vehicle to ride.

It edges forward, gouging fresh holes in the metal roof with its claws. Too hungry to sleep again, it waits as the long winter night passes. It watches as the pale, pulsing blue-white path writhes in the air, twisting and turning and spinning, but always showing the way to freedom.

At length, the driver stops again. Before the vehicle utters its final squeak and hiss, before the big black tires finish rolling, it drops to the ground near the front section, on the side opposite the driver. It projects its simplest glamour, the human image that approximates its own coloring, an old man in black clothes, and rips the door open. The hefty driver's head whips around from the other side to gape at it. Startled, he is more confused than intimidated by the sight of an old man. "What the hell!?"

It lunges into the vehicle, right hand flashing out, claws ripping into the tender human throat. With its other hand, it pulls the human meal forward, then it bends over and feeds.

CHAPTER NINE

Alex slept as Wendy drove through the early-morning hours, Lake Erie a vast darkness bordering I-90 off to her left. Seconds hung, minutes dragged and the hours were interminable. Almost two hundred miles from Cleveland to Buffalo, and each mile seemed to stretch farther than the one before, as if the space-time continuum were elastic and the longer she drove the farther away her destination. With Alex asleep, she couldn't engage in conversation to help pass the time. So much work ahead to prepare herself and yet how she should train remained a mystery. Even if she had a plan, her practice of magic was limited behind the wheel of a car, especially at night with the near-constant threat of snowfall and snow-clogged or icy roads.

After a long night driving through Ohio, crossing Pennsylvania's northwest *chimney*—couldn't really call it a panhandle—in less than an hour was sweet relief. Her energy flagged, however, once she reached New York, checked her maps and calculated the distance to Massachusetts, over three hundred and fifty miles. Despite the horrendous snowfall it had suffered this past week, Buffalo became her goal. They could pay for a hotel room, catch several hours sleep in a real bed, load up on coffee and have less than five hundred miles left to Windale. Five hundred miles wouldn't seem so brutal in the morning.

As she neared Buffalo, she scanned billboards advertising hotels near I-90 exits. She chose one, took the exit and tapped the brake as she checked the sign directing her to the hotel. The change in the hum of the tires roused Alex from what was, at best, a fitful sleep in a cramped position, hunched over in the passenger seat. Somehow, neither one of them had thought to climb into the back and stretch out on the bench seat. Discounting the safety hazards of a sprawled-out position in back, bailing from the passenger seat wouldn't have seemed sporting. *One for all and all for one*, Wendy thought inanely. *Musketeer code of honor. Two musketeers, unless I count astral Wendy. Okay, I'm a wee bit stir crazy.*

"Where are we?" Alex mumbled, rubbing sleep from his eyes. "And why are we stopping?"

"Buffalo," she said. "I'm stiff, hungry, bored and, frankly, a little bit delirious. Besides, we've gone far enough for one day. No point arriving in Windale totally wiped out." Wendy steered the Pathfinder into the Hampton Inn's entrance. "Pray for a vacancy." She parked the car in front of the lobby. "Wait here. I'll check in."

Fifteen minutes later they dragged their overnight bags out of the elevator and down the hall to their second-floor room. The only sound other than the squeaky wheel on Wendy's suitcase was the bass hum from the ice maker and vending machines. "Hungry?" Alex asked.

"Too tired to eat," Wendy said. "Crack of dawn, I'll be all over that complimentary breakfast bar."

"Hope my stomach grumbling doesn't keep me awake all night . . . or morning? What time is it, anyway?"

They stopped in front of their room. Wendy slid the key card into the lock, shoved down on the handle and pushed the door in with her shoulder. She flicked on the light, revealing a clean, well-lit, fair-sized room.

Alex stopped in the middle of the room and shook his head. "Double beds? What were you thinking?"

"Oh, daydreaming about real dreaming."

"Sleeping is for wimps," Alex said, trudging over to the foot of the far bed. He dropped his duffel bag where he stood, slipped out of his parka and tossed it at a chair across the room and missed, then he toppled backward onto the bed. "Sleep, huh?"

"What is it with guys? Can't you ever turn it off?"

"We're hardwired," Alex said, shrugging in his prone position. "Must raise the flag . . . even if we're too tired to salute."

"I intend to wash my face, brush my teeth, fall asleep and be back on the road by six."

"Six? Are you crazy? That's what, an hour from now?"

"Not quite," Wendy said. "Well, seven o'clock then." She ignored Alex's groaning as she dialed the number for a wake-up call and entered 7:00 AM into the automated system.

WINDALE, MASSACHUSETTS

Nightfall . . . and a dusk red smudge in the western sky fades to a purplish bruise.

She is flying over Windale, but a Windale divided by dirt roads with wagon-wheel ruts, as if she has flown into the town's past. She banks to the left, swooping down across a field of corn, her night-adapted eyes seeking any movement and finding . . .

A man in threadbare coveralls stumbles along the road, pausing every few moments to take a swig from a jug. Whiskey dribbles down his chin. He wipes it away with the back of a sunburnt arm. He is careless of his surroundings, oblivious to what is above, hunting him . . .

She drops from the sky with the deadly grace of a hawk pouncing on a rabbit, arms extended, fingers flashing wicked claws.

The jug shatters with the impact, bursting in the man's hand. Before he can react, both sets of claws tear into his flesh, cracking ribs, stealing his breath.

She arcs upward with her burden, into the branches of an old oak tree, shoving the stunned man into the Y-fork of a branch. With a swipe of her powerful claws, she savages his throat, rendering him mute. Her lips pull back from bristling rows of jagged teeth, and her dark, leathery skinned head darts forward. As her razor sharp teeth dig into the man's flesh, warm blood gushes into her mouth—

Kayla awoke with the taste of warm blood in her mouth. At first it seemed a sensory illusion, remnant of the terrible repeated dream. But the taste was real—because the blood was real! A frightening moment passed before she realized it was her own blood. Her tongue was throbbing; she must have bitten it while asleep. Nerves jangled, she continued to tremble for several minutes.

The LED readout on the bedside alarm clock glowed 2:13 AM. *Nightmares starting sooner,* she thought. *Closer to the witching hour.*

Blinds were down, curtains drawn, but she couldn't resist

peeking outside. Prepared to see Wither's face or the monster's face peering back at her, a sign that she'd had a false awakening. *Maybe I haven't bitten my tongue. One bad dream within another.* She pushed aside the edge of the curtains, slipped a finger under the blinds, pulled them inward and saw . . . nothing but the blanket of snow, almost glowing white in the reflected light of the waning gibbous moon. No surprises outside tonight. *Be thankful for small favors,* she thought, padding her way down to the kitchen. Unsure how to treat a tongue bite, she resorted to gargling salt water. Cold salt water, since warm water would kick-start the flow of blood. Salt stung, but she welcomed the discomfort, anything to take her mind off the dream.

She stopped in the bathroom down the hall from her bedroom and ran cold water, intending to splash some on her face, hoping it would help her stay awake long enough to avoid slipping back into the same dream. Closer to dawn her dreams seemed less . . . vile. Letting the water run, she examined her face through bleary eyes. This early in the morning her full lips seemed puffy. What caught her attention was her bottom, ring-pierced lip, in particular several flecks of dried blood staining it.

Dark flecks . . .

With an anticipatory squint, she flicked on the mirror lights, then pinched her lower lip between her thumb and index finger and tugged it out for inspection. The dried blood looked brown, not black, as she had feared. She scratched away the flecks with a black-painted fingernail and rinsed them down the drain. Next she stuck her tongue out and to the side to examine the bite. A little raw, but red, thankfully. Satisfied, she splashed water on her face, patted it dry with a hand towel and returned to bed.

Sitting there, she had an urge to peer outside her window again. *Shit! This is getting way too obsessive-compulsive.* Determined not to succumb to the urge, she whipped her blankets up over her Sorcerer's Apprentice nightshirt and rolled onto her side, away from the window. A minute passed, then another, and the growing itch in the center of her back made her shudder. *Okay, just this once!*

Hopping out of bed, she hurried to the window, grabbed the cord for the blinds in her hand, took a deep breath . . . and yanked down. The blinds flashed up—

—Nothing.

Just a blanket of snow, and snow-covered trees.

So why was her heart racing? Shivering, she lowered the blinds, climbed back into bed and, after a long time, fell asleep again.

TRAVELING: I-94 EAST
ENTERING WISCONSIN

After eating most of the plump driver of the long two-sectioned vehicle, it has no trouble finding another vehicle, leaving the rest area before other humans can discover the ravaged carcass.

Large, but not quite as long as the first vehicle, this one has only one section, and is painted white with windows along the side and back. Fortunately, the side and rear windows are covered with curtains. This new vehicle has a name painted on its side, an Indian name: Winnebago. Remarkably, a narrow metal ladder is bolted to the back of the vehicle, but the convenience is clearly intended for frail humans. When it climbs up the back, the metal rungs bend under its weight, one almost snapping free before it clambers over the top.

As it lies atop the roof, its claws sink into the smooth metal. It has the sense this vehicle is less sturdy than the first. With the slightest movement of its bulk, the metal creaks and groans in protest. For all its shortcomings, however, the new vehicle is as fleet as the first. It lies still, braced against the wind, yet enjoying the blast of invigorating cold air.

Through squinted eyelids, it watches the twisting, bending path, mesmerized by the pulsing blue-white thread and its promise of freedom.

The miles pass effortlessly.

BUFFALO, NEW YORK

Wendy shook Alex's shoulder. They'd both fallen asleep with their clothes on. Alex hadn't even bothered to crawl under the blankets of his bed. Just kicked off his boots, curled up on his side and nodded off. Wendy shook him again, harder this time. He mumbled, "Can't be seven o'clock. Still dark out."

She walked to the window, grabbed the metal rod and yanked the heavy drapes aside, flooding the room with daylight. Alex flinched, like a vampire locked in a greenhouse at sunrise, yanked the pillow out from under his cheek and clapped it over his head. "I'll drive first," she said. "But I can't carry you out to the car."

An unenthusiastic response, muffled by the hypoallergenic pillow. Appealing to his empty stomach, she said, "Complimentary breakfast bar downstairs." Another mumbled response that sounded like, "Bring me one of everything." She needed to get his attention out from under the pillow. Worst part of waking up was the first five minutes. "Wait here."

"No problem," was his muffled reply.

In the bathroom she undressed, then wrapped herself in a white bath towel, tucking the corner under her left arm. She took a moment to finger-comb the tangles out of her shoulder-length, auburn hair before returning to Alex's bedside. She sat on the edge, tapped his thigh with her index finger. "Time for your shower?"

"You're done already?" Perhaps he'd caught a glimpse of her bare thigh. Would explain why the pillow seemed less molded to his head, his voice clearer.

"No."

"Want me to go first?"

"Nooo," she said, drawing out the word this time. *Even sleep-deprived, he should figure it out in a couple seconds.*

Alex flung the pillow aside, pushed himself up on his right elbow. Intrigued at last, he said, "Co-ed shower?"

"Technically, I'm no longer a college gal, but . . ."

"This would be a really cruel trick, if . . ."

"No tricks," Wendy said, smiling. "Witch's honor."

"And we're not talking about a co-ed *cold* shower?"

Wendy slapped his thigh, stood up and walked toward the bathroom. "We'll make it as *hot* as you want," she said, glancing over her shoulder with a seductive smile. "If you're out of that bed in the next ten seconds."

He was off the bed and following her into the bathroom in less than five.

TRAVELING: NEW YORK, I-90 EAST

Despite taking time to sample the breakfast bar, as well as each other, they were back on I-90 before nine o'clock. Wendy volunteered to drive until the Crone appeared or she needed a break, whichever came first. With a full tank of gas and a brown paper bag full of mini-mart snacks and soda, they were ready for the long drive across the state of New York. "How many miles to Massachusetts?" Alex asked.

"About three hundred." Wendy noticed the serious look on his face. "What?"

"As much as I've enjoyed our time together," Alex said. "Especially your renewed passion for water conservation, because it's been a long time since . . ."

"Yes," she said. "A long time. But . . ."

"Twenty-twenty hindsight, but you could have flown to Logan International."

"I couldn't abandon my . . . car." *My mother's car,* she thought.

"I could have driven it back to Windale."

When she faced the trip alone, flying just hadn't entered her mind as an option. Then, when Alex asked to ride along, she welcomed the opportunity to reconnect with him, to reestablish their emotional ties. After their morning shower—her idea—she had to admit more than the practical reasons for allowing him to accompany her.

Also, in relation to the current crisis, she had to train and become familiar with new magic, and for that, location was irrelevant. But she had another reason for delaying her return to Windale. Another uncertainty, one that she dreaded facing. "I need time," Wendy said. "To train and cope with the idea that *she* might be back again, waiting for me in Windale."

Alex sat up straight. "Wait—you don't mean . . . ?"

"She came back once before, in a different body, long after I thought she was dead."

"You think Kayla might be—?"

"No," Wendy interrupted. *Speak of the devil,* she thought, *and the devil appears.* "No, I don't. But I have to be prepared, just in case." Wendy heaved a sigh, shook her head. "Something is happening with Kayla. She was infected with Wither's blood." *Now I've gone ahead and spoken her name!* "And maybe . . . maybe she'll never be the same. I need to find out. I suspect she's keeping something from me. But . . . maybe it's not important."

"Kayla's tough. She'll be all right."

Wendy nodded, though her intuition told her everything about Kayla might be important. *What if she becomes my enemy? I couldn't bear it.*

TRAVELING: NEW YORK, MASSACHUSETTS, I-90 EAST

Nearly three hours into their day's journey, approaching Syracuse, Wendy's legs were already stiff. *Road fatigue syndrome,* she thought. *Diminishing returns each day.* In Schenectady, they stopped for a late, drive-thru lunch, taking several minutes to stretch and visit a restroom. With Alex driving, they crossed into Massachusetts, still almost one hundred and fifty miles from Windale. Wendy called Kayla at the Crystal Path to tell her they'd be arriving in Windale early in the evening, depending on road conditions.

"You're making good time."

Was that a hint of nervousness in her voice? Wendy wondered. "Thanks to tag-team driving and tenacious sleep deprivation." *Here goes,* Wendy thought. "Kayla, will you have time to get together tonight? I'd like to talk about . . . what's happening."

Prolonged silence. "Sure. Um—just call me when you're near. We'll set it up. Drive safe. Alissa will be upset she missed you."

"See you soon," Wendy said. She ended the call and looked over at Alex. "Seemed a little nervous."

"With good reason," Alex said. "She's connected to some serious shit."

"You're right. I'm reading way too much into this."

Alex took her hand. "We'll figure this out, Wendy. All of us. Together."

One way or another, we'll have our answers, she thought. *But maybe not the ones we want.*

TRAVELING: MASSACHUSETTS, I-90 EAST, I-95 NORTH

As they neared the Worcester area, little more than an hour from Windale, the Crone finally appeared, resolving ghostlike in the seat behind Wendy. Relief evident in her voice, Wendy said, "Beginning to think you weren't gonna show."

"*This is no simple thing, Wendy,*" the Crone said. "*As your present nears an inevitable, major event in my past—an anchor point—I experience more . . . resistance when I try to manifest. The time stream, like water, flows in familiar paths.*"

For Alex's benefit, Wendy added, "Major events in the Crone's past, because of the number and degree of consequences carve deeper . . . trenches. They're harder to reroute."

"So, you can redirect a tributary stream," Alex said to the Crone, "but the Mississippi isn't changing course?"

The Crone nodded, accepting his extension of the water metaphor. "*Creatures of chaos—such as Wither and the wendigo— are temporal wild cards. What was a good outcome in my past may yet be altered by chance in your present. Evil and chaos will find a way. My goal is to prepare Wendy for what she must face.*"

"Right," Wendy said. "So let's stay focused on my training." She was concerned the Crone might not be able to appear again until after the anchor point. "You mentioned three areas where I need work: astral projection, protective spheres and border vision."

"*Yes. Have you been practicing?*"

Wendy nodded. "I was able to astral project, but aside from spying on people, I'm not sure how it's gonna help me fight the big-ugly."

"*Did Alex see your astral body?*"

Wendy frowned. "No. Should he?"

"*Not with first stage astral projection,*" the Crone said. "*In first stage, you would be invisible and your only astral sense would probably be sight, possibly smell too.*"

"I need to be visible?"

"*Yes,*" the Crone said. "*This is critical. Your astral body should be visible, and more opaque than I am right now.*"

Wendy glanced at Alex with a wry grin. "Told you she wouldn't be impressed."

"*Don't be concerned with impressing me, Wendy,*" the Crone said. "*The stakes here are your very survival.*"

"Point taken," Wendy said grimly. "You're the expert. Any tips?"

The Crone frowned. "*My manifestations here, because of the temporal rebound aspect, are dissimilar to pure astral projection. My technique won't help you. My advice is to treat stage two astral projection as an enhanced form of the visualization component. After you displace awareness, visualize yourself appearing. The better the visualization, the more opaque and realistic your astral replica."*

"Are there more than two stages?"

"Yes. Projection of an illusory glamour instead of a pure self-replica. And the development of astral senses beyond sight. Latter stages represent higher levels of difficulty. Fortunately, stage two should be sufficient for now."

"What if my astral body loses sight of my physical body?"

"Your physical body remains inert while your consciousness is displaced," the Crone said. *"If that consciousness was prevented from returning, the physical body, if left untended, would eventually die of thirst."*

"Waste away?"

The Crone nodded. *"But it is unlikely you would need to wander so far from your body that you could not find your way back again. And there are methods for finding a lost body."*

"Lost body? Don't like the sound of that. How . . . ?"

"If you wandered too far and became lost or if someone relocated your body while your consciousness was away."

"Shouldn't I learn about these locating methods?"

"At some point, that would be advisable. Presently, no," the Crone said. *"Soon, you might want to visualize a silver thread connecting your astral body to your physical body. But that's not critical for the present situation."*

"A silver thread? Like a psychic umbilical cord?"

"Somewhat."

"I'll put that on my Wiccan to-do list," Wendy said. "But right now, I need you to explain border vision."

"*You coined the phrase, Wendy,*" the Crone said, with a sly little smile. "*Or you soon will.*"

"What?" Alex said. "Sorry. Had to ask."

"She's always stealing my thunder," Wendy said with playful antagonism. "She comes back from the future to tell me things I will eventually tell her. Remember, it's only confusing if you adhere to strict rules of cause and effect."

Alex frowned, confused. "Don't you kinda have to?"

"When you're an astrally projected time traveler," Wendy said, "apparently not." She returned her attention to the Crone. "So, please explain this coined phrase of mine."

"*Border vision is a way of seeing that which resists being seen,*" the Crone said mysteriously. "*Or seeing through something that isn't real. The wendigo sometimes projects a glamour to appear human, to lull its prey before it attacks.*"

"And I have the ability to see through this?"

"*You will. You must. It's important that you learn how.*"

"Don't keep it a secret." *Need to move this along,* Wendy thought. The Crone's image had become fuzzy around the edges, and was losing translucency. The cloth pattern of the seat back was more distinct through the Crone's torso.

"*You once described border vision to me as 'seeing more by focusing on nothing in particular.'*"

"Like how you're supposed to see those hidden, Magic Eye, 3-D stereogram images?"

"*You also told me that border vision begins at the periphery of one's vision,*" the Crone said. "*And that glamour is least effective at the edges of your field of vision.*"

"Which is a border of sorts," Wendy said, nodding, "between what you can see and what's in your blind spot."

"*Perhaps that's how you came up with the name,*" the Crone mused. "*Just keep in mind, to combat a glamour, look at it indi-*"

rectly. Mirrors can foil a glamour, but only if one hasn't already viewed the glamour directly. For some reason, once the mind is fooled, the glamour is proof against reflective surfaces."

"Once I develop border vision, the *wendigo* won't be able to sneak up on me?"

"It . . . *a fearsome creature,*" the Crone said. *"Do not underestimate . . . possesses a shriek that paralyzes humans with fear."*

"Magically?"

"Unknown . . . might just be . . . unnerving."

"Before you leave, tell me what I need to practice with my protective spheres. Faster conjuration? Larger diameter?"

The Crone shook her head. The motion dissolved part of her left cheek and chin. Her blue eyes had gone pale. *"The sphere . . . origins in the protective circle. You . . . an offensive weapon, extending . . . striking. Think . . . -plications. Offensive . . . evasive . . . will need to escape . . . also . . . protect magic . . . devours . . ."* The Crone spread her hands—as if everything depended on Wendy's inventiveness with her protective spheres—and watched, helpless, as her fingers dissolved in the back of the Pathfinder. A moment later, the rest of the Crone's ghostly image faded away.

Wendy sighed and looked at Alex. That hadn't been the first time the Crone had told Wendy she would discover many creative applications for the protective magic sphere. At the moment, however, she wasn't feeling very creative. "Nothing's ever easy."

"Let me know if I can help."

Minutes later, when Alex left I-90, taking the exit for I-95, which looped around the urban sprawl of Boston, Wendy said, "Let's find a diner or something. We'll stop and eat. I need to call Kayla, tell her what I have in mind. Hope she can meet at the cottage."

"Is that the only reason we're stopping?"

"Well, I'm famished."

"And . . . ?" Alex asked, perhaps sensing her hesitancy.

Wendy shook her head, but didn't reply right away. She wasn't sure what to tell him. Not enough time left to practice astral projection in the car, or to compose the next chapter in 101 Uses for a Protective Sphere, and the promised wonders of border vision remained a mystery. Now that Wendy was so close to Windale, was she stalling, delaying an inevitable confrontation with . . . the past? Or the present? Was she afraid of stirring up painful memories of her parents' death? Or worried that Kayla wouldn't really be Kayla anymore? Why hadn't she pressed the Crone for information about Kayla? *She would have warned me if it was bad . . . unless a temporal anchor point prevented her from interfering. She did seem to fade out quicker this time. Might not see her again until . . . maybe not ever if I . . . What if . . . ?*

Taking a deep breath, Wendy tried to concentrate on what she knew. Kayla had discovered, or was about to discover information about Wither and her plans for a reborn coven consisting of Wendy, Abby and Hannah. Failed plans, as it turned out, but they were all still reeling from the after-effects of the original coven's machinations. If Wendy understood Wither's plans better, maybe she could figure out how to remove the curse. *Accentuate the positive*, she told herself.

"Wendy?"

"I need some time to collect my thoughts," Wendy finally admitted. More than one of those stray thoughts concerned the massive, cannibalistic snow demon, summoned by Wither with her dying breath, an evil force of chaos determined to snuff out Wendy's life. "And time is running out."

CHAPTER TEN

Wendy drove the last half hour into Windale. The quickest route to her cottage ran through the Danfield campus. She slowed on College Avenue and, as she approached the library, swung the SUV against the curb, shifted into park and applied the emergency brake. When she stepped out onto the slushy street, Alex directed her attention to the NO PARKING sign mounted on the nearest telephone pole. "Relax," she said. "I'll just be a second. Besides, I seriously doubt they'd give me a ticket here."

Wendy stared at the words on the side of the massive white stone building, bathed in wall-mounted spotlights to make them visible at night. Two rows of two-foot-high metal letters composed in small caps, gleaming silver, the bottom row centered beneath the top.

THE LAWRENCE A. WARD & CAROL G. WARD
MEMORIAL LIBRARY

They died together, she thought. *It's fitting that they're memorialized together.*

With one last look at the sign, she climbed back into the Pathfinder, released the emergency brake and paused with her hand on the gear shift. She sighed, then spoke to Alex without looking at him. She tried to clear her throat, but the lump remained. "Last year, the, um, provost sent me a letter . . . an invitation, actually, to attend the dedication ceremony."

"How was—?

Wendy interrupted. "I couldn't . . . make it. Was traveling at the time. Anyway, she—the provost, that is—said there's a . . . display, or something inside—pictures, plaques and stuff—commemorating my father's years as college president, my parents' involvement in the community. I've heard it's a great tribute."

Alex stared at her, realizing the truth. "It is, Wendy." He took her hand. "You should—"

She shook her head. "Not yet," she said, still avoiding eye contact. "I will, but . . . not yet." She shifted the SUV into gear and drove the last mile or so to Kettle Court. Several of the homes appeared only as Christmas-light silhouettes, some colors blinking, some not. Front lawns featured light-reindeer or glowing plastic snowmen. On one slanted garage roof was a life-sized plastic Santa in sleigh, pulled by an economy class complement of four reindeer.

At the end of the cul-de-sac Wendy's white, stone-faced cottage was subdued, a picture of rural, unlit understatement, with its wide yard and the lone red maple, denuded of leaves and, like the lawn, frosted with snow. Both the sidewalk and the walkway had been freshly shoveled and sprinkled with de-icing pellets. Wendy sent her former paperboy a monthly check to take care of the grounds, front and back, although she suspected he was getting too old for odd jobs. Probably subcontracted the labor to his younger brother. Not that it mattered, as long as the place was maintained.

Bundled in a black leather jacket adorned with silver studs, threadbare blue jeans and black biker boots, Kayla sat on the small porch, at the end of the curved walkway, a small nylon suitcase beside her. When the Pathfinder stopped at the curb, Kayla rose and strode several steps down the walkway. Under the cold, pale glow of the lone streetlight at the end of the cul-de-sac, she stood with her hip cocked and brushed the fingers of one hand through short, electric-blue hair.

Alex lowered his window and called out, "Cool hair!"

"Ice blue," she said, allowing herself the trace of a smile.

Wendy's mental image of Kayla still included coal black, gelled-hair spikes. *Hope that's the only change*, she thought ominously.

As Wendy climbed out of the SUV and walked to the back, Kayla said, "Welcome home, stranger."

"Thanks," Wendy said. "Brutal trip. And things only get worse from here."

Alex was shouldering more than his share of the luggage. He paused and shot her a concerned glance. Maybe he thought she was about to accuse Kayla of being the new and blue Wither. Wendy waited for him to say something, but he gave a minor shake of his head, took a careful step over the plowed snow and made his way up the shoveled path.

Kayla grabbed the few bags Wendy couldn't manage, allowing Wendy to lock up the car, then walked beside her. "You really think so?" Kayla asked, frowning.

"Unfortunately, yes."

Kayla nodded grimly and dropped back a step. Wendy fumbled with her keys before finding the right one. She unlocked the door and ushered everyone inside.

The cottage had an air of abandonment even though Frankie would have left for Christmas break less than two weeks ago. Everything was tidied and cleaned, placed in cupboards or closets, which gave the overwhelming impression that life was not being lived within these one-story walls. A freestanding lamp running on a random timer provided the outward illusion of occupancy.

Wendy dropped her luggage and bags near the closet door on her left, advising the others to do the same. She took in the deserted cottage with a stranger's eyes. While the dimensions and layout of the rooms were familiar, Frankie had redecorated since Wendy's last stay, making the place seem even less like *home* for her. The front door opened on the living room, separated by a half wall from the family room. The kitchen and dining area were situated to the left of the small family room and overlooked the stone terrace in back. To the left of the living room, beyond a closet and storage area, was a short hallway, with a utility room and Frankie's bedroom to the left, the bathroom and Wendy's room to the right. Wendy had chosen the right-hand bedroom because its two windows faced the backyard instead of the front lawn.

Though the carpeting was still forest green and the walls antique white, the selection of furniture had changed somewhat, while remaining minimal and eclectic, purchased from garage sales and second-hand stores.

Next to the floor lamp was a rickety recliner. *Frankie's new reading chair?* Near the recliner were folding chairs and the card table. In the family room a threadbare tan loveseat was backed against the half wall to face the television that had once belonged to Wendy's parents. Flanking the loveseat on the left was a ghastly yellow beanbag chair, which at one time had been crudely illustrated to resemble a smiley face with a tongue hanging out. *Frankie must have lost a bet.*

The walls remained relatively barren, a few nature prints Wendy had purchased more than a year ago, some framed photos of Frankie with friends whose names Wendy could not recall if she had ever known them. A wall clock hung in the kitchen, its quartz-precision ticking loud in the quiet house.

Wendy discovered another addition in the dining area: a small pine table with matching chairs in good condition. With a strange wave of melancholy, she pulled out one of the chairs and sat down, ignoring the slight wobble.

Alex looked around and followed her out to the kitchen area. "Anything missing?"

"No," Wendy said. "But some stuff I've never seen before."

Kayla entered the kitchen last, too casual with her fingers slipped behind her studded, black leather belt. "Hideous beanbag chair. We could burn it out back."

"Probably toxic," Alex said.

"Could be why my eyes burn when I look at it."

Wendy said, "Give me a few minutes to unpack; then we'll talk."

"Sounds good," Kayla said, nodding. "Need any help?"

The doorbell rang, followed by a loud knocking.

Wendy and Alex exchanged glances.

"Oops," Kayla said. "Hope you don't mind, but I ordered pizza before I came over. You're welcome to have some . . ."

"Thanks," Wendy said. "We've already eaten."

"I always save room for pizza," Alex said. "Special compartment in my stomach. On pizza standby at all times."

"Fine." Wendy laughed. "I'll unpack; you two enjoy the pizza."

Wendy's bedroom had white carpeting and powder blue walls, her attempt at a cloud and sky motif. A fine layer of dust coated her dresser, the cedar chest at the foot of the bed and the wooden pentagram hanging on the wall. Frankie probably hadn't disturbed the room since Wendy's departure.

Out of the several framed photos that had once decorated her bedroom walls, only two remained, both of Alex. In one, he wore his track uniform; in the other, he struck a pose with his old dragon-headed cane, a square of black electrical tape in place of a mustache. Overall, a weak impersonation of Charlie Chaplin, but it made her smile. Unlike the photos of her parents, which had caught her emotionally off guard one too many times. She'd finally stacked them in a cardboard box in the closet, where they would remain until she was ready to face them. Easier that way.

As Wendy placed clean clothes in her dresser and closet, tossing the rest into the white wicker hamper, she heard casual conversation down the hall—Kayla commenting how the town seemed almost deserted with the Danfield undergrads on break, Alex advising her to enjoy the peace and quiet while it lasted. He might have been talking about the coming of the *wendigo*, if not for his lighthearted tone.

After unpacking, Wendy sat cross-legged on her bed, running her fingers along the stitched pattern of the comforter, her mind adrift. She looked up as someone knocked on the doorjamb.

Kayla, alone. "Few slices left. Last chance."

"Thanks. I'll pass." Wendy could hear the television. *Alex getting his ESPN fix*, she thought and managed a half smile.

Kayla stepped into the room, sat on the edge of the bed beside Wendy. "Too late, right? To go out there and get it over with?"

"Out in the woods? Probably pitch black by now."

Kayla sighed. "So you think we should try this other stuff first?"

"Definitely. Dream magic is a safe place to start, usually." Wendy grimaced with the flash memory of clawing her own thigh during one of her Wither dreams.

"Probably a waste of time," Kayla said. "It's always the same dream. A . . . feeding."

"We need to explore the connection between this recurring dream and your urge to go into that clearing on Matthias Stone's land."

"Wendy . . ." Kayla paused, shook her head. "I really hope they're completely unrelated. But . . ." She sighed. "Damn her to hell!" Kayla slid her upper teeth back and forth across the steel ring that pierced her lower lip. "Wendy, I wish you could guarantee it's not gonna happen to me. I don't want to become like—like—" Kayla's voice caught.

"*I don't want to become like Gina Thorne.*" No need for Kayla to complete that sentence. The idea—the threat—of Wither coming back yet again had frightened both of them, but for Kayla it was a waking nightmare of losing her own identity. Wendy clasped Kayla's hand in hers and squeezed. "That won't happen," Wendy said, hoping her voice was strong enough to convince both of them.

On the verge of tears, her lips trembling, Kayla stared hard at Wendy, unwilling to accept a comforting lie. "How can you know that?"

"Because . . . we would know by now," Wendy said, trying simple logic. "Gina was completely possessed by Wither in

several months. It's been almost a year and a half since . . ."
Since Gina forced you to drink Wither's black blood from her veins.

A note of desperation entered Kayla's voice. "Then what's happening to me?"

"Kayla, when we talked before, that first time, after the Crone told me to contact you . . . I had the feeling you were . . ."—*hiding something*—". . . holding something back."

Kayla nodded. "I—that day Bobby and I were in the clearing, I—my nose bled." Kayla's hand rose nervously to her nose. "I thought—it seemed like—that my blood was . . ."

Black? Wendy wondered, Could it still be in her, after all this time? "Was it?"

"I—I don't know," Kayla said. "I passed out. Bobby cleaned me up. It was getting dark. He thought I might have imagined it. But I was still worried until . . ."

"What?" Wendy asked. Kayla shrugged off her black leather jacket and pushed up the sleeve on her Felix the Cat sweatshirt, revealing a gauze bandage on the inside of her left forearm. "Oh, no! What happened?"

Kayla flashed a wry grin. "I decided to make sure."

"God, Kayla!" Wendy said. "You cut yourself?"

"Sick, I know," Kayla said, frowning. "But not deep. Look . . ." She peeled back the tape and lifted the gauze to reveal a pink, puckered scab, almost healed. *As self-inflicted wounds go,* Wendy decided, *it looks healthy.* "Of course, Bobby's more than half convinced I'm looney tunes now."

"Kayla, maybe these . . . symptoms have nothing to do with evil. I'm not a psychiatrist by any stretch, but it could be a form of post-traumatic stress."

"I considered that. But how do you explain the clearing?"

"We don't know that it means anything magical," Wendy said. "You passed out. You're not sleeping well. Could be fatigue-related."

Kayla shook her head, unconvinced. "Wendy, I'd love to believe that, but I'd be kidding myself. Don't ask me how I know, but there's something in those woods, something that wants to reveal itself to me. Don't know why—hell, I'm afraid to know why! I have this sick feeling I won't like the answer."

"Wendy!" Alex called from the other room. "Come here! You gotta see this!"

Wendy and Kayla exchanged a startled look; then both jumped off the bed and hurried down the hall. Alex was watching CNN's *Headline News*. "What's up?" Wendy asked as she dropped onto the loveseat beside him; Kayla plopped into the garish yellow beanbag chair and nervously combed her fingers through her hair.

"It's about Fargo," Alex said. "They're talking about some guy named Lloyd Fetty, a motel clerk at the Fargo Motor Lodge. Found his body in a Dumpster. That's the guy, right? The scumbag?"

"Yeah, Lloyd." *Creepy Desk Clerk Lloyd.* "What happened to him?"

"Something ate most of him." Alex pointed the remote and turned up the volume.

"—comes word of a similar death near Minneapolis, Minnesota, where an independent truckdriver, George Mooney, was found almost completely devoured in the cab of his tractor-trailer." Here the head-shot of the expertly coiffed anchor was replaced with jittery footage of the interior of a truck's cab, a yellow tarp covering a body and, judging by the shape under the tarp, there wasn't much left to cover. A news ticker continued to run at the bottom of the screen, incongruously announcing sports scores. "Police originally attributed the Fargo attack to a wild animal, possibly a grizzly, but news of the second killing, hundreds of miles from the first incident, raises the specter of a cannibalistic serial killer or possible cult activity." Back to the anchor head-shot. "Christopher Hall, Minneapolis police chief, indicated in a press conference today that the FBI is already involved in what some sources are calling the Road Ripper murders."

Wendy shot a worried glance at Kayla. "Told you it only gets worse from here."

"So that—that's . . ." Kayla swallowed hard. "Because of the snow-dingo thing?"

"*Wendigo*," Wendy said. "It's a Native American word for—"

"We're fucked," Kayla said. "Royally fucked."

"Let's not panic," Wendy said. "We'll get through this."

"This thing likes the snow so much, let's buy one-way tickets to Hawaii."

"And then what?"

"Take up surfing!" Kayla shrugged. "Who the fuck cares? We'll be alive."

"Kayla, you're free to go anywhere," Wendy said. "Far as I know, I'm the only one on the *wendigo's* hit list."

"Okay, so you fly south for the rest of your life."

Wendy sighed. "It's not that simple."

"Why the hell not?"

"Because, she may have sent this monster after me, but it's murdering innocent people! And it will keep on killing to feed itself until it kills me or I find a way to stop it." Wendy looked down at her feet. "I'm partly responsible for this."

Kayla pushed herself out of the beanbag chair, started

pacing the room. "How can you be even remotely responsible for this?"

Wendy stared at her. "I reactivated the curse in Winnipeg. I couldn't let sleeping . . . *wendigos* lie. Wither tricked me, but I invoked it. I helped her set this nightmare in motion. And I have to stop it."

"Or die trying?" Kayla asked, agitated.

"Possibly," Wendy said. "My death might end the killing spree. If that's the only way, well . . . I won't be responsible for more deaths." She pressed her hands together. "If I run and hide, fly off to permanently warmer climes, I couldn't live with myself. Every day would be unbearable, knowing my cowardice was condemning more innocent people to violent deaths. If it were you, could you live with yourself?" Kayla lowered her head, silent. Wendy continued, "But I won't blindly sacrifice myself either. We have no evidence my death will stop the killing. And it's entirely possible I'm the only one who can stop this thing. I may not be running, but I haven't surrendered."

Alex squeezed her knee. He'd had time to adjust to the frightening reality closing in on them, on her in particular. She'd made the decision simple for him. If he couldn't accept the weirdness in her life, their relationship would never work. So, as much as it frightened him, he would support her choice. Maybe there was hope for them after all.

Kayla pressed her fingertips to her temples. She shook her head in mute resignation, took a deep breath, then exhaled forcefully. "This is so unbelievably fucked up, you know that?"

"I wouldn't blame you if you took your own advice. It's not your fight."

Kayla sighed. "I'd better stay."

"Why?"

Kayla quirked a wry grin. "Purely selfish reasons."

"Which are?"

"I need you to fix me," Kayla said. "I have this . . . dark cloud hanging over me, every minute of every damn day. Do you know how often I wake up in the middle of the night and wonder if Wither is setting up shop in my brain? If I'll still be me in the morning? It's like a fucking evil time bomb in my brain." She sighed. "I wish I could help you. I will if I can, God knows, but please, for the love of Christ, get this evil bitch out of my head once and for all."

Wendy walked over to Kayla and gave her a hug. "Kayla, I will do everything in my power to help you. Promise."

Kayla's eyes were bright. "Thank you," she said. "Thanks."

They watched the repeating newscasts until they were sure they'd heard all the relevant details the police had released concerning the two *wendigo* murders, alternately teased as the work of the "Road Ripper" or the "Road Killer." The police and the FBI had no suspects and no witnesses. Other than the location and condition of the bodies, the news reports were thin, at best.

"Not that there's a real upside here," Alex said. "But it's probably more than a thousand miles away. We have time."

From Kayla, "How could it travel hundreds of miles in less than a day?" A moment later, her face became ashen. "Oh, no! Wither could fly. Tell me this thing doesn't fly."

"No, but it could use a glamour to appear human and hitch a ride."

"What?" Alex said, standing.

"The pickup truck that crashed into the Fargo Motor Lodge," Wendy said, looking at him as realization dawned.

"For a moment, I thought I saw something in the truck bed . . . a figure, but it disappeared."

"But you said the bodies in the truck were both—"

"Beheaded," Wendy finished, nodding. "I thought it happened on impact. But if the *wendigo* was riding in the back and wanted them to stop . . ."

"What am I missing?" Kayla asked.

"It *knew*," Alex said. His voice was hushed, almost a whisper. He sank back down on the loveseat. "Jesus, Wendy, it knew you were there—right there! And it ripped their heads off to stop . . ."

"To stop the truck," Wendy said.

"Oh, shit," Kayla said. "Real subtle."

"The Crone said it's been hibernating," Wendy said. "I had a vision of a man, a man wearing buckskin."

"Like Daniel Boone?" Kayla asked. "Or the Village People?"

Wendy shook her head. "Authentic. It wasn't a dream, precisely, but I think it must have been him, how he looked before . . ."

"Who?"

"The man who became this particular *wendigo*," Wendy said. "If so, he's—it's hundreds of years old."

"Mere pup compared to Wither," Kayla said.

"And mighty spry," Alex said with a solemn glance at the television. The sound was muted, but the pictures of tarp-covered corpses were in regular rotation.

"Kayla, you brought the books from the Crystal Path?"

She nodded. "Even told Alissa you'd pay for them, but she said just return them when you're done."

"Good. I need to look for weaknesses in this thing. The books might help. Now, Kayla, if you're ready," Wendy said, glancing at the kitchen clock—*almost midnight!*—"we should get started."

Wendy Ward's Mirror Book
January 4, 2002
Moon: waning gibbous, day 20
Windale, Massachusetts

I've never tried anything like this before. Dream magic, lucid dreams, guided dreams, sure—but always before it's been my own dreams, my own mind I was exploring. This time I'll be trying to slip into someone else's dreams and nightmares, into her subconscious mind. I'm not sure if it will work or if it's possible. But I must try.

Have these few minutes—only a few!—while Kayla's changing in the bathroom, to record my thoughts. I have to wonder, though, if they'll be my final thoughts, my last words—let's engrave that tombstone now! Because, what if Kayla isn't really Kayla anymore? At least not deep down in her subconscious. For all I know, Wither is waiting there, growing like a poisonous toadstool in the dark, waiting to be reborn yet again. If I reach her at that level—the unknown battlefield of a foreign subconscious—will I be able to escape? Will she be able to snuff me out like a candle flame between her fingers? Another possibility. What if I slip so deep inside Kayla's mind I can't find my way out again?

Alex is worried. *Hell, I'm worried!* But I can't let either of them see my fear. Alex would try to talk me out of this—maybe I'd even let him. And Kayla, if she knew the extent of my reservations, might panic and back out of this experiment. (Wish I had the Crone's input on this, but

I can't exactly call her on my cell phone, and I have no idea if she'll be able to manifest again before this is over.) Nevertheless, I have to know. My life, Kayla's life . . . many innocent lives may depend on what's locked in Kayla's mind. Oops, she's coming—

WINDALE, MASSACHUSETTS

"Just think of it as a very exclusive Wiccan slumber party," Wendy said, smiling to put Kayla at ease. With a fleeting glance, she noticed the corner of her notebook computer sticking out from under the bed. She'd saved the unfinished mirror book entry but hadn't spared the time to power down the computer. Her attention flicked back to Kayla.

They sat cross-legged on Wendy's bed, facing each other, both in their nightclothes. Wendy wore a pastel green nightshirt with tiny, embroidered red roses along the V-neck and notched hemline. Kayla wore an oversized white Betty Boop T-shirt she'd brought along in her small suitcase, which also held a change of clothes. Wendy had told her on the phone to plan on spending the night.

Alex had also changed. Since the dorms were closed until January fifth, Wendy had invited him to stay overnight as well. Quietly observing, he stood barefoot in the doorway, leaning against the doorjamb, arms crossed over a gray Danfield T-shirt. He wore pin-striped pajama bottoms.

Wendy held two porcelain teacups, resting one on each knee, attempting to look calm and unconcerned to counter Kayla's nervousness. Kayla's brow was creased with a slight frown as she ran her left index finger up and down the ring piercing her lower lip. "It's still early," Kayla said. "Last time I had the nightmare was after two o'clock."

"We'll need time to fall asleep," Wendy said. "Besides, we don't know when or how the dream starts." She offered one of the teacups to Kayla. "Drink this." Kayla took the proffered cup and peered into its depths, and her frown deepened. "It's just an infusion for dream magic," Wendy explained. "Water with chamomile and valerian."

Wry grin from Kayla, which was an improvement. "You do realize I'm not Wiccan?"

"Doesn't matter," Wendy said, deadpan. "This will convert you."

About to take a sip, Kayla tensed. "What?"

"Relax, I'm joking."

Kayla cleared her throat. "Right. Of course you were." She downed the infusion like a shot of whiskey. "Don't feel any different."

"Good," Wendy said, drinking from her own cup. "Alex, can you take these?" Alex stepped forward, retrieved the empty cups and placed them on the nightstand.

On the bed between Wendy and Kayla were two linen sachets with long lace ties. Wendy picked up the first one and tied it behind her neck. The pouch rested between her breasts, close to her heart. "Lean forward," she instructed, then fastened the other pouch around Kayla's neck.

Kayla rubbed the pouch between her fingers. "What's inside?"

"Anise fruits to raise magic energy, and two stones. Amethyst and moonstone. Both aid dream magic." Even though Kayla wasn't Wiccan and Wendy was attempting, under the Crone's instruction, to divorce herself from ritual when accessing magic, in this instance Wendy believed the formality would put Kayla at ease, and help her believe it would work. As with most endeavors, belief was tantamount to success.

Wendy took Kayla's hands in hers, looked directly into her eyes and smiled confidently. "Ready?"

"Any chance this gets kinky?" Alex asked from the doorway, displaying a mischievous grin. "Because that's not necessarily a deal breaker."

"Good-bye, Alex," Wendy said, shaking her head but grinning anyway. "Turn out the light and close the door behind you. We need some privacy."

Kayla laughed. "That's right. We've got some serious sleeping to do here."

"Okay," Alex said, flicking off the lights. He grabbed the doorknob and started to pull the door shut, but paused. "Give a shout if you need—uh, anything." The door clicked shut.

Their faces pale in the moonlight streaming through the windows, Wendy and Kayla looked at each other for a moment. Then Kayla began to giggle. "Poor boy," she said. "Dying to write a *Penthouse* letter."

"Can't blame him for thinking about sex," Wendy said with a chuckle. "He is male and awake, after all."

"You should put him out of his misery."

"A little . . . anticipation won't hurt him."

"So. What now? How do we . . . ?"

Wendy scooted around to the side of the bed nearest the door. "Here," she said, patting the pillow on the opposite side. "Lie down." As if to demonstrate, she lay on her left side, legs stretched out, head on her pillow.

"Yes, Sensei," Kayla said, with a formal nod. She lay on her side, facing Wendy, her elbow on the pillow, head resting in her palm. "Ever done anything like this before?"

"No."

"First time for everything, right?"

"Mm-hmm," Wendy said, scrunching up her mouth to suppress a laugh.

"All for experimentation myself," Kayla said. "Never figured you for the type."

"Sometimes you just never know about people," Wendy said, arching a seductive eyebrow, then blowing her a kiss. "Hubba-hubba."

Kayla laughed, rolled onto her back and stared at the ceiling. She placed both hands over the linen pouch on her chest and said, "It won't be pretty."

"I know."

"Assuming, of course, it actually works." She looked thoughtful. "Do I have to believe in this"—holding up the pouch, she glanced at Wendy—"for it to work?"

"Try to stay open to the possibility. A person who resists a hypnotist can't be put into a trance. Don't actively *disbelieve* it. Just relax. And let me take care of the magic."

"You're gonna hypnotize me?"

"No," Wendy said. "Sorry, bad analogy. You'll just be sleeping, as usual—"

"Nothing *usual* about this scenario," Kayla said, smiling. "Got a hot little Wiccan chick in bed with me."

"You're as bad as Alex!" Wendy said, giving her a little shove. "Anyway, you'll be sleeping. The magic side of it, I hope, will open a doorway into your dreams, just enough for me to slip through. Then we'll take control of the dream."

More serious now, "Will I know you're there? Inside my dream?"

"You may not see me," Wendy said. "But if it works, the dream will change. I'll bump it out of its repetition, try to redirect it."

"Lucid dreaming?"

Wendy nodded.

"But if these dreams are real. If they're not figments of my subconscious imagination, will that mean . . ." Again she cast a sidelong glance at Wendy. "Will it mean that I'm . . . ?"

"Akashic records," Wendy said. Kayla frowned a question at her. "Some people believe all the memories of everyone's experiences since the beginning of time are stored in a spiritual substance called *akasha.*"

"A big psychic warehouse?"

"It's this idea that it's *all* out there. Maybe whatever she did via the blood contact simply attuned you to her memories, nothing more."

"So there's a chance I'm not . . . tainted?"

"A good chance." *Until we see evidence proving otherwise. Maybe I'll know in a few hours. Tell her that and she'll be too nervous to fall asleep.* "Let's figure this out together. Okay?"

Kayla nodded.

Wendy reached out to Kayla's face, stroked an errant lock of electric-blue hair away from her forehead. "Like it," Wendy said in a softer tone of voice. "Bold, definitely makes a statement and not as severe as the spikes."

Kayla grinned. "Are you making a pass at me, Wendy Ward?"

"Caught me," Wendy said, leaning over to kiss her forehead. "Now be quiet and go to sleep before I have to spank you."

"Knew there was an ulterior motive to get me into your bed."

"I'm devious," Wendy said. "So what's the protocol? Who ravages whom?"

"I'm fighting this, aren't I?"

"Um, a little."

"Nerves."

"Tell me about Bobby? Is it serious?"

"Except for the part where he thinks I'm crazy," Kayla said. "Yeah, it's kinda serious."

"Engagement plans?"

"Oh, God, no! Not that serious," Kayla said, chuckling. "Living in sin. I'm too young for marriage. Don't even have my Harley yet. Gotta experience a few Harley years before I think about tying a knot around my neck."

"Neck?"

"Freudian, maybe?" Kayla said. "Nah. He's a bit overprotective sometimes."

"Protect and serve," Wendy said. "Job requirement."

"I know, I know," Kayla said. "But I don't want to live my life under house arrest or constant police protection. That being unreasonable?"

"No. But sometimes you need somebody to lean on in a crunch."

"You're right," Kayla said, letting out a long sigh. "I get defensive. Maybe it's my inner outlaw. Bobby's cool. He is ... I don't know why I ..."

"You don't have to be afraid."

"What? Never said I was—"

"If the dream is bad, I'll wake you," Wendy said. "Promise." Another sigh. "Okay. Let's do this. Help me fall asleep."

"How about a relaxation exercise?"

Kayla nodded, eyes closed.

"Clear your mind of this extraneous stuff we've been talking about. Think of a peaceful place. A beach—a deserted beach. Nobody there, but you. It's near dusk. Gentle waves are rolling in, splashing foam on the smooth, cool sand. One wave after another, rolling up the sand with a soothing spray of foam . . ."

In a few minutes, Kayla's breathing steadied, then became deep with sleep. With a light, cautious touch, Wendy took Kayla's right hand in her left, interlacing their fingers. Kayla's fingers curled a bit, almost grasping Wendy's hand unconsciously. Placing her right hand atop Kayla's, so that she held it top and bottom, she raised it close to her chest, close to the linen pouch. Wendy closed her own eyes, took long slow breaths, letting natural lethargy wash over her, carry her down to sleep and into another woman's nightmare . . .

Nightfall . . . A blood-red smudge in the western sky darkens to a purplish bruise.

She flies over a Windale long gone . . . fewer homes and those present are separated by dirt roads with wagon-wheel ruts. She banks left, swoops down across a tall field of corn, her night-adapted eyes seeking movement, human movement.

A man in threadbare coveralls walks a drunken line, pausing every few steps to raise a jug to his fish-puckered mouth. The whiskey courses down his chin, fat drops staining his coveralls. With the back of one sunburnt arm, he wipes the whiskey from his stubble-covered jaw. The hour is late. Perhaps he is wandering homeward, careless of his surroundings, oblivious to what lurks above.

She drops from the sky with the ease of a bird of prey striking a furred morsel in the middle of a grassy meadow. Her arms extend, fingers flashing wicked claws . . .

The impact is sudden and fierce. The jug explodes, bursting in the man's hand. Before he can cry out, two sets of claws gouge into his flesh, crushing ribs and stealing his breath.

Arcing upward, she banks into the branches of an old oak tree, wedging the stunned man into the Y-fork of one strong branch. She swipes out with a flash of claws—and swipes again—but the man is gone!

Enraged, she flies around the tree, darting lower and lower, to find where her prize has fallen, fallen and died, probably, from a broken neck. She would feast while the blood is warm . . . down and around, down and around to the bottom, landing with a rushed impact on the loamy ground . . . and he is gone.

(Wendy?)

(I'm here.)

Then the tree disappears . . .

Alarmed, she takes to the sky (How—) (What?) (—does she fly?) (Oh.) with the speed of thought . . . Where has the tree gone, she wonders, what sort of magic works against her . . . who would dare?

From a high vantage point, she first scans the ground for movement. If he flees, she will spot him, snatch him up and pluck his eyes out for troubling her so . . . but where? She swoops low, beneath the treetops, zigzagging across the fields, into the woods, until she sees the barn, the roost, the nest, the lair . . . but she hungers, so why return? Darting up briefly, she drops down through a worn hole in the roof with practiced ease, lands in the loft with a weighty thud, attracting the attention of the other two . . . watching her with gleaming red eyes (Are they . . . ?) (Yes.), watching . . . and the barn is darker than before. She glances up and the hole is missing, sky is missing, hole repaired—never happened?—where, no when is she. This is before . . .

She runs across the loft, leaps up on the front wall, claws digging into the wood, but not deep enough to support her weight. Somehow, magically, she cheats the pull of gravity, scurries down the wall with the light, stalking grace of a spider. Above the double *doors, then she drops to the floor of the barn. Though her body's dimensions are smaller, she is more agile—less powerful—but much stronger than a human. So when is she? And the voices in her head—whose voices—what sort of magic—who dares—the year, the year before, the drunkard's year was 1899. Bigger then but not biggest, the biggest is the end of the cycle, the time for rebirth and a new body—a fresh body—but now is before, so this before must be 1799.*

Her powerful arm swats at the barn door and blackness yields to night, and she is flying again, hungry again, but where (Wendy, what's happening?) is she flying this time? Why? The forest (Where is the clearing?) spins beneath her, the keeper's house (What?) aglow with one light, but which keeper, which (Make her go to the clearing, trigger those memories!) Stone—which year?—is it? Voices, strange voices. What magic—who dares? She banks right, away from the house, to the special place, but why the special place now?

Encircled by trees, it seems to pull her down, down beneath the treetops, but she is already there with a keeper—which keeper?—not Matthias who will come—has died, was killed—the weak one before? The one who killed himself? No, it is before, the first keeper in the New World, the new line, the first Stone, but she is (What's wrong with her mind?) already changed, leathery black skin but only a foot taller than the—Ezekiel—Stone. So this is the first awakening (All her memories are available. She confuses past and future in this present.) and already hard to compose thoughts on human paper, hidden thoughts guarded here, her record, her legacy. No one must find or read—Protected! Secret! Hidden!—what she keeps here. They will grow change evolve experiment with the next coming cycle. No limits, new limits, known limits. She drops down inside the body, her body, first awakened body, she is the body. Ezekiel stands—wary—with a shovel, waiting for her to finish.

Stones and bones and stones and bones and blood her blood to seal her—Hidden! Secret! Protected!—thoughts on paper human paper. Why is she here now? Not the first time (Go to the first time!) when was the first time (You know.) for dirt and bones and stones (You know!) and blood—the hole, the secret place. You wish—

—she is human again!

This is before the sleep—the hibernation—the change, the darkening, before she was hanged—they were hanged—by those who feared her and the others, Sarah and Rebecca, her coven—the year she formed her coven, the year 1699. She is human—looks human anyway—and they are fallen—fallen women, not-women, once-human, inhuman, unknown—she wears human clothes, a head rail and widow's peak, a doublet and looped petticoat under a riding hood. Ezekiel's face glistens with sweat from digging the hole—wearing a jerkin and baggy leather breeches tied below the knee—and he is respectful, fearful, anxious, awaiting her command.

A hard rain begins to fall, pelting Ezekiel and Elizabeth Wither.

She is in the clearing, the dirt first turned in this—Protected! Secret! Hidden!—place by Ezekiel, her first Stone keeper. He will know (This is the beginning.) this place, but he fears, is trusted because he fears, will be a keeper for this place as he is a keeper for the coven. Know but not touch, only the blood may touch, only the blood (She hid something here!) may see, may feel beneath the stones and bones and dirt to the bottom. Only the blood! Others will know—he will know—only DEATH! It will be so, it will be so, it will be so, and she peers into the hole—the abyss!—and sees the dirt and stones and bones and down where it lies—where death awaits!—let no one know (It's a trap!) not of the blood . . . it will be SO!

The fat drops of rain turn red, turn to blood, soaking the ground, seeping into the dirt, becoming a crimson mud. Light bleeds from the sky and darkness looms. In the gathering shadows, crimson becomes black . . .

The ground heaves and roils and twists beneath her, pulling her down (WENDY!) but she is of the blood!—she reaches (Let's—!) for the sky, she sinks to her doom, she breathes dirt (PLEASE!) and gags, she struggles (get out!) in vain—but she is of the blood!?—worms burrow into her (HELP!) flesh, worms feast on her (of here!) flesh, she screams in agony, her chest (ME!) burns—burns!—BURNS!

Wendy gasped for breath, squeezing Kayla's hand hard between hers, pulling herself up and coughing.

Kayla was choking, gagging for air that was everywhere around her but not in her dream. Trapped in the nightmare, Kayla was now living and dying in the nightmare. Wendy shook her shoulders, shouting her name. "Kayla! Wake up!"

In the ambient light, she saw Kayla's lips turning blue.

Wendy straddled her waist, slipped her hands under Kayla's shoulders and pulled her up, shaking her without receiving any response. Finally, Wendy raised an open hand and slapped Kayla hard across the cheek. Kayla's eyelids flew open, the whites enormous, still living the dream, trapped in the suffocating darkness, buried alive, unable to escape the dream. "Kayla! Do you hear me? It's Wendy! Talk to me!"

"Uh—uh—uh!" Kayla shuddered and gasped, her voice hoarse. "Can't—br—breathe!"

"You can breathe here! That was a dream! Just a dream! It's over!"

"B—b—breathe!?"

Wendy nodded, vigorously. Kayla sucked in air, as if she'd been underwater for over two minutes and had just that moment surfaced. Wendy hugged her, careful not to squeeze too tight, alternately stroking her electric-blue hair and patting her back, rocking her back and forth in a slow, soothing motion.

"Dream—the dream," Kayla said, trembling. "You were there—I sensed you, spoke with you . . . in my mind. Her mind."

"Yes," Wendy said. And repeated, "You're okay now. It's over."

Kayla pulled away, just enough to look into Wendy's eyes. Tears had streaked Kayla's face. "You saved me. Jesus!—she tried to kill me! But you saved me. You!" She kissed Wendy's cheek, then found her lips once, twice, before pressing her cheek against Wendy's, holding their heads together, as if she were about to whisper a confidence. Instead, she just trembled, whispering over and over, "Thank you."

Wendy could taste the salt of her tears. "I saved us both," Wendy said. "Remember, I was trapped in there too."

"Seemed so real . . ." Kayla shook her head in disbelief. "What happened?"

"We started to experience the trap she was setting," Wendy said. "She was placing a spell on that clearing, on whatever she buried in that hole."

Kayla sat back on her heels, so she could see Wendy's face. She took a moment to wipe away the drying tear tracks with the heel of her palm. "A trap, huh? So what now?"

"We figure a way to disarm it."

"Wendy, I don't know. This stuff is too freaky. Maybe we should . . ."

"It's a spell for the unwary," Wendy said. "That's not us. We'll be protected."

"How? With bulletproof vests? Biohazard suits?"

"Magic," Wendy said.

"Fight fire with fire? Wendy, I don't know . . ."

"Kayla, if you want answers, you have to trust me. One more time," Wendy said. "Wither hid something there, protected it with magic, for hundreds of years now. You were drawn to that place. Strangely, I think she wants you to find it."

"That's what I'm afraid of."

Wendy covered her mouth, but had to laugh.

Kayla smiled, grasping for the humor, even the gallows variety. "What?"

"I was just thinking," Wendy said. "Alex would kick himself if he knew he missed that . . . kiss thing earlier."

"Kiss thing?" Kayla asked, arching an eyebrow. "What do you mean?"

"When you—before, when you . . ."

"Oh," Kayla said, smiling. "You mean, when I did this . . ." She leaned forward, an exaggerated pucker to her lips and batted her eyelashes comically.

Wendy grabbed a pillow, slipped it between them, and pushed Kayla away, squealing.

"What's this?" Kayla asked, feigning shock. "No, it couldn't be, not a—pillow fight!" Kayla grabbed her pillow and was about to swat Wendy's head when the bedroom door swung open.

Alex stood there, gaping. "Thought I heard yell—Ooh, lovers' quarrel?"

They both threw their pillows at him, laughing hysterically.

Wendy Ward's Mirror Book
January 4, 2002
Moon: waning gibbous, day 20 (continued)
Windale, Massachusetts

It's over now. Scared the hell out of me, but it's over. I experienced the nightmare with Kayla, in her mind, and something—someone?—tried to attack us. But maybe that's looking at it too simplistically. I don't really know if something . . . sentient was there, something malevolent. But somehow the dream took on a psychological or subconscious reality.

I was able to snap out of the dream, but I had a hard time waking Kayla, and all the while she was gasping for air. Unfortunately, I still don't know if we're safe from Wither's influence. Can't be sure, one way or the other. If Wither lurks within Kayla, in some nascent form attempting another rebirth, why would that life force try to kill her, its host? But it seems Kayla is in as much danger from this as I am, or anyone else. If it is sentient, it's indiscriminate. Guess that's part of chaos.

For Alex, I tried to downplay what happened. Minimized the risk I took, the danger we faced. Helps that I don't intend to attempt cooperative dream-walking again. Oops, alert the Crone! I've coined another phrase.

Tomorrow, we visit Wither's clearing and find what she's been hiding all these years. Tonight? This morning, actually . . . well, I need to learn a few new tricks. Kayla's asleep in Frankie's room. The dream-walking took a lot out of her. (I promised to check in on her, wake her if it looked like she was having another nightmare, but I believe we broke the nightmare cycle.) Told Alex I needed meditation time, so he's in the other room, watching some obscure sporting challenge on one of the twenty-four-hour sports stations. No matter the sport, if somebody's keeping score, he'll watch.

Enough procrastination. Need to start preparing myself to fight this winter demon. So much to do, and I'm running out of time.

CHAPTER ELEVEN

Wendy's focus was a flame.

Across the bedroom, on her dresser but visible from her bed, burned a tea candle in a glass holder. Sitting in the lotus position, she faced the flame. As an aid to concentration, she fingered a quartz crystal on her multi-bead bracelet. Now that she'd overcome the challenge of stage one astral projection, she was determined to learn the intricacies of stage two. *No time like the present,* she thought. House was quiet and she should be tired, but the frantic dream-trap experience had pumped enough endorphins into Wendy's system that she felt the after-burn of excess energy. *Best to try now before I flame out and collapse from exhaustion.*

Hardest part was clearing her mind of those recent events to achieve a state of total relaxation, and the total disconnect necessary for self-hypnosis. Fortunately, she'd had years of practice sinking into meditative states, in centering her mind and focusing on the magical task at hand. In less than five minutes, her astral body—her awareness—slipped loose from her physical self, floated past the foot of the bed and paused before her dresser mirror. She could *see* the mirror with the crystalline clarity of astral vision, but the only reflection in the mirror was her seated physical self. Very weird moment, because physical Wendy's eyes were closed, yet she was staring at her own reflection. *Just not my current one. If that makes any sense.*

Minutes passed, with her awareness hovering motionless right in front of the mirror. The Crone said she needed to will her astral self into visibility. Everything was an extension of belief and will, mind over matter, mind over ether.

If she concentrated long enough, her awareness spread from a pinpoint of consciousness to a complete sense of body. Glancing at the reflection of physical Wendy, astral Wendy thought it might help if she mimicked physical Wendy's current state. Simple to visualize an image that was right in front of her astral eyes.

Wendy imagined her astral body as light as smoke, then lighter, then weightless. She imagined airy limbs coming together, legs crossed, hands on knees, palms up. She continued to stare at physical Wendy's reflection in the mirror, acknowledging each detail, a long and growing list in her astral mind—creases in her nightshirt, a stray lock of auburn hair obscuring her right eyebrow, a fading dime-sized bruise on her left shin, the crescent moon and stars tattoo above her right ankle, the chip of puce fingernail polish on her right thumb and on and on—until the sum of the parts became a visualized whole. At some point, astral Wendy stopped concentrating on physical Wendy long enough to notice a ghostly duplicate reflected beside her in the mirror.

Had she the capacity to breathe, she might have gasped. *It's as if I composed an air painting of myself,* she marveled.

Focusing her awareness on her astral self, she unfolded her ghostly legs and tried to stand, but without mass she could only approximate an appearance of gravity's hold. There remained about her translucent image a sense of weightlessness, like an astronaut who might push off and perform several slow-motion somersaults through the space shuttle's cargo bay. Rather than trying to imagine herself planted to the floor, she concentrated on improving her opacity. Her astral replica appeared accurate in all the details, but as insubstantial as movie film projected onto a column of white smoke. Looking at the problem logically—"there are no problems, only opportunities" according to one of Alex's mystical managerial texts—all her colors appeared faded, washed out, from her flesh tones to the green of her spectral nightdress with its tiny, embroidered red roses. *It's all just a matter of will,* she told herself. *Just intensify my visualized colors.*

In a few moments, the colors in her astral image began to change, as though she were adjusting the hue, saturation and brightness controls of a color TV. The metaphor helped, in a way, made the adjustments seem natural and so, simpler to imagine. She began to glow, the colors radiating from her astral form as though she were illuminated from within. *Okay, maybe a little too much brightness,* she thought. *Bring that down and work on saturation.* Another few minutes' experimentation and she had deepened most of the colors to full opacity. Only her flesh tones remained a challenge, a trifle ghostly. If she remained motionless for more than a few seconds, details of the room, seen through her flesh, began to resolve. After a while, she found a compromise. While her true, physical reflection was healthy in a tan-free way, the astral analog would be alabaster white, like marble and thus unnatural. Her astral image was immune to the sun's harmful UV rays, so she decided to do a little visualized tanning. A few moments later the tan was complete and the translucency was gone.

After a satisfied inspection of the new and improved astral image, she attempted an astral walk but found that illusion impossible to create. She had no mass, felt no friction or resistance, and had no sense of physical balance, so the result was her limbs fanning the air in a freaky spacewalk pantomime. Instead, she held the opaque astral image of herself still and glided forward and backward by willing her awareness around the room. Much easier to manage but, if anything, a hell of a lot freakier.

Maybe the problem was that she appeared in her nightdress, her arms and most of her legs exposed to view. The illusion of walking might be easier to maintain if she visualized herself in a long flowing robe, maybe with only her hands exposed. Duplicating the sway and flow of loose cloth in motion would require much less precision than the articulation of human limbs. But, so far, she'd only been successful in establishing a visual image for her astral self by duplicating every detail of her physical form. For now, she would be satisfied with her astral glide. Maybe in her next exercise she'd visualize herself in a hooded cloak. Or, to keep it simple, put a cloak on her physical body before she began visualization. At some point, she would need to progress to higher stages of astral projection and that meant astral glamours, displaying different clothes and appearances for herself.

Satisfied with her stage two effort, she decided to take it on the road, literally. She willed her astral self through the closed bedroom door, noticing the slightest resistance—no, wrong word . . . hesitancy—as she passed through the physical substance of the wood. Hesitancy and a flicker of darkness, then she emerged in the short hallway. Before leaving the house, she decided to check in on Kayla, as promised, so she passed through the door to Frankie's bedroom, exercising a little caution in her entrance on the off chance Kayla was awake. *I could scare her to death after that dream from hell almost suffocated her.* But Kayla was asleep, sprawled on her back, chest rising and falling in the steady rhythm of sleep.

Reversing direction, astral Wendy backed out of the bedroom and coasted down the hallway, as silent as thought . . . and into utter silence. Hovering behind Alex, who had also dozed off, she stared at the flickering images on the television screen and realized that astral Wendy was deaf. According to the Crone, stage one astral projection had one sense, astral vision, but experiencing others senses was possible. Of the five senses, sight was the most informative, arguably the most critical, but hearing was right up there. Touch might prove counterproductive in the astral world—although astral control of objects in the physical world would definitely be useful. She could be a poltergeist for Halloween. Smell, since she couldn't eat on the astral plane, seemed least important. To hear and to be heard—*how can an astral body make sound?*—were priorities.

Astral sight had been automatic, a standard feature. She needed some optional equipment to make astral projection a viable tool in her Wiccan magic bag. Visual cues helped her create a visible form. Maybe aural cues would help her *hear* astrally. Between sports highlights, the anchors faces appeared, talking heads. While she had never learned to read lips, some words were obvious. As she *read* certain words, she began to imagine she heard them as well.

It began as a hushed whisper, expanded to a roomful of whisperers, almost like distant crowd noise, a rush of indistinguishable words, a wall of sound. But then those helper words, gleaned from the telltale movement of lips, started to pop up, rising above the white noise flavor of the ether around her. Sound was just vibrations, compressions and expansions in the air. Hearing was interpreting those vibrations, making audible sense of them.

The longer she watched the sports anchor's lips move, the shorter the gaps between popped words. "That's shushl-shush . . . for shush-shushl-shush. Coming shush next, we'll take a shushl-shush the league for NBA highlights. We're back in two!" A dandruff shampoo commercial came on and Wendy heard most of the words, even those spoken in voice-over. Sound heard astrally had an odd quality, probably because she was *listening* without the aid or limitations of organic ears. Almost as if the sounds were coming from everywhere at once. Everywhere? Or just inside—as part of her new awareness? Now that she was hearing astrally, she imagined she could distinguish the faintest sound, if only she concentrated long enough and hard enough.

Hear . . . and be heard.

She tried to talk, but nothing happened. *Of course, stupid,* she thought. *You don't have vocal chords!* But the Crone managed to talk in her astral form. She'd spoken directly to Wendy's mind before, even in dreams, a telepathic mode of speech. But she also talked aloud. Wendy imaged speaking aloud would be more difficult and more tiring than speaking telepathically. *Probably easier to learn sign language than to make sounds while in astral form,* she thought. *But most people*

don't understand sign language. Hand gestures, maybe, but not
sign language. Which made her wonder, *Why is there a univer-*
sal hand gesture for "screw you" but not one for "thank you"?

Employing her advanced visualization techniques,
Wendy spent several minutes experimenting with creating
her own sounds, vibrations from within the head and throat
of her astral image. Unversed with *Gray's Anatomy,* she
couldn't visualize how vocal chords worked in a strict medical sense, so she approached the problem from another
aural angle, playing games with the air, creating vibrations
in the air. Soon she could make various puffing, hissing,
blowing and whistling sounds. All faint, but with practice
she could mix, match and modulate them into near-words.
"Wenn-wee . . . Ahh-wesss . . . Hehh-wohh . . ."

Great, Wendy thought. *I can always find work in a haunted*
house attraction. Making sound without lips, she imagined,
was like trying to learn ventriloquism. *Only harder, so incred-*
ibly harder.

"Ahh-wehss . . . waayy-uhh!" Far from waking up, Alex
never stirred. Her words—her sounds, rather—were no more
than haunting whispers, breathy exhalations. "Cahh wuuu
heee-uh meee?" Apparently, not.

Abandoning astral speech therapy, Wendy decided to
continue exploring, not only out of body, but out of building. She floated forward with phantom grace, passed
through the sliding glass doorway out onto the terrace, and
discovered another benefit of having no tactile sense. She
couldn't feel the cold! If physical Wendy stepped outside
wearing nothing but a satin nightshirt and panties, she'd
promptly freeze her ass off, a shivering study in gooseflesh,
her teeth chattering like castanets. Astral Wendy, on the
other hand, could maintain every ounce—every *figurative*

ounce since, technically, she was weightless—of her dignity. *Not that floating outside in a nightshirt is that dignified to begin with*, she admitted. *But the wind chill can't touch my astral ass!*

A thought carried her straight up into the sky, but once she was above the highest treetops it seemed pointless to go any higher. Yet as she floated along, she thought of a potential complication. She was visible now, a scantily clad young thing skimming the rooftops like Tinker Bell without the pixie dust, and that meant anybody who happened to look up at an inopportune moment would probably jump out of their skin, swerve off the road or have a coronary. True, it was the wee hours of the morning, but all it would take was one accident . . . The simplest solution was greater elevation, high enough so she would be indistinct to anyone on the ground. At some point, she had to learn how to fade in and out of sight, but for now, she just soared up into the sky until the houses below seemed the size of milk cartons, the cars like Matchbox toys.

Speed was another variable she had some control over. She seemed to have a default floating or drifting speed. A touch of "will power" applied brisk acceleration. With just a little more concentration, she darted through the night sky faster than a bird. Anything faster and her thoughts started to become fuzzy and confused, as though the pinpoint of consciousness were expanding, spreading itself too thin. Fearing the consequences of losing self-awareness while disconnected from her physical body, she slowed her flight to average bird speed.

Her astral body was neither aerodynamic nor designed for flight, but none of that mattered. No physical effort was required for her to stay aloft; she encountered no friction; and she was immune to the pull of gravity. To fly in any direction at any reasonable speed, all she had to do was will it. She could stop in midair instantly, hover motionless—even upside down—pirouette, dive or soar. The possibilities seemed endless.

Gazing down over the sprawling town of Windale, Wendy tried to ascertain her location by examining the network of roads, the clusters of mostly dark houses, and the irregular lines of trees and clumps of forests. Using Main Street as a reference, she angled down and away, toward the Stone property. She descended until she was less than fifty feet above the tallest trees. From that vantage point, she located the charred timbers of the barn that had served as a lair for the monstrous coven. Though the structure had burnt to the ground, she sensed the evil of it. No other way to explain the nameless loathing she felt, the desire to be anywhere but there. *Are astral beings more sensitive to the presence or artifacts of evil?* She experienced the equivalent of an astral shudder. *Probably a mental compensation,* she thought. *Like an amputee who feels an itch in the missing limb.*

Floating away from the ruined barn, she rose higher and attempted to locate the clearing she'd seen in Kayla's dream. Flitting back and forth around the old house, she had no luck. Instead, she had the sensation of blacking out at brief moments, tiny flickers of emptiness or forgetfulness. After searching in vain for a few minutes, Wendy came to the inescapable conclusion that Wither's protective spell shielded her special area from astral spying. One more way, not altogether unexpected, to guard her secret cache. *Tomorrow is soon enough,* she thought. *Kayla will find it again in the morning.*

As Wendy looped up into the sky again, her attention was drawn toward something pleasant, a feeling of home and acceptance. An opposite sensation to being repelled from and repulsed by the wreck of the barn. She couldn't see what attracted her, almost called out to her, but she was aware of it. Drifting beneath the night sky she let the sensation guide her will, like a homing beacon. When she drifted farther from the source, she reversed direction until the *signal* became strong again. The process of zeroing in on the strange, welcoming sensation was almost completely intuitive. It felt right.

A stream, glittering with ice and a trickle of freezing water, reflected the moonlight back to her. Wendy swooped down from treetop level and spotted a flash of white fur slipping between the trees, seeking the water. Wendy descended to the grass and hovered an inch above the ground. The flash of white was a wolf, and Wendy knew. "Aaa-veee!"

The wolf's head swiveled on a powerful neck to stare at her, startled but unafraid. Wendy hung motionless in the air and wondered what wolf Abby would make of astral Wendy. Certainly the wolf couldn't smell her. In that sense she would be invisible and inscrutable to the wolf. But, clearly, the wolf saw her astral form. Then Wendy noticed some sort of modified khaki backpack on the wolf's back, with what looked like hair scrunchies sewn on the underside, taking the place of the arm straps. *Something Abby slips on before shape-shifting?*

"Izz mee . . . Wenn-wee!" The wolf's head gave a quick nod. Abby not only saw and recognized her, she heard her as well! "Izz harruh ooo sspeehuh." Wolf Abby rolled her eyes, as if to say, "Try being a wolf."

"Iiii-maa in Winnhail."

The wolf nodded again, taking a few steps toward her, sniffing the air in vain for a scent.

"*Buhh noo ree-lee hee-uh now. Thisss isss ahsssshruhl . . . pro-heshun.*" Even if she knows what I said, she probably won't understand. "*Yoo no sssmehhl.*"

Wolf Abby sat before her, cocked her head.

"*Cahn yoo beee-cuhm hyoo-mahn? We sspee-uh ooo-gehthur.*"

After a moment, the wolf nodded and backed up a step or two. Wendy watched, in a state of awe as the wolf's bones seemed to bend and twist in impossible ways, claylike in their malleability. The body contorted, joints popped, and skin rippled in ways uncomfortable to watch, making Wendy wonder how bizarre it must feel. Fur retracted into flesh or thinned to a light, human down, as skin became pink and tender. If the reforming legs had been unnerving to watch, the morphing face took it to another level. The skull collapsed into the now furless face, the cranium extending upward, rounding, the ears shrinking from tufted, twitching points to round girl ears with pierced lobes.

The whole transformation lasted no more than a minute; then Abby was human again, naked and chilled to the bone. With unself-conscious ease, she slipped the scrunchie-straps off her slender arms and pulled a wool blanket out of the backpack, wrapping it around her shoulders as she hunched over, trying to conserve body heat. "Not really dressed for January," Abby said, teeth chattering. "Being naked and all."

"*Sorree, Aa-vee.*" Wendy had been so determined to talk to her, she hadn't thought through the physical consequences of Abby's change to human form.

"That's okay," Abby said. "I'm getting used to it. I come out here late at night to attempt other shapes. I want to fly, Wendy, but I can't yet. I try so hard . . . Sometimes it almost works. My bones want to change, but I mess it up."

"Nooo fiii-ih," Wendy said.

"Don't fight it?" Abby asked. "The change, you mean?"

Wendy nodded. "*Lehh boness may-kuh new bohd-deee.*"

"Let my bones make my new . . . body? But I want to fly, to be a bird, an eagle."

Wendy nodded, agreeing with the goal. "*Lehh boness eee-cide.*"

"Let my bones decide." Suddenly, Abby smiled. "Let my bones decide what kind of bird they want to become!"

Wendy smiled. "*Yess . . .*" She was beginning to feel fatigue. Not physical weakness, but rather a lack of concentration, a gradual fuzziness of awareness, which was probably her cue to get back to her physical body soonest. The Crone talked about her consciousness being lost, but what if her consciousness became too unfocused to make the return trip. *Could my . . . essence simply dissipate on the ethereal winds?*

"Are you really in Windale?"

Wendy nodded.

"Can I see you tomorrow? After school? Good." Abby frowned. "Um, where do you live?"

"*Sssame place . . .*"

"Good. I'll come over, somehow. I'll find a way. As me, the wolf or, maybe as a bird!"

"*Bee carefuhl,*" Wendy said. "*Musss leave now . . . ohh-kay?*"

"Okay, Wendy," Abby said. "Thanks for the tip. I'll give it a try."

Wendy rose into the night sky, watching Abby's small form recede beneath her. Abby stuffed the blanket back into the backpack, struggled to slip her arms through the home-made shoulder straps again, then shifted back to wolf form. Before the change was complete, Wendy flitted across a row of trees. When she passed over houses, she soared upward at a forty-five-degree angle, gaining elevation and distance in one motion. In less than two minutes, her phantom flight brought her back to her own terrace.

Looking through the glass door, she saw that Alex was awake, remote control balanced on his knee. The sudden movement must have caught his eye. One second he was focused on sports highlights, the next he was staring at her through the plate glass.

He thinks I'm standing out here in my nightie!

Alex pushed off the loveseat, hurrying to the sliding glass door to admit her into the house, and probably wondering if he should add sleepwalking to his list of Wendy Ward oddities.

She passed through the glass door into the dining area, and had to smile when the remote control dropped from Alex's numb fingers. He blinked, rubbed his eyes and shook his head, all futile attempts to dispel what he perceived was a late-night hallucination. "Wendy . . . what? How?"

She really put a lot of effort into enunciating the words this time, and almost got it right. "S*stay-juh two.*"

"Stay . . . what?" Alex said. "You're voice is faint. And your lips aren't—they're not moving."

Oops, she thought. *Stay focused now. Two one syllable words. Just say 'em!* "Stage two."

"Stage two?" Alex's eyebrows rose, recognition dawning. "Oh! Stage two—your astral projection. You did it! Really! I can see you. It's like you're right—can I touch you?"

Wendy raised her right arm, palm out. *I come in peace,* she thought, and smiled.

Alex stepped forward, a little hesitant. He raised his left hand in front of her right, palm facing palm, and closed the gap millimeter by millimeter, not quite touching. *Probably afraid I'll shock him.* "*Booo!*" she said, and shoved her hand against his—against and through it! Two of her fingers poked out of his forearm.

Alex jumped back with a yelp, as if stung by a wasp. "Oh! God—that's freaky!" He rubbed his left forearm with his right and shivered.

Wendy smiled and shook her head. She felt tired, unfocused. Not good. "*Back to myy bohdee now.*"

"What about the bottom slap test?"

"*Whah-tess?*"

"The one where I slap your bottom to see if you can feel it," Alex said with a mischievous grin. "And . . . maybe a little payback for scaring the hell out of me."

Wendy shook her head and, with a thought, glided through the kitchen—literally *through* the kitchen. The lower half of her body passed through the dishwasher before all of her disappeared into the wall, reappearing in the hallway beyond. Alex barely had time to cup his hand and step forward to demonstrate his technique before she was gone. He ran down the short hallway to her bedroom just as she vanished through the closed door.

Wendy was surprised to see her physical body out of its lotus position, lying on its left side, head almost hanging off the side of the bed. *Not unconscious, precisely,* she thought, *more like a state of preconsciousness.* Physical exhaustion was taking a toll on her astral body, perhaps explaining her lack of focus, her fuzzy awareness.

Alex opened the door and stood there, gaping. The smile had slipped off his face.

With a thought, Wendy rushed into her prone body, like plunging into warm water, feeling her awareness spread throughout her physical form, her tingling extremities.

Again, she experienced the sudden drag of gravity on her torso and limbs, the uncomfortable and unnatural weightiness of physical being. She pushed herself into a sitting position and immediately yawned. "Hey," she managed. Speech, at least, seemed effortless and natural again.

"Are you okay?" Alex asked. "I was goofing around, but when I saw you lying there, I thought you were hurt."

"I'm okay," Wendy said, fumbling to pull down the blankets and sheets. "Well, bone tired. But okay."

"I can imagine," Alex said sympathetically. "Well, not really, but . . ."

"Yeah." Wendy arched an eyebrow. "Wanna snuggle?"

"Don't have to ask twice. Give me two seconds to turn off the TV."

"Might be . . ."—yawn—". . . asleep in two seconds."

"Hell with the TV," Alex said, and climbed into bed beside her.

By the time he slipped his arm around her waist and pressed his face into her hair to catch the scent of her shampoo, she had mumbled " 'Night, Alex" and drifted off to sleep.

Somebody was shaking her shoulder.

Whispered urgency. "Wendy! Wendy, wake up!"

She opened her eyes and focused on Kayla's face, still surprised to see the electric-blue hair above the twin eyebrow posts. Kayla wore her oversized Betty Boop T-shirt. Alex was lying on his side, facing the window, his back to Wendy, sound asleep. "Time is it?"

"Little after six," Kayla said. "I'm due at Crystal Path by ten. If we're really doing this, we should get rolling."

"Right," Wendy said, sitting up as she swept a hand through her hair. "Shower. Coffee. Or . . . the other way around."

"Pot's already on, some of my special double blend," Kayla said. "I'll hop in the shower while you're getting your act together." She indicated Alex. "Late night?"

"Yes, but not what you think, unfortunately," Wendy said. "Magic training. Advanced astral projection. Even visited Abby in . . . about several miles from here."

"Seriously?" Kayla asked. "Cool. Too cool. Fucking frigid, girl!"

"I'll remember that," Wendy said with a crooked smile. "Dreams?"

Kayla shook her head. "Not after that doozy we shared." She rapped the top of her head with her knuckles. "Knock wood."

"Super," Wendy said. She stretched her arms up and curled her toes down. "And . . . getting up now."

"What about Alex?" Kayla asked. "Coming with?"

"Suppose I should ask him."

"Ask him nice," Kayla said. "If you catch my drift." Wendy felt a blush rise to her cheeks. "Since you're a quick study," Kayla said, tossing a square silver foil packet on Wendy's pillow. "Enjoy."

Wendy laughed at Kayla, who sailed out of the bedroom with one last glance over her shoulder, complete with sly wink. Wendy sat there for a moment, listening to Kayla whistle as she made her way into Frankie's bedroom and out again, down the hall and into the bathroom, closing the door. A moment after Wendy heard the blast of shower water against the vinyl curtain she decided, *What the hell? Better seize the moment.*

When she whispered Alex's name in his ear, he mumbled something unintelligible in the "go away" or "leave me alone" family of dismissals. Obviously, more assertive measures were required. She grabbed the hem of her nightshirt, pulled it up and over her head, and tossed it on the floor near where the two linen dream sachets had fallen. She was without a bra, wearing only a pair of French cut, black silk panties. *That seems about right.*

This time, when she whispered in Alex's ear, she pressed her chest against his back, and slid her hand under the waistband of his pin-striped pajama bottoms. Kissing the back of his neck, she set about the pleasant task of arousing him in more ways than one.

As her feathery caresses progressed to firm strokes, Alex took notice, in more ways than one. "Oh—Ahh!" he said. Finally, despite the early hour, she had his full and undivided attention.

After a frenzied but delightful blur of preliminaries, Wendy found herself pleasurably breathless but ready to proceed, except for one minor detail. She reached up and found the foil packet now underneath the pillow, ripped it open and removed the latex ring inside. She waved it at Alex, diverting his attention from other important matters.

"Oops," he said, a little breathless himself.

"Almost," Wendy agreed. When he reached for the condom, she shook her head. "Come closer. Let me put it on." He was more than happy to oblige. When she finished unrolling the condom, she gave him a healthy squeeze and said, "You may now resume course, sailor."

Alex flashed a sly smile. "Full speed ahead?"

"Belay that," Wendy said with a mock frown. "Slow and steady as she goes . . . but we better finish this before Kayla finishes her shower."

Alex canted his head, as if hearing the running water for the first time. "I'm up to the challenge."

Wendy smiled. "Couldn't help noticing."

He lowered his mouth, taking her left nipple gently between his teeth as he slipped deep inside her in one nerve-tingling stroke. Despite her call for moderation, she found herself urging him along.

Later, as Alex lay trembling beside her, taking deep breaths, Wendy looked over and said, "By the way, Kayla wants to know if you're coming."

"Kinda personal, but I think I've answered that question."

Wendy chuckled, realizing she hadn't heard the shower running for quite some time. As if on cue, Kayla called from Frankie's bedroom. "Shower's free, sleepyheads."

Alex frowned. "Think she knows?"

"Who do you think left that little foil packet under my pillow, the condom fairy?"

"She—?" Alex scrunched his eyes closed. "Ah, this is embarrassing."

"Only if you let it be," Wendy said, essaying the sophisticated response, especially since Alex hadn't witnessed her bout of blushing. "Answer the question?"

"Will I be escorting you to the mysterious clearing? Of course I will."

"Good," Wendy said, grinning. "We need someone for shovel detail."

"I walked into that one."

Basking under the massaging jets of a hot shower, Wendy was thankful she'd permitted herself a small bit of personal time—intimate time—with Alex. Oh, she'd thoroughly enjoyed the experience on the physical level. But it was more than that. In the back of her mind, the clock was ticking, her time running out. She sensed the approach of danger with a renewed awareness of the fragility of life, the fleeting nature of things too often taken for granted and the everyday vulnerability of the people one comes to love. She would treasure those moments because she knew with grim certainty there were no guarantees. What had the Crone said? *Many will die . . .*

Despite the steaming heat of the shower, Wendy shivered with a sudden dread that seemed to infuse her bones with ice. A premonition of things to come . . . a presentiment of the dead of winter.

By 7:30 AM, they were dressed, bundled in coats, scarves and gloves, and ready to take the Pathfinder to Wither's clearing. Alex suggested breakfast, via drive-thru window if necessary, but Kayla vetoed the whole idea of food. "Believe me," she said grimly. "You don't want to go there with a full stomach, because you won't leave with one."

Wendy pointed her key fob at the Pathfinder, about to disengage the locks, when she noticed the approaching police car. "Somebody forget to pay a parking ticket?"

"It's Bobby," Kayla said, frowning at the morning complication.

The black-and-white squad car parked behind the Pathfinder, engine idling.

"Bobby is . . . ?" Alex said, glancing at Wendy. He was holding the shovel—conspicuously *not* a snow shovel—that he'd retrieved from the small maintenance shed in back of the cottage. "Oh, Bobby. McGee—no, that's the Joplin song. McKay!" Alex nodded. "Are we getting a police escort?"

"No," Kayla said, her voice harsh. "He's not coming."

"You'd better tell him," Alex said, looking about as guilty as a grave robber up to his knees in cemetery dirt.

A tall, square-jawed policeman with brown hair and an immaculate mustache climbed out of the squad car and looked over the roof lights, frowning at Kayla. After a moment, he flashed an unconvincing smile. "Hi, Kayla."

"Hey, Bobby," she said, with a quick, friendly wave.

"How'd he find you?" Wendy whispered.

Kayla spoke without moving her lips. "Told him I was staying over last night."

Wendy nodded. *Ask a simple question . . .*

As the deputy walked around the back of the police car, Kayla stepped forward to meet him halfway. "We were just heading . . . out," Kayla said. She reached up and gave him a peck on the cheek. After a quick hug, he stepped back, holding onto her right hand. Again, he frowned, leaving something unsaid. "I'll call you later, Bobby. Okay?"

"Mind telling me where you're headed?"

"Still a free country, right?" she said, canting her head and sporting a teasing grin to take the sting out of avoiding his question.

"All the same, the roads are a bit treacherous in places," he said. "Bad places, dangerous places."

"I'll keep that in mind, Deputy McKay."

Bobby sighed. "Enough games, Kay. I know what this is about."

A bit defensive, "Then why ask?"

"To see if you'd lie to me."

"Withholding information is not the same as lying."

"It's obstruction of justice," Bobby said.

"What crime?"

Bobby seemed flustered. "Trespassing. That area is posted—private property."

Wendy stepped forward. "Actually, that's not a problem."

"Wendy Ward, right?"

"Yes, but—"

"Knew it. Soon as she told me Wendy Ward was back in town, that she was staying here overnight, I figured this was what you had planned. So, tell me, why isn't trespassing a problem?"

Wendy cleared her throat. "Because I own that land."

"What?" all three asked simultaneously.

Wendy couldn't decide who seemed most surprised.

"The murder investigation turned up a will in the Stone house," she said. "I suspect Wither had Stone leave everything to me. Of course, she assumed she would be living her new life inside my body, so it makes sense. Matthias Stone probably wasn't too thrilled though. He seemed to stray from his faithful service and . . . okay, now I'm just babbling."

"But the victims? What about civil claims?"

"True, Sheriff Nottingham explained everything in a Matthias-was-a-serial-killer scenario for the official reports, but Wither wanted that land, so I thought I should keep it, at least until I found out why."

"But how?"

"I had the property appraised, then paid twice the market value to the victims' families, using funds from my parents' estate. Probably a lousy real estate investment, but I thought it might be important for Abby, Hannah and me, and Kayla now, of course."

Bobby looked at Kayla. "You think going back there solves anything?"

Kayla nodded.

"Then I'm coming with you."

"Bobby, this isn't police business."

"I'm beyond that," Bobby said. His voice softened. "If it's important to you, it's important to me."

Kayla lifted his hand and pressed it to her cheek. She had tears in her eyes. "Bobby, I need to do this without you. Please understand."

"I don't," he said, shaking his head. "I can't."

"I may not like the answers I find there," Kayla said. "And, if the worst is true, I couldn't bear for you to be there and see me."

"You'll be in danger," Bobby said. "I'm a policeman. I can protect you."

"Not from this," Kayla said. "Not from what might be inside me. Wendy might be able to help. But she's the only one."

"What should I do? What do you want me to do?"

"Wait," Kayla said. "Just wait for me. That's all. Just wait here and . . . hope for the best."

Bobby looked at each of them, his gaze settling on Alex and his shovel. "What's your story?"

Alex coughed and cleared his throat uncomfortably. "I'm, uh, manual labor. I mean, Alex Dunkirk. Friend of Wendy, junior at Danfield."

Bobby looked at Kayla for a moment, then turned his attention to Wendy. "I talked to Sheriff Nottingham," he said. "He explained some things to me. After Kayla and I were out there in those woods. This is all strange, to say the least. Don't know what to . . ." He sighed. "Well, I do know something isn't right out there. Not close to being right." Wendy nodded. She knew what he was trying to admit, even if his own logic fought him every step of the way. "What is out there? Can you tell me that?"

"An echo," Wendy said. "An echo of evil."

Bobby nodded. "Sheriff called the town a tuning fork, still vibrating."

"Well, that place is where the vibrations began. Intentionally laced with evil to keep people away." Wendy had been about to say *sane* people. "Because Wither hid something there."

"Something you believe will be . . . helpful?" Bobby asked Wendy the question, but he was watching for Kayla's reaction.

"Something of Wither herself," Wendy said. "Her plans for her coven. Plans which, eventually, included Hannah, Abby and me."

"What about Kayla? From what the sheriff told me, she wasn't supposed to be part of Wither's reborn coven."

"For all practical and magical purposes, Gina Thorne became Wither," Wendy said. "And Gina picked up where Wither left off. Starting a new coven with Jensen Hoyt and Kayla. But she also failed. Jen died in the explosion and Kayla . . . escaped before Gina could convert her."

Bobby sighed, a resigned sound, and nodded. He placed his hands on Kayla's shoulders and gazed into her eyes as if he might never see her again and needed to remember them forever. "Call as soon as you're out of there."

Kayla nodded.

Bobby looked them over again. "One of you damn well better have a cell phone."

Wendy patted her pocketbook. "Don't worry, Deputy McKay. I'll take care of her. Promise."

Alex drove to the old Stone property, with Kayla in the backseat staring out the passenger-side window, Wendy beside her, watching her facial reactions to their surroundings as the Pathfinder slowed, noticing the slight tic beneath her left eye. "Here," Kayla whispered.

"Pull over," Wendy instructed Alex.

A short walk to the charred timbers of the old barn, a place that made Wendy uncomfortable, but not to the degree it had when she hovered there in astral form. Kayla led the way toward the ruin of Stone's battered old ramshackle farmhouse, then veered off to the right onto the vague suggestion of a trail.

Snow crunched under their boots. The frigid air chilled their lungs with the crisp scent of pines and spruce, but seemed lacking in oxygen. Walking was a breathless struggle, and anxiety began to claw at Wendy's gut, equal parts dread and nausea. The others felt it too. Something wanted them to turn around and go away, run away, but they fought the impulse.

"Just ahead," Kayla said. "Almost there."

But hours seemed to pass before the press of trees opened and revealed the circular clearing, maybe ten feet wide, with a long flat stone the size of a bench lying across the far side. Alex glanced at his wristwatch and shook his head in disbelief. Wendy recalled Kayla's description of lost time on her first trip to the clearing.

Kayla's face was unusually pale. "So," she said, visibly trembling. "We made it, but . . . I don't feel so hot."

Bobby McKay had been half tempted to follow them, but he figured that would irritate Kayla no end. He thought he might be reacting emotionally, instead of logically, and wanted to give himself enough time to clear his head. The fastest way to regain objectivity would be to find a sounding board, someone he could trust enough to let himself come across as . . . well, crazy. He knew the perfect person. Turning the patrol car around, he returned to downtown Windale.

As he swung his patrol car into the parking lot of the Windale Public Safety Building, he saw Sheriff Nottingham descend the back stairs and stride toward his own car. Stopping perpendicular to the sheriff's car, Bobby lowered his window. "Sheriff! Got a minute?"

"What's up, Bobby? I have a situation at home."

"Serious?"

"Christina can't find Abby."

"This can wait," Bobby said. "Need help?"

The sheriff shook his head. "No, it's okay. Abby's done this before. Wanders off into the woods behind our house. I'm sure she'll turn up soon. Probably before I make it home."

"Good. I'll make it quick. I'm worried about Kayla."

"She's a tough girl," Sheriff Nottingham said. "Not much she can't handle."

"This might be one of those things."

"How so?" The sheriff blew into his hands and rubbed them together.

"Hop in," Bobby said, nodding toward the passenger door. "Heater's running full blast."

"Think I will," the sheriff said. A few seconds later he was in the police car, warming his hands at the vents. "What's on your mind, Bobby?"

"The evil tuning fork." Bobby stared at his own hands, which were white-knuckling the steering wheel. *Tell it plain and simple,* he coaxed himself. *According to the sheriff, he's seen a lot worse.* "She's heading back to that place . . . in the woods, where she passed out. The Stone property."

"Why?"

"Says she needs to find out something about herself," Bobby said. "Something I might not like."

"I'm not sure what that means, Bobby, but it wasn't a good idea to let her wander in those woods alone."

"Oh, she's not alone. The worst part, she practically admitted she was in danger, but said I couldn't help her. Said only Wendy could."

"Wendy Ward?"

"That's who she's with. Wendy and some Danfield junior, Alex somebody."

"Dunkirk," the sheriff said. "He is—was Wendy's boyfriend. But I wasn't aware she was back in town." The sheriff rubbed his jaw pensively.

"Apparently she rushed back from Minneapolis to talk to Kayla," Bobby said. "Kayla was upset, but I got the impression they *planned* this together. The trip to the woods. What do you think it means? Should I be more worried than I already am?"

"I honestly don't know what it means, Bobby," the sheriff said. "If I had to guess, I'd say it involves Wither somehow. By itself, I would chalk this trip up to simple curiosity, Wendy trying to learn more about Wither. Nothing wrong with that. After all, Wendy owns that land."

"So I heard."

"By itself, the threat from this trip would seem to be minor . . ."

"But?"

"But Wendy's hurried return to Windale, combined with the *haste* of the trip and Abby's sudden disappearance . . ."

"But you said—"

"That was before I knew about Wendy's return. She and

Abby are close, ever since the Wither business. All these separate pieces might be coincidence, but I distrust coincidence these days."

"Because of the vibrating tuning fork?"

"Yes. Think about it. Wendy's back, Kayla's worried about something in Wither's woods, and Abby's missing. It's time I had a serious talk with Ms. Ward, Bobby." He shook his head slowly, thoughtfully. "I have a bad feeling."

"Did I mention I have a bad feeling about this place?" Alex said.

He stood with the shovel clutched high in both hands. Kayla thought he looked like a hockey player about to commit a cross-checking foul. His nervous gaze traveled from one end of the clearing to the other and back again.

Wendy's reaction was mixed, curiosity at her own aversion, along with concern for Kayla. Wendy looked at her and frowned. "Are you okay?"

"A little light-headed," Kayla said. But it was more than that and Wendy seemed to read it in her face. "Don't worry. I'm cool. I'll get through this."

Wendy gave Kayla a probationary nod. After a moment, she crouched and ran her palm along the barren ground—no grass or snow, just packed earth—before scratching some of it up with a fingernail. Kayla experienced a flash of last night's dream image, the blood rain making crimson mud out of this soil. Eventually Wendy made her way to the long flat stone with its stain-mottled surface, and knelt before it. "This wasn't in the dream."

"Probably came later." Kayla approached Wendy, but kept her gaze on the stone, as if expecting it to shatter the moment she stopped paying attention. At the thought of touching the stone again, she felt a wave of dread and . . . desire, selfish desire. She needed to possess what lay beneath, while keeping it from anyone else who would dare to touch it. "It's a seal," she said to Wendy, indicating the stone. "A magical seal."

"How do you know?"

"I just do," Kayla said, hugging herself. Wendy shrugged, then reached out to touch the stone. "No!"

Alex stepped forward, concerned. Wendy's hand was inches from the splotchy surface of the stone, poised there. "Kayla?"

"Don't you remember? The dream? 'Only the blood. Others will know only death.'"

"The trap," Wendy said, nodding. "Tell me again what happened when you touched it?"

"It's crazy, I know, but I thought . . . I felt the stone vibrate. Then my nose started to bleed . . . and when I tried to stand up, I passed out."

"Let me try," Alex said, hefting the shovel. "I have the proverbial ten-foot pole here. Granted, as ten-foot poles go, it's only about five feet, but it should make a good lever anyway." Wendy and Kayla stepped back. Alex aimed the pointed tip of the shovel blade under the corner of the stone, placed his Timberland boot heel against the flat top edge of the blade and pushed the tip down into the dirt. He changed position, placing both hands over the wooden shaft of the shovel, pushing down to pry up the stone. Metal screeched against stone and a blue spark ignited into a jagged blue bolt of electricity that lanced up the length of the shovel, seized Alex and tossed him across the clearing.

Kayla screamed.

Wendy uttered a strangled cry, but rushed to Alex's side

the moment he landed. She kneeled beside his convulsing body, but instead of touching him, she pulled off her multi-bead bracelet. Pinching a stone or two between her left thumb and forefinger, she closed her eyes and extended her right hand to Alex's chest. After a few moments, Alex's convulsions subsided. Kayla blinked several times at a trick of the light, thinking she'd seen a momentary aura of golden light surrounding his body.

Sitting back on her heels, Wendy appeared winded, taking several deep breaths, but she smiled as Alex rubbed his head and sat up. "Feel better?" she asked.

A tentative nod at best. "Yeah, but talk about a kick-ass static shock!"

This is stupid, Kayla thought. *It wants me.*

Resigned, she walked around to the far side of the flat, stained stone—the seal—acknowledging at last the likely source of those dark splotches. After all, Wither had come back to this place more than once. She kneeled before the stone and pulled off her gloves, stuffing them into her jacket pockets. Taking a deep, tremulous breath, she held her hands over the surface, palms down.

"Kayla!" Wendy called, starting toward her. "No!"

"It has to be this way, Wendy," Kayla said. "It's the only way."

Wendy had healed Alex all too well. Before she could take two full steps toward Kayla and the seal, he caught her around the waist and pulled her back. "She's right! You know she's right."

"Let me conjure a protective sphere around her!"

"Won't work," Kayla said. "Can't touch the stone if I'm sealed in your magic bubble."

"Then I'll think of something else! Just give me some—"

"No, Wendy," Kayla said. "Shield yourself and Alex, if you want. I don't have a choice. I have to give this bitch what she wants, or we'll never know the truth."

"Fuck!" Wendy shouted, out of pure frustration.

Kayla couldn't really blame her, but Wither would not be denied. She wanted her pound of flesh or, in this case, blood for a stone.

"Alex," Wendy said. "Stay close to me!" Apparently she was taking Kayla's advice to conjure a protective sphere around the two of them.

A shudder twisted Kayla's spine, a wave of nausea roiled in her stomach, but she'd made up her mind. "Here goes!" She slapped both palms down on the coarse stone. "Oh, shit," she moaned, her arms trembling.

"What's happening?" Wendy asked, edging closer.

"It's vibrating again," Kayla said. "Down to my bones . . . *can't you feel it?*"

"No," Wendy said. "From here, you're shaking, but the stone is still."

"Suppose that makes more—" Kayla swooned, but caught herself before her face smacked the stone. Took some effort to raise her head. Made her wonder if she had hit the altar after all, since blood was flowing from her nostrils, across her lips, and dripping on the coarse gray stone, forming an uneven puddle between her splayed hands. Even as she stared at the dark puddle, the rock seemed to absorb it, like an offering. All at once, the stone stopped vibrating. She raised her palms from the stone and wiped the blood from her face with the back of one hand. "It's safe now . . . safe to move the stone."

Wendy nodded, but her eyes were wide, her face a shade or two paler than it had been moments ago. Kayla forced a bitter smile and said, "You saw it?"

Wendy swallowed hard, nodded.

"What?" Alex looked back and forth between them. "Saw what?"

"Isn't it obvious?" Kayla asked, uttering a harsh little laugh.

"Her blood," Wendy said, her voice soft and flat. "Her blood is black."

Alex stared at Kayla's face, noticing what was left of the smudged dark blood, already drying on her lips and chin. "Black? Like . . . does that mean . . . ?"

"Kayla?" Wendy said. "How do you feel?"

"Light-headed," Kayla said. "Weak as a kitten . . . and hungry. But that's all." *In other words, it's safe to lower your protective sphere.* Kayla left that last thought unsaid, afraid to confirm that Wendy no longer trusted her. "Can't prove it, but I still feel like me inside."

Wendy nodded cautiously, her fingers sliding across her bracelet again. "Alex, you okay for shovel duty?"

"Whatever you did before, I feel great. Hungry, but great."

"We'll brunch later," Wendy said. "Right now, let's see what's in Wither's pit and get the hell out of here."

"Can't be soon enough for me," Kayla said.

Alex wedged the shovel blade under the rock again, but this time gave only a tentative push down on the handle. Metal scraped rock, but without any sparks or energy bolts. As promised, Kayla had disarmed the trap.

Alex pried the flat stone up to a forty-five-degree angle, then Kayla and Wendy kneeled on either side of him and flipped it over. With the stone seal out of the way, Alex was about to push the shovel tip into the dirt, but Kayla stopped him.

"Let me check first," she said. "Might be another booby trap." She brushed her hands across the ground that had been covered by the stone, from one end to the other and back again. No vibrations, odd sensations or premonitions. She felt only a human sense of dread at what they'd find at the bottom of the pit.

Within five minutes of digging, Alex discovered the first human bone, what looked like an adult femur, split in half. Kayla clapped a hand over her mouth in revulsion. Wendy shook her head and grimaced. Kayla thought, *This is only the beginning.*

Alex cursed when he found the other half of the femur, then again when he found the finger bones, and a fractured jawbone. Near the bottom, he uncovered what looked like a mound of round stones but were actually human skulls, some of them too small to have belonged to adults, all lined up carefully, like eggs in a carton. Kayla staggered away, fell to one knee and vomited a bitter string of bile. She was still trembling, her breathing ragged, when Alex called, "Found it!" He'd removed the skulls by this time, and had tossed the shovel aside. "Need help with this."

Kayla returned to the gaping hole. Mercifully, Wendy had pushed the skulls and assorted bones past the tree line. Kayla could still see them, but only if she made an effort. Instead, she peered over their shoulders down to the bottom of the hole and saw a small ironbound chest. Though the metal had rusted in spots, the chest seemed structurally sound and in remarkable shape considering its age and where it had spent those years. *Magical preservation?* Kayla wondered. *If so, what else?* "Better let me check it," she said. "Wouldn't put it past her to pack one more whammy into her pit of doom."

They backed away, giving her space to lie on her stomach and extend her arms straight down into the hole. Her fingers touched the surface of the chest. The iron bands were cold as ice, making her fingers ache. The wood felt spongy, strangely organic. But she sensed no threat or power emanating from the chest. Spreading her arms to grip the sides, she pulled the chest from its earthen vault, but she could only lift it so far. "It's slipping. Somebody grab it!"

Alex circled to the other side of the hole and lowered himself across the mound of loose dirt. He reached down and together they brought the chest out. Couldn't have weighed more than thirty pounds. Kayla glanced at the bottom of the hole, half expecting to see a squirming nest of eels or snakes or, worse, more human remains, and was relieved to see only dirt. She turned her attention back to the black, ironbound chest, basically a three-hundred-year-old safe-deposit box. She uttered a bitter laugh. "We're guilty of making an unauthorized withdrawal from the First Infernal Bank of Wither."

Alex kneeled in front of the chest and discovered a heavy but crude padlock securing the contents of the chest. "Old-fashioned lock," he said. "I could smash the lock plate with the shovel, or chop through this old wood."

"Better not," Wendy said. "We don't know what's inside or how fragile it is."

"What then? Look around for a key? Or phone a locksmith?"

"Neither," Wendy said. "Allow me."

Alex stepped aside and Wendy kneeled before the chest. She pulled her crystal necklace out from under her coat, held the crystal in her left hand and extended her right to the face of the lock. "Shouldn't be too complicated."

Kayla looked a question at Alex, who smiled and said, "She never told you she was a Wiccan safecracker-in-training?"

Thirty seconds later they heard a loud ratcheting click.

Wendy removed the lock from the plate, tossed it aside, then flipped open the top of the chest. They gathered around and peered at the only item it contained.

"Some kind of ledger," Kayla said, disappointed.

"It's so old," Wendy said. "Maybe it's her Book of Shadows or the equivalent. Safe to touch?"

Kayla pressed her fingers to the dark surface. Nothing. She nodded to Wendy, who lifted the tome out of the chest and ran her fingers across the stained, dark leather cover, engraved with the letter W. Kayla recalled her vision in the diner.

Less than an inch thick, it was possibly the crudest sort of book imaginable, hardly worthy of the designation. The leather cover was more of a protective wrap—*a Puritan dust jacket,* Kayla thought—and the pages inside were loose, with brittle yellowed edges. After a moment, Wendy tried to lift the cover. She frowned. "It's stuck!" Her fingernails clawed under the edge of the leather wrap to no effect. "Like it's petrified."

Kayla shook her head, understanding now. "Not petrified. Sealed. Look at the stains."

Wendy paused in her attempts to pry the book open and examined the coarse leather cover again. "Oh—that means it wants . . ."

Alex kneeled down beside them. "What?"

"'Only the blood,'" Kayla repeated, taking the book from Wendy. *It will never open without more black blood. Each time I bleed black for this bitch, what is it doing to my insides? Wicked irony there. Only way to find out is to bleed a little more.* She struggled to find her voice. She needed to be sure she was making the right decision. "You really think this will help us?"

"It has to, Kayla," Wendy said. "She's still a mystery, a millennia-old mystery. The more we find out . . ." She shrugged, reluctant to make guarantees. "It has to . . ."

"Okay, I'll try," Kayla said. "But, not here. Not again."

"I'm all for leaving this godforsaken place behind," Alex said. "And never coming back."

Wendy nodded. "It's unanimous. Let's go."

As they embarked upon the narrow path back to the old Stone farmhouse and the remains of the barn, Kayla held the book and rubbed her hand across the leathery cover, hoping it contained some sort of closure for all of them. "This is all that's left," Kayla said, her voice harsh with disgust. "Wither's damned legacy."

TRAVELING: I-80 EAST, I-69 SOUTH
OUTSIDE JAMESTOWN, INDIANA
POKAGON STATE PARK AREA

"There's our exit, Eleanor," Sal Orsini said, pointing out the windshield of the Winnebago. His other hand made a nervous pass through his thinning gray hair. Hated turning the wheel of the RV over to Eleanor, but he'd been driving for five hundred miles and his eyes weren't getting any better. "We want south sixty-nine. Puts us fifty miles north of Fort Wayne."

"I can read the sign, Sal," Eleanor said. "I'm not blind. Go sit in back and relax." She applied the brake and swung the RV onto the exit lane.

Not likely, he thought. Eleanor was a distracted driver under the best of conditions and this trip was an anxiety-inducing nightmare. Snow squalls seemed to follow them wherever they went, their own personal storm clouds. And all this madness because Rachel decided to get married in the dead of winter. *What we put ourselves through for our grand-children,* he thought.

"Don't stand there, hovering over my shoulder," Eleanor said. "Watch something on the TV."

"In this storm? Reception will be lousy."

"Put in that Jack Lemmon video you brought," Eleanor said, exasperated. "My word! You are the world's worst back-seat driver."

With a noncommittal grunt, Sal lumbered over to the table and slid into the booth. The TV/VCR unit was mounted on a Lazy Susan, plugged into one of the RV's overhead electrical outlets. Without much hope, he turned on the set and tried to find a clear VHF station and saw mostly snow, caught the random word or two of audio. Anything would be better than slipping *The Out-of-Towners* into the VCR. When they'd left Minneapolis, it had seemed an appropriate choice, especially humorous. But the long nerve-wracking drive had sapped his appreciation for humor right out of his bones. And Eleanor hadn't wanted him to bring along any violent war films or thrillers.

Disgruntled, Sal crossed his arms over his barrel chest and attempted to make sense out of the crumbling, distorted television images. *Waste of time,* he thought. *Better off behind the wheel no matter how damned tired I am.* He'd brought along a copy of the new Hawking, *The Universe in a Nutshell*, but his eyes were too bleary to look at fine print, even with his bifocals. *Fine print? Hell, I can barely read traffic signs any —*

Whap—BANG! Whap—BANG! Whap—BANG!

"Sal!?"

"I hear it." *Coming from the roof,* he thought.

"What is it?"

"Sounds like something's come loose."

"I'm worried. What if it falls off?"

Sal grunted. "Then it won't make any more noise."

"Salvatore Orsini! What if it flies off and smashes some-body's windshield!"

"All right, all right," Sal grumbled. "Pull over. I'll check it out . . . and freeze my ass off in the bargain."

"Rachel offered us plane tickets," Eleanor reminded him.

"Told you a hundred times, Eleanor, I'm not getting on no damn airplane."

Two minutes later, bundled in his navy blue parka and black leather gloves, Sal walked around to the back of the RV. The darkness on this deserted section of highway was relieved only by their flashing hazard lights. Worse, the snow had kicked up a bit, driving the big wet flakes straight into Sal's face, nearly blinding him.

Climbing the narrow ladder on the rear of the Winnebago, he paused when he noticed the damaged metal rungs and cursed under his breath. "Damned teenagers. Destroy every-thing."

As his head cleared the top of the camper, he thought he saw a blur of movement, of darkness in the swirl of snow. He looked left and right but—coming right at him! Nerveless fingers lost their hold on the maintenance ladder. But pow-erful, furred arms lashed out and claws sliced through his parka, ripping into his flesh and hauling him up to the roof as easily as a bear might snatch a fish from a mountain stream. Sal never had a chance.

From below, a woman's voice calls, "Sal? Salvatore!"

Two of them, traveling together. Now one is dead. But it must silence both before feeding. It had to act fast when they turned away from the pulsing blue-white path. Once they turned south, it had to stop them. Having stopped them, it would feed.

It leaves the gutted old man lying atop his vehicle, eyes glassy in death, but first it stares at the undamaged face, learning its features . . .

"Sal? What's taking so long?"

Eleanor had already grown tired of Sal's complaints. *Let him drive the rest of the way, for all I care. I'll relax and watch the stupid movie.* Besides, she hated driving a car in the snow, let alone the ponderous Winnebago. *But the old fool had better not fall asleep at the wheel.*

She sat in the booth and tried to listen to a special news report, made incomprehensible by the poor signal and the ungodly racket Sal was making on the roof. "Sal? Salvatore!" No answer. *In five minutes he'll be yelling for his tool chest.*

Long moments of quiet followed, enough time for her to hear bits and pieces of the news story about a cannibalistic serial killer that had already struck in Fargo and Minneapolis. For once, she was glad they were far from home.

Rapping on the passenger door.

"For heaven's sake, Sal! The door isn't locked! Take off your gloves, and—" She sighed in frustration. "Oh, never mind, I'll get it."

She moved forward again, caught a glimpse of his gray hair fluttering in the wind, and pushed the door open. "They're talking about a serial killer on the news."

He shoved the door aside and scrambled over the passenger seat toward her. "Sal, you left the door wide open!" Too late she noticed something odd about him. *He's too big, and fast . . . his arthritis . . .* "Sal . . . ?" Her voice seemed small to her own ears.

Sal smiled, and his teeth grew long and sharp.

When he shrieked, Eleanor's blood ran like ice water in her veins.

It grabs her throat and takes her down, ripping and tearing until the floor of the vehicle is soaked with blood and entrails. After gorging, it notices tiny voices, hissing and popping. On the table, it sees a small box with colored images, pictures of people moving and talking, images of the plump driver's vehicle, the seat where it killed the man, men in uniforms with badges.

Slowly, it reaches an understanding. These humans are physically weak and helpless, but they have other magic, magic to send moving images to one another. They are warning their kind about its hunting. It has been too careless, leaving human remains out in the open wherever it travels and kills.

The uniformed men carry modern firearms and would turn the hunter into the hunted. But it still has the advantage. They do not know its destination, cannot see the pulsing thread of light that leads to its special prey. They only know where it has been, not where it will be. And it will no longer provide a trail of half-devoured bodies for them to follow. Yes, it has been careless, but it will adapt. If will wait longer between kills and, when it is finished with the carcasses, it will conceal them. By the time the humans discover the hidden remains, it will be too late for them to stop it from reaching and destroying its special prey.

With a large, furred fist, it smashes the picture box. One powerful blow silences the hissing and squawking. It has nothing to fear from humans. They will always be its prey. Their tools may have changed, but their raw, warm flesh and hot blood are as sweet as ever. It reigns as master of this season, the bringer of frigid winds and blinding snow. Despite their fast machines and their picture magic, it is the humans who should be afraid.

All fear the wendigo in the dead of winter.

PART THREE

DEAD OF WINTER

CHAPTER TWELVE

Almost absently, her gaze rarely wavering from the centuries-old book she carried, Kayla led Wendy and Alex away from the clearing, through the dark forbidding woods, to the dilapidated farmhouse. Seemed as if Kayla had walked the path a hundred times or more. *Maybe,* Wendy thought, *some unknowable and alien part of her has done exactly that.* Somehow the twenty-year-old woman with the electric-blue coif and a dozen body piercings was linked to a millennia-old creature of darkness.

They turned left at the farmhouse and proceeded toward the burned wreck of a barn. Wendy hoped the old journal—spell book, Book of Shadows or whatever it was—would shed some light on what Wither planned for her modern-day coven, and offer an explanation and cure for Kayla's . . . infection. *And maybe it will show me how to revoke Wither's curse.*

Whatever answers the book contained, they needed them fast.

"Wendy!" the sheriff's voice called, startling her. "I'd like some answers."

Kayla stopped short, Alex and Wendy flanking her.

The sheriff and Bobby McKay had been waiting for them, standing side by side beyond the ruined barn, seemingly unperturbed by the cold or the light snowfall. The sheriff's arms were crossed, his face a fierce scowl. Bobby's features were a mix of emotions. He stood with his thumbs hooked over his belt, his hat tilted low.

Wendy hoped she and the others didn't look as guilty as she felt, though they hadn't broken any laws. Well, *tampering with a crime scene,* she thought. *But it's hundreds of years old.* "Hello, Sheriff," she called. "Deputy McKay."

"Bobby," Kayla said. "I asked you to stay away."

"I—the sheriff, that is—considering the history of this area, we thought an investigation of the situation was warranted."

"Enough bullshit cop-speak," Kayla said, flaring. "You couldn't respect my privacy? I told you I'd call."

"Easy on him, Kayla," the sheriff said. "If this situation is as serious as I think it might be, he was right to come to me." Kayla looked away, unconvinced. "Well, Wendy? Want to tell me what's going on?"

"We unearthed that book," Wendy said. "It belonged to Wither."

"Where were you? We looked everywhere."

"In the same damned clearing," Kayla said, looking at Bobby. "Oh . . ."

"So why couldn't we find it?"

Wendy answered, "It's protected. Only Kayla can find it."

"Why?"

"That's what we hope to learn," Wendy said. She looked at

the sheriff. "That book might tell us what Wither's coven planned for Hannah, Kayla, me and Abby."

"Was Abby with you?"

"No," Wendy said. Then, "Is she missing?"

"She was, earlier. I thought she might be with you, until I received word from Christina via the police switchboard. Abby's fine. She was wandering in the woods again and lost track of time."

"She had no part in this, but obviously I'm glad she's okay," Wendy said. Though Wendy and the sheriff were aware of Abby's shape-shifting, she'd asked that they guard her secret.

"Is that old book all that you found?"

Wendy sighed, then shook her head. "Bones. Lots of human bones and skulls."

The sheriff took the information in stride, while Bobby gaped in disbelief. The deputy hadn't lived in Windale during Wither's reign of terror. With grim purpose, the sheriff framed the most relevant question. "Any of them recent?"

"No," Wendy said. "They were buried more than a hundred years ago." She couldn't be sure how long it had been since Wither last opened her secret cache. "Possibly two hundred or three hundred years ago."

"Most likely no practical way to identify the remains," the sheriff said, resigned. "However, we will need to see the crime scene."

Kayla was shaking her head. "I'm not going back there right now. Not anytime soon." She glanced at her watch. "We've lost time. I'm already late for work. Besides, Wendy and I need to . . . figure this book out."

Bobby was sympathetic. "If those bones have waited centuries, I'm sure they can wait a little while longer."

The sheriff nodded in grudging agreement. "What exactly is this book?"

"It's magically sealed," Wendy explained. "We'll need time to unlock it."

"Fine, Wendy, but you'd better bring me up to date," the sheriff said. "I have a bad feeling some nasty history is about to repeat itself."

"Trust that feeling, Sheriff," Wendy said. "We're almost out of time."

"I really hate it when I'm right," the sheriff said.

Back at her cottage, Wendy poured fresh coffee for Alex and Sheriff Nottingham, who sat opposite each other at the small pine table, divvying up the sugary spoils from a Dunkin' Donuts box. The sheriff had his eye on the jelly donuts, Alex the cream-filled, leaving the chocolate-frosted up for grabs. Wendy took the dietary high road, however, leaning against the sink to eat a bowl of bran cereal in skim, with a banana chaser.

Wither's journal—which is what they'd taken to calling it—remained magically sealed on Wendy's countertop, a mystery whose resolution was necessarily delayed. Via Wendy's cell phone, Kayla had tried to beg off work at the Crystal Path, but Alissa was swamped with holiday returns and exchanges and needed all hands on deck. She promised Kayla an early exit if she would just get there as soon as possible. Bobby drove Kayla to work in his squad car, straight from the old Stone property, which left her battered Neon parked in front of Wendy's house, along with the Pathfinder, Wendy's blue-tarped Honda Civic, and the Sheriff's black-and-white. Regardless of her work situation, Kayla needed time to recover from her ordeal in the clearing, to regain her sense of self after bleeding black to open Wither's secret cache. If anything, a few hours at the Crystal Path might help her regain her perspective. While they were trudging back to the Pathfinder, Kayla had whispered to Wendy that she couldn't possibly try to open the journal in front of Bobby. Until she was sure of her own identity, that she was not a threat to anyone, Kayla was too vulnerable to expose something potentially detestable inside herself to the man in her life. "I can't let him see me that way." Wendy had replied, "I understand. We'll wait. But not too long, okay?" Grasping the urgency of the situation, Kayla had agreed to make the attempt soon.

While Kayla was away, Wendy briefed Sheriff Nottingham on the details of the past week. The more the sheriff heard, the deeper his frown became. Finally he said, "A lot's riding on the contents of that damned book."

"I hope it has answers for us," Wendy said. "I believe it will. As far as providing a way to revoke Wither's curse or stop the *wendigo* in its tracks . . . I don't know."

"This thing has been hunting you across half the country," the sheriff said in amazement. "How is that possible?"

"A witch's smart bomb," Alex offered.

"Is the creature intelligent?"

Wendy pulled up a folding chair and sat down. "Here's the deal. I have access to three sources of information . . ." In descending order of reliability those sources were: the Crone, who provided the real scoop from a future perspective, but with gaps and time-line uncertainty; the brief vision of the man in buckskin; and the Crystal Path books Kayla had borrowed and brought to the cottage. Wendy explained the Crone's input as psychic premonitions, a concept the sheriff, given his experiences in Windale, was perfectly willing to accept. "Some of the information is reliable, but the rest comes from myth, folklore and legend, which could be skewed or pure speculation. This particular *wendigo* was once a man, probably infected by a pure-bred demon *wendigo* or another possessed-slash-infected *wendigo*. Supposedly purebreds are bigger, but this one is plenty big. It eats raw human flesh, and has the ability to camouflage itself."

"How?"

"Two ways," Wendy said. "A glamour, which is a magic illusion that makes it appear human to its prey. Not sure how sophisticated the glamour is, but theoretically I suppose it could appear as any one of us."

The sheriff grunted. "That's comforting."

"Also, it travels within snowstorms and, because of its mostly white coloring, is camouflaged by snow the way a lion is camouflaged by tall savannah grass. The *wendigo* is adapted for winter, and prefers that season, which is why Wither's original curse, in August, 2000, was only partly successful."

"And you think Wither's curse has a Murphy's Law aspect to it?" The sheriff sipped his coffee. "Whatever can go wrong, will go wrong?"

"Casting the spell did not require proximity to the *wendigo*. I believe it would have worked anywhere. My presence in Winnipeg, however, increased the likelihood of the *wendigo* killing me in record time. Wrong place at the wrong time. Fortunately, I left Winnipeg the same day I inadvertently recast her spell. That gave me a head start. But the *wendigo* nearly caught me in Fargo."

"Could that work against you in other ways? The Murphy's Law thing?"

"God, I hope not. But it's possible, yes."

"And this . . . *wendigo* has already killed four people?"

"Four that it's eaten," Wendy said. "At least since it woke from its long hibernation. But it also beheaded the two guys in the pickup truck. Not eaten, still dead."

"Now the FBI is involved."

"For all the good that will do," Wendy said. "It can't be profiled like a serial killer. They won't be able to catch it and won't know how to kill it. Did I mention its paralyzing shriek? Freezes victims in their tracks."

"We have an advantage the FBI doesn't," the sheriff said. "We don't have to track it. We know its destination. Just a matter of time before it shows up in Windale, looking for you."

Sounds a lot worse when somebody blurts it out like that, Wendy thought.

"The answer's obvious," the sheriff said. "We set a trap for it. When it comes knocking on your door, we punch its ticket."

"So simple," Wendy said with a veneer of sarcasm. "I feel much better now."

"Of course, the plan only works if there's a way to kill it," the sheriff said. "What is this thing's Achilles' heel?"

"Not sure it has one," Wendy said. "Some of the accounts advise throwing excrement at it."

"The old shit grenade," Alex said. "Maybe we should leave a flaming bag of dog crap on its doorstep."

Frowning, the sheriff asked, "Why excrement?"

"Apparently it confuses the *wendigo*."

"Makes two of us," the sheriff said. "What's the point of confusing it?"

"Gives you time to run away," Wendy said. "However,

even if I was the type of girl who flings excrement about, running would only delay the inevitable."

"Give me something else to work with."

"Well, if Windale had a local shaman, he or she might have some sage advice," Wendy said. "Barring that, silver bullets might kill it."

"It really is like the abominable snowman crossed with a werewolf," Alex said.

"Also, not a real happy time if you become infected by a *wendigo*'s bite."

"I'm guessing rabies shots won't cure that."

"No mention of a cure. But the accounts describe how to stop the spread of . . . infection. It was seen as a demonic possession. But no discussion of an exorcism."

"Which means what? You kill this possessed person?"

"First you kill," Wendy said. "Then you chop the corpse into pieces. Finally, you burn said pieces in order to—you hope—kill the spirit so it can't infect others."

"Remind me not to get bitten," Alex said, a little stunned.

"Here's my idea," the sheriff said. "We lay a trap using Wendy as bait—"

"So far, not loving it," Wendy said. "But, continue. Maybe it gets better."

"My men will be armed with silver bullets."

"Where can you buy silver bullets?" Alex asked.

"Never tried," the sheriff said, grinning. "But I know a guy tinkers around with firearms and bullet molds. I'll have him fill hollow point rounds with silver. Don't worry. That's the easy part."

"Could this guy modify a sword?"

"Maybe. You have a sword?"

"Well, usually it's a cane," Alex said. "Sometimes, it's a sword."

The sheriff told Alex to give him the cane-sword before he left, then asked Wendy. "Anything else we can throw at this thing? Holy water, crosses, garlic cloves?"

Wendy shook her head.

"Couldn't hurt to ask. Anyway, once we're set, I'll have my guys keep an eye on your place round the clock. Bobby understands, at least I think he does. Not sure if the others are willing to accept the unexplainable, at least not till they've seen it with their own eyes. In this case, that would be too little, too late. So you know, I'll probably explain the threat as a stalker, big guy, with a fondness for PCP."

"Should put them in the right defensive frame of mind."

"Good," the sheriff said. "Now what about you? Any magic hocus-pocus up your sleeve?"

"A protective spell, which only goes so far. Fire conjuration, which I'll practice, since I have doubts this winter warlock can tolerate fire. And some stuff in the works."

"Worst case," the sheriff said. "We'll be ready to douse it in gasoline." He looked at Alex. "You'll be with Wendy?" Alex nodded. "Familiar with handguns, Mr. Dunkirk?"

"Couple trips to a shooting range."

"Revolver or automatic?"

"Automatic."

The sheriff scratched his jaw. "Might have something for you. A Glock 23, .40 caliber, compact, packs more punch than a nine millimeter. Department's plan is to switch over to the Glock this year, make it our standard firearm. I'll load some silver-tipped rounds into the clip for you. But it stays in the house. And you return it soon as we put this thing down." Alex nodded again. "And God help us all."

Before Sheriff Nottingham left, Alex's gargoyle-headed cane-sword in hand, he made Wendy promise to advise him if Wither's journal provided any useful information. Wendy walked him to the door and locked it behind him, while Alex cleared off the small dining table. Returning to the kitchen, Wendy placed the journal on the table, where she sat in one of the pine chairs, and stared at it for a while. Alex sat down opposite her, silent but, she thought, holding something back. "What?"

"Nothing. It's just . . . I think we should warn them."

"Who?"

"The FBI, for one."

"And tell them what, exactly? There's a dangerous serial killer on the loose? They already know that. That it consumes human flesh? Ditto. Alex, what can we add?"

Alex frowned in thought, first interlacing his fingers, then cracking his knuckles. "We could tell them about the silver bullets."

"I'll rephrase the question. What can we tell them that they'll believe?"

"What's wrong with telling them to use silver bullets?"

"And when they ask *why* silver bullets?"

"I see your point. Suddenly we're candidates for the loony bin."

"Nothing you say will make them listen," Wendy said. "In a way, I hope it eludes them. It won't be stopped. And whoever gets in its way will die."

"It kills to feed," he reminded her.

"I know," Wendy said bitterly. "So I probably shouldn't try to revoke the curse."

"Why?"

"Because, right now the curse is compelling it to get here fast—"

"Yes! To kill you!"

"Believe me, I'm not overlooking that little detail," Wendy said. "But think about the alternative. What happens if I whip up a spell that takes me off its most wanted list?"

"You'd be safe."

"Yes, I would be safe."

Alex pursed his lips. "That was a trick question, wasn't it? Because, if it's not after you, it would probably wander around aimlessly all winter working up an unhealthy appetite every few days."

"Not knowing where it will strike next, we would be helpless to stop it. With the curse in force, the fewest number of innocent people are in danger."

"Yeah, but you're one of the few."

"Wrong," Wendy said. "I'm partly responsible for this, which is all the more reason for me to stop it." Once again, Wendy tried to peel back the leather covering on Wither's journal, but she couldn't raise a single corner. It might as well have been a ceramic sculpture. Until Kayla made an attempt to open it, the journal was about as useful as an oversized paperweight. "Few hours to kill," Wendy said. "I should train."

"Can I help?"

Wish I knew a way to practice border vision, but that's out for now. Further progress with astral projection would require time and patience but, according to the Crone, stage two should be sufficient for her encounter with the *wendigo*. Sphere conjuring was a possibility. And maybe . . . "Fire," Wendy said. "The rest of my magic is defensive."

"Best offense is a good defense."

"Maybe," Wendy said. "But I'd feel better having some offensive—as the sheriff would say—hocus-pocus up my sleeve, something to knock this thing on its ass."

"And you're thinking fire?"

"I've conjured fire balls . . . sort of. But I need to learn how to throw them. Not something to try indoors."

"They don't make oven mitts big enough for me to catch fireballs."

Wendy laughed. "I'll also need practice conjuring fire in the cold. Remember the trouble I had in Minnesota with a simple flame?" Alex nodded. "The *wendigo* is shielded by snow and ice, but that shouldn't prevent me from drawing heat from the air."

"Ah, because we're hundreds of degrees above absolute zero?"

Wendy flashed a grin, nodding. "Yes, Crone logic. She said my use of fire wouldn't play a large part in the upcoming battle. Maybe in her past I was unable to conjure fire in the extreme cold and that was why so many people died."

"It's a theory."

"It makes sense, Alex. It really makes sense. I'll need to pick up a few things, then find a place to practice. Somewhere isolated . . ."

"I might know a place."

They stood in the center of Schongauer Hall's deserted parking lot, which had been cleared of snow in readiness for student arrivals the following day. The plows had pushed huge mounds of snow around each lamppost, and against the back corners of the lot.

Wendy parked the Pathfinder at the front of the lot, and Alex had unloaded the supplies, suggesting they confine their activities to the west side of the lot to remain hidden from street traffic. Wendy would need an hour or so to determine if she was ready for fire conjuring in frigid weather.

Every time she looked at Alex, she fought the urge to giggle. He'd draped the flame-retardant blanket over his shoulders like a cape, and clutched the rifle-sized Super Soaker with the resolve of a Green Beret. He'd filled the jumbo water gun with warm water to delay it from freezing. "Honest, Alex," Wendy said. "I promise not to hurl any fireballs your way."

Alex gave a shrug that nearly dislodged the blanket. "Hey, accidents happen."

"You do realize the water gun and blanket are for *my* protection."

"You?" Alex said with mock astonishment. "The wise and powerful Wiccan?"

"Yeah, that works," Wendy said sardonically. "Last time I tried this, I nearly lit my pajamas on fire. I was wearing them at the time."

"Ah," Alex said. "Well then, I stand ready to hose you down the second you look too hot . . . too late!" He shifted his double-handed grip on the large water gun and took a bead on her.

In a warning tone, "Alex . . ."

"False alarm," he said. "As you were."

As soon as she wiped the smile off her face, Wendy took hold of her crystal pendant and began the process of centering herself, beginning with her deep-breathing exercise. Each inhalation was a startling reminder of how cold it was outside, how little heat there was for her to draw upon. Though she was focused, her visualization technique suffered from the harsh reality of the current New England windchill factor. *No such thing as cold,* she reminded herself. *Only the absence of heat. Much, much hotter here than in outer space.* And maybe that was the way to overcome her visualization impasse. Begin with absolute zero in mind, with the frigid, lifeless depths of outer space. She imagined temperatures so low that air itself froze, liquid oxygen, liquid nitrogen . . . she imagined the landlocked frozen depths of Antarctica. Cold so deep that blood froze solid in human veins. Image upon image of unrelenting cold until . . . she came back to Windale in early January and she saw heat all around her, radiating from their bodies, streaming out in their breath, rising off the hood of the Pathfinder.

She extended her palms and imagined all that heat swirling toward her, a vortex of heat mirages spiraling down into her palms, roiling balls of energy, almost glowing. She closed her eyes and filled her mind with heat images as a kind of magical bellows for the energy coalescing above her hands, envisioning sun-scorched beaches and pizza ovens, steamy saunas and hot griddles, campfires and funeral pyres, welders' torches and molten lava, erupting volcanoes and sun flares . . . Her mind filled with one fiery image after another until perspiration beaded on her brow.

"Wendy!"

She opened her eyes and gasped, nearly losing control of the twin fireballs roaring above her outstretched palms, swirling globes of fire the size of basketballs. They burned without smoke because they remained in her control and away from a fuel source. Also, as magical flame, they would emit no heat until they left her control or ignited something. "Wow . . ." she whispered, almost breathless. She hadn't even needed to visualize compressing the heat into an igniting pinpoint. *This is incredible,* she thought. *But is it anything more than a sideshow act?*

"Stay calm," Alex said, stepping forward and pumping up

the air pressure in the water rifle. "I'll hose you down before—"

"Don't!" Wendy said quickly. "I need to know if it's a legitimate weapon."

"I peed myself," Alex said. "Does that count?"

"Stand back," Wendy said, ignoring his joke . . . if it was a joke. She took a hesitant step forward, then another, balancing the flames. Then she turned toward the nearest lamppost and faced the cardboard box Alex had wedged into the mound of snow. As she brought her left hand back to her side in a slow motion windup, she kept the flame well away from her body, clothes and hair. "Ready . . . aim . . ." She flung her cupped hand forward and yelled . . . "fire!"

The fireball left her palm with a lazy topspin, hurtling toward the cardboard box. But less than three feet away from her hand the sphere evaporated in the cold air. The cardboard box, lodged in the mound of snow, seemed to mock her. The remaining fireball still glowed and roiled above her right hand, as impressive as the first had been a few seconds ago.

"I see what you mean," Alex said. "All sizzle, no steak."

"No fuel source," Wendy said. "Once I throw it away, it becomes real flame or vanishes like a cheap stage trick. If I was better at this, I might be able to maintain control longer, long enough to . . ." Wendy sighed. "Or . . ."

"What?"

"Unfortunately, this may be a short-range weapon . . . a very short-range weapon."

"Try it."

Wendy nodded, balancing the fireball as she took a careful step or two up the mound of snow. Now the cardboard box was about five feet away. Allowing for her reach, that should be just about right. Any closer to the *wendigo* would be suicidal. She swung her right arm back, but took a moment to imagine the perfect throw and follow through. Then, exhaling, she hurled the fireball in a looping arc, *releasing* it as her arm flew straight out, pointing at the target. The glowing orange sphere spun through the air with the same lazy topspin, but this time, before it could dissipate, it *whumped* into the top third of the cardboard box and seemed to wrap around it before igniting it.

"Hot damn!" Alex cheered, firing burst after burst from his Super Soaker into the air, like a delirious freedom fighter celebrating a coup d'état.

"It worked," Wendy said quietly, unable to wipe the smile off her face. The box burned and wilted under the *real* fire, smoke curling up and whipping away in the gusting wind. Only the bottom flap of the box, sodden with snow, refused to burn. She turned to Alex, "It's something, right?"

"It's freaky-amazing!" Alex said incredulously. "Remind me never to get you mad at me."

Wendy practiced for over an hour and, as a consequence of her new visualization techniques, hardly felt the cold. Alex wasn't as fortunate. While Wendy managed to work up a literal sweat conjuring fireballs, Alex's face became numb from the cold, his ears as red as tomatoes. When his voice became thick, Wendy urged him to take shelter in the Pathfinder, but he took his safety duty too seriously to abandon her. One moment of lost concentration and her coat could go up in flames.

That moment nearly came when her cell phone rang—BBRREEEEEPP!—interrupting her concentration. Her first, wrong instinct at that moment was to reach for the cell phone in her jacket pocket. The distraction, combined with bringing the fireball in contact with the fuel source presented by her coat, would have been the height of magical idiocy. She should have known better.

Fortunately, as soon as Alex heard the phone ring, he anticipated her reflexive grab for the phone and ran forward, the water rifle clattering to the asphalt as he pulled the flame-retardant blanket off his shoulders.

Seeing Alex charge, blanket flapping, brought Wendy back to the danger of the moment. With a thought she released the heat energy she'd harnessed with her conjuration. Alex wrapped the blanket around her hands and wrists a split second later. Fortunately, she survived the error without any burns.

The call was from Kayla. She'd clocked out early as per her agreement with Alissa, and would be waiting in the bus stop shelter on Theurgy Avenue in ten minutes. "That should give us just enough time," Wendy said to Alex.

They both hurried to the Pathfinder. Now that Wendy had finished channeling enough heat for fireballs, the sweat on her body was evaporating, sending chills down her spine. She turned on the heater and flipped the blowers to high.

"Have you thought about Kayla?" Alex asked, his voice still thick from the cold. "About the black blood?"

"Don't have any answers," Wendy said. "At this point, it could go either way. I keep praying Kayla stays on our team."

"Amen," Alex said.

Kayla was silent on the drive back to Wendy's cottage. She stared out the rear passenger window, following the aimless track of random snowflakes as they marshaled their forces to blanket every surface for miles.

When Kayla first climbed into the backseat, Wendy gave her hand a friendly squeeze, but neither she nor Alex mentioned Wither's journal. They all knew it was waiting there, and that Kayla was the only one who could possibly open it and reveal its secrets. Each of them worried that by tapping into her connection to Wither, Kayla might be giving Wither's life force an inroad into her psyche, a lever to corrupt her soul or take over her mind. What could they say that wouldn't seem trite? *Spare me the platitudes*, Kayla thought.

At the cottage, they piled out of the Pathfinder and started up the walkway, silent if not grim. Wendy, in the lead, stopped and looked at them. "You guys hear that?"

Kayla and Alex exchanged confused glances, but a moment later all three of them heard the sound, which began high pitched, then dropped low. "KEE-*arr!*"

Wendy walked back to the curb and stared up into the overcast sky.

"What is it?" Alex said. "Not the *wendigo* . . . ?"

"No," Wendy said, a nascent smile tugging at the corners of her mouth.

"It's a bird," Kayla said. "Big one."

"KEE-*arr!*"

"Not just a bird," Wendy said. "A hawk." She pointed at the sky, directing their attention to the white-feathered hawk flying lazy circles above the cottage. It banked gracefully, descending in a smooth spiral.

"Some kind of omen?"

"It's not an omen," Wendy said absently. "It's Abby."

Kayla stood beside Wendy. "Um . . . you have a pet hawk named Abby?"

"Not exactly," Wendy said. The hawk had glided lower, not far above the rooftops, and the center of her circular flight had shifted from the cottage to Wendy herself. Wendy held out her arm, forearm parallel to the ground, braced in front of her. The hawk swooped down and, with a great flapping of broad wings, latched onto Wendy's coat sleeve with powerful claws.

After a cautious step backward, Kayla whispered, "Could have fooled me."

"Hi, Abby," Wendy said. She was proud, beaming. *Maybe she taught it that arm-landing trick*, Kayla thought. *Teach it a trick, toss it a mouse?*

A neighbor two doors down had been unlocking his car door and witnessed the display. He shook his head in amazement, but climbed into his car and drove away. Kayla figured the old coot would be on the phone to animal control before the end of business.

Wendy said, "We'd better go inside."

Inside the cottage, Wendy transferred the bird from one forearm to the other so she could slip out of her coat. Its underside was snow white, while above it was brown with white streaks, along with a reddish tail, and yellow legs and toes, with sharp black claws.

Alex and Kayla both kept their distance. Kayla, for one, had a hard time not staring at the sharp beak, which looked more than capable of plucking out an unwary eye. And the way the hawk's head twitched from side to side, staring with an eerie intensity at Kayla then Alex and back again, Kayla had the impression it was deciding whose eyes would be juiciest.

"Don't be afraid of Abby," Wendy said to them. "She's . . . tame. Aren't you, Abby?"

Amazingly, the hawk's head bobbed down and up once, an avian nod.

"Smart bird," Alex said.

The hawk's head bobbed twice more.

"Abby . . . ?" Wendy said, almost as if she were trying to read the bird's thoughts. "You know Alex and Kayla, right?" One bob. "They're both good friends." Another bob. "Trusted friends." A bob, followed by a head tilt. "Would you like them to . . . get to know you better?"

"I'm not feeding it mice," Kayla said, shoving her hands in her pockets.

For a long moment the hawk stared at Alex, then it swiveled its piercing gaze to Kayla for an equal length of time, head cocked, before returning its attention to Wendy. After another moment, a slow, minimal bob of the head. To Kayla, it almost seemed like hesitant agreement to Wendy's question. *I had way too much exposure to Disney at an impressionable age*, she thought. *I could anthropomorphize a toilet brush.*

"Excuse us for a moment," Wendy said. She walked down the hall to her bedroom and closed the door.

Kayla looked at Alex with an arched eyebrow. He shrugged.

Less than a minute later Wendy returned without the hawk. "Sorry," she said. "She needed privacy."

"Are hawks bashful by nature?" Kayla asked. "Or just this hawk?"

"Just this one," Wendy said with a mysterious smile.

"Maybe she should see a hawk whisperer," Alex suggested, grinning.

Kayla hooked her thumb toward Wendy's bedroom. "You left a bird of prey alone in your room."

Wendy nodded.

"As we speak, it's probably shredding everything you own."

"Or wearing one of her robes," Alex said. He'd been looking down the hall and was now frowning in evident confusion.

"Wearing—?" Kayla followed his gaze. "Oh . . ."

Towheaded Abby MacNeil stood outside Wendy's bedroom door in a belted forest green robe, which fell to her ankles, unsuccessfully attempting to roll up the long, roomy sleeves. With a shrug, she gave up and padded down the hall toward them in bare feet. "Hi, everyone!" she said, grinning ear to ear. "How cool was that?"

"Abby is a shape-shifter," Wendy explained. "Until now, she could only assume a wolf form."

"Promise not to tell anyone else," Abby said. "Okay?"

"Uh, sure," Alex said. He was accustomed to keeping Wendy's and Windale's secrets. Abby's secret shape-shifting life probably seemed one more aspect of that.

"Zipped lips," Kayla said, and had to smile. Abby looked like a girl trying on her mother's clothes, pretending to be a grown-up. *Would a ten-year-old girl who can turn into a wolf or a hawk have the slightest fascination with high heels and lipstick?*

"I thought it would be okay for you to know, because you know about Wendy and Wither and everything. You understand," Abby said. "You won't think I'm a freak, like the kids at my school would, if they knew."

"Of course, we understand, Abby," Wendy said. Kayla and Alex nodded.

"I've been trying to shift into a bird for, like, forever," Abby said, with an appropriate but unconscious flapping of her big-sleeved arms to accompany her enthusiasm. "First, I tried forcing the change, making wings and feathers. Ugh, what a mess! Almost turned myself into a pretzel, instead of a bird."

"You're quite the expert now," Kayla said.

"Thanks to Wendy," Abby said. "She told me to stop forcing my bones and let them decide."

"You talk to your bones?" Alex asked.

"Well, not out loud," Abby said. "But sometimes I can feel when they want to change. If I fight it, the feeling gets worse and worse until I have to give in."

"Sounds like my problem with chocolate," Kayla said.

"Anyway, I wanted to shape-shift into an eagle," Abby continued. "That's all I thought about. Cut pictures out of newspapers and magazines. I drew pictures of eagles, read library books about them, dreamed about them and everything." Abby paused to catch her breath. "But my bones didn't want to be an eagle."

"They wanted to be a hawk?" Alex said, catching on.

"Actually, a red-tailed hawk," Abby said. "I changed for the first time this morning, before school—forgot about the time and got in trouble—but, anyway, I stood on the deck rail and studied my reflection in the glass so I could look it up later at school. My bird back is lighter than the book pictures, maybe because my girl hair is so light. So, don't know why, but my bones wanted to shift to a red-tailed hawk. I came here to thank Wendy for helping me fly."

"Abby, does the sheriff or Mrs. Nottingham know you're here?" Wendy asked.

Abby frowned. "I left a note. For the sheriff. Asked him to bring clothes if I wasn't home for dinner. Guess I should call, huh?"

"Good idea," Wendy said. "Alex could you take the portable phone in the living room and help Abby with that call, while Kayla and I take a look at the . . . other thing."

"Other—? Ah, sure! No problem."

Kayla cast a nervous glance at Wendy. "That time, huh?"

Wendy nodded. They walked into the kitchen area, while Alex grabbed the phone and stayed with Abby in the living room. After Wendy and Kayla sat opposite each other at the small table, Wendy slid the ancient book to Kayla and said, "If I could do this myself..."

"I know," Kayla said. Looking down at the dark, blotchy leather wrap, she exhaled sharply to steady her nerves. "I'm ready. Wish I knew what to do," she said. "When I touched that stone in the clearing, it vibrated under my hands and it made me bleed." She made an exploratory pass with her hands across the coarse cover, but shuddered at the thought that, in all likelihood, Wither had made the cover not from cured animal hide, but from flayed human skin.

Wendy leaned forward. "What?"

"Nothing," Kayla said quickly. "One of those creep-out moments." She sighed, shook her head. "Touching it and ... nothing. No vibrations, no visions, no speaking in tongues, *nada*." Maybe she could never unlock the journal, no matter how hard she tried. If she lacked some metaphysical ingredient in her psyche needed to open the journal, wouldn't that be the best news she'd had in weeks? *Meaning, I get to stay me, after all,* she thought.

"You've touched it," Wendy said. "But have you tried to open it?"

"Of course," Kayla said indignantly. "What are you implying?"

"Do you *want* to open it?"

The direct question made Kayla squirm. *Do I? Am I secretly resisting because I'm afraid of the consequences? How can this stupid book know I don't want to ... I don't want to open it. Shit! I've been kidding myself. That's the problem.* Kayla frowned at her lack of resolve and flashed Wendy an abashed smile. "Great time to go all chicken-shit, huh?"

"I'd be scared too," Wendy said, "if it were me, trying to face what you're facing."

"But you're facing something worse," Kayla said. "Something deadly."

"Don't think for one minute I'm not scared."

"Scared shitless?"

"Terrified shitless," Wendy said. They both smiled. "If it helps, remember this isn't a Pandora's Box we're trying to open. Except for the hope part. This journal should have answers, maybe solutions, cures. Abby is excited about her shape-shifting right now, but we don't know what the consequences are for the rest of her life. She hasn't thought that far ahead—she shouldn't have to—but I do, and so does the sheriff. Hannah is aging too fast. She could need a walker and dentures before her Sweet Sixteen birthday party. Wither used me, more than once. She used you. Wouldn't you like to turn the tables, rip aside the veils, the secrets, and ruin her plans, whatever the hell they were?"

"Damn straight!" Kayla said, smiling. "Okay. All right, I'll try." She raised her palms over the book, not surprised to see them trembling above the engraved W, but she was determined now. She wanted to read Wither's diary, violate the bitch's property and privacy as payback for Gina Thorne's violation of her life. *Wish me luck, Bobby,* she thought as she slapped her hands down on the bloodstained leather cover.

Her forearms began to tremble. She held the book in a white-knuckled grip, the fingernails of her right hand slipping under one folded edge of the dark wrap. Wendy had been unable to peel aside even a corner of the leather cover, but Kayla already felt some separation under the top flap. As she pulled, the quivering sensation spread along the entire length of her arms, into her shoulders, up her neck and down her spine. Her muscles ached, her jaw snapped shut and wouldn't open again, and soon her entire face became a trembling, agonized grimace.

"Kayla . . . ?"

Kayla's vision began to blur and darken, a loss of focus at the periphery of sight that crept toward the center like a spreading ink stain. Tears welled up in her eyes, spilling down her cheeks, dripping on the backs of her outstretched hands and on the leather book cover. To Kayla, everything looked black. She tried to speak but her jaw was locked. "UH—*uh—uh—*"

Wendy came out of her chair, mouthing "*Kayla, let go!*" but all Kayla could hear was the roaring of blood in her ears.

She looked up at Wendy, beseeching—

—but darkness surrounded her—the room tilted, sliding sideways and away—then nothing but—silence and the . . .

. . . darkness . . .

Wendy hadn't been sure what to expect. At first Kayla began to tremble, then she became rigid, her face stiff as petrified wood. Her jaw was clenched shut and she couldn't speak, could only grunt. Then it seemed as if she was about to cry, but the tears that flowed from her eyes were not clear. They were black—tears of black blood.

As Wendy jumped out of her seat to help Kayla, to try to pry her hands from the ancient journal, Kayla teetered in her chair, falling sideways, literally blacking out. But as she spilled out of the seat, with her last conscious act, her hand convulsively pulled back the top flap of the leather cover.

Wither's journal was unsealed and open at last.

Kayla sprawled on the floor.

Wendy dropped to her knees beside Kayla, checking her pulse and respiration, all too aware of the drying tracks of black blood tears on her cheeks. "Kayla? Can you hear me?"

"Hey," Alex said as he walked into the kitchen. "Thought you'd keep it quiet in here with—whoa! What happened?"

"She passed out," Wendy said, distracted. "She opened the journal but fainted. Fell out of the chair."

"Should I call 911?"

"No—no, wait. Let me try to heal her first. Stay out there with Abby."

Kayla moaned softly, started to lift her head, then clamped a hand over her eyes. "Ouch!" she said. "Aspirin—God!—aspirin!"

"Bathroom medicine cabinet," Wendy instructed Alex.

Wendy helped Kayla into a sitting position. Her head hanging forward, Kayla ran a trembling hand through her electric-blue hair. Alex returned with a cup of water and two Extra-Strength Excedrin caplets, which he passed to Kayla. "Let me know if you need anything else," he said before returning to the living room to stay with Abby.

Kayla popped the aspirin in her mouth, gulped down the water, then crumpled the cup into a ball and tossed it in the general vicinity of the trash can. "Why couldn't monster witch bitch invest in one of those tiny padlocks for her fucking black diary?"

"Somehow I doubt she'd have that much trouble unsealing the journal."

"Unsealing? It worked?"

"You don't remember?" Kayla shook her head. Wendy smiled. "Yes, it worked."

Kayla laughed with relief. "Son of a bitch!"

"I'll make a Wiccan safecracker out of you yet."

"Don't do me any favors," Kayla said. Then, "On second thought, you could help me up. Legs feel like overcooked noodles."

Wendy put one arm around Kayla's waist, the other around her elbow, and helped her into the chair. Kayla stared at the open book, took a deep breath, her smile long gone. "I should be thrilled . . . so why am I suddenly scared to death?" Kayla pushed the book—which was no more than a stack of yellowed pages inside the leather wrap—to Wendy. "You first," Kayla said. "I don't have the stomach for it."

Wendy pulled the journal near. The first page was blank, discolored with crumbling, brittle edges. With great care, Wendy picked up the page by a corner and turned it over, laying it to the left of the main pile. The second page was also blank. But the third had a large W scrawled on it. At the bottom right-hand corner was the number 1699. *That's the year she started this*, Wendy thought. Another blank page followed. As she flipped that page over, she glimpsed the next page, full of text. Thick, blotchy letters—*the ink must have bled into the paper*—made by a cramped hand. Wendy attempted to read the writing, but shook her head in disappointment.

Kayla had watched each flipped page with growing anxiety. When Wendy seemed to give up, Kayla leaned across the table on her elbows. "What's wrong? Not English?"

"Definitely not English."

"Middle English? Greek? Latin? Aramaic?"

"No language I've ever seen," Wendy whispered.

"From upside down it looks kinda Cyrillic. Maybe it's Russian," Kayla said. "Any Russian language profs at Danfield?"

"It's not Russian," Wendy said. "It's not . . . anything."

"What about ciphers? Maybe it's encrypted or . . . What do you mean it isn't anything?"

Wendy spun the book around and pushed it toward Kayla. "Read it."

"I don't know the lang—"

"Just . . . examine the first sentence. Closely."

"Okay, that would be gibberish, gibberish, gibberish, and gibberish, gibberish."

"Now read—examine that same sentence again."

Kayla's eyes scanned left to right, twice. "It's not . . . That's impossible!"

"It's different each time you read it. Every character, each time you look at it."

"Any chance it ever switches to English?"

"The language isn't changing," Wendy said. "Each character position is randomly cycling through the same set of symbols. Runes, maybe, but none I'm familiar with."

"Maybe it's like opening it. I have to really want to read it to make it legible."

"Try it."

Kayla pulled the stack close to her, concentrating on the page of changeable text. "Pass me some napkins," she said. "You know, in case I start to bleed from my ears this time."

Wendy shoved the napkin holder her way and waited. With apparent single-minded determination—brow furrowed, upper teeth scraping nervously against her lip ring—Kayla examined the page before her. After almost two minutes, she shook her head in disgust and pushed the journal away. "Please tell me this hasn't been a big waste of my time and your aspirin."

Wendy had no answer for her.

"Hey," Alex said, standing there with Abby at his side. "Now it's too quiet in here. What's happening?"

"Nothing much," Kayla said. She pushed out of her chair and walked away from the table with her hands clasped behind her neck.

"It's open. That's progress."

After Wendy explained the changing pattern of mysterious glyphs, Alex slid into Kayla's vacated seat and studied the page. "Okay to touch?" Wendy nodded. Alex flipped to the next page, which Wendy hadn't tried. She leaned forward, but he shook his head. "Same rotating jumble." Just to be certain, he flipped ahead several pages. "Some kind of encryption. But how to decrypt it when it's never the same letters twice . . . unless . . ."

"What?"

"Grab some paper and pencils and sit your sweet self down beside me."

"What do you have in mind, Alex?"

"Humor me. This will take ten minutes, fifteen tops."

Wendy retrieved the requested supplies from the kitchen junk drawer, a pencil and a blank sheet of paper for each of them. She listened to Alex's idea and thought it worth a try. Apparently Kayla thought so as well, for she returned to the table and looked over Wendy's shoulder. Abby stood on Alex's right, as curious as the adults.

"On three, begin," Alex said. "One . . . two . . . three!"

They both started writing down the symbols in the first line on their own sheet of blank paper, focusing on one letter at a time. When they reached the end of the first line, they returned to the beginning of that line and wrote down the changed version. It took some practice, because some of the symbols resembled complicated ideograms and were difficult to draw. Once they were both comfortable transcribing the strange language, if that's what it was, they repeated the first line twenty times, then compared their sheets, line by line. Wendy's first line differed from Alex's. Her second was also unlike his. Line by line, not one match. Worse, even though they had been writing the same line over and over, as they saw it, none of their twenty lines matched any of the others.

Alex sighed. "Well, it's too small a sample of the entire text, but I have to say, it's completely random. We never saw the same grouping of letters, symbols, whatever they are, at any time. Encryption can't be random, can it? I mean, maybe if we ran this through a Cray supercomputer . . ."

"Encryption is technology based," Wendy said. "I think the only way to decrypt this is with magic, with a spell or incantation."

The doorbell rang.

Alex looked at Abby. "You're busted, young lady."

The sheriff had come for Abby, with a bag of clothes. None too pleased about her disappearing act, he was unaffected by her excitement at being able to shape-shift into a red-tailed hawk. He kneeled down beside her and whispered, "Abby, you need to be more responsible with this ability. Or we need to tell Mrs. Nottingham."

"No," Abby said, almost a squeal.

"You told these people."

"Because they know about this stuff. They don't think I'm a freak."

"Mrs. Nottingham is your mother now, kiddo. She worries about you. If you insist on disappearing, we need to tell her what's happening in your life."

"Okay, I'll . . . I'll think about it."

"Glad to hear it," the sheriff said. "Now go put some clothes on. I need to talk to Wendy." He stood up, patting Abby's shoulder to send her on her way. He waited until the bedroom door closed. "Here's the deal. I want Abby out of here pronto. She can't be here when—"

"Agreed," Wendy said quickly.

"Good. Now, I should have silver bullets tonight. Least enough for one full load per man. And maybe half a clip for the Alex's loaner Glock. Starting tonight, I'll have one of my men posted on this street, in an unmarked car. I'll have the patrol car on duty make regular passes as well. If you decide to go out, call me first and tell me where you'll be. Then tell whoever is parked outside. I'll introduce you to each guy so you know everyone. When the *wendigo* comes for you, we want to be wherever you are. Got it?"

"Got it."

"Good," the sheriff said. "Have you been watching the news?" Lately, none of them had. "Early this morning, Indiana state police investigated an abandoned RV on the shoulder of I-69 South, near Pokagon State Park. They found two bodies, half eaten."

"Oh, God," Kayla said softly.

"Husband and wife," the sheriff continued. "Salvatore and Eleanor Orsini. Traveling from Minneapolis to Fort Wayne for their granddaughter's wedding."

"When?" Wendy asked.

"Exact time of death is unknown," the sheriff said. "Ten, maybe twelve hours ago. And this one answers the intelligence question."

"How so?"

"They were on I-80 East for a while," the sheriff said. "It killed them minutes after they took I-69 South."

"And what?" Kayla asked. "I don't get it."

"Somehow, it knows where I am," Wendy said. "I-80 East takes it toward Windale, more or less. I-69 South takes it farther away. It killed them to stop and hitch a better ride."

"How far is that," Alex said. "From here?"

"About eight hundred miles," the sheriff said. "If it has continued in this direction at an average speed of fifty miles per hour—"

"Sixteen hours to Windale" Wendy said. *To me* . . .

"Since the RV murders, which were twelve hours ago," Alex said. "It could be four hours away now . . ."

"Remember, we're talking estimates all around," the sheriff said. "Estimated time of death, estimated time for the *wendigo* to hitch another ride. It could face delays . . . or it could find a lead-footed driver and make the trip in twelve hours. As of right now, people, be on guard!" He waited a long moment to let that sobering thought sink in. "Have you had any luck with the Wither journal?"

Wendy showed him the indecipherable, changeable text. "Bunch of rotating nonsense, is what it is," he said, flipping back and forth between two pages. "Like an optical illusion. Reminds me of holographic trading cards Max and Ben are collecting. The images change as you tilt them back and forth."

Alex said, "Too bad border vision doesn't work on paper."

Wendy grabbed his arm. "What?"

"Well, it's supposed to help you see through a glamour, right? To reveal the *wendigo's* true form. I figured if—"

"Excellent, Alex!" Wendy said. "Maybe it is a glamour, a spelled illusion to keep the book's contents disguised as random nonsense. Magical encryption! But . . . minor problem. I haven't quite mastered border vision."

Abby returned from the bedroom wearing a powder blue sweater, jeans and boots. She was dragging a red parka behind her by the hood. "I'm ready to leave now," she announced with the impatience and imperial self-importance that comes so naturally to children.

"Yes, we should go," the sheriff said. "Once Abby's safe at home, I'll stop back. Before I leave, let me introduce you to James Kirkbride. He'll be watching your place until eleven tonight, followed by Angelo Antonelli. The men will be taking shifts in an unmarked car outside, so as not to alarm your neighbors. Look for a navy blue Crown Victoria, a few doors down." The sheriff depressed the transmit button on the radio mike clipped to his epaulet and said, "Jimmy. Step inside for a moment."

A minute later, Deputy Kirkbride was at the door, stomping clumps of snow off his boots, brushing a light coating of flakes from the shoulder and sleeves of his coat, a brown leather jacket with a sheepskin collar worn over dark gray uniform pants with gold piping. A big man, he had curly red hair cut short, a pale complexion, gray-blue eyes, acne scarred cheeks and an aquiline nose that overpowered his other features. "Pleased to meet you," he told Wendy, shaking first her hand then Alex's.

"Hi, Jimmy," Kayla said in a familiar tone. "You see Bobby, tell him I'm fine."

"Will do," the deputy said. "So you're stayin' out of trouble?"

"Trouble has a way of finding me, Captain Kirk."

"Aw, Kayla, you know I hate that," he said, chuckling as he put his hat back on with a minor adjustment or two. "Anyway," he said, turning his attention back to Wendy. "Anything suspicious, strange phone calls, noises in back or whatever, you let me know right away. Understood?"

"Sure," Wendy said. "But this crea—creepy guy is not big in the subtlety department. When he shows up, you'll know it."

"We'll nail the perp before he knows what hit him," he said with a confident wink, then turned to the sheriff. "We good, Sheriff?"

The sheriff thanked him and sent him back outside. Then, before he left with Abby, he said, "Don't worry, Wendy. I'll make sure my men realize how dangerous the situation is. Meanwhile, you have my cell number. Anything urgent comes up, call me direct. That goes for anything, uh, magical in nature. But don't fool around with medical emergencies. Use 911. You can always call me later. Clear?"

"Thanks, Sheriff. I appreciate everything."

"Lock the door behind us," he said as he led Abby outside.

"Bye, Wendy," Abby called, waving a bulky mitten in farewell.

"Bye-bye."

Wendy closed the door against the cold and flipped the dead bolt, for all the good a slab of metal would do against a rampaging *wendigo*. Time to assess her situation. She had round-the-clock police protection. Later in the evening, the entire Windale police force, along with Alex, would be armed with silver bullets, which was a good start. Responsible for the magical side of the crisis, she was ill-equipped for the challenge. Too many unknowns. What new and improved protective sphere tricks would help her against the *wendigo*? How did astral projection figure into a battle strategy? And just how was she supposed to develop . . . "Border vision. Thank you, Alex!"

"Maybe you should wait to thank me," Alex said. "Border vision might not work on the book."

"A glamour is just an illusion, a magical disguise," Wendy

said as she walked to the kitchen. Kayla and Alex followed her, attentive. "If an illusion is disguising the text of Wither's journal, then border vision should neutralize it. Anyway, that's my theory and I'm sticking with it." Wendy smiled. "Unless I come up with a better one."

"But you still don't know how border vision works," Kayla said.

"The Crone said the ability is easiest at the periphery of vision, which is a border itself, between that which is seen and unseen by the human eye. It's a common theme. Borders are special places in magic, the borders between inside and outside, darkness and light, between one day and the next, the witching hour."

Wendy turned her chair sideways, facing Kayla and Alex, the table on her right, with the pages of the journal stacked near her elbow. Keeping her gaze forward, she placed her hand on the right edge of the pages and inched them forward, toward the front of her field of vision. Too far forward and the strange glyphs came into focus as cycling gibberish; too far back and she couldn't focus on the large blotchy symbols at all. She continued to make incremental adjustments in the placement of the pages, while keeping her eyes front and center. Although she could see the pages in the periphery of her vision, the image was blurred and useless. Without moving her head, she shifted her eyes slightly to the right, like a second hand moving from twelve to three, with the book at the three o'clock mark. By the time she had adjusted the direction of her gaze and the position of the journal pages to approximate 2:15 on a clock face, she already had a splitting headache. She squeezed her eyes shut against the throbbing pain, but when she opened them again, she let out a gasp.

"Don't tell me," Kayla said. "You see dead people."

"No, smart-ass," Wendy said, but had to laugh. Until that moment, she hadn't been sure which was worse, the tension in the room or her throbbing headache, and if forced, she would have called it a draw. "Words! I can see her goddamn words!"

CHAPTER THIRTEEN

"Tell us," Kayla urged. "What's it say?"

"Says . . . 'Wednesday'," Wendy said. "'Pick up dry cleaning.'"

"Now who's the smart-ass?"

"Sorry, couldn't resist," Wendy said. "Oh, damn . . . I can read this, but it's giving me a splitting headache."

"I know a cry for aspirin when I hear it," Alex said and slipped away.

"Not sure how long I can concentrate on this."

"Skip ahead," Kayla said. "Look for the juicy stuff."

"It's bizarre . . . fascinating. Each symbol is only a fragment of a letter. Before, it seemed like twenty lines per page, but looking at it this way, I see half as many. The symbols change continually; they're almost liquid, like ripples in a pond, but instead of expanding, concentric circles, these ripples are the shapes of letters and words and sentences. The illusion is that the symbols are ever static! We saw the letters change each time we looked at them, but it was like looking at a series of stills from a motion picture reel. With border vision the projector is running and all the movement makes sense." Wendy rubbed her eyes. "Okay, less incoherent babbling and more reading . . ." She squinted at the page. "She's talking about some members of the town, her impressions of their character, who might be dangerous, who might be corruptible, who might be . . . vulnerable." Wendy flipped through some pages.

Alex returned with a bottle of aspirin and a paper cup filled with water. He set both on the table, but Wendy was unwilling—as much as her temples and forehead throbbed in protest over that decision—to take her border vision focus off the pages.

"It's all in here . . . how she enlisted Ezekiel Stone as her keeper with promises of gold and long life, sending him on various . . . 'dark errands' to test his competence and loyalty to her, while 'turning him against the interests of the community, against the interests of his fellow man.' " Wendy flipped through more pages. "Okay . . . here she's talking about checking her body for signs of the change, the 'ascendance of the beast within' . . . how she won't be able to pass as human anymore." Wendy shook her head. "Obsessed with checking the veins in her forearms . . . 'forearms and inner thigh will show the first trace of the black blood within.' "

Wendy stopped reading, aware of Kayla in front of her, pushing her sleeves up to her elbows. "So far," Kayla said. "I'm cool."

Alex said casually, "Feel free to check your inner thighs."

"You wish!"

Wendy turned a few more pages, stopping when she noticed a familiar name. "Oh! Here she mentions Sarah

Hutchins, how she believes Goodman Hutchins might be beating Sarah . . . skipping ahead, skipping ahead—yep, she's confirmed it through . . . 'other sight'? She might be talking about astral projection. Yes, and whispered conversations with Sarah. She offers to help Sarah kill him and make it look like an accident . . . wants to turn Sarah against man, against her nature . . . okay, okay. She mentions the power of the coven, strength in numbers and strength in magic, in corruption . . . skipping again . . . Now she's talking about Rebecca and her seizures, and the lecherous magistrate, Cooke . . . wait, I must have missed an earlier mention, but I think Wither's admitting to killing Rebecca's husband in a church collapse . . . he was crushed and she indicates that was her plan— 'a simple matter really, to arrange the corruption of the structure just where he would be'—to isolate Rebecca, make her vulnerable and desperate because of her seizures."

Wendy stopped reading to unscrew the aspirin bottle cap. She swallowed two caplets with water. "These can't possibly work soon enough," she said, closing her eyes momentarily to help matters along, to try to ease the pain.

"Take a break," Alex said.

"Not yet," Wendy said, continuing to rest her eyes. "I thought this might be a book of spells and rituals, a Book of Shadows, basically, but I'm not seeing much along those lines. Mostly she visualized corruption. She could subvert nature, the natural order of things, bend nature to her will. Her ability to fly must have worked that way. She needed ritual sometimes, apparently . . . but maybe only for subtle magicks."

Finally, Wendy opened her eyes, but spent frustrating minutes regaining her border vision focus. She became impatient with the unfolding tale, and started flipping pages faster, skimming more. She could always revisit sections later.

"Some of this I remember from the lucid dreams, the veridical dreams I had a couple years ago . . . Wither wanting to go into hibernation before the change becomes apparent, she makes enough mistakes in the commission of their murders to be discovered. 'I let these simple folk see what even fools would see to damn us in the eyes of their justice . . ' Looks like Wither wanted them caught to force the hand of the other two women, to convince them to join her coven by mixing their blood with hers, then drinking her black blood. 'These two I have chosen have damned themselves already to survive their station. 'Tis unlikely they will succumb now, given a choice to thrive, given a choice of life everlasting.' She promised them their changed bodies would survive the hanging. She's already made plans for Ezekiel to dig up their ensorcelled bodies. She relied on his greed and selfishness."

Wendy skipped ahead. "I'm in 1799 now . . . they've awakened after their first long hibernation. Black leathery skin, seven feet tall, most of their hair has fallen out . . . they hunt at night and they still speak English, to one another and to Ezekiel. These entries are shorter, sporadic. They're already looking ahead. Rebecca is troubled by the unborn fetus she carries. Wither believes it has changed to scar tissue, harmless, but Rebecca insists it has a mind, a child's mind that speaks to her in her sleep. 'She raves and raves, losing what little mind she herself has left.' She believes if she . . . consumes enough children, she'll restore form to the baby's body and finally give birth. Oh, God, that's horrible! Skipping, skipping, thank you! Okay, here . . . Sarah has become fascinated with tales of humans who can assume animal forms, either by wearing skins or by applying ointments. She's talking about therianthropy."

"Like Navajo skinwalkers?" Kayla asked.

"Exactly," Wendy said. "The Navajo skinwalkers were witches who could mimic different kinds of animals, wolves, coyotes or bears, while maintaining human intelligence. But tales of were-creatures and shape-shifters come from many cultures, all over the world. Let's see . . . the *eigi einhamir* of Norway and Sweden changes into a wolf by wearing a wolfskin, as does the *ulfheobar* of Scandinavia, similar to their berserkers, which become bears by wearing bearskins. Here's a slight twist: Celtic selkies are seals that become human by *removing* their sealskins. And in Iceland, they have the *hamrammr*, which can shape-shift into whatever creature it's most recently *eaten*. Closer to home, Mexican folklore talks about *nahuales*, warlocks who can shape-shift into various animals, usually coyotes." Wendy tapped a finger on the journal page. "But this may predate all that folklore—or be the source of it! Because Wither doesn't reference any of those terms. Sarah's interest seems to arise from tales Wither has told her. And Wither has been all over the world, for thousands of years."

Wendy skimmed more pages. Black spots were dancing the tarantella before her eyes. "Okay . . . more on Sarah and her fascination . . . 'young bones are changeable bones.' Oh, shit! That's why she chose Abby . . . Sarah complains that her adult human bones were set, that she won't be able to 'run on four legs or fly with wings' even with her corruptive powers. Wither tells her to choose a child in her next cycle to inherit bones that are 'still growing and may yet learn the way of beasts.' She must have figured out a way to transfer that ability into Abby, and some residue of the power remained . . ."

"After the car accident," Alex said. "Abby was paralyzed for a while, but her bones started growing and changing."

"Sarah prepared her ahead of time, anticipating her new cycle in Abby, never dreaming it wouldn't happen, that she would fail and die." Wendy skimmed down the page, flipped to the next. "Rebecca seems intrigued with Sarah's plan . . . she's forgotten about trying to give birth, but she says her mind could merge with her child's if she were to choose a newborn for her next cycle. Listen to Wither: 'She now plans for the next cycle, but as an infant. Sheer foolishness. I tell her she will be as helpless as the babe she becomes, killed for a demon child before she is weaned.'" Wendy skipped ahead. "Ah—she's talking about Rebecca again and . . . oh, here it is! 'A babe that grows apace she will be' and 'a babe to start, but only a start.' Rebecca becomes secretive, talking about a corruption of internal time. Wither keeps calling her a fool. Rebecca insists folding 'many days into one will raise babe to woman as fast as need be.' Wither goads her, asking who would 'suffer this weed of a demon child to live after only a year of these many-folded days?' Rebecca says a mother will protect the child until Rebecca, as that child, can protect herself. Wither says 'such a freak child will be put down like a rabid dog' and calls Rebecca 'a complete fool to believe otherwise.'"

Wendy groaned, squeezing her eyes shut. Alex suggested rest again, but Wendy wanted to continue as long as humanly possible. She still hadn't come across Wither's plans for her own next cycle, plans that would include stealing Wendy's body. "A little while longer."

"Guess it's safe to assume Rebecca found a way to fold time and included that ability in the preliminary stages of her transfer into Hannah's body."

"An ability or an effect?" Wendy wondered. "Is this something Rebecca planned to switch off once she grew to maturity? If so, maybe Hannah can learn to switch it off. But . . . if Hannah has to switch it off herself but never learns, she'll keep folding days until she grows old and . . ."

"Save that worry for another day," Kayla said. "You'll have time to figure it out. That switch might even be somewhere in this book. A spell to stop or reverse it."

"Reversing might be dangerous," Wendy said. "I'm sure Karen would settle for simply stopping the acceleration at this point."

Wendy turned a few more pages, and was now more than three-quarters of the way through the pile. "They're getting ready for the next hibernation, the one that will take them to 1899. Wither hasn't been able to convince Sarah or Rebecca to change their next cycle plans, plans that won't be fulfilled, if successful, until 1999. Now she's talking about herself . . . 'And what of me? Yet another cycle like the last, and the one before that, and the one before that? What might I change? For too long I have followed the same pattern with similar results and similar power. Need it always be so? Instead of choosing a random female, suppose I select a young woman with flashes of power herself? A human female with powers attuned to nature would present an interesting vessel. Will my corruption subvert her power to darkness and chaos? Or will her natural powers enhance my corruption to unimaginable levels? Delicious to think so!'"

Wendy took a deep breath.

"She's talking about you," Kayla said, in case Wendy was in denial mode.

"She just doesn't know you yet," Alex added.

"Not surprising," Wendy said grimly. "Since I was one hundred and eighty years from being born when she wrote this." Another thought occurred to her. "But she assumes someone like me will exist. That means there had to be women in her time who were like me, women who could do what I do. It couldn't have been pure speculation on her part."

"You're probably right. But those women would be long dead by the time she was ready for a new cycle," Kayla said.

"But if she expected someone like me to be around in two hundred years, there are probably more women like me out there now. Kindred spirits."

"Others maybe with untapped potential," Alex said. "It's possible she jump-started your magical abilities for her own eventual gain."

"Tenderizing meat," Kayla said. "Except she wanted to eat your mind, not your flesh."

"This is weirding me out all over again," Wendy said, with a half-suppressed shudder. "Let's move on." She turned pages. "Not much left before the next awakening . . . she's talking about the dark instincts taking over as the 'beast within becomes ascendant.' She doubts the journal will be continued much longer until the new cycle. 'The beast in us is all power and force and arrogance. There is little of subtlety, less of flexibility. The courses we have chosen guide us, and we shall not be denied. The beast of two hundred years will feed and fury, but rarely question what it has chosen in saner times.'"

Wendy turned the page and found the next one blank. The page after the blank had only a year scrawled on it.

"It's 1899 now," Wendy told them, flipping to yet another page, which was only half filled with the rippling symbols, and those partly illegible, as if transcribed with a clumsy or arthritic hand. "She's angry. Mad at her own inability to continue the journal. Disorganized thoughts, interrupted continually with talk of feeding, and half-formed conclusions about which part of the human body is—yuck!— 'sweetest to the tongue.' " Wendy turned the last several pages, stopped to read a few lines aloud. " 'Useless, useless! Why write? Why? Need only to feed— not write! Words mush mush MUSH! together—hate words and clumsy hands, not human writing hands. Done is done! We will find what we seek. NO MORE BOOK! Nothing changed . . . but everything has changed. We are THIS!' " Wendy turned the last page over. "That's it . . . Hope I caught the important stuff. It's just . . . there's so much more, especially the 1699 section. How much helps us, I don't know."

Kayla looked dejected. "Mistake to get my hopes up for a cure."

Wendy grabbed her hand. "I'm not done. This border vision must get easier with practice. Otherwise, I would have named it 'thundering headache vision.' " That, at least, elicited a smile from Kayla.

Alex said to Kayla, "Personally, I think Gina screwed up your conversion."

Intrigued, "How so?"

"Yeah," Wendy said. "What's your idea?"

"Remember, I was there," Alex said. Kayla nodded, not likely she'd forget anything about that incident. "She made you drink her blood."

"Yeah, that's kinda my problem."

"But she didn't mix your blood with hers," Alex said. "When Wither was in that cell with Sarah and Rebecca, they mixed their blood together, then they drank Wither's blood. That's how they became like her, joined her coven."

"He has a point," Wendy said. *Although,* Wendy realized, *Gina was an aberration in the Wither—for lack of a better term—reproductive cycle. More like an evolution than a continuation. Gina's powers and limits seemed less constrained than those of Wither's prior incarnations. Gina was a wild card.* Still, Kayla's *blooding* difference was something to cling to, something to explain how she continued to retain her own identity, despite the black blood episodes. "Maybe drinking her blood, by itself, isn't enough to convert you. Especially since you purged it right away."

Kayla nodded, hopeful.

"You had difficulty unsealing the stone, even more so unsealing the book. I mentioned earlier that I doubt Wither would have had as much trouble with her locks and traps. Something's not right—more to the point, something's not *wrong* with that."

"So I won't be ultimate evil. Maybe just pull-the-legs-off-flies evil?"

"Seriously," Wendy said. "Stay positive. We'll beat this."

Wendy stood up and the headache transformed into a light-headedness that made her stagger. Alex caught her in his arms, supporting her until she regained her balance. "So, we've answered a few questions," she said at length. "But have some major disappointments. Aside from the limited information on the blooding ritual, there was nothing related to a curse. Not that I was expecting anything specific, since the curse came through Gina, long after Wither stopped recording her thoughts in the journal . . . but I kinda hoped there'd be more info on her magic, her spells, potions and powers."

"Something like Wither's full-blown Book of Shadows."

"Or even something less formal," Wendy said. "She took so much of her power for granted."

"She wasn't writing for posterity," Alex said. "Just herself."

"You're right," Wendy said. "I believe she kept that record to remind herself—her future-cycle selves—what had happened before with her and her covens. Maybe, in the latter stages of her cycle, when she's in full monster mode, she loses memories. This journal may have been a new twist, a written record she could review to avoid past missteps and calamities."

Kayla quoted, "Those who forget the past are doomed to relive it."

"Exactly."

"And for someone whose past dates back thousands of years," Alex said, "forgetting mistakes would be a major pain in the ass."

They decided to monitor cable news again, hoping for an update on the Indiana murders, but fearing news closer to home. Alex and Wendy sat on the loveseat, while Kayla lounged in the beanbag chair, legs extended and crossed at the ankle. Wendy kept her eyes closed, a hot washcloth draped over her forehead while she waited for the aspirin to work its pharmaceutical magic. She wanted to familiarize herself with Wither's entire journal and thought maybe the best approach would be to read it aloud while someone else transcribed it on a legal pad—better yet, audio-record her reading. She was a competent typist and could always transcribe it later, right into her laptop computer's word processor. Or find a speech to text program to—

BBRREEEEEPP!

Wendy jumped at the sound. Her cell phone, where she'd left it on the kitchen counter. "Sit! I'll get it," Kayla ordered, struggling out of the beanbag chair as if she were thigh-deep in quicksand.

BBRREEEEEPP!

Kayla answered the phone before the third nerve-jangling ring. "Just a sec," she said, walking it over to Wendy. "Prof lady."

Wendy opened her eyes and frowned. "Hi, Karen," she said. "Hannah okay?"

"Yes, Hannah's fine," Karen said. "She's with me."

"Wait a minute," Wendy said, sitting up straight, alarmed. "Where are you?"

"Don't worry. We're not in Windale."

"That's good," Wendy said. "For a minute there, I thought—"

"We're in Boston."

"What? Why are you in Boston?"

"Hannah was worried. She said something awful was coming, that she should help you."

"Keep her away, Karen."

"I know, Wendy. Believe me," Karen said. "Before we left, I had to promise Art we would stay in Boston and come no closer to Windale. Our flight just landed. Seems we beat a major snowstorm closing in from the Great Lakes. Anyway, we're staying at the Copley Plaza Hotel. You might need to reach us. Pencil handy?"

Wendy asked Kayla to grab a pen and pad from the kitchen drawer, then wrote down Karen's information. "Karen, why . . . ?"

A long pause on the other end of the line. "Last time, with Gina Thorne, Hannah's proximity seemed to help you. I mean, it helped her help you, right?"

"Yes, but—"

"And Hannah was never in any real danger then," Karen said. "If anything were to happen to you now because I selfishly kept her too far away . . . I don't pretend to understand your relationship with Hannah. Gives me a headache whenever I think about it. But I was there when that . . . monster, Rebecca Cole, came crashing through the skylight in the birthing center. I saw what she was. I'm beyond doubting the unexplainable exists. My ostrich life ended the day Hannah was born."

"Thank you, Karen," Wendy said. "I appreciate the support—as long as you two stay in Boston! And I have some news. Not enough, by far. But I've learned some things about Wither and her coven." Wendy gave her the short version of how they'd discovered and decrypted Wither's journal. Then she explained what she'd learned of the coven's plan, specifically Rebecca's plans.

"At least that explains why this acceleration is happening to Hannah," Karen said. "Now if only it told us how to stop it."

"I've only had one quick pass through the journal," Wendy said, trying to sound hopeful. "The answer may be there."

"If not, we can hope the acceleration will cease when— when . . ." Karen's hushed voice fell silent. Wendy thought she could hear the older woman weeping for a while before regaining control. "It's horrible, Wendy . . . to rob a baby of her childhood. Who knows how this will affect her in the long term."

Robbing Hannah of her childhood hadn't been Rebecca Cole's plan, though. Her real intention was far more insidious. She had intended to take over the child's body, subsuming or expelling Hannah's mind and identity, replacing it with her own. Had Rebecca succeeded, Hannah would have ceased to exist moments after her birth. Of course, that was poor consolation for Karen now. Thinking of her relationship with the Crone, Hannah's image of her future self, Wendy was encouraged. "Whatever happens, Karen, I know Hannah will turn out fine."

"I pray for that every day, Wendy."

Wendy had good reason to believe those prayers would be answered.

Before she hung up, Karen asked Wendy to keep her in the loop. It was the least Wendy could do, considering that Karen had, at a relative moment's notice, hopped on a cross-country flight from San Francisco to Boston to help Wendy in a time of crisis.

After Karen's call, they resumed channel surfing for information, catching one wave of news cycles after another. When the latest round of *Headlines News* reiterated, for the umpteenth time, the few known details about the Indiana murders with a brief recap of what had happened in Fargo and Minneapolis, Kayla had an optimistic spin. "At least there haven't been any more murders."

Wendy had a more chilling conclusion. "Or it's getting better at covering its tracks."

Bobby McKay wasn't off duty until eleven, but he decided to stop by Wendy Ward's house to check on Kayla. She hadn't spoken to him much since she and Wendy and Alex had located the old witch's journal—just a few monosyllabic words when he drove her to the Crystal Path. *Probably still pissed at me for following her to the woods,* he thought. But he couldn't help worrying about her, couldn't turn his concern off like an alarm clock. Especially when she'd seemed so afraid of what might be in that journal. It had been bothering him all day. No, he thought, *it started before that. On New Year's Eve when she took that knife to her arm. Actually, she hadn't been quite the same since she first wandered out to that damn clearing.*

As expected, Jimmy Kirkbride was parked a few doors down from Wendy's house, ensconced in the old blue Crown Vic. White smoke streamed from the tailpipe of the idling sedan. Jimmy probably had to run the motor every fifteen minutes or so, just for the heat. Windows fogged, which meant the lame defroster was losing the battle. Kirkbride had given the old circular forearm rub to the windshield and driver's-side window.

Bobby parked behind the unmarked car, walked up and tapped on the glass and waited for Kirkbride to roll down the window. "Hey, Jimmy, how's it going?"

"Besides freezing my balls off?"

"Besides that, yeah?"

"Peace and fucking quiet," Jimmy said. "Not that I'm complaining." He glanced at his watch. "It's early. You're not here to relieve me, are you?"

"No such luck, sport," Bobby said. "Just stopping by for a minute." He started to walk away, then paused. "She's still in there, right?"

"The incomparable Ms. Zanella? Hard to miss with that new blue look. Yeah, partner, she's still there. Unless she snuck out the back."

"Thanks," Bobby said and frowned. If the sheriff thought the threat to Wendy Ward was that credible, maybe they should have two officers watching the place, front and back. Suddenly, he wasn't too thrilled with the idea of Kayla hanging out at the cottage tonight.

He rang the bell and smiled when Kayla answered the door with, "Well, hello, Officer Handsome! What can I do for you?"

"The not-biting-my-head-off is a good start," he said, returning her smile. "Glad you're in better spirits. Good news, I hope."

She grabbed the collar of his jacket and pulled him inside. After she closed the door, she planted a rough kiss on his lips. "Not great, exactly."

"Kiss me again, I'll try harder."

"Not the kiss, you dope," she said. "I was talking about the journal."

"Hi, Deputy McKay," Wendy called from the family room. Alex waved with a casual, "Hey!"

"Sit here," Kayla said, indicating the threadbare recliner by the front window. As soon as he complied, she dropped into his lap and looped her left arm around his neck. "Sorry if I was bitchy earlier. Lot on my mind."

"But the . . . situation is better now?"

"I—we," she said, indicating Wendy, and maybe Alex as well, "have reason to be hopeful. I may never be normal as the next gal—not that I was going for that, mind you—but maybe I've seen the worst of it."

"Good," he said. "I'm glad. That's terrific."

"Long as you can tolerate my present and prevailing level of weirdness."

"I'll manage," he said. "I have another concern, though." He cleared his throat and continued softly. "I hope you don't plan on staying here overnight again. The sheriff is convinced there's a credible threat against Wendy."

"That's the consensus."

"Don't you think you'd be safer at home or . . . ?"

"Your place?" Kayla asked with a knowing smirk.

"Now that you mention it, I get off at eleven."

"And you were hoping to get off again soon after?"

"Such a demure young lady."

"Yeah, that's me!" Kayla laughed. "But . . . I hadn't really thought about it."

"You have your answers from the book?"

Kayla nodded, a little hesitant.

Bobby thought there might be something more there, but wasn't about to press that issue. "Is there any way you can help here? Besides . . ."

"Playing the role of cannon fodder?" Kayla frowned again. "I don't know. If I leave, I'll feel as if I'm deserting—" Sensing movement to her right, Kayla looked up and saw Wendy approaching. "Wendy?"

"Deputy McKay—"

"Please, call me, Bobby."

"Okay, Bobby. Tell me you've come to take this young lady home."

"Well, I was—we were . . ."

Kayla cocked her head at Wendy. "How did you—?"

"Kayla, you don't need to hang. You should go. Really."

"But what if . . ."

"If I thought you could—I mean, you've already helped as much as you can, unsealing the vault and the journal at great personal risk. I appreciate everything you've done. But it's enough. Go home and get some rest. I'll call if anything develops."

"Thanks, but I'll stay for a bit," Kayla said. "Rather not be home alone and, besides, Bobby's on duty till eleven."

That was how they left it. Kayla would stay at Wendy's place until Bobby's shift ended. Wendy thought it would be safe at the cottage, at least until midnight. Bobby debated switching duty with Captain Kirk in the Crown Vic, but decided the time would pass quicker if he kept on the move, patrolling the streets of Windale. He kept reminding himself that this threat, whatever it was, was not after Kayla.

Later, after the sheriff flagged him down at the intersection of Main Street and Familiar Way to give him six silver-filled hollow point rounds for his service revolver, Bobby began to seriously wonder what the hell was happening in Windale.

As promised, the sheriff returned to the cottage to give Alex the Glock 23 automatic handgun. He told Alex the modifications to his cane-sword hadn't been completed, but should be soon. Then the sheriff made sure Alex knew how to handle the gun. "Couldn't get you a full clip. You only have six silver-tipped rounds, any one of which should be enough to drop an average man in his tracks," the sheriff said. "Unfortunately, if Wendy's right—and I suspect she is— we're not dealing with anything resembling an average man. One round's already in the chamber. Let's hope the silver will pack the supernatural punch the bullets themselves lack." He looked to Wendy. "Find a demonic Achilles' heel yet?"

"No, but we cracked the journal. And it explains, indirectly, why Sarah chose Abby." Wendy explained Sarah's desire to begin her next cycle in an immature body, one with a developing skeleton, to pursue her interest in shapeshifting."

"Abby had the misfortune of being the female child who lived closest to the witches' lair," Kayla said.

"Rotten luck in itself," the sheriff said. "But Sarah never finished transferring herself into Abby's body. So why does Abby have her shape-shifting ability?"

"Been thinking about that," Wendy said. "My guess is that Sarah had to use the magic inherent in her current body to endow Abby's body with therianthropic abilities. Maybe the transfer of consciousness had to be the very last act of the old cycle's body. Rebecca seems to have prepared Hannah's body in a similar fashion. In both cases, the witches—oh, I really hate using the term *witches* for those demonic creatures, but whatever—in both cases, the witches were killed before they could transfer their . . . essence into the newly prepared bodies."

"Thank God for small favors," the sheriff said.

"Those magical preparatory changes, however, remained inside Hannah and Abby."

"Does this mean . . ." He took a deep breath, bracing himself for the answer to his next question. "Is there any possibility Abby will become like Sarah?"

"Sarah's body and her life force were destroyed. I see no evidence Abby will ever become like her. Of course, because of what happened she's unique—well, definitely uncommon—in her shape-shifting abilities."

"So the worst case for Abby is that she'll have to accept shape-shifting and be comfortable in her own skin. Skins, I should say."

"Three skins and counting. And I'd say she's adjusting fairly well."

"Three's plenty," the sheriff said, shaking his head in wonder. "As of now, each of my deputies—including Jimmy outside—has silver-filled rounds for their guns. And Alex, I hope I can count on you to be responsible with that weapon."

Alex held the black gun flat in his palm. "Guns scare the hell out of me."

"That's a good start," the sheriff said. "Simple piece of advice? Respect the damn thing or you may not live to regret it. Remember, you're the last stand. Something happens, you stay in here. Let my men handle the situation. Tonight, at least, should be long and uneventful. Maybe our last calm night before all hell breaks loose. In addition to the officer parked outside, expect to see my car or another black-and-white cruising your street on a regular basis."

During Sheriff Nottingham's brief stay inside the cottage, the outside temperature had dropped several degrees and the sporadic flurries had escalated to a heavy snowfall. Fat snowflakes dotted the shoveled walkway and speckled the hoods and windshields of cars parked along the street. He turned up his fur-trimmed color and blew warm air into his hands. The lone streetlight at this end of the cul-de-sac seemed unequal to the task of banishing darkness. Anyone with common sense had retired for the evening.

As he drove past the old Crown Vic, the sheriff waved to Jimmy's pale face, framed in the only clear section of the fogged windshield. *Helluva night for surveillance,* the sheriff thought as Jimmy returned the wave. *Let's hope it's uneventful.*

Jimmy Kirkbride checked his watch for the hundredth time. Still fifteen minutes before he was relieved. Might as well have been an hour. Cold seemed to seep into his bones and take up residence. Chalk it up to his lanky frame or high metabolism or low body fat, but whatever the reason, once a chill took hold, he couldn't shake it off without ducking inside, out of the elements. Instead, he had to be content with running the car's heater at intervals to warm the interior. As the night wore on, he had to leave the engine idling longer to warm the car, and it seemed too damn cold again thirty seconds after he shut it off.

Half a dozen times he'd been tempted to knock on the door of the cottage and ask for a hot cocoa or coffee, but he thought that would look unprofessional. *Wouldn't hurt them to bring something out,* he supposed, but they probably thought he'd stocked up on all the coffee, donuts and fast food the average cop would need for an evening's curbside surveillance. Whatever, his shift was almost over. No sign of a stalker, peeper, masher or whatever the sheriff was so damn worried about. *Special bullets?* He thought. *Okay, so a guy burnin' PCP is more than a handful in a 'fuck you, I feel no pain' kinda way . . . But silver-tipped bullets? C'mon! What the hell's he expecting, Dracula or the Wolfman, for Christ's sake? Sometimes I really wonder about that man.* He rubbed his hands together in front of the vent for the two hundredth time and thought, *Weird fucking witch town.* Another check of the clock. *Ten more minutes of this crazy bullshit and I'm outta—*

Knuckles rapped against the driver's-side window.

Auto Club's early, was his first thought as he lowered the fogged window. But it wasn't Angelo. "Hi, Sheriff. Forget something?"

Beneath his dark hat brim, Sheriff Nottingham stared at him blankly, unresponsive.

Why is he on foot? Left a moment ago in his sheriff's car and it's . . .

Then the deputy saw something dead in his eyes and wondered if the sheriff was ill. "Sir, are you okay?" *More than the eyes, his whole face seems . . . off somehow. Like a bad copy.* "Is something—?"

Jimmy Kirkbride gagged on the rest of his question. An arm had flashed through the open window, clutching and ripping into his throat, tearing flesh. With rapidly graying vision, Jimmy understood that the vague simulation of the sheriff's pale features, along with the hat and jacket, had been part of some weird fucking disguise for someone or something inhumanly strong. With the weak and trembling fingers of his right hand, he clawed at his holstered .357 Magnum, loaded with the silver-tipped slugs, wondering—*What the fuck is it?*—as his throat was torn out.

Kayla hung up the portable phone and said, "That was my mother. Her car's in the shop. She said the snow's really coming down and she needs a ride home."

"Better get moving," Wendy said. "Your Neon's not exactly an all-terrain vehicle. On second thought, take the Pathfinder."

"No, thanks. You might need it. Besides, the Stewpot's not that far."

"Be careful," Wendy said. "And call me when you're safe at home."

"Will do," Kayla said, shrugging into her coat. "Take care, guys. Call if you need anything." She hesitated, sighed. "I feel like I'm aban—"

"You're not abandoning us! You're rescuing your mother. Go! Before the snow gets worse."

"Okay, okay. If Bobby calls, tell him I'm headed for the Stewpot, then home."

"I'll send him your way."

"Cool. Thanks." As Kayla slipped out the front door, with Wendy there to lock it behind her, she heard Alex ask about switching to ESPN for a bit. Wendy laughed, but Kayla couldn't blame him. The wall-to-wall news coverage had become mind-numbing.

Once outside, Kayla understood her mother's concern. Low cloud ceiling. And the air was thick with snowflakes, dizzying in their abundance. At least an inch had accumulated on the formerly shoveled walkway. Her car was a big white mound, with only sections of black tires visible. She fumbled her key into the hidden lock, retrieved her ice scraper from the car floor and used the bristled end to uncover her windows and lights. As she climbed into her car and slammed the door, she glanced over at Jimmy Kirkbride, sitting in the unmarked car. His driver's-side window was down, exposing his pale face and red hair. *That's odd*, she thought. *Staring at me like a lunatic. Face probably numb from the cold, but still . . .* She took hold of her door handle and for a moment entertained the idea of walking over to bust his chops. *Is he really that pissed I called him by his nickname?*

With the storm worsening, she knew she should make tracks to the Witches' Stewpot. Besides, couple more minutes and she'd have to clear the windows again. "Screw it," she said and drove away. Gave a halfhearted wave as she drove by the idling car, then frowned when Jimmy didn't return the gesture. *Jeez, hold a stupid grudge, why don't ya?* But there was something else troubling about his vacant stare.

Much later she would realize she hadn't seen his breath misting in front of his face, as it would have had he been breathing, had he been warm . . . or human.

It has never felt so powerful. Or so confused.

Disguised as its most recent victim, it sits in the man's place, in the front seat of the dark rumbling vehicle, amazed by what it has witnessed and by what it continues to experience. Without bothering to feed off the cooling corpse, it stuffed the dead man under the vehicle, out of sight, his blood already blanketed by the swift falling snow. Though its hunger is considerable—since witnessing the moving pictures magic box, it has fed only once and was careful to hide the carcass in a shallow pit off the main road—it now focuses on what it must do to reclaim its freedom.

Since entering this quiet, unremarkable town, its power over cold and storms has grown tenfold. It wonders if the surge in power comes from the place itself—which it senses is the origin of the dark magic that has driven it to the special prey—or if the intoxicating bounty comes from the special prey herself. More likely it is a final effect of the dark magic, to ensure its success in killing the girl. If so, it will lose the extra power when she is dead . . . and yet it will be free again. For now, it savors the power flowing through its veins and wonders how much of a threat this special morsel will be.

The glowing blue-white path disappears through the near wall of the small white dwelling. This close to her, the line is the size of a hawser, and it pulses and throbs with energy. If it remains still long enough, it can sense the thudding of her heart, the pull and release of her breath. So close . . . But what of the other girl, the one with the strange blue hair who stared at it from the small vehicle? She trails a black thread, a black path that slips back from wherever she has gone and wraps around the pulsing blue-white cord right before its eyes. Instinctively, it knows that the two women are linked, and that the blue-haired one is somehow responsible. Is she the one who cast the dark magic that roused it from hibernation and set it on this guided path of destruction? Is that why she flees, knowing the other one's doom is at hand? After the special prey is gone, maybe it should follow the black thread for answers and more. As long as the *black thread flows from her to its eyes, it will find her. But first, it must claim its freedom.*

It steps out of the rumbling vehicle, slams the door and takes long strides to the small dwelling. A thought, filled with surging energy, pulls the cold around it like a cloak of ice, a freezing wind and a wall of snow.

"Headache's better," Wendy said shortly after Kayla left. "Mind if I go back and work on my astral projection? Need to practice realistic body motion."

"Sure. Can you come out here and keep me astral company?"

"We won't be able to snuggle."

Alex pursed his lips, as if he hadn't considered that logistical problem. "Then sit on the beanbag chair," he said. "I'll pretend you're mad at me."

"If I were mad at you," Wendy said, "you'd be the one sitting on the beanbag chair."

As she started down the short hallway, someone banged on the door, three deliberate knocks. "Can you see who that is, Alex?"

Wendy—!

Wendy stopped in her tracks. "Who's . . . there?"

Wendy, I . . .

A voice in her mind. The Crone? But why hadn't she manifested if Hannah was as close as Boston. Unless . . .

Wendy's breath plumed in front of her face.

"It's Deputy Kirkbride," Alex called. "Probably to tell us the shift's changing."

—glamour!

Time line anchor point interference! Wendy had already turned back toward the living room. "Ask his nickname!"

"What?"

"Ask him—NO! Don't let him in!"

But it was too late. Alex had already flipped the dead bolt and started to turn the doorknob. The door almost seemed to explode inward, striking Alex so hard he stumbled backward. Deputy Kirkbride took two long strides into the room; then his gaze whipped around, as if magnetically drawn to Wendy's position. A gravelly hiss, "YOU!"

Weird, Wendy thought, *he's fuzzy around the edges!* She turned her head just to the side, focused with border vision—and saw the other image, the true outline, like a three-dimensional silhouette, almost a foot larger than Kirkbride, taller and wider. *Fuzzy because it's covered in fur!* Her next thought was as grim and inescapable as they come. *The wendigo! It's too soon. I'm not ready!*

Alex jumped forward in an attempt to grapple with the man-who-was-not-a-man, but a powerful backhand staggered him. Backpedaling to stop himself from falling over, Alex crashed into the half-wall divider and nearly toppled over it.

Wendy heard a loud thump, but couldn't spare a glance to determine the source. The *wendigo* ignored Alex, who was no longer an obstacle, and turned its full attention to Wendy. Powerful arms raised in the weird silhouette revealed by border vision. She could almost look directly at it and still see the stark outline of vicious claws. One swipe could rip out her throat or disembowel her. She reached for the crystal pendant around her neck.

"Wendy! Down!"

After the sheriff left, Alex had placed the Glock on the half wall, within arm's reach of the loveseat. When he struck the wall, the gun must have fallen to the floor at his feet.

Wendy dropped into a crouch—

The *wendigo's* mouth—which, eerily, still resembled Deputy Kirkbride's mouth—stretched too wide and the creature emitted a hideous shriek through jagged teeth.

—and her left hand, still on her pendant, trembled at the sound. *Concentrate!*

BLAM!

In the confined space, the Glock's roar was deafening.

As was the *wendigo's* roar of outrage that followed.

In that instant—like a still-water image scattered by the drop of a pebble—the *wendigo's* glamour fell away. The oversized silhouette shimmered and resolved into the *wendigo's* actual appearance. It stood at least seven feet tall, was massively muscled and covered in thick, matted fur, white at the head and torso, black-streaked along the limbs. The glowing yellow eyes hardly distracted Wendy's attention from its mouthful of jagged teeth, and its fierce, black, twitching claws. For a heartbeat, that true image was frozen clarity in her mind, like a digital photograph of pure evil.

The *wendigo* whirled around to face Alex, flinging a stream of pus yellow blood from its wounded shoulder to splatter against the wall above Wendy's head. Although the wound bubbled and sizzled, it seemed too high to have resulted in a punctured lung. Unless the bullet fragmented. Or the silver—

With another shriek, the creature charged Alex.

Time slowed to a crawl, the pace of inevitable doom.

Everything seemed too bright.

Alex aimed the black handgun at the *wendigo*, right hand cupped in his left, in the two-handed shooting stance he'd practiced with Sheriff Nottingham. But during the practice session, Alex's hands hadn't trembled as they were now. He wasn't firing—he seemed petrified with fear!

Wendy raced down the hallway, clutching her pendant in her left hand.

Angelo Antonelli had underestimated the intensity of the snowstorm. Five minutes after leaving the Public Safety Building, he guessed he'd be late relieving Kirkbride. But, as his wife, Carla, told everyone, Angelo had an optimistic streak a mile wide most days, and two miles wide on Sundays after the family attended the early service at Holy Redeemer. His church had suffered a series of setbacks—the loss of its steeple in 1999, followed by the loss of its spiritual leader, Father Murray, in 2000—but the church had always managed to bounce back from adversity. And Angelo believed, if at first you don't succeed, you aren't trying hard enough. So he nurtured the slim hope that he'd make it to Kettle Court, even without chains on his squad car's snow tires. When it became obvious to such a born again optimist that he would in fact be a few minutes late, he radioed ahead to give his apologies to Jimmy. Except Jimmy wasn't answering.

He turned onto Kettle Court, into the brunt of the winter storm, and could make out the unmarked Crown Vic because it was the only car on the block not buried under mounds of the white stuff. *Heat from the idling engine melting the snow*, Angelo thought. For a supposedly inconspicuous car, it stood out like a sore thumb. Not that he begrudged his fellow officer the right to avoid a frostbitten rear end. Still, his cop instincts began talking to him, telling him something was wrong.

As he neared the back of the dark Crown Vic, he noticed

the driver's-side window was down. Snow whipped into the interior of the car. Without bothering to pull in behind the unmarked car, Angelo left his squad car double-parked and pushed his door open into the driving wind and swirling snow. He climbed out into the hostile night, flashlight in his left hand, handgun in his right.

He played the beam of the flashlight across the front seat of the car. Everything was wet with melting snow and—blood! Nobody in the front, or in back behind the cage. Even as a devout optimist, Angelo suddenly had cause to worry. Regretted not having called for backup already. And he was about to kick himself for dropping his special bullets into his jacket pocket instead of loading them into his handgun at the first opportunity. He played his flashlight beam across the quickly filling footprints, which led to the cottage under surveillance, but also on the pattern of disturbed snow along the side of the car.

Angelo dropped to one knee to look underneath the Crown Vic—

—into Jimmy Kirkbride's pale, frozen face with its unblinking eyes. Kirkbride's throat looked like raw meat, ripped open so deep, the white gleam of his spinal cord was exposed.

Shouting from the cottage—

BLAM!

Angelo climbed to his feet and raced for the door as he grabbed the radio mike and reached for the transmit button.

Bobby McKay decided to change his plans. Originally, he'd intended to drop off his police cruiser at the Public Safety Building, go off duty, strap snow chains on his

Mustang GT and swing by Wendy's cottage to pick up Kayla. Unless, of course, she wanted to take her Neon home or back to his place. Once the storm throttled up, he decided the prudent course would be to pick Kayla up in the cruiser and drive her back to the PSB. Little chance she'd want to drive alone in the freak snowstorm with near white-out conditions. But he had another reason for Plan B. He wanted her out of that house and, if he let the situation stand much longer, she would probably bunk at Wendy's place for a second night in a row. Any other time, no problem. When faced with what promised to be one humdinger of a blizzard, the best advice was, usually, stay at home. Definite exception to the rule arose when the home in question was a prime target for a rampaging winter demon attack.

The sooner she's outta there, the better.

By the time he turned down Kettle Court, he'd set his wipers to their maximum speed. The frenzied cycle—KA-THRUMP! KA-THRUMP! KA-THRUMP!—provided ominous stroboscopic images of the scene at the end of the cul-de-sac. Bobby hunched over the steering wheel in concentration.

Angelo, down on one knee, peered under the unmarked car. Whatever he saw spooked him, because a moment later he was up and running toward the cottage. Bobby's radio crackled with static, then a frantic voice.

"—333 Kettle Court! Shots fired! Officer down! Officer needs assistance!"

Bobby flicked on his siren and overhead lights, tapped the accelerator briefly, then brought his police cruiser to a skidding halt beside Antonelli's, effectively barricading the end of the street.

Antonelli reached the door of the cottage.

As Bobby jumped out of the patrol car, a tumble of concerned thoughts and emotions filled his mind with gnawing panic. *Oh, God—Kayla! Damn it! Should've taken you out of there when I had the chance!*

BLAM! BLAM!

From inside the house came a thunderous crash.

The *wendigo's* shriek was said to paralyze its victims, freezing them in their tracks. Less than three long strides from Alex, the *wendigo* had shrieked with bloodcurdling fervor.

Alex's gun trembled in his hands.

His eyes were wide with shock.

Wendy's racing heartbeat seemed sluggish as she registered each horrifying detail of the tableau in front of her. She wondered if Alex had enough presence of mind to get off another shot, wondered if it would even slow the creature down.

Clutching the crystal pendant in her left hand, she raised a protective sphere with a moment's concentration. Imminent crisis equaled instantaneous focus. Yet wrapping a protective bubble around her body wouldn't help Alex. She had to think of something, something fast. *No time to conjure fireballs!*

BLAM!

Alex fired! The realization was a flash of triumph, snuffed out as a chunk of plaster exploded high, to her left. *He missed!*

BLAM!

The *wendigo* flinched, stumbling backward, but the bullet had only grazed it. Wendy's shield took the brunt of the modified, large caliber slug's impact, with a flash and protesting squeal, an instant before the ricochet shattered something in the kitchen.

Wendy fell back on a sphere trick she'd learned during her battle with Gina Thorne. From the outside, the sphere was an impenetrable bubble, like bulletproof glass, but she could mold it from within. Back then, she'd struck out with a portion of the sphere—what she visualized as an amoeba-like pseudopod of protective energy. Easy to visualize the same projection again—*there!*

Now what? she asked herself, then immediately answered, *Make a better weapon—fast!*

That's it! Fast! Make it spin!

Running within her sphere, she imagined it rotating, blurring with the speed of a circular saw, spinning on its vertical axis as she advanced. But the sphere had a projection—now two! One on each side for balance, as she molded her weapon with the speed of thought.

Had the *wendigo* charged through Alex's position, bowling him over or smashing him into the wall, Wendy would have been too late. Instead, the *wendigo* stopped before him, swatting aside his gun arm to send the Glock caroming across the floor, before raising its other set of claws to strike him down.

At that moment, Wendy's spinning sphere collided with the demon. The first energy protrusion slammed into the massive creature and it crashed into the wall. Alex pressed himself down against the half wall as the *wendigo* stumbled past.

Wendy hadn't counted on recoil. The moment her spiked protective sphere struck the fur-covered demon, the sphere came to a violent stop and, since she hadn't visualized it spinning counterclockwise, she was hurled backward, bouncing off the wall outside the kitchen and slamming into the small pine table, toppling it and scattering the loose pages of Wither's journal across the floor. The sphere had protected her, but the jarring impact left her dazed and snapped her concentration. Unable to maintain focus, she inadvertently released the sphere's energy.

Groggy, she was still on hands and knees when a short, swarthy police officer—Angelo *something*, Wendy remembered—burst through the doorway, gun drawn.

A torrent of snow swirled into the house around him, accompanied by a teeth-chattering breeze. Brittle yellow pages fluttered around Wendy like crazed butterflies.

Officer Angelo's darting gaze took in the scene: Wendy, dazed on all fours; Alex, by the half wall, down and unarmed; and a furred, seven-foot-tall, enraged creature with a mouthful of jagged teeth and two sets of fearsome claws rising to its feet. Angelo whispered, "Sweet Jesus!" and started firing, emptying his gun into the *wendigo*.

The *wendigo* shrieked in rage, not in pain.

Undaunted, it charged the stunned police officer—

—and chopped down with a massive, furred hand, shattering his wrist.

Angelo's empty gun dropped from nerveless fingers as he fell to his knees, moaning in pain. He dropped his flashlight to cradle the ruined arm. The *wendigo* caught him with a backhand, spilling him back into the bitter night. A moment later, the *wendigo* spun around to face the room again, its yellow-eyed gaze tracking for a moment before locking onto Wendy with a growl of satisfaction.

Alex leaned over the half wall. "Gun!?"

Wendy looked around frantically before spotting the automatic wedged under one side of the beanbag chair. She pointed and Alex pounced on it, rolling onto his back and bracing the gun with both hands.

His earlier shot had injured and enraged the creature, despite his two misses. Yet the cop had scored at close range with every shot, and the bullets had had no effect whatsoever. Sheriff Nottingham said everyone was armed with silver-tipped bullets, so why—? *Pointless questions*, she realized, turning her attention and magical focus on generating fireballs, at the risk of torching the cottage in the process.

The *wendigo* took a threatening step forward before noticing Alex was again in possession of the Glock. Wendy thought she saw something in those odd, yellow eyes. Grudging respect, maybe. *Or caution.*

Alex took a bead on the *wendigo* and fired, ripping a hole high on its left shoulder. Yellow blood sprayed the wall and the *wendigo* roared in pain, staggering backward through the doorway. Another shot gouged the doorjamb.

From outside, "Oh, fuck!"

Wendy glimpsed a brief struggle, heard a man scream and then a gunshot, followed by the sound of a body falling. Climbing to her feet, she renewed her attempt to summon fireballs, but sensed it was too late. If she'd ever had an opportunity to use fire against the winter demon, it was gone now. Nonetheless, she staggered through the doorway into the raging storm.

"Wendy—NO!" Alex yelled.

But she kept walking. She had to . . . she had to stop it.

She became aware of the squawk of police radios and, for the first time, realized a police siren was wailing in the night. Outside, Angelo writhed on the ground, clutching his shattered wrist, moaning softly. The *wendigo* had vanished into the driving snowstorm and . . .

. . . Bobby McKay was lying on the ground, still as death.

CHAPTER FOURTEEN

As it lopes into the freezing night, its white-furred form a blur against the snow-covered landscape and the snow-laden sky, it is—in pain!—confused. Recent events flash through its mind as it seeks answers . . .

The special prey, the one called Wendy Ward, was expecting its attack. But how? Even if she saw the images of its other victims in one of the magic boxes, how could she know she was its target? And her house . . . guarded by men with guns—guns loaded with silver!

Silver burns on impact, and burns more while its body tries to heal itself. Enough wounds from silver-edged weapons or silver projectiles could inflict mortal damage. How could she know this, and be prepared?

Silver! It has little fear of ordinary guns. Lead projectiles are minor distractions, a slight discomfort, as the man at the door discovered! Its body would expel the lead projectiles, completely healing the injuries they inflicted in a few hours. In this special place, where its powers are magnified, the wounds heal in scant minutes. But not wounds wrought by silver, those wounds burn, and the silver projectiles, where they remain lodged in its body, are like red-hot pokers. Eventually its body will expel them, but at the expense of strength, and possibly only after a fevered sleep of healing.

Another surprise was the young woman's physical strength. She was no more than a wisp of a girl. Yet somehow, she slammed its body into a wall with enough force to stagger it, dropping it to its knees, stunned. Incredible! It is accustomed to vast superiority over frail humans, depending on its speed and strength to take down its rightful prey with ease. Yet one blow from a slender girl felled it!

As it bounds through the town's deserted streets, through the fierce torrent of snow and the shifting drifts, through the frigid whipping wind and endless patter of snow, its confusion is replaced with a certainty, a belief that its special prey is indeed special, and no ordinary human at that. Just as it possesses what humans would consider magical or supernatural powers, this one called Wendy Ward must have powers of her own. To anticipate its attack and plan the best defense against it, she must have the gifts of a seer. Too, she must have access to formidable, magic-assisted strength. But she is not invulnerable, and it is not finished with her. Even if it could rid itself of the compulsion to kill her, it would still choose to kill her, to avenge its injuries.

Nevertheless, it decides to retreat, to decide how best to proceed. For too long, it has only had to choose a victim, vanquish that victim and feed.

Now it believes it was deceived, led unsuspecting into a trap, just as it once trapped small, furred beasts in another life. And it knows who set this particular trap, if not why. The one who roused it, spurred it on for many miles to kill the special prey. It remembers this other one, she who trailed the thin black thread. She was inside the special prey's dwelling moments before its attack. To warn the *special prey? To protect her with the secrets of its destruction? But why? Why bring it here with her dark magic only to make it fail, to try to destroy it? Why...?*

The time for questions has passed. It makes a decision.

Before it kills the special prey, it will visit this other one and make her do its bidding for a change. First she will tell it how to maintain its heightened powers. Then she will explain why she led it into an obvious trap.

It sees a bend in the black thread, and veers its course to follow the feeble path to her. It senses her presence nearby, ever so close.

Once it has her secrets, only one question will remain.

How sweet is the taste of her raw flesh?

Fearing the worst, Bobby crouched down, sparing one anxious moment to see what Angelo had discovered under the unmarked car. He was ashamed to admit a moment of relief, along with shock, at seeing Jimmy's dead face staring back at him. *Thank God, it's not Kayla...*

More than likely, whatever had killed Jimmy wasn't finished. Bobby pushed himself up and ran to the cottage. His boots crunching the heavy snow, handgun unholstered, Bobby focused on Angelo Antonelli, silhouetted in the doorway. Less than two running strides later, Bobby witnessed Angelo firing every round in his gun without a warning. That was the moment that Bobby, without confronting any visual evidence himself, finally and completely accepted the truth. The murders in the Midwest were not the result of a cannibalistic serial killer, at least not a human one. A supernatural force, a supernatural creature, really was to blame. And that supernatural creature had been set loose on a cross-country vendetta via a last-ditch magical curse by one Gina Thorne, who happened to be the last incarnation of Elizabeth Wither, the lead witch of Windale's notorious and murderous colonial coven. It was all there. He accepted it. If there was another, rational conclusion, it utterly eluded him.

A moment later, his grim assessment proved correct.

A massive, furred shape loomed over the short and stocky Angelo, chopping his wrist with a clawed hand. Antonelli dropped his spent revolver, moaning in agony as he fell to his knees. The creature dealt him a backhand blow that bowled him over, sprawling out of the doorway as he twisted and moaned.

While Angelo had been emptying his revolver into the massive creature, Bobby closed the distance to the cottage. With Angelo down, Bobby had a clear shot. The creature had turned back to face the interior of the cottage. Two more shots rang out from inside the house, one striking the creature, the other ripping a chunk out of the doorjamb. A moment later the creature whirled around, attempting to flee.

Bobby was waiting for it.

The yellow-eyed creature—a *wendigo*, Nottingham had called it—took one long stride to close the distance and swatted Bobby's arm aside. He retained possession of the gun, but the *wendigo* wrapped powerful arms around him, crushing him in a bear hug—a *wendigo* hug! Bobby fought for breath, struggled in vain, tried to bring his gun into play. He squeezed off a shot, but the barrel was pointing down and the slug just burrowed into frozen ground.

Fortunately for Bobby, the creature was wounded and seemed frantic to escape. With an enraged growl, it bit down through the shoulder of his leather coat until he winced in pain; then it hurled him to the ground with enough force to knock the wind out of him. Helpless, he watched as the white-furred creature with black-streaked arms and legs loped off into the fury of the snowstorm.

Bobby cast about for his gun, saw it a few inches from his knee. Might as well have been in another time zone. A shadow fell across him. Though he hurt like hell, he doubted it was the grim reaper. *I'm in much better shape than Angelo.*

"Officer McKay? Bobby?"

Wendy, he realized. *Still alive. But . . .* "Kayla—is she . . . ?" he croaked, his voice almost lost in the buffeting wind.

"She's fine," Wendy said. "Left a few minutes ago. How bad are you hurt?"

"Wind knocked out . . . of me. Angelo . . . is bad. Call EMS . . . and Sheriff Nottingham. Tell him . . . Jimmy's dead."

"Call an ambulance," Wendy shouted over her shoulder to Alex.

As for Nottingham, she saw his sheriff's car emerging from the thick curtains of snowfall, tire chains clinking and crunching through the twisting drifts, even as she knelt over Angelo's writhing form.

She had her multi-bead bracelet off, the rose quartz bead between her left thumb and forefinger. As gently as possible, she placed her right hand over the deputy's ruined wrist, wincing in sympathy at its gruesome appearance, all puffy and mottled red and blue. He moaned and yanked it away. "Please, try to be still!" she shouted. "I can help you." Even shouting, she worried he might not hear her voice over the howling of the wind, the wail of the sirens and the roaring of his own pain. She managed to keep a few fingertips near the damaged location, and tried to concentrate on drawing the healing energy she needed into her body so she could pour it out through him.

She heard the sheriff shouting at curious neighbors to go back inside their homes. With the fierce storm whipping snow and ice in their faces, they weren't putting up much of an argument to stay out and gawk. Before Wendy could focus her concentration and generate the healing energy, she had to block out the distractions of cold—she wasn't wearing a coat—and noise, including Angelo's pitiful moans. But she was getting better at slipping into her meditative state. The feel of crystal and rose quartz between her numb fingers helped block out the outside world. Soon she felt the warmth building inside her, imagined the pulsing sphere of golden power waiting to be shaped and applied. With her fingertips touching Angelo's forearm, she visualized bones free of fractures, blood flowing unhindered through veins and arteries, skin smooth and undamaged ... Then she released the energy through her projective hand into Angelo's forearm.

He shuddered beneath her, gasping one moment, shivering the next. Then he lay still. "How ... ?" he sat up, left hand delicately probing his right wrist. "It's healed! And the pain's gone! But how ... ?"

"It was nothing," Wendy said, a little light-headed and breathless herself. She tried to stand, swayed and caught herself on the doorjamb before toppling over. *Must have released too much energy*, she thought. Same thing had happened when she'd healed Abby long ago. Despite wobbly legs and dizziness, she returned to Bobby. He'd already managed to sit up and pushed himself up from one knee as the sheriff approached.

"Bobby?" Wendy said.

"Relax, I'm okay," he said. "I'd feel a lot better if I'd managed to wing it with that one shot. He—it tossed me aside like a rag doll. Ran off with its tail between its legs. I don't know—that might be literal. Did it have a tail?"

She flashed a wry smile, shook her head. *Cracking jokes,* she thought. *Must feel better than he looks.*

He massaged his left shoulder, as if working out a kink. His jacket leather was torn there. *Must have ripped it when he fell,* she thought.

"Where is it?" the sheriff asked.

"Gone," Bobby said. "Only one way to go, but damned if you'd see it in this mess. We'll have a foot of snow on the ground within the hour."

"Ambulance is on its way," Alex said, standing behind Wendy in the doorway.

"Everybody inside," the sheriff said. "I want to know what the hell happened here."

From his harsh tone, Wendy interpreted the subtext of the question, *What the hell went wrong?* After everyone came inside she closed the door, but the cottage still felt like an icebox. Not that it would help, since the heater was already running nonstop, but she increased the temperature setting on the thermostat for the small amount of satisfaction the gesture provided.

Alex helped her right the small pine table, then gather the scattered pages of Wither's journal, many damaged during the *wendigo* attack. Some were torn others were damp, their symbols blotchy and smeared. A few were so sodden they crumbled under the gentlest handling into wet pulp. Wendy lamented the amount of Wither's history lost in one fell stroke. *What's done is done,* she thought with bitter resignation. *I'll wrap up what's left, stash it away in a safe place until I have time to transcribe it.*

Everybody began talking at once but as confusing as it

should have been, the exchanges filled in the picture of the sudden and brutal *wendigo* attacks. Angelo couldn't stop massaging his healed wrist, casting a curious glance Wendy's way every half minute or so, no doubt wondering if she were some sort of miracle worker. "What in hell was that thing?" he asked the sheriff.

"Think of it as a rabid grizzly on steroids," Alex said.

"Actually, it's worse that that," Wendy said. "It's intelligent and apparently it has control over winter weather."

Angelo shuddered and spoke softly, "Whatever it is, it killed Jimmy."

"Where the hell is that ambulance?" the sheriff asked for the third time, glancing out the front window to keep an eye on the crime scene. "Hate to leave him out there . . ."

"Does he have family?" Wendy asked.

"None local. Think he was dating a girl worked at the One-Stop Mini-Mart." He rubbed the stubble on his jaw, contemplating an unpleasant task. "I'll have to call his parents in Rhode Island."

Angelo said, "I put six slugs into that thing at close range and . . . nothing. Like I had a peashooter."

"Silver must have no effect, Sheriff," Bobby said. Then, abashed, "Although, my only shot is lodged somewhere in the front lawn."

"That's wrong. About the silver, I mean," Wendy said. "Alex hit it twice. I saw the blood. It staggered, became enraged. Tangible effects."

Angelo cleared his throat. "I, uh, never actually loaded the silver, um . . ."

"I left you silver bullets, Angelo!" the sheriff said angrily.

"I know. Got 'em right here in my jacket pocket." He couldn't have looked more embarrassed. "I was planning . . .

I'm sorry, Sheriff. Figured . . . one bullet was as good as anoth—"

"Well, they're not. Both of you make sure you have every silver round loaded and ready," the sheriff said. "And if you see Curtis before I do, tell him the same. This thing is too dangerous. We can't afford any more screwups!" He paused, took a deep breath. "Look, I know this is like nothing you've ever experienced as law officers. Don't look for a rational explanation. You won't find one. Accept this thing on its terms and deal with it accordingly. This is not something I could have prepared you for in a way you could accept. You never would have believed me. Not really, not where it counts. Not without doubts about me or about this thing, doubts that would have impaired your effectiveness. Now, at least, I hope you realize what we're facing is the unknown. And I hope you will be ready for it. As ready as you can be."

Wendy looked at the two deputies. Of the two, Angelo remained a bit shell-shocked, overcoming disbelief slowly. Bobby, who already had some knowledge of Windale's secrets, sported the determined, grim face of a true believer. Almost unconsciously, he rubbed his sore shoulder. She'd offer to heal it for him, but she was still a little shaky herself and it seemed like no more than a bruise. *Best to conserve my energy*, she thought. *This night isn't over.*

"What now?" Bobby asked, as if reading her mind.

The sheriff looked at Wendy. "What's your read? Don't suppose this thing will head for the hills never to return."

"No. We just spooked it. Probably wasn't expecting the silver. It will come back, but probably not through the front door again."

"I'll leave someone here, inside the house," the sheriff said. "Angelo?"

"Sure."

Bobby looked at Wendy. "You said Kayla left a short time ago?"

"She went to the Stewpot to pick up her mom. Then home, I believe."

"Mind if I use your phone?"

Wendy handed him the portable.

Ambulance lights strobed the front windows, accompanied by the angry, truncated bleat of a siren.

Bobby had switched off his own cruiser's siren and lights, and the sheriff had notified the dispatched EMS team that they would be picking up a corpse so they could run silent, but asked them to kindly haul their asses to Kettle Court. All but the last instruction must have sunk in. Either that or the roads were becoming treacherous.

The sheriff stood, zipping his jacket. "I'd better get out there," he said, then tightened the chin strap on his hat and braced the cold.

Wendy—

The voice, inside her head again.

Angelo was asking Alex, "How many silver rounds left in that automatic?"

"The machine picked up," Bobby was saying.

—can you hear . . . ?

"Excuse me for a minute," Wendy said. She gathered up the remains of Wither's journal, wrapped in the leather covering which, fortunately, did not resume its former petrified state, and walked down the hall to her bedroom.

With her bedroom door closed, she placed the journal on her dresser, rubbed her hands together for warmth, and called, "Crone? You out there?"

Wendy . . . ?

The voice was still only in her mind, faint.

"I'm alone, if you want to pop in."

Difficult . . . but better than before . . .

A hazy image of the Crone shimmered into existence in front of her, visible but almost transparent. From the waist down, she had the opacity of a heat mirage. "*Best I can do . . .*"

"We were attacked," Wendy said. "Alex hit it twice with silver-filled bullets. And I sort of . . . thumped it with a blunt sphere."

"*You were fortunate . . . to surprise it. But, it's not over . . . it is alive . . . and enraged . . .*"

"Any idea when it's coming back?"

"*Strange . . . not there where you are,*" the Crone said. "*First Kayla . . .*" She seemed surprised by her own future memories, of what was about to happen in Wendy's present. "*Not just you . . . it wants to kill Kayla!*"

"Kayla! But she wasn't here when it attacked. Why?"

"*It believes Kayla is other . . . is Wither? Blames her . . . the curse. Why . . . ?*" The Crone shook her head, confused.

"It's the blood," Wendy said. "It found me through the curse, magical breadcrumbs or something, but it must also sense the black blood in Kayla. It assumes she started this. Oh, damn it!" Wendy shook her head in disbelief. *How much worse can this get?* "I have to tell Bobby. He's already worried about her."

The Crone was shaking her head, "*Too late . . . it's already taken her . . .*"

"No! God—no!" Wendy said. "I was supposed to be the target!" She wanted to pound her head against the wall, but settled for falling back on the bed and gripping the comforter in white-knuckled hands. *Damn it, me. Not Kayla . . . but something she said—what?* "Wait. You said 'It's already taken her? Not already killed her. Where is it? Where has it taken her?"

"I *don't know . . .*" Again, she shook her head, but this time she lost substance with the motion. She was fading out. "*Can't remember . . .*"

"Try! Before it's too late."

"A . . . *a place that doesn't exist . . .*" She frowned, confused herself. "*Strange . . . dark rows, white . . . wall . . . hole in the sky . . . Abby saw . . .*"

Then the Crone was gone and nothing Wendy said or willed could bring her back. Throwing open the bedroom door, she ran down the hallway and saw Bobby, portable phone clutched in his hand, shaking his head. Before she could speak, Bobby said, "No answer at the Stewpot or her house. She could be stranded somewhere in this storm."

"Worse," Wendy said. "The *wendigo* is after Kayla."

"What? Why?"

"It thinks she's responsible for the curse," Wendy said. "That Kayla is who called it here."

"Oh, Christ!" Bobby said, his voice strained. "God—Kayla . . ."

At that moment, they heard an urgent call over the police radio, reporting at least one murder at the Witches' Stewpot on Main. The sheriff burst through the door, his face red from the bitter cold outside, and twisted into a grimace. "This whole fucking town is cursed!" he said. "Bobby, you're with me."

"We'll follow you," Wendy said, reaching for her coat.

"Not without me," Alex said.

"You'll both be safer here with Angelo."

"Sheriff," Wendy said. "You need me for this."

"What?"

"It's the *wendigo,*" she explained. "It's hunting Kayla."

The sheriff stopped in his tracks, hands clutching the doorknob on his way out. He never bothered to ask how she knew. Didn't have to ask. He was an admitted believer. "Let's go!"

Kayla arrived at the Witches' Stewpot at 11:45.

For the last mile or so, the rooftop neon-cartoon sign of the three witches hunched over their steaming cauldron had been a garish beacon of hope. If she could see it, maybe she could actually reach it. Finally, after what seemed hours of tense driving, she pulled into the parking lot.

As she parked beside the only other car on the lot, Wild Bill Borkowski's old white Taurus station wagon, she heaved a huge sigh of relief. Several times on the ride from Wendy's place, the car had foundered in deep snow, tires spinning with a frustrated whine. Happened every time she had to bring the car to a halt, at red lights and stop signs. Since the streets were deserted, she began to cruise through intersections. Her only concession to traffic law was a brief downshift into first gear for better traction. *Fuck it*, she'd thought. *I'm dating a cop. None of the guys would dare give me a ticket. Hell, Sheriff Nottingham would let me off with a stern warning.* She frowned. *Well, Jimmy might write me up, since I'm apparently on his shit list.*

She pushed open her car door and started to climb out, only to have the door slammed back at her by a fierce gust of wind. Already the lot was covered with four to six inches of snow, and the storm gave no indication of abating. If anything, the downfall had increased in intensity and the wind drove the big flakes down at a forty-five-degree angle. Visibility was horrendous.

As she reached for the black metal broomstick handles

on the double doors, she noticed somebody had switched off the orange neon OPEN 24 HOURS sign. *Not tonight, folks,* she thought. *Tonight, the most intrepid of Windaliens will have to look elsewhere for a cheeseburger and fries.* The gusting wind made a preemptive grab at the door, rattling it against protesting hinges, but Kayla managed to slip inside the small vestibule and pull the outer door shut behind her. The chimes hanging from the interior door rang as she pushed through into relative comfort, wondering if sensation would ever return to her numb face.

Aside from her mother and Wild Bill, the place was deserted. Lena Zanella was sitting in Kayla's usual spot, the stool near the cash register. She still wore her black waitress uniform, but she'd removed the orange apron. Folded over the next stool were her red parka, black hat and gloves, a mound capped by her black leather pocketbook. "Hi, babe," she said, sipping from a Styrofoam cup of coffee. "Sorry to drag you out in this mess."

"No biggie," Kayla said, her lips stiff from the cold. "Was about to head home anyway." Actually, she'd been thinking of driving to Bobby's place, but that called for more winter driving than she wanted to experience in her little Neon tonight.

Wild Bill stood opposite Lena, his meaty hands gripping the edge of the counter. He wore his cook's whites—soiled with grease spots after a full day's work behind the griddle and ovens—and he had a dish towel slung over one shoulder. "How's my little girl, huh? That John Law treatin' you right?"

As he squeezed through the opening in the counter, no doubt intending to bestow on his surrogate daughter one of his patented rib-popping hugs, Kayla held up her hand. "I'm frozen solid and if you squeeze me right now I will shatter into a hundred pieces. And, by the way, his name's Bobby McKay and he treats me fine."

"Splendid," Wild Bill said. "Now I have just the thing to fight off the chill." He held up a finger to request a minute's patience. He ducked into the kitchen and returned shortly, carrying a cardboard basket of crinkly French fries and a Styrofoam mug of hot chocolate. "Had to nuke 'em for you, Miss Kayla. Hot chocolate was your mother's idea, but I want you to know those fries were cooked in the finest of aged greases. An artery-clogger with personality. Last batch before I cleaned the deep fryer."

"Thanks, Wild Bill," Kayla said, hopping on a stool two down from her mother's. She cupped the steaming hot chocolate in both hands, then put it down. With a kick of the foot rail, she spun one complete revolution. "For luck," she said to them, shrugging. *Yep. One silly superstition,* she thought.

The hot chocolate was heavenly, defrosting her from the inside out. After circulation returned to her fingers and toes, she decided to risk a few killer fries. Aside from snacks at Wendy's place, she hadn't had anything to eat in quite a while. She talked while she wolfed down the French fries, ever conscious of the worsening storm conditions on the other side of the long plate-glass windows. "You're really closed for the night?"

"Owner called," Lena told her. "Said the roads looked to be impassable and only crazy people would be out on a night like this."

"What's that make us?"

"Loony birds," Wild Bill said. "But, hey, we're three of a kind. We gotta flock together, right?"

"And we should get the flock out of here."

"So you know, Miss Kayla, I did offer to drive your lovely

mother home. Told her, soon as I finish cleaning the grill, we can leave. Turned me down flat."

"Bill, you live over in Harrison," Lena said. "You'd be driving the wrong way. Besides, you'd just finished telling me your car heater was broken." Lena whispered to Kayla, "Have you seen the way he drives?"

Kayla smiled. "So, Mother, you ready for the frozen tundra?"

BRRINNGG-RRINNGG!

Bill cast a disgusted look at the old black AT&T telephone mounted on the wall behind the cash register. "Jeez!" he said, without making a move to pick up the receiver.

BRRINNGG-RRINNGG!

Lena placed her hat, gloves and pocketbook on the counter and slipped into her red parka. "Ready in two shakes, babe."

"Aren't you gonna answer that?" Kayla asked Wild Bill.

BRRINNGG-RRINNGG!

"Nah," he said. "Been ringing off the hook ever since we decided to close. 'Do you deliver?' Over and over again. As if we got a dogsled team out back. It's a blizzard, people!" Bill shook his head and jabbed a finger toward the far window, pointing toward Harrison. "Soon as that grill's shiny and new, I'm hitting the road."

BRRINNGG-RRINNGG!

Kayla's breath plumed in front of her face. *Feels like the heater quit.*

Her gaze followed Bill's pointing gesture in a conversational knee-jerk response, which was why she happened to be looking right at the side window when it appeared. Gooseflesh rippled across her body, making her shudder with fright. She jumped off the stool, shaking. "Oh, my God! What the fuck is that!?"

They followed her startled gaze—just as the broad plate-glass window imploded, spraying glass everywhere in the Witches' Stewpot.

BRRINNGG-RRINNGG!

Jeff Ryan and Daniel Wilkins tore a refrigerator box in half and trudged to the top of Witch Hill, a favorite Windale sledding locale, which the kids at Harrison High often referred to as Witch's Tit. And, on this first Friday of January, 2002, it was—if never before—certainly as cold as one.

As seniors at good old HH, Jeff and Danny thought riding actual sleds would make them look like prime dorks. On the other hand, riding down the steep hill in this mother of all snowstorms on a section of a Frigidaire carton had to be the height of bad-ass cool. "This is wicked, man," Danny said as he struggled to keep his flapping sheet of cardboard from sailing out of his hands. "Can't even see the bottom of this bitch. And we got it all to ourselves."

"First thing tomorrow," Jeff said. "Getting me a snowboard."

"First thing tomorrow, this place will be covered with losers. Enjoy it while you can, dude!" Taking his own advice, Danny folded up the front of his makeshift cardboard sled, then dropped down on it and pushed off. He rushed down the hill for about six feet, then started to spin sideways. After that, Jeff lost sight of him. Last thing he heard before the wind stole Danny's voice was, "Woo-HOO! This fucking rocks!"

Jeff nodded, grinning like a fool. The snow swirled

around his head, a million flashes of white in the darkness. The wind buffeted his body, thrashing his hair across his face. He folded his piece of cardboard as Danny had and tried to drop down on it for his first run down Witch's Tit. Something snagged his shoulder. But the trees were a few feet back, farther up the hill. Confused, he turned around . . .

Yellow eyes glared at him from a massive furred face.

Dark claws flashed—

—and Jeff's brief scream was lost in the night.

Its hunger temporarily sated, it drags the boy's carcass into the trees, pushes it into a snowdrift in a hasty attempt at concealment.

The extra energy required to heal its silver-inflicted wounds has made it ravenous. Had it waited much longer before feeding, it would have succumbed to the healing sleep, thwarting its chance to extend its power and avenge itself. Purpose blazed at the front of its mind. Just when hunger threatened to distract it from its pursuit, it stumbled across the boy, standing atop the hill, a morsel too convenient to ignore.

It sprints down the isolated, snow-covered streets, surprised when it sees moving lights ahead. Blinking yellow lights. A large, sturdy yellow vehicle, with a massive metal scoop attached to the front, angled to shove the snow to the side of the road. The driver's purpose is to thwart the power of winter, to make the roads passable for smaller vehicles.

It chases the lonely vehicle at first out of anger, but soon it realizes that its healing hunger has not yet been sated. The lonely driver who would defy winter represents another opportunity to feed.

Pacing the slow-moving vehicle, it leaps to the platform under the driver's door and shoves its fist through the glass. The man inside yells and continues to shout as it pulls his bulky body through the shattered window.

In the middle of the deserted street, it eats the best parts.

With no one to guide it, the large vehicle careens off the road, jumps onto a walkway and smashes into a red brick wall.

In haste, it stuffs the driver's body under the nearest stationary vehicle. Careless, but she is so close now—the black thread is more vibrant, almost pulsing—and it must be at full strength and in complete command of its powers when it takes her and the other one, the special prey.

For a few minutes, it runs with the wind at its back, then it sees a long building with a strangely colored picture-sign mounted on top. But the sign holds only secondary interest. The pulsing black thread pierces the building itself.

She is there. It is almost close enough to see her.

Inside the Witches' Stewpot, glass rained down around them, driven by a fierce wind and chased by a heavy snowfall, now mixed with sleet and freezing rain. The embodiment of all that winter fury stood before them, where it had landed a moment ago after hurling itself through the plate-glass window. Kayla knew what the furred beast must be, that it couldn't be anything else. *Wendigo!* All seven feet of it, the slashing claws and razor teeth, the tufted ears and glowing amber eyes, the inhuman, seething rage—this was the winter demon!

In that first frozen moment of terror, Kayla noticed several gruesome details, the dapples of bright red blood, frozen on its chin, and yellow fluid—its own blood?—on its shoulder and side. *Wounded,* she thought, *but it's recently fed.* Then, *Who? Has it already attacked Wendy? Killed her?*

But *why is it here?* Then a moment of black humor, *It's still hungry, so it came to a diner.* "Sorry, we're closed," Kayla said, surprised that she'd actually found her voice without screaming, even if she sounded like a bad Minnie Mouse impersonator.

Cautious, the *wendigo* stalked forward, as if suspecting a trap. Its large head swiveled to take in all three of them, Wild Bill behind the counter, Kayla and Lena in front. As it walked, the fierce wind at its back stirred its matted fur, blasting a fetid odor through the diner. Kayla thought the diner would never outlive the stench. *Most likely, neither will I.*

"Oh, my God," Lena whispered, hand to her mouth. "It's some kind of a . . . monster."

"It's a *wendigo*," Kayla said.

"A what?"

"Never mind," Kayla said. "It's bad. Real bad."

With calm deliberation, Wild Bill reached under the counter and brought out a long ax-handle. Unfortunately, it was a weapon better suited to dispersing teen vandals than battling cannibalistic winter demons.

Lena stepped into the aisle. She whispered, "Kayla, get behind me."

"Better idea. Let's all get the hell out of here!"

"I like Miss Kayla's idea," Wild Bill said. "You two run for the door."

"What about you?" Kayla asked.

"Oh, I'll be right behind you," he said, then tapped the ax-handle against his palm. "And I'll have a little surprise for that son of a bitch if it tries to stop me."

The *wendigo* took two more steps, its yellow-eyed gaze flicking from the ax-handle to Kayla, but settling on her.

Kayla swallowed hard. *Okay, so this isn't the world's worst fucked-up luck. It's after me. Me—but why? And if it only wants me, maybe I can lead it away—*

"Go!" Lena shouted, pulling Kayla after her.

Kayla stumbled, turned on her heel. The door chimes rang. Her mother was standing there, holding the door to make sure she was safe. "Fuck it, Mom! Run!"

Wild Bill sidestepped through the gap in the counter, then backed away from the *wendigo* while brandishing the ax-handle. He'd also picked up a glass sugar dispenser, which he hurled at the beast's head.

The *wendigo* swatted the glass container, shattering it and spraying sugar everywhere. Then it shrieked a bloodcurdling sound, like an injection of pure fear into their veins. "G—go!" Wild Bill shouted.

Kayla passed through the vestibule and pushed open the outer door with her back, fighting the gusts of wind. Her mother followed, but Kayla gasped at the speed and strength of the creature. Wild Bill was six-four, barrel-chested with powerful arms. But his age betrayed him. He managed one overhand swing, hard enough to crack the ax-handle across the *wendigo*'s shoulder. The demon ignored the blow, grabbing Wild Bill's head between both its large claws and slamming it against the countertop, two times, hard. When it released Bill's head, Kayla saw the shape was all wrong. The *wendigo* hoisted the large man over its own head and hurled him against the wall with a bone-crushing impact. Bill's body fell to the floor behind the counter, knocking over a bulletin board, smashing glasses and scattering condiment containers.

"No!" Kayla wailed. "It wants me! It's after me!"

"Run!" her mother cried, her lips stretched wide, her face bloodless.

The *wendigo* snagged the back of Lena's red parka and plucked her off the ground, tossing her back against the row of stools, where she lay too dazed to move. Kayla had a moment to look at her mother's still form, before the *wendigo* pushed through the inner door, popping it off the top hinge as it crammed its bulk into the small vestibule. "YOU!"

It *talks!* Then she remembered Wendy talking about the buckskin man in her vision, that this thing had been human once. Not that she hoped to reason with it. *Unstoppable rage and insatiable hunger for raw human flesh kinda gets in the way of reason.* Kayla staggered through the outer doors, into the full brunt of the storm.

A moment later the *wendigo* smashed the windows, wrenching one of the doors loose in the process. As it stalked her, mouth gaping, drool freezing as icicles under its chin, she continued to back away. If it was determined to kill her, the least she could do was lead it away from her mother. Wild Bill was dead. The head trauma alone had been devastating. But Kayla's mother might survive her injuries. At worst, some busted ribs. Kayla just had to lure the abomination far enough away that it forgot all about the helpless victim inside the diner.

"Why?" she yelled. "Why me?"

"You . . . trick!" it bellowed, its voice a tortured rasp. "*You want kill—but trick . . . and make strong. How?*"

"I don't know what you mean."

"*You trick . . . so kill you.*"

That part was plain enough. She turned and ran down Main Street, across snow and ice, head bowed against lashing winds and the blinding snowfall, with a seven-foot-tall winter demon charging right behind her. She never had a chance.

* * *

Back in the Witches' Stewpot, Lena Zanella struggled to catch her breath. Each attempt brought a scorching flare of pain to her chest. The monster had probably cracked more than a few of her ribs. For long, agonizing moments, time when her only concern was for her daughter, out in the blizzard at the mercy of that . . . the *wendigo*, she couldn't even sit up.

Eventually, she willed herself to endure the fresh spike of pain, like a white-hot poker, that came with every little shifting movement. She climbed to her feet, using a stool for support. When it creaked and began to spin, she almost toppled over, but managed to lunge at the counter with both hands and grab hold, screaming with the sudden pain. Inched along the counter. Slipped through the gap. Reached . . . reached for the wall phone, her breath coming in ragged, painful gasps.

She sobbed when she saw Wild Bill lying prone on the floor behind the counter, a pool of blood around his head. Regained control of her emotions. Then began to cry all over again when she thought of Kayla, outside in the storm, pursued by the *wendigo*.

With weak, trembling hands, she picked up the phone and dialed 911.

WINDALE, MASSACHUSETTS
JANUARY 5, 2002

The sheriff led the convoy out of Kettle Court, siren wailing and roof lights strobing the night. Bobby followed in his cruiser, roof lights flashing but without the siren. Angelo came third, his squad car also participating in the light show. The green Pathfinder brought up the rear with flashing hazard lights.

Alex was at the wheel of the Pathfinder, with Wendy in the passenger seat, staring out the side window at the endless falling snowflakes. She planned to use the hypnotic effect to her advantage, to reach the disconnected state of self-hypnosis needed for astral projection. By necessity, she kept her attention away from the treacherous road conditions and the tight procession of cars.

Before they piled into the cars, the sheriff instructed Angelo to call Deputy Curtis Johnson, at home. "Get his ass out of bed," the sheriff said. "We need him now. Not at seven o'clock." The sheriff planned to call the FBI field office in Boston himself, but considering the blizzard conditions, he doubted any additional manpower would arrive before morning, if then. Not that he expected the FBI—or any neighboring police departments, for that matter—to be much help without the proper ammo. The sheriff took a moment to load several more silver-tipped rounds in the ammo clip of Alex's Glock. "So far, you're the only one who's managed to wound the damn thing," the sheriff said in an approving tone, clapping Alex on the back. "Oh! Nearly forgot." He reached into the passenger side of his squad car and gave Alex back his gargoyle-headed cane-sword. "Silver-plated special. Man said it was decorative only. Likely to chip in prolonged combat. Figured that wouldn't be a problem."

Ready to clear her mind, Wendy continued to stare into the brunt of the storm. At some point, her eyes stopped following the spinning downward path of individual snowflakes and instead focused on the random motion of the visible mass itself, seeing it as a mesmerizing whole. Moments later, her astral self slipped free of her physical body and soared up through the roof of the Pathfinder.

Before she began her meditation exercise, she'd warned Alex not to leave the Witches' Stewpot with her entranced. She needed to know where to find her body, and was not confident in her ability to locate the SUV at night in a blinding snowstorm while it wandered the streets of Windale. Placing her trust in Alex, she rose into the freezing, blustery night sky. In her astral form, she was immune to the elements, and she secretly hoped she'd be able to return to her physical body long before the procession arrived at the diner.

Though astral Wendy was unaffected by the ravages of the powerful storm, her vision was obstructed by the millions of snowflakes swirling and spinning their way down from the low cloud cover. She relied on her familiarity with her hometown, noting large landmarks in passing, as she willed her astral self toward the Witches' Stewpot. On a clear night, its neon roof sign could be seen from miles away. Tonight, in blizzard conditions, she couldn't make it out until she was a quarter mile away.

Unhindered by slippery roads, unencumbered by the drag of gusting winds, she soared effortlessly as close as she dared to her awareness cohesion speed limit. Hovering over the parking lot, she saw the shattered window and knew they were too late to stop the *wendigo*. She darted inside the exposed diner, noting in passing the snowdrifts under some booths and stools. At first the place seemed deserted, but a splash of blood on the countertop caught her attention and, when she flew down the length of the diner to investigate from her elevated vantage point, she saw a large man in a cook's uniform sprawled on the floor behind the counter. One glance at his crushed skull and she shook her head.

"Are you . . . an angel?"

Wendy turned to her left and looked down. Lena Zanella sat on the floor behind the counter, back propped against the wall, hand clutching her side in obvious pain, with the telephone receiver dangling from its cord beside her.

"You look . . . like Wendy?"

Wendy nodded. "I *am*," she said, her astral voice in good form. Good diction, but a bit ghostly hollow in timbre. "*But too complicated to explain now. Help is on the way. What happened here? Where's Kayla?*"

"Monster attacked . . . Killed Bill," she said, looking at the cook. The slight head motion caused her to wince. "Kayla ran . . . it followed her . . ."

"*Is she injured?*"

A tear spilled down Lena's cheek. "Don't know . . . Please . . . help her."

"*I will,*" Wendy said. "*But what about you?*"

Lena nodded. "You say . . . help's coming . . . I'll keep. Go . . ."

Maybe it's witch's intuition, Wendy thought. *But I know Kayla is alive. Terrified, no doubt, and possibly injured, she is alive. But for how long? The wendigo was too unpredictable and dangerous to outguess. To save Kayla, they needed to act fast. Wendy needed to act fast! What had the Crone said? "Abby saw . . . the hole in the sky"?*

"*Hang in there, Mrs. Zanella,*" Wendy said.

Lena's pale blue eyes, a match for Kayla's, stared in wonder as Wendy floated straight up and through the ceiling. She probably had another five-minute wait for the sheriff, probably less for the ambulance that would have been dispatched.

Wendy flashed through the storm, not even attempting to hide or make her astral image transparent. Even though she was barely skimming over the treetops, visibility was so poor she doubted anyone could see her from street level. In less than thirty seconds she traveled the few miles to Sheriff Nottingham's home. Recalling where Abby shared a bedroom with Erica, Wendy looped around the house and peered through her window. She pulled back, startled, with the sudden movement of a hummingbird. Expecting both girls to be sound asleep after midnight, Wendy stared at Abby's face, looking back out the window at her. With a quick glance at the bed on the other side of her room, Abby gestured for Wendy to come in.

"*Expecting me?*" Wendy asked once she was inside. "*Or getting ready to roam?*"

Abby shrugged. "I had a feeling something was happening tonight," Abby said. "That you needed me. Like when that bad man attacked you with a knife." That premonition had saved Wendy's life. "But this time," Abby continued, "I wasn't sure which . . . version of me you needed."

"*I have an idea,*" Wendy said. "*Something bad took Kayla and it plans to kill her.*"

"I remember her smell," Abby said, smiling. "Maybe wolf Abby could track her."

Could that be right? Wendy wondered. "*No . . . The Crone said you saw or will see a hole in the sky. Dark rows and a white wall. Sounds like a hawk Abby job to me.*"

"It's really windy," Abby said. "But I'll try. Where should I start?"

"*Taken from Witches' Stewpot diner. Know it? Good. Start*

there." As Abby started to unbutton her pajamas, Wendy realized Abby would have to stand outside in the freezing
weather and shape-shift into a hawk, then brave a nasty
storm. "*Abby, maybe this is a bad idea. Too dangerous . . .*"

The uncertainty Wendy had seen in Abby's face when she
first arrived was gone, replaced by a confidence and determination beyond her years. "I'm supposed to do this. We both
know it."

In the end, Wendy acquiesced, slipping quietly back out
into the blustery night. If she had had an astral stomach
right then, it would have been playing host to a squadron of
butterflies in tight formation. A nameless dread crept
through her. *If this is the right thing,* she thought, *why does
everything suddenly feel wrong?*

Wendy intercepted the Pathfinder with the precision of a
guided missile, a phantom-guided missile, as the SUV pulled
into the Stewpot parking lot beside the three police cars and
an ambulance from Windale General. Before she slipped
down through the roof of the SUV, she paused a moment to
examine the crime scene. On the far side of the ambulance
she saw the county medical examiner's black station wagon
and a blue Jeep Cherokee. A tall black police officer stepped
out of the Jeep—Curtis Johnson, fresh out of bed and seven
hours early for his morning shift. EMS workers had already
strapped Lena on a stretcher with collapsible legs. The medical examiner was inside the diner, probably making a preliminary cause of death finding. Shaking her head with
impatience, Wendy shot down through the ceiling of the
Pathfinder as it came to a complete stop, and reacquainted
her astral self with her physical body. The gravity adjustment
seemed less bothersome this time, because of her impatience
maybe, or due to the relative brevity of her astral mission.

"Welcome back," Alex said in a subdued tone as she stirred, sat up straight in her seat and stretched her arms and legs. She told him about Lena's condition, Kayla's flight and Abby's imminent assistance. "No way Kayla outruns that thing in its element."

"I know," Wendy said. "If it hasn't killed her yet, it's taking her somewhere."

"If it thinks she's Wither, it probably wants her to lift the curse and set it free."

"Yes."

"What happens when it realizes she's not Wither?"

"We have to find her before that happens," Wendy said. "And sitting here waiting isn't getting us any closer."

"Suggestions?"

"Glad you asked."

Deputy Bobby McKay entered the Stewpot's restroom and locked the door behind him. He'd been ignoring the fine tremor in his hands, a nervous reaction that had begun on the torturous drive from Wendy's cottage, attributing it to anxiety and tension. But that hardly explained the dizziness he'd experienced climbing out of the car and the ache in his joints. He stared at his reflection in the mirror. Face flushed but not from the cold. He was feverish, his eyes burning and tender in their sockets. *Fever*, he thought. *Helluva time to catch the flu.* "Not a good time to fall apart, McKay," he cautioned himself. "Kayla needs you. Don't fuck up. You hear?"

He tried to work the stiffness out of his left shoulder, but when he massaged it with his right hand he winced in pain. Where the *wendigo* had tried to take a pound of flesh, his jacket was torn. Its teeth had really clamped down. *Doubt the collarbone fractured,* he thought. *But it's gonna be one Technicolor bastard of a bruise.*

Grimacing, he shrugged off the jacket and draped it over the hot-air hand dryer, temporarily clipping his radio mike to his shirt epaulet. Both his charcoal gray uniform shirt and his white T-shirt were ripped. Unbuttoning the shirt, he pulled it down from his shoulder. Through the tear in the undershirt, he saw where several of the *wendigo's* sharp teeth had punctured his skin. The white undershirt was stippled with blood, but the puncture wounds had stopped bleeding. In fact, they already showed signs of scabbing. The surrounding flesh, however, was red and sore, tender to the touch. "Shit," he said, wincing again. "I'll probably need rabies shots."

Now was not the time to worry about a few needles in his stomach, or the round of antibiotics a doctor was likely to prescribe. Kayla's safety was foremost in his mind. She was out there somewhere, with that monster, but still alive, if Wendy's instincts were right. For now, that was all that mattered. *Kayla first.* "Suck it up, McKay," he told himself as he buttoned his shirt and pulled on his leather jacket. "Find this godforsaken furry bastard and kill it before it hurts Kayla. Worry about the rest later."

Huddled under a blanket to shield her nakedness from the brutal cold of the storm, Abby had crouched outside her closed bedroom window until the change was complete. When the blanket fell away, revealing the red-tailed hawk, she gave a cry of delight—"KEE-arr!"—and launched herself into the sky.

Abby had read that birds possessed thousands of feathers and were well insulated against the cold, migrating not because cold weather was a danger to them but simply because their food sources grew scarce in the winter. Waterfowl migrated because their lakes and ponds froze. So Abby was pleased but not surprised at how well her avian form tolerated the severe cold. Wind, however, was another matter.

Against the gusting winds, she fought a continual battle to stay aloft and maintain her altitude. Although she was larger and more powerful than a true hawk, she had her hands—well, wings—full just navigating to Main Street. Fortunately, she not only had eyes *like* a hawk, she literally had hawk eyes. And the Witches' Stewpot was hard to miss, especially surrounded by flashing police and ambulance lights.

Abby circled outward from that starting point, struggling against the wind and the rush of snow in her face. The reconnaissance was giving her bird form a healthy appetite. *So hungry I could eat a rat*, she thought. Then, *Yuck!*

To take her mind off her stomach, she tried to recall Wendy's exact words. "*Dark rows . . . white wall . . . hole in the sky.*" Abby wondered, *What exactly is a hole in the sky?* And would she see dark rows and a white wall too? *Hard to see much of anything in this storm*, she thought, *even with hawk eyes!*

She flew over the ACME parking lot, caught a glimpse of the green-striped awnings of Gibson's Package Store, and experienced a disquieting moment of déjà vu. *Something about this is familiar . . .* The rotating 1-STOP sign passed beneath her. *My dream!* Abby remembered. *Before I learned to fly for real, I dreamed of flying over these same buildings. Maybe that dream was another vision . . .*

Spiraling down past the One-Stop Mini-Mart, she

directed her flight to the building on the next corner, the one with the damaged roof, damaged in Wither's hailstorm back in 1999, and partially caved in from subsequent water damage. From her lofty vantage point, she peered down into the black stormy night and saw—a hole! *The hole in the sky!*

Kayla remembered running . . . and not getting very far before the massive bulk of the *wendigo* slammed into her, knocking her to the ground with enough force to leave her lying dazed in about a foot of snow. Though conscious, she was too weak and disoriented to stand or resist. At that point, she figured she was *wendigo* chow. Game over. Sayonara. Now, go inside and redeem those karma points!

Fortunately, she was too stunned to care. State of shock. Whatever. Just hanging onto consciousness took all her mental capacity. And at that moment, maintaining consciousness seemed like a fucked-up idea, at best. Better to be oblivious during those few horrific moments between being eaten alive and being a cannibalized corpse. Ignorance is bliss, baby! A bit delirious, she nevertheless fought for consciousness, for the chance to escape, to survive. Something deep inside refused to give up.

Although she had the potential to be a rich source of *wendigo* protein, Kayla soon realized the winter demon had other plans. A *Kayla-free diet*, she hoped. It scooped her up from the snow, slung her over its uninjured shoulder, and her added weight hardly seemed to burden the creature. Its loping strides revealed no hint of distress or fatigue, its powerful body apparently immune to exhaustion.

In her semiconscious state, Kayla had no idea where it might be taking her. Draped over the creature's back, Kayla's view—during fleeting moments of lucidity—consisted of anonymous snow-covered ground and the *wendigo*'s furred ass.

A moment of disorientation as the *wendigo* ducked into an alley and began to climb up a red brick wall. The ground receded, providing a view of a toppled trash can and garbage covered with snow. She realized the *wendigo* was no longer holding onto her, that her body was balanced precariously over its shoulder. It needed both hands to scale the wall. If she fell from such a height while still groggy, she'd probably break her neck. Choosing to avoid the more immediate danger, Kayla grabbed two fistfuls of matted fur and hung on tightly. So what if she looked like a Fay Wray wannabe in a bizarre remake of *King Kong*? She would survive a little longer.

Once the *wendigo* climbed onto the building's roof, it wrapped its arm around the back of her thighs again, its claws scoring her jeans. A few long strides across the roof of the building, then it paused to kick a loose cinder block out of its way. The cinder block had been pinning down one corner of a black tarp, mostly covered with snow. Freed, the corner of the tarp flapped in the gusting wind. The *wendigo* crouched to peer under the flap, then grunted in apparent surprise. It stood upright, took a few more steps, and struck aside another cinder block. Now the tarp billowed in the air, whipping and snapping like a flag at full staff. Kayla could also hear the creak of the sagging roof under the *wendigo*'s weight. The tarp had covered a gaping hole in the roof, through which she could see rotted timbers and darkness below. The *wendigo* stood on a natural depression in the roof, a place where water had gathered over the years, seeping into the building materials, compromising their integrity and precipitating a partial collapse of the roof.

I know this place! We're on the roof of the Palace Cinema.

The *wendigo* leaned over the gaping, yard-wide hole, and peered into the darkness. Its glowing yellow eyes were obviously better adapted to the dark than her human eyes were, because it gave another satisfied grunt. For all Kayla's eyes revealed, they might just as well have been standing over the foulest pit of Hell.

The *wendigo* thrust its foot down, snapping free some of the rotted beams and planking. She heard the debris crash in the darkness. The next moment the *wendigo* brought her down off its shoulder, pressed her to its chest, and jumped into the newly expanded hole. Kayla squeezed her eyes shut and grimaced as they fell thirty feet or so to the bottom. Their descent seemed at once endless and instantaneous.

They landed with an earsplitting crash of shattered wood and screeching metal. As the *wendigo* climbed over this new wreckage, Kayla's eyes began to adjust to the deeper darkness. They had landed in the first two rows of the theater, destroying about four padded seats in the process. The massive white rectangle of the movie screen gleamed ghostly white in the darkness, bordered by the folded lengths of a retracted curtain. In front of the screen was a walkway that resembled a foreshortened stage, with curved steps providing access at either end. The Palace Cinema had featured comfortable seats and a large balcony but only one—admittedly massive—screen. The variety of films offered by the multiplexes in Harrison and Peabody had put it out of business. The hail storm and subsequent flood damage to the uninsured roof had just been the final nail in the coffin. A coffin, Kayla thought, that had now become hers.

The *wendigo* dropped her unceremoniously on the truncated stage in front of the wide movie screen, then it jumped up and crouched beside her. "*Tell now . . .*" it rasped in its sandpaper-on-cement voice.

Naturally, Kayla was afraid of the creature, but even more afraid that anything she said might be enough to send it into a murderous—and ravenous!—rage. She moaned softly, a bit of improvisational acting on an abandoned stage, pretending she was semiconscious or delirious, to stall for time.

The *wendigo* grabbed her jacket in its clawed fist, bunching it tight under her throat and lifting her face up to its horrifying head. "*Tell now . . . or DIE!*"

Wendy's plan was simple. Two sets of eyes were better than one. While Abby soared over downtown Windale as a red-tailed hawk looking for a hole in the sky, Wendy would assist the aerial search using her astral form. Meanwhile, Alex would rely on the Pathfinder's four-wheel drive and snow tires to provide ground level reconnaissance, using the diner as the focus and expanding the search radius a block at a time in each direction with every circuit. The *wendigo* was afoot, dragging or carrying Kayla, which would hinder its progress. There was a chance Alex would intercept them before the *wendigo* could hide with its captive.

Before Alex left the diner's parking lot, Sheriff Nottingham gave him a spare police radio, with instructions to call for assistance the moment he spotted anything unusual. Alex now carried a police issue automatic and radio. Although he had not officially been deputized, he was essentially, as the police might say, on the job.

With Alex navigating the snow-clogged streets, Wendy's astral form rose through the roof of the SUV and into the stormy night. Not sure what a "hole in the sky" meant or where she should look for such a phenomenon, Wendy floated above the level of the buildings and the trees planted during Windale's last bout of urban beautification. Since the *wendigo* was incapable of flight, the "hole in the sky" reference was even more perplexing. *Or misleading,* she thought. *It must be down* there *somewhere.* She mulled over the clues the Crone had left her, *White wall . . . dark rows . . .* She saw rows of businesses, upscale town houses, more modest row homes and rows of trees. In a storm at night, everything seemed dark . . . and hopeless. They were running out of time.

Kayla most of all.

CHAPTER FIFTEEN

Confronted with the *wendigo*'s lambent yellow eyes, flattened nose and fetid mouth filled with uneven rows of jagged teeth, Kayla's voice came out as little more than a frightened whisper. "What—what do you want?"

"*Tell . . . why? Why bring here to kill . . . Wenn-dee!*"

"That—that wasn't me," Kayla said. "I didn't bring you here."

It squeezed the coat bunched at her neck. "*You . . . LIE!*"

Kayla croaked, "No! Wither called you—and she's dead!"

"*You lie . . . you SHE!*"

"She died. A long time ago," Kayla said. "Two summers ago!"

Curious, loosening the grip. "*Summer . . . ?*"

"That's right. In August. So you're, uh, free to go back—back home. Okay?"

"*No home, not free . . . until Wenn-dee dead!*"

"No! Wendy is dangerous. Very powerful Wiccan. Leave, before it's too late."

"*No choice. MUST kill.*" It shoved her back in anger and frustration. Her head struck the hardwood floor of the shortened stage. "*You . . . not one who make kill?*"

Kayla shook her head. *A rhetorical question? New facts sinking through thick skull. Just shut up, and let it get on about its business.*

"*If you not she . . .*" It paused, thinking. "*You no help . . . Not need you.*"

Kayla realized her error too late. She had steered a potentially dangerous conversation down the definitely lethal fork in the road. For some reason, the *wendigo* had been under the mistaken impression that she was Wither, and it had wanted something from her, something other than essential vitamins and iron. Now it thought she was useless, except as a possible midnight snack.

It turned its horrible visage full upon her. In the ghostly light reflected from the white screen above her she couldn't be certain, but she thought it was drooling. "*Not need you . . . alive.*"

"Uh—um, wait—wait a minute . . ."

KEE-ARR!

Both Kayla and the *wendigo* looked up toward the hole in the roof, through which swirling torrents of snow continued to fall. Perched on one of the rotted and split joists at the edge of the hole was a large, mostly white bird. *Oh, God!* Kayla thought with a flood of relief. *It's Abby—she found me!* "Abby! Get help!"

With an enraged roar, the *wendigo* swung at Kayla. She managed to turn away from the brunt of the blow, but it caught her shoulder and the impact slid her across the floor to slam into the wall under the movie screen.

The red-tailed hawk stretched its wings and launched itself through the hole, fighting a sudden downdraft before vanishing into the night sky. *Oh, God,* Kayla thought. *Hurry, Abby! Hurry!*

Before Wendy found anything remotely suggestive of a "hole in the sky" she saw the shape of a white bird struggling against the fierce winds, but veering toward her. Wendy willed herself toward the hawk, and was coasting at her side in seconds, attempting to mirror the bird's erratic flight as best she could. "*Abby, have you found it? The hole in the sky?*"

KEE-ARR!

"*And Kayla? She's alive?*" The hawk screeched again. "*Show me!*"

Hawk Abby wheeled around almost 180 degrees, then pounded her powerful wings into the teeth of the storm. After a block or two, Abby dropped down toward the roof of the Palace Cinema, which had closed in late spring and never reopened. *Structural damage,* Wendy recalled. In a moment, she saw the gaping hole in the Palace's roof for herself. Wendy pointed. "*Kayla . . . down there? With the wendigo?*" Another affirmative screech. The details clicked for Wendy. "*Dark rows*" of theater seats, a "*white wall*" movie screen. "*Abby, listen to me. Find Alex! Green car. Big. Bring him here. Then YOU go HOME. Understand?*" The hawk screeched yet again, but something about the sound seemed unconvincing this time. "*Promise!*"

The hawk banked away, spiraling down closer to the deserted streets.

For Abby's own safety, Wendy had to hope she would show some common sense and return home after locating Alex. At the moment, Wendy had her hands full. She had to stay and assess the situation and determine if Kayla was in immediate danger. *Have to find a way to help her in my astral form! Give her time to escape. Guess this is where I'm supposed to have some excrement to fling at the* wendigo, *to confuse it and . . . Wait a minute! Confuse it. That's all that matters. Maybe it will be enough.*

Wendy gazed into the hole in the roof, into the darkness. The snow swirling above the roof seemed to be drawn magically to that hole, spiraling down, like water rushing down a funnel, into the pit . . . with its master. *Stop stalling!* First she visualized her astral self completely transparent; then she sank her astral consciousness into the pit.

Alex thought he was hallucinating. Rubbed his eyes twice to convince himself that in the midst of the heavy snowfall a large white bird was swooping back and forth in front of the Pathfinder. "Christ, it's Abby!" One of Wendy's astral errands had been to enlist her aid in the search for Kayla. *Wendy must have stayed, sending Abby to find me and guide me there,* he realized. After flashing his high beams at Abby to indicate his understanding, he glanced worriedly at Wendy's entranced body slumped in the passenger seat beside him. *She's safe in astral form . . . isn't she?*

He fumbled with the police radio, almost dropping it when Abby banked to the left, and he had to make a sudden turn to stay with her. Pressing the call button, he spoke in a rush. "Sheriff, it's Alex. Abby's found something. She's taking me there now. I'll call soon as I know the location. Over."

The sheriff's voice came back over the radio. "Abby? What the hell are you talking about, Alex?"

Wary of revealing too much about Abby's current physical form over the open police band, Alex said, "Wendy's, uh, pet hawk. Named her Abby, remember?" *So lame*, Alex thought. He released the button and thought he heard the sheriff curse.

The hawk banked right and Alex turned at the intersection. Ahead was the wedge-shaped white marquee of the Palace Cinema. The hawk swooped down to the large marquee and perched on its tip. Alex picked up the radio again.

Alex's excited voice crackled over the police radio. "The Palace! They're in the Palace Cinema!"

"Wait for backup!" the sheriff replied. "Don't do anything foolish." He was about to sign off, but changed his mind. "And get Ab—that bird the hell out of there!"

The sheriff made a U-turn in the middle of Main Street. He'd been heading in the opposite direction, toward Harrison. Bobby and Angelo were probably on the far side of the Public Safety Building by now. Having heard the urgent call, they would be looping back. When Alex and Wendy left the diner ahead of the police, they had promised to call as soon as they found anything, but Wendy had neglected to mention Abby's involvement. That didn't sit well with the sheriff. Shape-shifting powers aside, Abby was his adopted daughter, a ten-year-old child.

He forced himself to concentrate on the deployment of his forces. Lena's ambulance had already left for Windale General and would return for Borkowski's body. Curtis would remain at the crime scene until the medical examiner cleared the body for removal and the EMTs took it away, then he'd wrap the diner in crime scene tape, pick up his silver-filled bullets from his mail slot at the PSB and, finally, join in the manhunt. Demon-hunt, technically. Made no sense for him to join the fray until he had the proper ammo. With his standard-issue rounds, he'd be defenseless.

That had been the plan, sandlot caliber as it was. But as the sheriff was leaving the scene, the WTKN news van appeared, emerging through the relentless wall of snow for an exclusive on the diner murder. Curtis's instructions for handling the press were simple. One response for every question: "No comment."

Stonewall tonight, he thought. *One way or another, this will be over by morning.*

"Not need you . . . *kill you* . . . *eat you*," the *wendigo* rasped, its maw stretching to approximate a clever smile, but the result was horrific. Maybe that was the point.

Pressed against the wall just under the movie screen, Kayla had backed up as far as possible. She looked across the wide, dark theater. Aside from its unusual size and architectural flourishes, it was fairly standard in design. Three wedge-shaped sections of seats, angled toward the screen, divided by two wide aisles that rose to double-door exits beneath a wide balcony, supported by several ornate columns. The rising mounds of snow on the first few rows of seats, however, added a surreal quality to the opulent décor.

She'd seen a couple dozen movies in the Palace in its day, and knew the layout as well as any Windalien. *I could run for the exit*, she thought, *but I'd never make it through the theater doors, past the concession stand and across the lobby fast enough. Even if I happened to make it that far, I'd have to smash through the exterior doors to escape.*

Bad as her flight option seemed, the fight option was worse. How could she not acknowledge the severe physical mismatch? The *wendigo* was bigger, stronger, faster than the best physical specimen humankind could offer by way of comparison. *What chance do I have?* she thought grimly. Then, *About as much chance as a balloon in a pin factory explosion.* Nevertheless, she had to do something fast, if only to distract the *wendigo* from its grumbling stomach.

"Wait, wait, wait!" Kayla said, holding out her hands. "True, I'm not the one who called you, but she—she infected me with her blood."

The *wendigo* loomed over her, dark claws twitching but not striking. That had to be encouraging. "*Her blood . . . ?*"

"Yes! It means I can do . . . things—things she did." *Maybe that's what caught its attention.* It was a supernatural creature, the scope of its powers and perception unknown. "I opened her secret place and unlocked a book, her book of spells." Slight embellishment, but more intriguing than the cold truth. *Keep stalling!*

"*Spells . . . magic? You know her magic?*"

"Some of it . . . comes naturally. From the blood. Her blood inside me."

"*Stronger here . . . powers stronger . . . much snow falls . . . how keep power?*"

Fuck if I know, Kayla thought. "Okay, that . . . that's a tricky one."

. . . Kayla . . .

It brandished its claws in front of her face and nodded. "*Make you bleed . . . then keep stronger powers?*"

Oh, shit, not this again. "No! That's not how it works!"

. . . Kayla . . . Listen to me . . .

A voice. So faint. "Wendy?" Kayla whispered. "How?"

"*Then show . . . Show now!*"

. . . I'm astral projecting . . . will distract . . . ready to run . . .

"Okay. Okay, I'm ready."

"*Show now! Or DIE!*"

"I'll need to stand," Kayla said, climbing cautiously to her feet. The *wendigo* tensed and took one step backward, but stayed within arm's reach. She experienced a flash memory of the creature smashing Wild Bill's head into the counter, and shuddered.

"OVER HERE, YOU BIG SMELLY APE!"

Growling, the *wendigo* turned its back on Kayla to confront the new arrival.

A moment earlier, Kayla had seen Wendy's astral image appear on the opposite side of the stage. Wendy's astral feet floated an inch or so above the wood floor of the shortened stage. Otherwise, the illusion looked real, solid.

The *wendigo* believed it. "WENN-DEE!"

"*You're supposed to kill me, Fluffy. Remember?*"

"Kill you . . . YES!"

"Well . . . *what are you waiting for?*" she said, flashing a meaningful look past the *wendigo* at Kayla. "*You want to end Wither's curse? Come and get me!*"

Mortified that she'd missed her cue—*on a stage, no less!*—Kayla edged away from the *wendigo*'s back. She slipped over the lip of the four-foot-high stage, dropped soundlessly to the carpeted floor and crept along the front of the theater to the right aisle. She stopped when she remembered there were fire exits on either side of the movie screen. Emergency lights were extinguished, so they weren't as obvious, but they were still there, and much closer than the double doors at the back of the theater. A quick glance at the stage . . .

The *wendigo* stalked Wendy with a show of caution. *Wary of her magic or suspicious of her confidence?*

Kayla padded down the ramp to the steel door and shoved down on the push bar. The metal bar squealed and—stopped short with a rattle of chains. *Oh, fuck! It must have heard that racket!* Kayla reversed direction and raced up the right aisle, sparing another glance at the stage.

The *wendigo* slashed at Wendy's astral form, wild swipes of its claws, a furious attack that passed harmlessly through her astral image. Wendy's astral form shimmered, however, after every frantic blow. Unfortunately, the roundhouse swings turned the *wendigo's* head enough for it to see Kayla sprinting for the exit. "Ghost body! TRICK!" the *wendigo* rasped. "KILL *witch pretender . . .*"

The floor shook beneath Kayla when the *wendigo* jumped down from the stage and continued to shake with every thunderous stride it took to close the distance between them. Too afraid to risk another look over her shoulder, she lunged at the double exit doors. Grabbed the nearest handle. Pulled it toward her and . . .

. . . the door was wrenched from her grasp with a protesting squeal of hinges and the splintery shearing of wood. Kayla stumbled into the long lobby, fought for and kept her balance—and ran!

Ahead, she saw Alex climb out of Wendy's Pathfinder and rush to the glass entrance doors. He saw her rushing toward him a moment later. His eyes went round when he saw what was right on her heels, causing the hair on the back of her neck to rise. She passed the empty glass display cases of the refreshment counter on her right, the door to the projectionist's booth on her left.

Alex yanked the glass doors, which rattled against their locks. Chained besides. He kicked the lower panel with the toe of his boots. His second kick cracked the glass. Too little, too late. Kayla made it as far as the opposing restroom doors before the *wendigo* caught her. Its long, powerful arm looped around her waist and hoisted her into the air with ease. "Freaky fucking son of a BITCH!" Kayla screamed. "LET—ME—GO!"

As if it had all the time in the world, it turned and lumbered back through the damaged door into the dark theater. When they were halfway to the stage, Kayla heard glass shattering, almost an explosion. Again, too little, too late. Astral Wendy had vanished, yet even if she'd hung around, the *wendigo* wouldn't fall for the same trick twice. *Too gruesome to watch your friend be eaten alive. Can't blame her for slipping out before the macabre portion of the show.*

As if to underscore the futility of her escape attempt, the wendigo tossed her back onto the stage, then jumped up beside her again. *Back to square one,* she thought miserably.

"*Make you bleed for trick . . . pretend witch.*"

One raised claw flicked across her face and sliced her cheek open from her ear to her nose ring. She gasped at the sudden, burning pain and pressed her hand to her cheek, but the *wendigo* grabbed her wrist and exposed the wound. "*Human blood,*" it said. "*Red blood . . . no power in . . . metal face girl . . .*"

Metal face . . . ? She realized its eerie yellow gaze had fixated on the right side of her face, specifically on the gleaming surgical steel post that pierced the skin at the outer edge of her eyebrow. Panicked, she thought, *No! Don't—!*

It pinched the short metal post between two pointed claws and ripped it out of her face. Kayla's scream echoed in the condemned theater.

My astral form is a one-trick phony, Wendy thought bitterly. Once the *wendigo* realized it was attempting to disembowel a bodiless form, Wendy could no longer help Kayla. As her friend ran up the aisle with the *wendigo* in pursuit, Wendy streaked across the theater, up through the roof and down through the marquee into the Pathfinder, settling into her physical body, which startled awake. Fighting gravity lag, she pushed open the car door as Alex was kicking his way through the theater's front entrance.

Not only were the doors themselves locked, padlock chains looped through each paired set of handles. Given time and some finesse, Wendy could probably pick the locks with magic. Instead, she resorted to her new sphere trick, creating surface protrusions and rotating the sphere so fast that, had it been visible, it would have been a blur.

Commanding Alex to step aside, she strode forward and struck the door with her spinning protective sphere. The glass shattered instantly, spraying shards of various sizes all over the red-carpeted lobby.

"Couldn't shoot it out," Alex said. "I'd waste the silver bullets."

She noticed he had his cane-sword tucked under his arm as well. "Let's go!"

"Sheriff said to wait."

"We wait," Wendy said. "Kayla dies."

"Right," Alex said, then ducked through the broken door.

Wendy followed. As they dashed across the red-carpeted lobby, they heard Kayla scream. They stepped through the broken interior door, into the deeper darkness of the theater. Wendy glimpsed the *wendigo* looming over Kayla's cowering form. Kayla's hand was pressed to her forehead. The right side of her face was covered in blood. The *wendigo* looked as if it was about to pluck something off her face with its claws. *Oh, God!* Wendy thought. *It's ripping out her piercings!* She whispered, "Alex, how good a shot are you?"

"Not good enough," he whispered back. "From here, I might hit her."

"It wants to kill me more than it wants to terrorize her," Wendy said. "I'll cross to the other side of the theater and lure it away from her."

"That's your plan?"

"When it comes after me, shoot it," Wendy said. "And, uh, try not to miss. Okay?"

"Take this," Alex said, handing her his cane-sword. "Just in case magic isn't enough. Don't argue. I need to get closer. Wait until I'm in position. Go!"

Taking the cane, Wendy slipped the tip through a belt loop in her jeans, palm resting on the gargoyle head to keep the shaft against her leg. She sidestepped along a back row of seats, all the way to the opposite aisle. Crouching low, Alex scrambled down his aisle to the front of the theater. Wendy waited until he stopped, beside the center section, third row of seats, and nodded in her direction. Taking a deep breath, she stood up, stepped into the open and began the long, slow walk to the front of the theater. "Hey, *wendigo!* I'm over here!"

The *wendigo* looked over its shoulder at her, yellow eyes ablaze. It rasped in disgust, "*Same trick?*"

"No tricks this time," Wendy said, her voice remarkably calm. Remarkable because she was terrified. She stopped, removed the cane from her belt loop and rapped it against the nearest seat-back. "Solid. Real me. Meat on the hoof."

Kayla had inched back from the creature, but was still within its considerable reach. Blood shone on her cheek, diluted by tears. She was almost panting with fear. The *wendigo*'s claws were twitching, anticipating a kill . . . but not taking the bait. To lure it away from Kayla, Wendy would have to get closer. Close enough for it to grab her instead. She resumed the long walk to the front of the theater. The *wendigo* dropped a clawed hand on Kayla's hip, startling her, but its burning amber gaze remained fixed on Wendy.

"You know you want me," Wendy said. She stood at the right corner of the center section, first row. "Kill me, the curse ends, and you're a free range demon."

"Kill . . . BOTH!"

"NO! If you kill her, I'll fly away . . . someplace tropical. Under the baking sun." She continued to talk so it wouldn't notice Alex, on the other side of the theater, rising up from behind the cover of theater seats, taking careful aim. "Look, how often does dinner serve itself?" Less than nine feet away from the demon, Wendy's left hand slipped over her crystal pendant. "Here I am, all hot and juicy. Come and get me!" The *wendigo*'s body shifted toward her. It lifted its possessive claw from Kayla's hip as it rose from its crouch. "Besides, you don't want to eat her. All those metal bits will chip your pointy teeth. C'mon, take me instead. And let her go away."

Kayla heard the emphasis on the word "go" and this time seized on the cue. Hopping down from the stage, she veered up the aisle where Alex had assumed a shooter's stance. Her sudden flight caught the *wendigo*'s attention. Too late, it turned toward Kayla, spotting her as she passed Alex who, at that moment, squeezed off a shot.

BLAM!

The *wendigo* roared as a yellow furrow blossomed on its right arm—a flesh wound. Kayla squeezed through the broken exit door. Relief flooded through Wendy, but it was temporary. Instead of charging Alex, who had the gun, the *wendigo* leapt from the stage in Wendy's direction. The abrupt change of course caused Alex's second shot to miss and the bullet tore a long, dark gash in the white movie screen.

Wendy had started to back away after the first shot, not wanting to be within reach of the enraged *wendigo*. As it jumped off the stage, Wendy pressed the recessed button that snapped up the gargoyle-head handle, releasing the short sword from its cane scabbard. Even with the silver weapon in hand, the idea of poking at a creature whose arms seemed long enough to swat low-flying planes had lost its appeal. Consequently, before she approached the stage from the first row of seats, she'd raised her protective sphere.

Taking care to keep Wendy out of his line of fire, Alex circled around the first row of seats and approached the creature. The *wendigo*, sensing his approach, ripped an armrest off the nearest seat and flung it at Alex's head with deadly force. Alex ducked, but the wood struck his shoulder, staggering him. "My shield's up, Alex! Shoot!"

The *wendigo* lunged at Wendy, crashing into her protective sphere with its considerable strength. Her sphere slammed into the front row of the far section. Several seats bent or shattered on impact. Inside her sphere, Wendy was disoriented but unharmed. Seeing her dazed within the shield, Alex was reluctant to test the shield's bullet-proof capacity. Only her focus maintained its integrity. "Alex! Shoot!"

With a grimace, he took careful aim and fired—

—into the meat of the creature's thigh. The *wendigo* roared in pain, but refused to attack its tormenter. Instead, it reached up with both hands and dug its claws into the surface of the sphere, finding the layer of magical resistance. Wendy doubted the creature could claw its way through the magical barrier, as long as she remained focused. With Alex in no immediate jeopardy, focus wouldn't be a problem.

"*Magic . . .*" the *wendigo* rasped, spattering her shield with its thick saliva. "*Eat . . . magic . . . make stronger.*"

Wendy frowned. Eat magic? Was it bluffing? *It's a meat eater, a raw meat eater, not a . . . Is there such a thing as a magic eater?*

Wendy's sphere was pinned between the broken seats and the *wendigo's* digging claws. She tried her spin technique, but the sphere was lodged tight in the cramped space. She struck out with pseudopods, like fists of energy, but the *wendigo* grunted, absorbing the blows as it gnashed its teeth. Something odd was happening. Perspiration beaded her brow. Maybe her imagination was running wild, but it seemed as if her sphere had contracted, become just a little bit smaller. And the *wendigo's* claws and drooling maw were that much closer.

Wendy suddenly remembered something the Crone had said about her protective sphere. The Crone had been fading at the time and the thought had been incomplete: "*More versatile . . . not vulnerable to . . .*"

My sphere, vulnerable to . . . ?

Oh, *no,* she thought grimly, *It's true. The wendigo's absorbing my magical energy!*

Bobby reached the Palace Cinema before the sheriff or Angelo.

Despite the frigid temperature, he continued to perspire. His arms and legs trembled as he climbed out of his police cruiser. He scratched an itch on his face and noticed the skin felt rough, like animal hide, almost numb to the touch. But he'd worry about his own course of treatment later, when Kayla was safe.

The green Pathfinder was angled toward the curb and, strangely, a white hawk perched on the movie marquee. As if aware of his scrutiny, the hawk shrieked and flew up into the stormy sky, circling over the roof of the cinema. Something about a hawk on the radio, but he couldn't remember. Hard to concentrate. He ducked through the broken glass door into the dark lobby, gun in hand.

Kayla, her blue hair almost iridescent in the ambient light, stumbled through a dangling theater door into the lobby, clutching her face, which was smeared with blood. Rage filled Bobby, the sudden need to kill, kill whatever was responsible.

"Bobby! Oh, God—oh, God, you're here! You have to help them!" She ran into his arms, savoring the fierce embrace. "It's in the theater! With Alex and Wendy—they saved me, but I couldn't . . ."

"Have to . . . get you out of here first." Bobby's voice was raw with emotion. He shoved his gun into its holster, then grabbed her upper arms. "To—to a . . . hospital."

"Help them first!" She winced in his grip. "You're hurting me!"

He shook his head. She didn't understand. Had to make her understand. The rage . . . "Must kill it now . . . got away before . . ." His eyes burned, throbbing in their sockets, and his teeth ached. He stretched his jaw wide until he felt it crack. "Must kill . . ."

"Bobby . . . what's happening to you?" Kayla said, her face a mask of new fear, fear of him. "Your eyes . . . they're glowing . . . yellow."

"I'm sick . . . just sick," he swallowed hard. "I'll go later—I'll . . . you're confusing me!" He shook her hard. Letting out that small bit of rage filled him with relief. Giving in to the strong desire to hurt and . . . to kill.

"Let me go!" she said, hands at his waist, trying to shove him away. Her gaze dropped to his hands, where they clutched her arms. "Oh, Christ, Bobby—your hands! There's fur on your fucking hands!"

Bobby stared at them, at the white tufts of fur that had sprouted through the coarsening skin. "No!" he screamed at her, as if it were her fault. He shoved her away, so forcefully she staggered across the lobby. Giving into the rage was intoxicating, liberating, like a shot of single malt scotch. "What's—what's happening . . ." His hands stroked his face, felt coarse hair sprouting there as well, beneath his sideburns, along his jaw. And his fingernails had darkened, like an animal's claws. "What's happening!?" he shouted, stalking her, trembling fists clenched at his sides.

"You said it got away before, Bobby," Kayla said. "You've seen the *wendigo*, haven't you? Did—did it bite you?"

He wrestled off his leather jacket, ripped open his shirt to expose the teeth punctures. His skin was roughest there, and covered with thick white fur. "It made me . . . What am I becoming?"

Kayla nodded, tears spilling from her eyes. "You're infected."

"What—what's the . . ." He struggled to find the words, even as the rage rolled through every corner of his mind, spreading like a toxin. "What . . . cure?"

Knowing the truth, Kayla sobbed. She had backed up to the far wall, was pressed against the projectionist's door, and now slid down to the floor, defeated. The brass door handle gleamed just above her head. Bobby stood over her, trembling with confused rage. "Bobby . . . there is no cure."

He struck out, slamming his fist into the door, splintering the wood. "No! A fucking monster . . . I won't! No, no,

NO!" He pulled his gun out and shoved it under his chin. "Kill myself first." Kayla wailed, knees drawn to her chest, fisted hands pressed to her face. Something round, metallic clutched in her hand. Seemed familiar, but he couldn't focus beyond the surging rage and self-loathing. Somehow, it all seemed to be her fault. She was the reason. She'd told him that—thing had infected him! She was responsible for the hate, the rage, for why he wanted—needed to kill . . .

But not himself. No . . .

He tossed the gun aside. It landed with a heavy clunk and skidded a short distance on the nappy red carpet. Kayla looked up at him, her eyes wide with fear. He could almost smell her fear, could almost taste—her. That fresh, glistening blood on her face . . . the smell of it! He licked his lips.

"Bobby?" her voice was so small.

Kayla whispered, "Bobby?"

Her forehead was a throbbing drumbeat of pain, oozing blood, as she sat huddled with her knees drawn up to her chest, perhaps trying to make herself as small a target as possible. She held her fisted hands pressed to her cheeks, warm blood against the right, the cool touch of metal a small comfort in her left. A sliver of hope.

"Bobby, don't . . ." But she knew it was too late. He was too far gone. She could see the inhuman bloodlust in his eyes. He'd been bitten by a *wendigo* and its evil spirit was in complete possession of him. He wasn't Bobby anymore. He no longer cared about protecting her—*and why had that ever been such a bad thing?*—he no longer cared about her, period. She was a different species now. She was meat. *Escaped one monster to run into the arms of another,* she thought bitterly. *World's worst fucked-up luck!*

With an inhuman snarl, Bobby's right arm darted out, his hand clamping around her throat to slam her head against the door. "Bitch! You did this to me!" he rasped, completely irrational now, his face a mask of misdirected rage. Moment by moment, tufts of fur sprouted on his cheeks, surrounding those eerie yellow eyes.

Kayla's hands twitched, fumbling with the metal ring . . .

"Bobby!" the sheriff shouted from the theater entrance. "Let her go!"

Although Bobby's grip remained tight on her throat, his head whipped around to glare at the intruders, Sheriff Nottingham and Angelo Antonelli. That was Kayla's sliver of hope, all the distraction she needed. She slapped one ring around Bobby's wrist, then jerked his arm up and clamped the other ring around the rectangular door handle. The metallic ratcheting sound snared Bobby's attention. His rabid gaze flashed to his wrist—handcuffed to the door—and he roared in frustration.

He'd been so distracted earlier while holding her arms and shaking her that he hadn't noticed the telltale tug when she pulled the cuffs from his belt case. Now he shoved her away, releasing his grip on her throat as he yanked his arm back and forth, rattling the cuffs against the rectangular door handle. Even bolted shut, the door shook on its hinges.

"He's possessed!" Kayla shouted as she rolled to Bobby's left.

He lunged at her with his left hand but came up short, wrenching his right arm in its socket. Kayla hurried across the lobby, scooped up his discarded gun and aimed it at him. With his inhuman strength, he might be capable of ripping the brass handle right off the door. Until that happened, she couldn't bring herself to pull the trigger. Somebody else would have to finish it.

The sheriff and Angelo took positions beside her, well away from Bobby's screaming, kicking rage at being chained. For Bobby's sake, Kayla prayed the irrational fury would continue. While the raging beast remained dominant, the rational, human side of Bobby was unable to pause and think through the problem and resolution of lock and key. *Chained or not*, Kayla thought, *if he reaches for his keys, I'll have to shoot him.*

"*Wendigo* bite?" the sheriff asked. Kayla nodded, not bothering to wipe away the tear that tracked down her bloodless left cheek. "There's no cure." Kayla shook her head, not trusting her voice. "Alex and Wendy?"

"Inside," Kayla said. "They need help."

"You're okay here?"

Kayla indicated the gun with a nod. "I know how to use it."

After one last, grieving look at Bobby, the sheriff nodded to Angelo and they both hurried into the theater—just as another shot rang out.

The *wendigo's* growling face was close enough for Wendy to see the bits of dried human blood on its dark lips and furred chin. Its vicious claws were closing in around her as her protective sphere continued to contract at an alarming rate. In her early days of sphere conjuring, the diameter of her spheres had been limited. Only through months of practice had she been able to sustain larger spheres and even mold portions of them to her will as needed. Now she needed total concentration simply to keep her sphere from collapsing. Worse, as she became weaker, the *wendigo's* power increased. Wind howled down through the hole in the ceiling, scattering the accumulated mounds of snow in erratic whirlwinds. On either side of Wendy, a thin sheen of ice coated the broken theater seats. No longer sweating from exertion, she was shivering with cold, her teeth chattering. The *wendigo* was not only absorbing her magic energy, it seemed to be siphoning her body heat.

Her flow of magic had reversed, and she was helpless to stop it. Hard as she tried to draw magical energy into her body, and wield it, the *wendigo* was pulling it away from her, depleting her magical reserves and her physical strength moment by moment. *Can't hold out much longer.*

Sensing her distress, Alex rushed forward, breath pluming in front of his face, gun held high in the double-handed grip as he sought a good angle for a point-blank shot. By now, Wendy was uncertain if her magical shield was proof against bullets. Doubt led to faulty visualization, which was the same as failure.

BLAM!

Wendy flinched, but not as much as the *wendigo*, with a chunk of its shoulder blown away. With a ferocious roar it clamped its arms around the contracting sphere and tried to tear into the energy barrier with its teeth. Wendy shrieked—but her shield held.

Alex closed the gap between him and the *wendigo*, coming dangerously close.

"Alex—NO!"

Too late. Alex took the final step and pressed the sleek black muzzle of his Glock 23 against the creature's right temple. "Die, fucker!" Alex shouted, almost a command. He squeezed the trigger and—

CLICK!

—on an empty chamber. The clip was empty. Frantic, Alex pulled the trigger repeatedly. CLICK! CLICK! CLICK!

Out of silver bullets, and Wendy had his silver-plated cane trapped inside the—

Alex raised the gun in a desperate attempt to pistol-whip the *wendigo*, but a clawed hand snatched Alex's wrist and wrenched it hard, snapping bone. With Alex gasping in pain, the *wendigo* pulled him by his damaged wrist and, with a motion like cracking a whip, flung him against the front of the shortened stage. Alex dropped in a heap.

Wendy was about to lose her protective sphere altogether. She decided not to wait. Gripping the silver-plated sword hilt in both hands, she dropped the shield, absorbing the remaining energy into herself. The *wendigo's* weight had been resting against the magical barrier, pressing against it, in a sort of reverse tug of war. When she released the energy, the *wendigo* fell against her. Wendy rode the surge of energy to meet its fall with a stiff upward thrust of the silver-plated sword. The *wendigo's* own weight worked against it, driving the sword under its ribs, into its body up to the gargoyle hilt.

Several things happened at once. Unsupported by her own shield, Wendy fell into the wreckage of the broken theater seats, a piece of which slammed into her head, dazing her. Another chunk gouged into her side, while a twisted piece of metal sliced her right arm open from wrist to elbow. But she had fallen into a collapsed pocket of chairs, which formed a small shelter for her upper torso around which the *wendigo* collapsed, supported inches above her by the surrounding, intact chairs. She was spared the full brunt of its weight, if not its rage. It shrieked in agony, even as it reared up to bring its vicious claws into play, to disembowel her where she lay too stunned to move. It's *wound might eventu-*

ally prove fatal, she thought bitterly, *but not soon enough.* Alex and Sheriff Nottingham were both shouting her name, fearing the worst. And finally, above the *wendigo's* fearsome head, Wendy saw a flutter of white—wide white wings stroking the snow-laden air. "Abby, no . . ." she whispered.

Two gunshots rang out in quick succession—too close together to be from the same gun. Yellow blooms appeared on the *wendigo's* fur, one on its chest and one above its right hip. But Abby had committed herself to attack a moment before the gunfire, before she realized help had arrived in the wake of Alex's crippling injury. Fearing Wendy was in immediate danger, she swooped down from the balcony level, diving at the *wendigo's* head, claws extended to rake its face, to ravage its burning yellow eyes. When the *wendigo* staggered back in pain from the silver-laced slugs, it spotted Abby's fateful approach, her threat nothing more than a nuisance. But it was angry, very angry.

"Abby—NO!" the sheriff yelled. To his deputy, "Hold your fire!"

Abby flew within inches of the *wendigo's* face. A swipe of its claws snapped her wing, high up near the shoulder. The red-tailed hawk flipped over in midair, one wing struggling to right a body no longer aerodynamic. An errant, spiraling descent and she was on the ground, squirming and almost helpless at the *wendigo's* feet. With a vicious snarl, the *wendigo* raised a foot to stomp the life out of the crippled bird.

As soon as Abby had sustained the injury, the sheriff sprinted toward the *wendigo.* Afraid to shoot and hit her as she fluttered down, his only concern was to shield her, then move her to safety.

When the *wendigo* raised its foot to stomp the hawk,

Sheriff Nottingham began firing, striding closer with each devastating blast. The creature staggered two steps backward, enough for the sheriff to position himself between the *wendigo* and Abby's prone form. His last bullet ripped away part of the *wendigo*'s lower jaw. Too close now to retreat, the sheriff seemed to know what was about to happen. He looked at Alex. "Get her out of here!"

Alex climbed to his feet, darted behind the sheriff and scooped the fallen hawk into the cradle of his good arm. Angelo ran by him, toward the sheriff, sparing a confused glance at the hawk. Wendy had the worst seat in the house, staring in shock as the *wendigo* gripped the sheriff's head between its massive clawed hands. Wendy concentrated, tried to draw heat, to conjure fireballs to hurl at the creature, to ignite the smelly, matted fur that covered its entire body, to distract it, to save the . . . *too late!*

Dark claws gouged into the sheriff's cheeks, drawing blood, slowly crushing his face. The sheriff had time to grab the hilt of the sword protruding from the *wendigo*'s abdomen and yank it free, eliciting another shriek of pain and fury from the creature. At that point, the *wendigo* must have decided enough was enough. One clawed hand clutched the sheriff's chin, while the other grabbed the back of his head.

Angelo shouted, "Let him go! NOW!"

The sheriff yelled, "Don't reason with it! Shoot the son of a bitch!" as he gripped the sword hilt in both hands and pressed the tip of the sword under the creature's ruined jaw.

In one agonizing moment, the sheriff shoved the silver-plated sword upward, through the roof of the demon's mouth, and into its brain, and the *wendigo* twisted the sheriff's head in a violent clockwise motion, severing his spine with a sickening crunch.

Angelo emptied his revolver, scoring three of his remaining five shots in the *wendigo*'s face, creating a yellow explosion of blood, gristle and bone.

Sheriff Nottingham's body slumped to the ground and toppled sideways. Driven back by the force of the bullets, the *wendigo* staggered three steps, then fell backward with a thunderous crash.

A moment later, the winds calmed and the snow ended.

Wendy crawled out of the broken theater seats, bleeding from her right arm, her side a throbbing cacophony of pain. None of it mattered. She stumbled over to the sheriff's body and, as she kneeled down beside him, Angelo caught her elbow. Rolling the sheriff onto his back, Wendy stared into his lifeless eyes and began to cry. After a moment she closed his eyelids. With her magic she could heal injuries, but she had no answer for death.

A crash sounded from the lobby.

Alarmed, Wendy looked up at the short, swarthy deputy.

"It's Bobby," he said. "He's turning into one of the creatures."

They kept their distance from Bobby, or whatever it was Bobby had become. Curtis Johnson, the tall black deputy, had just arrived and stood with gun drawn, beside Alex, who had laid the red-tailed hawk on the empty refreshment counter, where the bird twitched, making a clicking sound with its sharp beak. Kayla stood with her legs apart, arms braced with her gun trained on Bobby. She'd been careful to stay out of his reach. But he'd managed to extend that reach significantly. Handcuffed to the door handle, he'd ripped the dead bolt free of its housing and was now violently swinging the door back and forth, one hinge splintering wood as it tore loose from the doorjamb.

"If he breaks free," Curtis said. "We have to put him down."

Her voice strained with conflicting emotions, Kayla said, "I know."

Wendy was stunned at the changes in Bobby: tufts of white fur on his face and hands, his eyes that throbbing yellow color, and his canines extended, giving his face a vampiric cast.

Angelo stood behind her, loading his gun with regulation bullets, no doubt wondering if they would have any effect on this new, demonic Bobby McKay. "Are we sure there's no cure?" he asked Wendy.

She nodded slowly, reluctantly. Wendy doubted her magic could cure *wendigo* possession, even if she could get close enough to try. Bobby would kill anyone foolish enough to step within reach. *Maybe if we had tranquilizer darts,* she thought. *If we could knock him out, I could try to heal this.*

"What can we do?" Angelo asked.

Wendy was numb, thinking of what must come next. Her voice was hollow, drained of emotion. "Only one way to end . . ."

"What?"

"We have to . . . have to kill him, dismember the body and burn the pieces."

Bobby roared, thrashing the door back and forth, pummeling the wood panels with his fists, desperate to free himself and inflict his rage on someone, anyone, even the woman he loved. Her face a mask of drying blood, Kayla's lips trembled, and tears coursed down her cheeks. "Oh, God, Bobby. I'm so sorry. So sorry . . ."

She knows she'll have to kill him, Wendy thought. *And if not her, one of us. There must be something, anything . . . damn it!*

"The sheriff thought this might happen," Curtis said. "Had me bring gasoline and fire axes from the station."

Kayla sobbed. "Sorry, Bobby. It should be me. I'm the one . . ."

Bobby's hair color changed before their eyes, turning a dull white.

"God, he's still changing," Angelo said. "Wish there was something we could do to stop this."

Wendy looked at him, grabbed his sleeve. "What?"

"A way to stop the transformation, before it's finished."

Wendy smiled. "That's it. Before it finishes. Stop the infection!" They all looked at her, not quite daring to hope. "I'll explain later," she said. "Curtis, get those supplies. Hurry! We're running out of time."

Kayla glanced at Wendy, her eyes wide with fear and something else. "Wendy, if you're about to . . . I—I don't think I can watch."

"It's all right, Kayla," Wendy said. "I have an idea. I think we can save him."

Curtis returned with two red-handled axes and a two-gallon red and yellow gasoline container. "Alex, carry Abby out to the car. Kayla, wait here with Bobby."

"What if he breaks free?" She'd allowed room for hope, a flicker of hope that she wouldn't need to kill the man she loved. But what were her options?

Wendy grimaced. "Then . . . shoot his foot, his knee. Slow him down." She motioned for the deputies to follow her. Curtis gave Bobby a wide berth, slipping behind Kayla so as not to cross her line of fire.

Bobby growled, spewing saliva and, with one great heave,

ripped the top hinge plate loose. The door leaned forward. Kayla backed up, bumping into the refreshment counter. Alex picked up the hawk and backed toward the entrance. Kayla yelled after Wendy, "There's no time!"

"Give me two minutes!"

Kayla looked doubtful. Two minutes could be an eternity.

Wendy led the deputies down to the front of the theater, shouting instructions as she pulled the sheriff's body away from the dead *wendigo*. In seconds, she heard the heavy wet *thunk* of axes chopping into flesh, the sharp crack of bones split in two. They set aside their axes after the creature's torso was separated from its head, arms and legs. Both deputies doused the pieces of the furred corpse in gasoline. "Anybody have a match?" Curtis shook his head; Angelo said he'd given up smoking last year.

Curtis suggested, "Road flares in the squad cars."

"No time," Wendy said.

She conjured a fireball. A small one. But it was enough.

Wendy returned to the lobby just as Bobby ripped the door free of the last hinge.

Kayla jumped back just in time. With a tremendous heave, Bobby swung the door around, smashing it into the glass cases of the refreshment stand. Kayla fired a warning shot into the ceiling, wasting a silver-filled round. "Bobby, don't make me shoot you!"

He stomped on the door, kicking out the last panel, then smashed the frame until only the brass handle and its plate remained, sporting jagged pieces of wood, like a crude, homemade mace dangling from the end of the handcuff ring. With a roar of triumph he charged her. She aimed at his foot, fired and missed.

Wendy tried to maneuver around him, to reach Kayla in time to raise a protective sphere around both of them, but realized she'd never make it in time. "Kayla! You don't have a choice!

Kayla had a pained expression on her face, hesitating . . .

"Stop him! Give this ritual time to work!" Wendy shouted. "Before he does something he'll regret." *Like killing you!* "Fire! I'll heal the wound."

But Kayla continued to hesitate. Until her back collided with the theater's damaged front doors. With an anticipatory grimace, she aimed and fired.

Bobby collapsed, howling in pain as he clutched his left thigh above the knee. Blood seeped through his fingers. Red blood, not yellow! He rocked back and forth, gasping and moaning. Kayla looked horrified. She tossed the gun aside and began the agonizing wait. She dared not approach, and was afraid to try.

Ominously, the theater began to vibrate. Bits of broken glass fell from the display cases and jittered across the lobby carpet. The walls began to shake and particles from ceiling tiles rained down on them. An eerie green light spread from deep inside the theater, slowly expanding into the lobby, then flashing out into the night. At once, the building fell still. *It's the curse,* Wendy knew. *Released from the* wendigo. *But where did it go? And what happens to Bobby?*

Within thirty seconds, she had her answer. The white tufts of fur on Bobby's face started to fall out, and his eyes lost their inhuman yellow glow. Then, despite the continuing pain of the gunshot wound, the tension seemed to melt out of his body. The core of rage, coiled inside him since the beginning of the transformation, was gone.

Kayla reacted first to the change. She pounced on him.

"You stupid son of a bitch!" she said, pounding her fist against his chest before hugging him. "You made me shoot you!"

"Guess it hurt you more than me, huh?" he said in a pained voice, somehow managing a smile despite the pain. He winced, then added, "No, not possible."

Curtis and Angelo rushed outside and returned moments later with fire extinguishers and blankets gathered from the trunks of the squad cars. They hurried through the hanging door into the dark theater, hoping to contain the fire inside before it raged out of control.

Alex returned to the lobby, cradling hawk Abby in his good arm. His own face was white with pain, and his right wrist was swollen, a motley crimson and puce.

Kayla looked up at Wendy, her face streaked with blood and tears, but full of gratitude. She whispered, "Thanks."

Wendy slipped off her multi-bead bracelet. Taking the rose quartz between the thumb and forefinger of her left hand, she concentrated on building magical energy inside her for what promised to be a marathon healing session. They were all physically wounded, some worse than others, but she began with Abby, who had suffered the greatest loss of all. Wendy could heal contusions, broken bones and broken wings, but looking down into the hawk's alert, soulful eyes, she admitted to herself there were some wounds she was helpless to repair. As she had learned herself, some wounds respond to no treatment save the passage of time. And some not even then.

EPILOGUE

Alone, Abby sat in a wicker rocking chair by her bedroom window, staring out at the woods, her knees drawn up to her chest. She looked to the trees every day, but that was all. Either her changeable bones were tired, or they were content to let her be a girl and nothing else for a while. She had no desire to roam the forest or to claim the sky. While Erica, Max and Ben played out front in the snow, Abby wanted to stay in the house and spend the long hours trying to forget she was responsible for the death of her adoptive father. But she couldn't forget. Every time her mind felt numb and blank, she would remember how kind and patient and trusting he'd always been, and she would break down and cry all over again. Everyone must hate her. Any day now, she expected Mrs. Nottingham to call her a lying troublemaker and a freak, and ask her to leave.

A knock on the door. "Abby?" Mrs. Nottingham, at last.

Abby wiped her nose on her sleeve and, with a brief acknowledging glance, said in a lost, lonely voice, "Hi."

Mrs. Nottingham sat on the edge of Abby's bed and patted the space beside her. "Come sit with me."

Abby abandoned the comfort of the rocking chair to sit on the bed next to Mrs. Nottingham. Shoulders hunched, head hung low, Abby was afraid to make eye contact. "It's okay if you want me to leave now," she said softly.

"Abby!" Mrs. Nottingham took the girl's hand. "You're part of our family."

"So . . . you'll let me stay?"

"Of course," Mrs. Nottingham said. "But we need to talk."

"I'm sorry," Abby said, and began to sob. "It's all my fault."

Mrs. Nottingham hugged Abby to her black dress and stroked her hair until she calmed down. "Let it out, Abby," she said. "Let it out. But don't blame yourself."

"But I . . ."

"Wendy told me what happened," Mrs. Nottingham said. "That she needed your help. That this goes back to Wither and those other witches, that Bill—Mr. Nottingham . . . your father died trying to save you from something horrible."

"I know. But if I had stayed here, he would still be . . ."

"Abby, you can't know that. Wendy said this horrible creature could have killed many innocent people if he hadn't helped put an end to it. Abby, he died protecting people. That was his job, and he believed in it with all his heart. Wendy said you were trying to protect her, is that true?" Abby nodded. "Then you're just like him. You couldn't bear to let something bad happen to people you care about, to people you love." Mrs. Nottingham stroked Abby's ash blond hair. "Abby, I would sacrifice myself to save you or your brothers and sister. When you love someone, you worry more about that person than you worry about yourself. You would risk your life to save that person. Because that's how much they mean to you. Understand?"

"Yes, Ma'am," Abby said, thoughtful. "I would never let anyone hurt you or Erica or Max or Ben, or Rowdy even."

"Bill—your father, was a hero practically his whole life," Mrs. Nottingham said. "And that's how he died, as a hero. We'll always miss him, but we'll always keep him in our hearts and be very proud of him."

Abby sniffled. "Always." She looked up into Mrs. Nottingham's eyes, which were moist with unshed tears. She gave Abby a brave smile, a smile Abby returned. "Mrs. Nott—I mean, Mom—there's something Wendy didn't tell you. Something I made Wendy and Mr. Nottingham promise never to tell. But he thought I should tell you my secret. And I think I'm ready now."

"What secret, Abby?" Mrs. Nottingham asked. "Is it about Sarah Hutchins?"

Abby nodded, then finger-brushed hair from her red-rimmed eyes. "She changed me, made me different. She did it for her, but it stayed inside me after she died. She was bad, but that doesn't make me bad, does it?"

"Of course not, Abby."

"If something was meant to be bad or to hurt people, but you only use it in good ways and to help people, then it's a good thing, right?"

"I would say it's a good thing."

"Because, that's kinda what happened to me."

Mrs. Nottingham—Abby's mother—squeezed Abby's hand gently, and planted a kiss on her forehead. "Nothing you tell me will make me love you any less, Abby. Because I know in my heart you are a wonderful little girl."

Sheriff Nottingham died to save my life, Abby thought. *So maybe he thought so too.* With a sudden warm feeling inside, Abby knew she could trust Mrs. Nottingham with her life. And so, she shared it with her. All of it.

WINDALE, MASSACHUSETTS
JANUARY 12, 2002

Kayla couldn't help staring at Bobby as he steered his cherry red Mustang GT against the curb on Theurgy Avenue, shifted into park and engaged the emergency brake. Aware of this unwavering attention, he asked, "What?"

"You look so much better without the mangy fur and yellow eyes."

He laughed. "Well, I figured since you have the electric-blue hair, my having yellow eyes wouldn't be all that unusual."

"No, not at all," Kayla said, grinning. "Thanks for driving me to work, Mr. Acting Sheriff."

"That's not an official title, but a ride was the least I could do after that home-cooked breakfast."

"Consider it my apology for, you know, trying to blow off your kneecap. By the way, how's the leg?"

"Good as new," Bobby said, unconsciously reaching down to where the bullet wound had been. "No pain, no scarring, no rehab. Wendy should work in the ER." He studied Kayla's cheerful face, his fingers reaching up to touch the spot above her right eyebrow where she had once worn a surgical steel post. "She definitely does good work. Even healed the piercing hole."

"Yep. And for some strange reason, I shudder at the thought of having it re-pierced."

"Can't imagine why."

Kayla grinned. "I should get inside before Alissa docks my pay." She leaned over and gave him a properly thorough kiss. "Think about me."

"How could I forget the woman who shot me to prove her love?"

She punched his arm. "Don't blame me if you can't handle extreme dating."

When she reached for the door handle, he caught her arm. She quirked an eyebrow, the pierced one. "Kayla, I just want to say . . . I understand what you were going through before. Thinking Wither was inside you, wondering if you were still you."

"What about you, Bobby?" she asked. "Feel any different now that you've experienced your own inner demon?"

"I definitely have a new appreciation for life . . . and for who I have in my life."

She smiled. "Nightmares?"

A slight frown. "Now and then."

"Trust me, Bobby," she said solemnly. "The nightmares go away. Eventually."

Wendy Ward's Mirror Book
January 12, 2002
Moon: waning crescent, day 28
Windale, Massachusetts

Although I hadn't seen Sheriff Nottingham in recent months, his death made me realize that he had become something of a father figure to me. Though my real parents were unaware of my magical abilities, the sheriff knew about and accepted them. In hindsight, I regret not sharing that part of my life with my parents. My mistake was assuming we had years together ahead of us. I thought I needed to define myself before I would have to explain myself. But I never had the chance. I let time slip away. Sometimes, it's as if there's a part of me my parents never really knew. But *if* they knew—as I'm sure they know now, watching over me from a better place—I believe they would be proud of me. The most important lesson they ever taught me was to be a good person, one who is loyal, dependable, honest and trustworthy. I strive for that ideal every day.

Sheriff Nottingham was as proud of Abby MacNeil as any father could be of his daughter. Lately, I see the belief of that in Abby's eyes. And I think it comforts her. Though she's been comfortable in her many skins (and bones) for a while, seeing her now with Mrs. Nottingham and the other Nottingham children makes me smile. She really has found a warm, accepting home. If any good can result from tragedy, it will be in making those familial bonds even stronger.

Once the coast was clear, Karen and Hannah paid a short visit to Windale before flying back home Sunday afternoon. Karen has decided to keep Hannah in a home-schooling environment as long as her accelerated aging continues. Meanwhile, Karen is optimistic I'll find a cure in the remaining pages of Wither's journal. I'll revisit it again, soon, though I don't share her level of optimism. The soiled and torn pages are useless now. The encrypting glamour that made them readable through border vision is gone. On the damaged pages, the symbols have been reduced to true gibberish. I will keep them on the chance that someday I will find a means to reactivate the illusion that made them legible. Okay, maybe that is too optimistic. Sue me.

After Karen and Hannah left Windale, the Crone popped in. She gave me some tips on how I could use my protective sphere to climb by shaping virtual energy steps with the malleable interior. When I asked her about flying, she explained that one achieves magical flight via the controlled displacement of gravitational forces. Unfortunately, that explanation sounded way too Theoretical Physics Land for me. I'll stick with protective-sphere stair exercises for now.

Of course, the Crone remembers the past time line that matches mine, since that period is no longer in flux. She once told me many would die. I wonder now if our shared past is better or worse than what she originally experienced. While the Windale death toll could have been much worse, it was bad enough. Kayla lost a friend and father figure of her own in Bill Borkowski. And we all lost Sheriff Nottingham, along with Deputy Kirkbride. Bad indeed, and I hate to dwell on how much worse it could have been, so I won't. Our shared path is hard enough, thanks.

Odd as it sounds, after Bobby tried to kill Kayla and she reciprocated by blowing a hole in his leg, their relationship is closer than ever. Talk about tough love! Bobby is free of the demon's possession. And Kayla . . . Kayla is still as irrepressible as ever. But that's all. No more black blood incidents and why not, since there's been nothing to trigger them. Is she free of Wither's evil? She's asked me more than once. I keep coming back to the difficulty she had bypassing Wither's traps and locks, even with the aid of black blood. And the blood itself is not quite the same. It lacks the sentient, *seeking* quality of Wither's pure blood. Maybe it's lost its bite. Or become some sort of antivenom.

We now have a few more believers in town, and Kayla's mother is among them. Even if she were to convince herself my astral form at the Stewpot was a delirious hallucination brought on by extreme pain and fear for her daughter's life, she can't deny the existence of the *wendigo*. Yet she's been strangely silent about that night. Achieving believer status is a big adjustment. Kayla and I will give her the time she needs. If she asks, we won't deny what she witnessed, but we'll wait for her to come to us with the inevitable questions. Keeping secrets is a lot of work, especially among loved ones. Lena is a tough lady. She'll adapt to the new reality.

And me? I've been back home, in my shared cottage, for over a week now. Frankie arrived Sunday afternoon to reclaim her room, ready for spring session, but unprepared for the story I had to tell her. She stood tall at Wither's end, but I don't think she feels the slightest bit left out of this latest madness. If she's anywhere near as smart as I think she is, she'll start looking for a new roommate.

Finally, I've been wondering about the mystical green light that flashed through the theater lobby and out into the night. I'd like to believe it signaled the end of Wither's curse, but that Wiccan intuition of mine warns me otherwise. Can't help but remember one particular line in her vindictive spell, *"One by one—and by one more—seek her out forevermore."* Makes me think the *wendigo* was only the beginning. And that maybe I shouldn't overstay my welcome here in Windale. But first, there's something I need to do.

"It's time," Wendy said.

Alex sat beside her, in the passenger seat of the Pathfinder, aviator glasses down on the tip of his nose, index fingers tapping the dashboard in a drumbeat accompaniment to a song on the radio. "What time is that?" Alex asked. "I thought you were taking me to lunch. Treating me to the steak lover's special."

"It's time," she repeated.

Alex looked out the window and noticed the street sign for College Avenue. "Ah, *that* time." Wendy parked the SUV illegally, again. "This is good, Wendy. But is this a hello or a good-bye to Windale?"

"Well, Alissa's been hinting that if I would be inclined to buy the Crystal Path from her, she would be inclined to move to Italy. Florence or Rome, she hasn't decided."

"That would be great. For both of you. And for us."

"Becoming a business owner means planting some deep roots," Wendy said. "Not sure I'm ready for that. Besides, you only have a year and a half left in this bizarre little town. Then you'll return to Minneapolis and take over the financial district."

"Maybe." Alex smiled cryptically. "You never know."

Wendy slapped the top of the steering wheel in what she hoped was a decisive gesture. "Suppose I should go in before they *do* decide to give me a parking ticket."

"They wouldn't dare."

"In this town, you never know what to expect."

"Want some company in there?"

"No," Wendy said. "Thanks . . . but no. I can do this. I'll be all right." She climbed out of the SUV, slammed the door shut and walked around to the sidewalk, where she took a few moments to read the sign again.

THE LAWRENCE A. WARD & CAROL G. WARD MEMORIAL LIBRARY

She remembered how important her parents had been to her in shaping her life, and the influence they still had on her. Maybe that's why she'd been unable to come to this place, to view the exhibit honoring their memory, telling every visitor just how important Larry and Carol Ward had been to Danfield College and the Windale community. She'd wanted to be sure she could live a life that measured up to their high standards. Instead of admitting that to herself, she'd run away from everything and everyone but, in the end, she couldn't run away from herself and her responsibilities. Because of who she was. And Wendy had her parents to thank for that.

Some things in life people should never have to face alone. We need special people in our lives, she thought. *As much as we need to remember the special people we've lost. Memories of what we have meant, and will always mean to one another. Our memories are how we honor them.*

And because she could walk up those stairs and face this moment alone, she knew she didn't have to, not anymore. She looked back over her shoulder, reached out her hand to Alex, and said, "Come with me."

www.gsdw.net), JOHN resides in Logan Township, New Jersey with his wife and three children.

ABOUT THE AUTHOR

John Passarella won the Horror Writers Association's prestigious Bram Stoker Award for Superior Achievement in a First Novel for the coauthored *Wither*. Columbia Pictures purchased the feature film rights to *Wither* in a prepublication, preemptive bid. Barnesandnoble.com named the paperback edition of *Wither* one of horror's "Best of 2000." At Amazon.com, *Wither* was an Editor's Choice and a horror bestseller.

John's other novels include *Buffy the Vampire Slayer: Ghoul Trouble* (a *Locus* bestseller), *Angel: Avatar*, *Wither's Rain*, and *Angel: Monolith*. *Wither's Legacy* is the third book in the Wendy Ward series.

An active member of the Horror Writers Association (www.horror.org), the Science Fiction and Fantasy Writers of America (www.sfwa.org), the Authors Guild (authorsguild.org), and the Garden State Horror Writers (www.gshw.net), John resides in Logan Township, New Jersey, with his wife and three children.

For more information on John Passarella's books and events or to subscribe to his free author newsletter, please visit www.passarella.com. John welcomes email from readers at author@passarella.com.

Not sure what to read next?

Visit Pocket Books online at
www.SimonSays.com

Reading suggestions for
you and your reading group
New release news
Author appearances
Online chats with your favorite writers
Special offers
And much, much more!

10421